HOUSE OF MIRRORS

A Fenton House Novel

Ben Cheetham

The characters and events portrayed in this book are fictitious. Any similarity to real persons, living or dead, is coincidental and not intended by the author.

ISBN-13: 9798497322316

Cover design by: M.Y. Cover Design

Find out more about the author and his other books at bencheetham.com

Zig, zig, zig, Death in cadence,
Striking with his heel a tomb,
Death at midnight plays a dance tune,
Zig, zig, zig, on his violin.

HENRI CAZALIS, DANSE MACABRE

1

Thieves

The landscape was dissolving into dreamy twilight tinted by the afterglow of the sun. A patchwork of fields sloped away from one side of the road towards a navy blue ribbon of sea. To the opposite side of the road, a swathe of purple heather climbed towards a horizon punctuated by towering wind turbines and vast satellite dishes. Although the sky overhead was clear, the columns of dark clouds gathering to the south suggested it wouldn't stay that way for long.

Natalie stared vacantly out of the windscreen. Swallows swooped across her field of vision. She paid them no attention. Nor was her gaze attracted to the profusion of pink, yellow and red flowers bursting from the verges. She puffed her cheeks. "Boooring," she groaned in a slightly reedy voice. "God, I hate the countryside."

A grin split the orange-tanned face of the man behind the steering-wheel. "Oh really?" Leon's thick East London accent was laced with sarcasm. "I'd never have guessed. You've only told me twenty times today."

"I didn't realise you were keeping count."

"I keep count of everything, babe."

Natalie's honey gold eyes slid across to him. "What's that supposed to mean?"

"In my line of business, you get used to keeping track of things in your head." Leon tapped his temple with a finger whose knuckles were ridged with scars. "It's all in here – every penny I'm owed, everything I've ever done for anyone. As my dear mum used to say, there's nothing free in life. Even gifts have their price."

A faint frown disturbed Natalie's flawless forehead. She lifted her left hand to display a gold ring set with a sparkling diamond. "So how much do I owe you for this?"

Leon let out a sandpapery laugh, his baby blue eyes twinkling at her from beneath a mop of brown hair. "How much have you got?"

Before Natalie could reply, a loud yawn drew her attention to a man stretched out on the backseat. Jamie's eyelids blinked open, revealing hazel-brown irises.

"Look who's back with us," said Leon. "Did you have a nice nap, sleeping beauty?" The question had a snarky edge to it, as if he hoped the answer was no.

Jamie responded with the silent indifference of someone used to letting such comments wash over him. Rubbing a hand across the bristles of his sandy crewcut, he sat up and squinted out of the windows. "Where are we?"

Leon jerked a thumb at Natalie. "Ask her."

"How am I supposed to know where we are?" she retorted.

"This is your gig, isn't it?"

"Yeah, but you know I don't do maps."

Leon gave a soft snort. "Can't read maps. Can't drive." He glanced at an anaemic-looking sandwich languishing in cling film between the front seats. "Can't even make a decent sarnie."

"I enjoyed my butty," Jamie offered in a consoling tone.

"Then why don't you marry her?" asked Leon.

Jamie let out an awkward little laugh, unsure what to make of the suggestion.

"I'm serious," continued Leon. "She costs me an arm and a leg. And what do I get in return? Sod all." His grin broadened. "Tell a lie. She is good for one thing." Curling his fingers into a tube, he moved his hand back and forth in front of his mouth, pushing his tongue into his cheek as he did so.

"Pig," exclaimed Natalie, jabbing a long gold-painted fingernail into the hard ridges of Leon's stomach.

Laughing and grimacing, he swatted her hand away. "I'm only winding you up."

Her eyes thinned to slits. "Are you?"

"Of course I am. You know I'm mad for you. I must be. Why else would I be out here in the arse-end of nowhere?"

"To get rich."

Leon made a doubtful noise in the back of his throat.

"You think I'm full of shit, don't you?" said Natalie.

"Well you have to admit, babe – a secret vault full of gold – it's pretty far out there."

Natalie took a cracked and faded leather-bound book out of a jewel-encrusted handbag. As if it was a valuable artefact, she carefully flipped through its yellowed pages to a ribbon bookmark. Her sultry eyes traversing lines of spidery handwriting, she read aloud, "15th November 1914. Mr Lewarne does not seem himself. Indeed, with each passing day, as news comes in of the terrible casualties inflicted on both sides at Ypres, he seems more out of sorts. Kindermond–"

"Kindermond?" interrupted Leon. "Don't they make

chocolate eggs?"

"Just shut up and listen," snapped Natalie. "Who knows, you might learn something."

Flashing a wink at Jamie, Leon motioned for her to continue.

With a breath of strained patience, she picked up where she'd left off. "Kindermond. He keeps muttering that foreign-sounding word to himself. Mr Burton tells me it's a German word meaning the murder of children. It's said that of the many thousands of German soldiers killed in recent days, the majority were student volunteers. These students supposedly marched into battle four abreast singing whilst our machine guns cut them down. In one day alone, up to seven thousand of the brave young fellows were killed. According to the newspapers, the corpses were heaped so high that their comrades had difficulty climbing over them. Tonight Mr Lewarne drank so much brandy that Mr Burton and I had to help him to bed. God help me, Mr Lewarne kept saying. There was a strange, hunted look in his eyes."

"Why did this Lewarne bloke care about Krauts getting what they deserved?" asked Jamie.

"He owned the factories where the guns killing them were made."

"He sounds like a proper wet blanket," said Leon. "He should have been proud. We didn't start the war."

Natalie gave a sighing shake of her head as if both men were a lost cause. She lowered her gaze to the diary again. "I should not be writing this," she resumed. "If Mr Lewarne ever chances to read it, God only knows what he will do. However, I feel I must record tonight's events in ink or tomorrow I may come to believe they were naught but a bad dream."

"Give it a rest, will you, babe?" Leon broke in again. "I'm

not in the mood for Jackanory."

Compressing her artificially plump lips, Natalie clapped the diary shut hard enough to signal her irritation.

"I want to hear the rest of the story," Jamie said with a slight wobble in his voice, like a boy challenging his father's authority.

Leon's thick fingers flexed on the steering-wheel. "Christ's sake, Jamie, you're as bad as her." He heaved a sigh. "Go on then, but light me a ciggie first."

Natalie dug a packet of cigarettes and a lighter out of her handbag, sparked one up and placed it between Leon's lips. Sucking in a lungful of smoke, he nodded permission for her to carry on reading.

She stared at him inscrutably for a moment before opening the diary and continuing from where she'd been interrupted. "What seems a lifetime ago now, my sleep was disturbed by a sobbing as wretched as a soul suffering the torments of Hell. The pitiful sound seemed to issue from within the very walls, as if the house itself was in mortal agony. My first instinct was to cower under my bedsheets, but then I thought to myself, what if Mr Lewarne has taken ill? He's been very good to me. I wouldn't be able to forgive myself if any harm came to him because I was too afraid to go to his aid. I lit a candle and put on my dressing-gown. I'm not ashamed to admit that the candle was trembling in my hand as I made my way to Mr Burton's bedroom door. He didn't answer when I called his name, so I opened the door. His bed was empty. I can't say I was surprised. Mr Burton has become very friendly with a fisherman's widow down in the village. For some months, I have suspected that he sneaks out at night to visit her. My heart knocked hard at the knowledge that I was the only servant in the house. Even though Mr Lewarne has never mistreated me, I do not feel at ease in Fenton House. There is something about this place that–"

"Jesus Christ, will you just cut to the chase?" groaned Leon. "I couldn't give a monkeys about how the dozy cow–"

Now Natalie interrupted him. "Hey, don't call my Great Grandma a dozy cow."

"What do you care what I call her? You never even met her."

"Just don't. OK?" Natalie stared at Leon, her perfectly plucked eyebrows angling into a sharp V.

He chuckled and ran his tongue over his lips. "You know it turns me on when you get angry." Cords of muscle flexed on his heavily tattooed forearm as he squeezed her thigh. She squirmed as his hand climbed her skin-tight black yoga pants to grope between her legs.

"Pack it in, Leon," Jamie piped up from the backseat.

Leon eyeballed him in the rearview mirror. "What did you say?" The question was both a dare and a warning.

The wobble found its way back into Jamie's voice, more pronounced. "I said, pack it in."

For several seconds, uncomfortable silence reigned. Leon drew his hand away from Natalie in an exaggeratedly slow movement. "You know what, little brother, you're getting to be a proper cheeky fucker. Keep it up and you and I will have to have a good long talk."

Jamie met the barely disguised threat with silence, his jaw muscles flexing like he was chewing on something indigestible. A crimson flush climbed his neck and stained his boyishly smooth cheeks.

Laughter erupted from Leon. "Look at your face, you daft sod. I'm only messing with you." He swept a hand at the rolling landscape and the sea beyond. "Smile. Both of you." The words had the ring of a command. "We're on holiday."

Natalie pushed out a thin smile. Jamie slumped down in the backseat, staring at his lap.

Leon took a drag on his cigarette and spoke through a plume of smoke. "Come on then, Nat. Stop sulking and finish your little story."

She pursed her lips for a second at the condescending remark. Focusing on the spindly handwriting, she resumed in an annoyed monotone, "There is something about this house that leaves me cold. Often when I'm alone, I get a feeling of being watched. I tell myself, Emily you're being silly. You're not used to living in a big house. That's all it is..." Natalie tailed off, skim-reading the rest of the page. She threw Leon a barbed glance. "Just making sure I don't bore you with stuff you don't need to hear."

A corner of his mouth crooked up. He blew smoke out of it at her.

"You're not boring me," said Jamie.

Leon silently mimicked him like a schoolboy taking the mickey out of a teacher's pet.

Blanking him once again, Jamie asked Natalie, "What kind of stuff do you mean?"

"Emily was an East Ender like us. She talks about how she grew up in a little house in Spitalfields. She was only nineteen when she was taken on as a maid at Fenton House and upped sticks to Cornwall. She'd never been out of London before. She could barely read or write."

"Must run in the family," quipped Leon.

Flipping him the middle finger, Natalie continued, "Mr Lewarne brought in a tutor for her. That's why she didn't up and leave when weird things started happening at the house. She felt like she owed him."

Leon snorted. "Nothing's changed there then. Every rich

prick I've ever met has a talent for making you feel like you owe them something."

Arching an eyebrow, Natalie slid him a look that said, *You're not too bad at that yourself.* Her gaze moved past him to a young woman pushing a pram along a short stretch of pavement. The woman had the zoned-out expression of someone in a trance of tiredness. Natalie craned her neck to try and get a glimpse of the pram's blanket-swaddled occupant. Her gaze lingered in the direction of the woman and pram even after they'd disappeared from view.

Leon pointed to a lane hemmed in by hedges to the left of the main road. "Is that our turn?"

Natalie blinked like she'd snapped out of a daydream. "Ruan Minor," she said, reading the sign adjacent to the turn off. "No, we want Treworder. It's the next village along."

The road undulated between heaths of reddish grass and yellow-speckled gorse. Fat-bellied black clouds swept in from the coast, blotting out the sun. The wind picked up, shivering the hedges.

"Looks like it's going to hammer it down," observed Jamie. Even as he spoke, globs of rain hit the windscreen. Their pattering intensified to a drumming as the heavens opened. An ominous rumble of thunder rolled in behind the clouds.

"The forecast didn't mention rain," said Natalie, running a hand through her long black hair.

"What's the matter? Afraid your hair will get wet?" Leon asked with a chuckle. His voice took on a serious note. "The more rain the better. Fewer people out and about."

A little cluster of homemade signs emerged from the downpour – 'The Smuggler's Inn Fish BBQ Every Wednesday 6pm', 'Serpentine Café Pasties and Cream Teas', 'The Loft Art Gallery and Café Fresh Crab Sandwiches'. Alongside them was a road sign for 'Treworder'.

Leon licked his lips. "I could murder a pasty and a pint."

"Not sure that'd be a good idea," said Jamie.

Leon rolled his eyes at him as if to say, *You think?* "We need to find somewhere to lie low until dark."

They turned past the signs onto a ruler-straight road. After passing a handful of cottages, the road narrowed to a single lane. Massed ranks of clouds charged at them from the English Channel.

Natalie pointed to a muddy farm track. "What about there?"

"That'll do," agreed Leon, easing the sleek black BMW onto the track. He pulled around a bend, putting a hedge between the car and the road before cutting the engine.

"Wow, it's really coming down," said Jamie, watching rain bounce off the bonnet.

Natalie lit a couple more cigarettes and gave one to Leon. A flock of gulls with black-tipped wings flew overhead, fleeing the clouds. Their shrieks sliced through the drumming rain. She rested her head back, sucking on her cigarette as she watched the birds dwindle to specks.

"So..." prompted Jamie.

"Mm?" She lolled her face towards him.

He pointed to the diary.

She eyed it languidly, like a cat wondering whether it could be bothered to move. After an extended moment, she picked it off her lap. Exhaling wisps of smoke with each word, she read out, "I descended the attic stairs to the first floor landing. The sobbing had fallen to a murmur and now seemed to be coming from somewhere below. I began to wonder if it was nothing more than the wind keening through the house. An orange light was visible under Mr Lewarne's bedroom door. No sound came from within. I knocked quietly so as not to disturb Mr Lewarne if he was asleep. I received no response, so I opened the door. Coals were glowing in the hearth. Their light flickered on bedsheets that were twisted and tangled as if Mr Lewarne had been wrestling with them. The bed was empty. I was about to shut the door when I saw something that made me do a double-take."

Natalie tapped ash into the ashtray before going on, "To either side of the fireplace are stone pillars decorated with cherubs. The right-hand pillar had somehow moved sideways several feet. Closer inspection showed that it was mounted on metal runners. There was a hollow behind the fireplace. To my astonishment, I found myself peering into a narrow passageway with brick walls and a low ceiling of wooden beams and plaster lathes. The sobbing reached me again, carried on a chilly breath of air from deep within the passageway. Cupping my hand around the candle flame for fear it would be blown out, I entered the passageway. After a short distance, a steep stairway led up to the eaves. At its top, a small square of wood with a brass handle was set into the interior wall. I pulled the handle and the panel came loose, revealing a pin-sized hole. I looked through the hole and what I saw filled me with disgust, anger and fear all at once. It was a peephole that gave a view of my bedroom! Had Mr Lewarne stood there watching me? During the summer months, it is often so hot and stuffy in the attic that I sleep naked atop my bedsheets."

Grinning sleazily, Leon eyeballed Natalie's more than ample breasts. "If Great Granny was built like you, I'd have been there every night." He turned to Jamie. "Wouldn't you?"

Jamie shrugged.

"Don't give me that," sneered Leon. Jamie's cheeks reddened again as, jerking a closed hand up and down over his groin, his brother added, "Of course you would, you dirty little perv."

"Leave him alone, Leon," said Natalie.

"What are you? His mum?" Leon was still smiling, but there was a testy edge to his voice. "Jamie's a big boy. He can stick up for himself. Can't you, Jamie?"

Jamie muttered something under his breath.

Leon cocked an ear towards him. "What was that?"

"Nothing."

"Are you sure? Cos I could've sworn you told me to go fuck myself."

Jamie sat silent, not looking his brother in the eye.

There was something affectionate and proprietorial in Leon's manner as he thrust out a hand to rub Jamie's bristly hair. Jamie flinched. Annoyed with himself for reacting that way, he shoved at Leon's hand.

Natalie wafted the brothers apart with the diary. "For Christ's sake, can I please just finish reading this to you?"

Leon treated her to another of his wolfish grins. "I'm all ears, babe."

Jamie retreated to the far side of the backseat, his expression aggrieved and downcast, as Natalie once again carried on from where she'd left off. "Mr Lewarne has done so much for me. Not only has he given me a job, but he has provided me with an education so that when I return to London I will be qualified to seek a secretarial position. Only a year ago, I was resigned to leading the same life of drudgery as my mother. Now the future is full of possibilities. If not for this, I would have returned to my room that very instant, packed my belongings and fled Fenton House. Instead, my heart heavy with apprehension, I put back the wood panel and proceeded along the passageway. Cobwebs festooned the ceiling. I shuddered as they brushed against my face. At about the midpoint of the attic, a stairway branched off to my right. The sobbing seemed to come from that direction. I descended the stairs to a broader passageway whose walls were draped with red velvet curtains. I drew the curtains aside revealing tall arched windows that looked into the east wing bedrooms. It took me a moment to realise I was in fact looking through the back of the mirrors that adorn the walls in those bedrooms. Alongside each mirror was a brass button. I pushed one and the adjacent mirror swung inwards. I thought about the many friends and business acquaintances Mr Lewarne has over from London. The lavish parties he throws for them. Suddenly my mind was flooded with images of naked bodies entwined together on the beds the mirrors overlook. Never before have I had such thoughts. They made my face burn. The sobbing had transformed into moans of pleasure. I'm ashamed to admit that as the obscene thoughts assaulted me, the fire in my face spread downwards through my chest and stomach to my groin."

The rain was becoming more torrential by the minute. It was as if a river in the sky had burst its banks, but neither brother appeared to notice. Their eyes shone, seemingly spellbound by Natalie's breathy, intense voice.

"I don't know how long I stood there. Time melted away. It was only when I became aware of candle wax scalding my hand that I came back to myself. I rubbed off the wax. The skin beneath was scalded. Dazed and lightheaded, hardly aware of what I was doing, I continued on my way. My instincts warned me to turn around and leave before it was too late. I had an unshakeable feeling that there was something evil in the air."

"Evil?" Jamie echoed uneasily. "What kind of evil?"

With a guffaw, Leon said, "The same kind that makes porn the most popular thing on the internet." His eyes traced along

Natalie's toned curves. "Good old-fashioned lust."

Jamie stared at her too, then quickly looked away. His gaze skipped over the countless puddles dotting the fields. "The rain's stopped," he observed. "It's like someone turned off a tap."

"It'll be dark soon," said Leon.

Natalie tapped the diary's age-curled pages. "This is where it gets really interesting."

"Why?" Leon asked with a lascivious twinkle in his eyes. "Does Great Granny get it on with her boss?"

Refusing to rise to the bait, Natalie resumed reading, "I descended a third stairway. At the bottom of the stairs, another peephole looked into the living room. At that instant, such a shrill wail rang out that I stiffened as if someone had tipped ice water over me. The dreadful sound drew my eyes to a narrow gap between the stairs and the wall. In the space behind the stairs a wooden trapdoor stood open. Steep stone steps descended into darkness beneath the house. More wails issued from the aperture. Once again, my mind commanded me to flee. And once again, I disobeyed it. I squeezed through the gap and crept down the steps. They led to a passageway hewn out of solid rock. The candlelight glittered on streaks of the scaly green serpentine that gives the Lizard Peninsula its name. The cold, damp air had a salty tang that reminded me of the caves on Treworder beach. The passageway sloped downwards, passing under and surely beyond the house. I wondered if it was an old smuggler's tunnel. It wasn't so long ago that the smuggling of brandy and other contraband was rife in these parts. Indeed, it is said that the village is haunted by the ghosts of smugglers whose disembodied footsteps echo through the streets late at night."

"Woo-ooo-ooo," Leon interjected, waggling his fingers.

Natalie subjected him to a deadpan glare, like a mother

refusing to indulge an attention-seeking child. She cleared her throat and continued, "I pictured the ghostly smugglers wailing as they wandered the passageways. It was less frightening than the thought that Mr Lewarne was the source of the blood-curdling wails. I saw the flicker of a candle or a lantern up ahead. Some instinct of self-preservation compelled me to blow out my candle and advance on tiptoes. With every step, the temperature dropped. I had to clench my teeth to keep them from chattering. An open door of iron bars came into view. Beyond it was a rock chamber whose walls were lined with thick wooden shelves. My jaw went slack and I had the feeling that my eyes were trying to pop out of their sockets. The shelves were stacked with what must have been hundreds of gold bars."

"How much is a gold bar worth?" asked Jamie.

"Depends on its purity and weight," Natalie answered with the certainty of someone who'd done their research. "A 24-carat 12.5 kilogram bar currently goes for about £620,000."

"£620,000!" Awe and scepticism mingled in Jamie's big brown eyes. "And there were hundreds of them?" He glanced around the BMW's interior. "If that's true, we're going to need a bigger vehicle."

"*If, if,*" stressed Leon.

As if presenting incontestable evidence of the gold's existence, Natalie countered forcefully with more words from the diary, "It occurred to me that just one or two of those bars would be enough for me to live a life of ease. Instead of waiting on a master, I would be the master with servants attending to my every need and whim. The thought was driven out by the sight that next greeted my eyes. A naked man shuffled into view as if his ankles were shackled. Mr Lewarne was hunched over so that his spine looked like knotted rope. His face was so pale and contorted that it took me a moment to recognise him. His bloodshot eyes passed sightlessly over me. 'Kindermond,' he wailed, clawing at his chest savagely enough to draw blood. It was as if he was looking upon those far away battlefields where thousands have perished from bullets made in his factories."

Leon mimicked an eye-rubbing motion. "Oh boo-hoo, I got filthy rich off dead Krauts."

Jamie gave a low laugh, for once agreeing with his brother's sentiment.

"I wanted to help Mr Lewarne," Natalie pressed on. "Honest to God I did. It broke my heart to see him in such a pitiful state. But fear rooted me to the spot. All I could do was watch him tear his chest to bloody ribbons. 'They are no more,' he cried out. 'They are no more. They are no more.' The same awful words over and over. Finally, his arms dropped to his sides and he stood there panting like an exhausted animal. The silence freed my feet. I said his name and approached him. His eyes swung towards me. They were huge and jet black. 'Get out!' he bellowed. What else could I do but obey? I fled the vault. Without matches to relight the candle, I had no choice but to grope my way through the dark. I couldn't catch my breath. It felt like a lion was sitting on my chest. The tunnel seemed to go on for miles. I began to question whether I was losing my grip not only on my sense of distance, but on my very sanity."

"I know how she feels," muttered Leon, gloomily eyeing the coffee-coloured water bubbling along the sides of the farm track. "I'm gonna lose it too if I have to listen to much more of this depressing crap. I thought there was gonna be some shagging going on."

"Be a good boy and shut your gob and maybe later there will be," said Natalie.

His gloom flipping to glee in an instant, Leon made a mouth-zipped gesture and flashed a leering grin at Jamie.

Natalie's attention returned to the diary. "My fingers trailed along endless rock walls. My head reeled with questions. What if I couldn't find my way back out? How long would it take to succumb to exhaustion? If I died, would my spirit be doomed to wander that place for eternity? Was I ensnared in a labyrinth? Or did the passageways possess some strange power beyond my comprehension? The darkness seemed to leach the strength from my limbs. My legs gave out and I crawled onwards, stricken by the uncanny feeling that I was lost inside Mr Lewarne's black eyes. After what might have been minutes or hours, I collapsed sobbing onto my face. It was at that moment, when all hope had deserted me, that a soft, hollow voice spoke up. I could not tell whence it came. It seemed at once to be inside and outside of my head. 'You're not alone, Emily,' it said. 'I can help you, but first you must accept me into your heart. Put yourself in my hands and I will carry you away from this place.' The voice froze my blood for I knew to whom it belonged."

"Mr Lewarne?" said Jamie.

"No, you plonker," said Leon. "Not Mr Lewarne, Mr Devil. The big man himself. Satan or whatever you want to call–" He broke off, clapping a hand to his mouth and giving Natalie an apologetic look.

A smile playing at the corners of her glossy pink lips, she continued, "'All you need do is say Master help me,' it promised. I was sinking into those black eyes. I was drowning in their darkness. Soon my breath would stop and my life would be over before it had properly started. I would never know what it was to love and be loved by a man. I would never be a mother. It would be like I'd never even existed. I wish I was a strong person, but I am not. I want to experience everything life has to offer. I want to laugh, sing, dance, eat, drink and make love. So I said, 'Master help me. I put myself in your hands.' And suddenly I wasn't sinking anymore, I was floating.

Hands as gentle as my own father's were carrying me. At last, the darkness fell from my eyes and I found that I was lying on my bed. My body was as warm and heavy as when I once took laudanum to dull a toothache. By the silvery moonlight shining through the window, I saw that my dressing gown was hanging on its hook. My eyelids were sticky with sleep. It occurred to me that it had merely been a dream. The sobbing and wailing, the secret passageways, the gold, Mr Lewarne, the seductive voice, all of it a dream. 'Thank God,' I said, putting my hands together in prayer. It was then that I felt the soreness. With trembling fingers, I struck a match and lit a candle. The flame revealed a blistered red patch on the back of my hand."

Natalie fell silent, looking back and forth between the brothers as if expecting to see astonishment written large on their faces.

Jamie's forehead creased. "I don't get it. So was it a dream or not?"

Leon threw his head back and groaned, "Who gives a shit?"

"But if it was a dream, there's no gold. Right?"

"And if it wasn't a dream, then Great Granny gave her soul to the Devil," Leon added with a snigger.

Natalie slid him a look that warned him not to test her patience any further.

He held his hands up in mock innocence. "Hey, I think it's cool. I can just imagine Great Granny taking it in every hole during some satanic orgy."

"Yeah well, keep on imagining, Leon, because that's as good as it's going to get for you tonight," Natalie said coolly.

Smirking, he shifted his attention to the world beyond the windscreen. The waterlogged fields were fading into darkness. A new wave of storm clouds was marching inland.

"It's time," he said, starting the engine.

He reversed to the road. The wheels kicked up spray as he sped towards the coast. After about half-a-mile, the road curved sharply around a cottage with a B&B sign hanging outside it. In the distance, a grey church tower reached towards the heavens.

Silence held sway in the car as its occupants watched for other vehicles. A few fat Jersey cows sheltering under a tree were the only witnesses to their passing. The road began to descend towards a deep wooded valley. Lights twinkled in the windows of houses strung out along the valley bottom.

Natalie pointed to a lane whose hedgerows were so overgrown that there was barely enough room for a car. "I think this is our turn."

"*I think* isn't good enough," said Leon, braking to a stop. "We haven't got time for wrong turns."

She took a dog-eared paperback and a mobile phone out of her handbag. She shone the phone's torch at the book. A tall mirror in an ornate silver frame dominated its cover. A black curtain was drawn halfway across the mirror. An eerie hint of a disembodied face floated in the glass. 'Between Worlds' was scrawled in blood-red above the mirror. 'Adam Piper' was printed in white below it. 'Based on a terrifying true story' proclaimed the strapline. Natalie opened the paperback at a bookmarked page and read out, "The road ran parallel to the coastline until it met up with a lane that snaked through fields grazed by cows and horses."

"Another sodding book," grumbled Leon. "Who wrote this one? Your great grandad?"

Natalie let out a little fake laugh. "The guy that wrote this owns Fenton House. Thing is, some of the locations in it have been changed. He's had problems with ghost hunters."

"Ghost hunters?" Leon parroted with a snort.

"Yeah, some ghost hunters broke in and tried to summon a demon. One of them went missing during the ritual. She reappeared days later covered in scratches like something had clawed her half to death."

"Give me a break. Sounds like some bullshit made up to sell books."

"That does kind of sound like bullshit, Nat," Jamie agreed with a touch of apology.

"The girl was so scared that she jumped off the cliffs near the house," Natalie told them. "How's that for bullshit?"

Leon's lips curled contemptuously. "I didn't take you for the gullible type, Nat."

Her eyebrows bunched together in irritation. "It was in the newspapers. Her name was Faith Gooden. Google it if you don't–"

Natalie fell silent as headlights blinked into view a few hundred metres up ahead. Leon swiftly cut the BMW's lights and turned onto the overgrown lane. As the car climbed towards the brow of a low slope, fingers of hedgerow scraped along its doors.

"If the paintwork gets scratched, you're paying for the repairs," Leon muttered at Natalie.

"Who cares about the paintwork?" said Jamie. "If Nat's right, you'll be able to trade this in for an Aston Martin."

Leon gave a despairing shake of his head. "Yeah, and Santa will deliver it gift-wrapped to my front door."

Natalie read aloud from the paperback again. "The lane passed between windswept hedges before curving down towards the rugged coastline." As she spoke, the car tipped over the brow of the slope. Leon switched the headlights back on. Beyond hedges whose tops were curled like waves, grassy fields sloped away into a black expanse.

"This *is* the right way," Natalie exclaimed in a vindicated tone as, rounding a bend, they found their progress blocked by tall wrought-iron gates. Ivy spiralled up the rusty black bars and stretched across the brick walls to either side. A padlock dangled from a thick steel chain coiled around the central bars.

Jamie peered up at the stone ball-topped gateposts. "No CCTV."

Leon got out of the car, fetched a pair of long-handled bolt-cutters from the boot and went to work on the chain. Thick muscles flexed against his polo shirt as he squeezed the handles together. With a clunk, the blades sheared through the chain. He turned his attention to the big old lock at the centre of the gates. After studying it for a moment, he inserted a flat-head screwdriver into the keyhole. He gently moved the screwdriver's blade up and down, feeling for the opening lever. With a sudden twist, he popped the lock. Flashing a grin over his shoulder, he thrust the gates open.

"God, he's a smug git sometimes," said Natalie.

"Sometimes?" Jamie echoed sardonically.

The hinges squealed in protest as the gates scraped along well-worn furrows in the gravel driveway.

Leon beckoned the car forwards. Natalie shifted across to the driver's seat and eased the BMW between the gates. The headlights revealed a weed-speckled driveway flanked by shaggy sycamores and lawns that looked like they'd never seen a mower.

Leon shut the gates and wrapped the chain back into place so a casual observer would see nothing out of the ordinary. Wafting Natalie aside, he ducked into the driver's seat. He lifted a black holdall from the rear footwell and took out three plastic Halloween masks. He handed Jamie a ghost mask with a yawning mouth and eyes like black candle flames. Natalie copped for a warty, hook-nosed witch with straggly black hair. He kept a grinning red demon with stubby black horns and sharp white teeth for himself.

"We don't need these," said Natalie. "The house is empty."

Leon tilted an eyebrow at her. "Know that for sure, do you?"

"Look at the state of the place," said Jamie, motioning to the tall grass. "No one's been here in a long time."

"Either that or they just can't be arsed to mow the lawn."

Natalie tapped the paperback. "Adam Piper brought his family to live here after one of his sons died. They only lasted a week. That was two years ago. No one's lived here since."

"Why did they leave?" asked Jamie.

"Depends on what you believe."

"Bollocks to what you believe," said Leon. "I'll tell you what I know. They lock you up for a long time for burglary. So how about we give the ghosts and ghoulies a rest and keep things real?"

"There have been three murders and the same number of suicides here over the years," countered Natalie. "Is that real enough for you?"

"Bloody hell," said Jamie. "Is that true?"

A flicker of satisfaction passed across Natalie's face at his awed tone. "One hundred percent. Adam Piper hates the place so much that he'd rather let it rot than sell it."

"Then he's even more of a headcase than your great granny was," said Leon.

Natalie sucked her lips as if to hold back an angry retort

before saying, "The point is, that's how I know the house is empty."

"Maybe you're right, but until I'm certain there's no one in there, we wear the masks. Agreed?"

"Agreed," said Jamie, sliding the ghost mask down over his face.

Natalie and Leon did likewise with their masks. "Trick or treat," chuckled Leon, dipping a hand into the holdall and pulling out a pistol with a stubby red barrel and a black bullet cylinder.

"What's *that* for?" exclaimed Natalie, her eyes widening within the witch mask's wrinkled eyeholes.

"It's for just in case."

"It's only a starter pistol," said Jamie. "It fires blanks."

"Loud and scary as hell," explained Leon. "Fire off a round and people will do just about anything you tell them to do."

"Anyway, Nat, it looks like you're right." Jamie motioned to the blackness beyond the headlights. "I can't see any lights on. So what's to worry about?"

She gave a far from reassured, "Hmm."

"Listen, we've been doing this for donkey's years and no one's gotten seriously hurt yet."

"Except for that bloke whose skull I had to crack," corrected Leon. "You remember? The big bastard who came at us with a–"

"OK, fine," Natalie cut him off, not wanting to hear it. "Let's just get on with it, shall we?"

"What's the matter, Nat?" Leon's voice rasped through the devil mask's pointed teeth. "I thought you liked scary stories."

She fixed him with an unamused glare. "I'd rather go to

prison for burglary than murder."

"Relax, babe, nothing's going to go wrong." He patted his mask's horns. "You're riding with the Prince of Darkness."

Jamie raised his hands and bowed. "All hail Satan."

"Hail Satan! Hail Satan!" the brothers chanted in chorus before bursting into laughter.

Natalie put a hand under her mask and pinched the bridge of her nose as if she had a headache. "I just knew I should have done this on my own."

Leon's laughter became incredulous. "Said she who could get lost on her way to the bathroom."

"I found the way here, didn't I?"

"Yeah, by luck more than anything else."

Natalie flipped him the middle finger again. He stuck his tongue out at her and waggled it lewdly. Heaving a sigh, she shook her head as if to say, *I give up*.

Leon squinted at the driveway, his face suddenly intense with concentration. "OK, no more mucking about," he said, as if it was Natalie who'd been laughing and joking. "It's show time."

2

Demons

Thirteen hours earlier…

Adam's fingers danced over the keyboard, piling sentences into paragraphs and paragraphs into pages. Every so often, he leaned back in his chair to read what he'd just written. He always took a mouthful of coffee and cracked his knuckles before resuming writing. There was something almost ritualistic about the way he repeated the process over and over.

The *briiing-briiing* of a phone jolted him out of his routine. He sidled along the narrow space between his desk and the footboard of a double bed. After dodging around a dressing table, he exited the cluttered bedroom and opened a door at the end of a short landing. His nostrils flared at paint fumes. The walls of the small room beyond the door were a pristine pastel pink. The window frames and skirting boards glistened with drying white gloss. Brushes, rollers, trays and tins were stacked alongside a stepladder on the dustsheet-covered floorboards. The only furniture in the room was a gun-grey filing-cabinet with a cordless phone on top of it.

Adam picked up the handset. 'Number Unavailable' said the screen display. He put the receiver to his ear. "Hello?"

He waited for the sales patter that usually accompanied unavailable numbers.

Silence.

"Hello?" he repeated.

Still nothing.

A frown touched his forehead. He started to lower the phone, but hesitated. On the edge of hearing, as faint as a whisper of wind in trees, he caught the sound of breathing.

"Who is this?" he asked.

Softly, ever so softly, the quivering breaths tickled his ears. Was someone crying?

"Who am I talking to?" The question was tinged with hesitation as if he wasn't sure he wanted to know the answer.

The breaths receded beyond hearing. Doubt flickered in Adam's eyes. Maybe all he'd heard was static. A faulty line. He remained on the line for a moment, but there was only silence. He returned the handset to its base unit and stared at it pensively.

The creak of rapid footsteps on the stairs drew his attention. As he moved to peer over the banister, the front door clunked shut. His gaze shifted from the gloomy square of hallway at the bottom of the stairs to a door behind him. He called out tentatively, "Henry?"

No reply.

He opened the door and stepped into a bedroom that felt as if it hadn't seen the sun in a long time. A blackout blind covered the window. Wrinkling his nose at the stale air, he surveyed the room. A duvet was scrunched into a ball on a single bed. Cereal was congealing in a bowl on a bedside table. Socks, boxer shorts, t-shirts and jeans were strewn across the carpet. He peered around the door at a desk cluttered with a computer keyboard, a flat-screen monitor, pens, pencils, books, empty crisp packets, sweet wrappers and Coke cans. An electrical hum told him that, although the monitor was blank, the hard drive under the desk was running.

He pressed the monitor's standby button. The Google search bar appeared on-screen. Hovering the cursor over 'History', he scanned down the 'Recently Closed' list – YouTube, Inbox, Demonology: List of Demons' Names.

His frown returning, he clicked the last link. It took him to an alphabetical list of demons topped by 'Abaddon'. An exquisitely detailed drawing depicted a winged man with a muscular chest, scaly legs, sharp teeth, a hooked nose, pointed ears and bulging eyes. A brief bio described him as 'an angel of the abyss'. Other names, both unfamiliar and familiar, followed – Adramelech, Asmoday, Azazel, Beelzebub, Belial, Belphegor, Lucifer, Melchiresa, Ornias, Satan, Xaphan. They too were accompanied by grotesque illustrations – a man's body with a horse's head; a squat-bodied monstrosity with the heads of a man, a bull and a ram; numerous variations of a man, sometimes muscular, sometimes scrawny, sometimes fat, sometimes bearded, always with wings and horns. Of the names Adam recognised, Beelzebub 'Lord of the Flies' was a repulsively bloated fly-like creature; Lucifer 'Light-bringer' was another demon of the winged, horned variety; as too was Satan himself. The goat-headed, cloven-hooved 'Prince of Darkness' was illustrated sitting cross-legged between two sickle moons, one white the other black.

Adam's gaze fell to a corner of paper poking from under the keyboard. He pulled the sheet of paper free and read out the sentence written on it in a familiar scrawl, "To know the name of a thing is to have power over that thing." He gave a little start at the sound of footsteps plodding up the stairs. Quickly, he turned off the screen and left the room.

Ella's flushed face appeared at the uppermost step of the

stairs. Although it was pleasantly cool in the house, sweat dappled her forehead. Her light brown hair was scraped back into an Alice band. “Is Henry in his room?” she asked, slowly rising further into view, one hand clutching the banister, the other cupping a belly that bulged against stretchy maternity leggings.

“No.”

“Well is Edgar up here?”

“I haven’t seen him.”

“I wonder if Henry’s taken him for a walk.”

“Wouldn’t surprise me. I heard the front door not long ago.”

Ella clicked her tongue. “He’ll be late for school. Who was that on the phone?”

“The phone? Oh, no one. I mean, just a wrong number.”

Ella’s almond eyes narrowed a fraction at Adam’s fumbling response. “Is something the matter?”

He blinked, fighting an impulse to avoid her inquiring gaze. “No. Why?”

She heaved a sigh. “You don’t have to wrap me up in cotton wool, Adam.”

He tenderly placed his palm against the dome of Ella’s belly. “I know, but I like to. I don’t want you worrying about anything.” A smile spread across his face as he felt a flutter beneath his palm. “She moved.”

“Tell me about it. The little bugger never stops moving. All day and night, twisting, turning, wriggling. It’s knackering me out.” Ella sighed again. “I’m too old for this.”

“What do you mean, too old? You’re only forty. Besides, pregnancy suits you. You’re–”

"Don't you dare say I'm blooming," interrupted Ella, amusement and warning mingling in her tone. "When I see the young mums with their little bumps at the antenatal class, I feel like an old whale."

Adam's hand slid around to Ella's thickly padded bum. "I like something to get hold of," he murmured, leaning in to kiss her neck.

She gave a "Mmm," of pleasure, but then drew back and treated him to another searching look. "You're not keeping anything from me, are you? You know how worried I am about Henry."

"I'm worried about him too, but what can we do?" wondered Adam, his gaze drifting past Ella and descending the stairs. His mind was suddenly back in *that* horrifying moment – the slam of a door; the crash of breaking glass; himself racing downstairs; finding Jacob sprawled amongst the shards of the plate-glass door he'd just smashed headlong through. Blood was gushing from gashes in Jacob's wrists, saturating the air with its sweet, metallic scent. Henry was standing by his twin brother's head, his eyes as big as full moons.

Adam's memory spooled onwards – the frantic drive to Whipps Cross Hospital; Jacob being whisked away into surgery. It was like watching a horror film on fast forward.

What happened? Even now, almost three years on from that day, the question he'd asked Henry as they agonisingly awaited news of Jacob was always lurking just below the surface of his thoughts.

Every word of Henry's tearful, rambling reply was seared into him – *He hit me so I hit him back and made his lip bleed and he got really angry. I was scared so I ran into the porch and shut the door to keep him out but he ran into the glass. It was an accident, Dad. Honest.*

Ella's voice brought Adam back to the present. "We can talk

to him. Find out what's going on in his head."

He thought about the list of demons. Did he even want to know what was going on in Henry's head? "He's fourteen. You remember what it was like to be fourteen? When I was his age, I was a moody sod too."

"Yes, but you hadn't been through what he's been through."

Ella's voice was matter-of-fact. Not so long ago, Adam knew, it would have been choked up with tears. Time had chipped away at her grief, though, sculpting her into a more resilient version of her old self.

"We've worked so hard to get him back on track," she continued. "But ever since we told him about…" She trailed off, looking down at her bump with mixed emotions.

"This isn't our fault, Ella. We didn't plan for this. It was an accident." As if fearing the bump would take offence, Adam stooped to speak to it. "You're our wonderful accident, Zara."

"Zara," Ella repeated, testing how the name felt on her lips. "I'm still not convinced that's the right name. It makes me think *clothes shop*."

"Well I think it's perfect. She's our Zara, our new beginning." Adam crooned at the bump again, "And I couldn't be happier that you're almost here."

Ella feathered the backs of her fingers over the dark stubble on his cheeks. "Is that really how you feel?"

"Of course it is." He gave a wry laugh. "I can't say I'm looking forward to the sleepless nights and dirty nappies, but after the twins, one baby should be a walk in the park."

Ella smiled. "They were certainly a handful. I don't think we slept for the first year. Do you remember? Just when we got one of them off to sleep, the other would wake up."

Adam puffed his cheeks as if the mere thought of it made him tired. "Yeah, well this time it's going to be different. And not only because we're having just the one, but because *we're* different."

Ella's hand dropped away from him, her thick brown eyebrows pinching together. "What's that supposed to mean?"

"It means we won't make the same mistakes." Adam regretted the words the instant they left his mouth. He braced himself for the inevitable follow-up question.

"And what mistakes might those be?" Ella asked in a prickly tone. "Do you mean the mistakes that left one of our sons dead and turned the other into a miserable loner?"

Adam pursed his lips, resisting the temptation to dig himself deeper into the hole he'd made. He was usually so careful to keep his fears and doubts about Jacob's death stowed out of sight. After all, what good could come from reopening old wounds? What could it possibly achieve besides upsetting Ella?

Henry's protestation of innocence echoed back to him again – *It was an accident, Dad. Honest.*

But was it? Was it really?

Of course it was a fucking accident, he silently shouted at himself. Likewise, the phone call *was* just a wrong number. As for Henry's interest in demons, was it really that difficult to understand? Blaming demons for the bad things that happened in life was as old as sin.

"I love you," he softly told Ella. "And I love Henry."

She stared at him like she was trying to decide if he was telling the truth. Her head turned at the click of the front door opening. A stout, sandy-coloured pug with a squished black face waddled into view. Edgar was followed by a gangly boy, his shoulders hunched as if against a biting wind. Baggy black trousers and a half-tucked in white shirt hung off Henry's skinny frame. His brown eyes peered morosely through a fringe of loose curls. Freckles dotted his pale cheeks and sharp nose. A fuzz of bumfluff on his upper lip cried out for a razor. He stooped to unclip Edgar's lead.

Eager as always to get to his feeding bowl, Edgar nosed open the living room door and scampered from view. His eyes never leaving the floor, Henry mooched after the pug.

Adam and Ella exchanged a glance. Without a word, they headed downstairs.

They passed through a bay-windowed room furnished with a comfortable-looking old three-piece-suite. A wire mesh fireguard was screwed into place across a cast-iron fireplace. Cushioned corner protectors and edge guards were fitted to the window ledge, coffee-table, TV stand and anywhere else a baby might fall and bump itself. Ella had pointed out that there was a long way to go before that was necessary, but Adam hadn't been able to stop himself. Even before starting work on the nursery, he'd gone around the entire house, checking for danger zones and baby-proofing them.

A door at the rear of the living room led to a small kitchen with fitted units, appliances and a dining table squeezed into it. A window above the sink overlooked a sunless paved backyard. Edgar was snorting like a pot-bellied pig, his face buried in his bowl. It always made Adam smile to see the pug attacking his food as if he was perpetually starving. Henry was pouring himself a glass of orange juice at the fridge. He glanced around as his parents entered the kitchen, but said nothing. The sight of his son's downturned lips and unreadable eyes wiped the smile from Adam's face.

Ella reached to stroke Henry's brown curls. "Where have you been?"

He shied away from her touch. "Park."

Irritation prickled Adam at the monosyllabic response, but he made an effort to keep his tone light. "I bet you didn't get very far." He glanced at Edgar. "Fatty fudge cake here has got to be the laziest dog in the world."

"Don't call Edgar fat, you'll hurt his feelings," Ella playfully chided. With a little grimace of effort, she bent to stroke the pug. Wagging his stubby tail, Edgar rolled over for his belly to be scratched.

Henry looked on, stone-faced.

"Would it kill you to crack a smile?" Adam couldn't resist the urge to ask. "You do remember how to smile, don't you?"

Henry obediently curled his lips into a joyless simulation of a smile.

"Have you had any breakfast?" Ella put in, swiftly moving the conversation on.

"I'm not hungry," said Henry.

"You need to eat breakfast, Henry." Ella straightened to remove a box of cereal from a cupboard. "How do you expect to be able to concentrate in class if your brain doesn't have the energy it needs?"

"I said I'm not hungry." There was a sullen edge to Henry's gruff, recently broken voice, as if he resented being fussed over. He gulped down his drink, dumped the glass in the sink and, eyes once again fixed on the floor, headed for the living room.

"Where are you going?" asked Adam, no longer bothering to hide his annoyance.

"School obviously."

Don't get clever with me, Adam opened his mouth to retort. The words died on his lips as Ella threw him a pleading glance.

"Don't I get a kiss goodbye?" she asked, moving to catch hold of Henry's hand.

He stood stock still, allowing her to kiss his cheek. Her belly drew his gaze as it brushed against him. Adam caught a flicker of something in Henry's eyes. What was it? Jealousy? Animosity? Whatever it was, he didn't like the look of it.

As if she saw it too, a vertical cleft appeared between Ella's eyebrows. Instead of drawing away from Henry, though, she leaned in to hug him, saying, "You know you'll always be my baby."

Seemingly untouched by her tender words, Henry squirmed from his mum's clutches and slouched away.

She stared after him with troubled eyes. At the sound of the front door opening again, she called out, "Bye, love. Have a good day."

Henry didn't reply. The door thudded shut. Supporting her belly with both hands, Ella hurried to the front window. Edgar scurried after her, then flopped to the carpet, panting from the brief exertion.

Ella waved to Henry. Adam made no move to do likewise. He knew only too well that the gesture wouldn't be reciprocated. It didn't matter how many times Henry snubbed Ella, though, she was always at the window with a smile and a wave for him. Holding in a sigh, Adam came up behind her and nuzzled her neck. His hands slid around her belly. He felt another tremor of movement. "Not long now," he murmured to both Ella and Zara.

"Twelve days," said Ella.

"Twelve days and seven hours to be precise."

Their voices were a matching mixture of excitement and apprehension. Tuesday the week after next, 3:00 pm – that was the day and time when Ella was booked in for a caesarean at The Royal London Hospital. It was a few miles further away than Whipps Cross Maternity Unit, but neither of them could stomach the thought of Zara being born in the hospital where Jacob died.

Adam's hands descended over Ella's belly button, feeling for the slight ridge of scar tissue where, after two days of futile labour, they'd cut her open to pull the twins out. Even fourteen years on, he could vividly remember being led into the operating theatre to sit by Ella's head amidst a bewildering array of beeping, humming machinery. A green plastic curtain had been draped across her abdomen. He'd put on a smile for her, but a nauseous terror had seized him as the surgeon set to work on the other side of the flimsy barrier. The operation had seemed to go on forever, but then suddenly a tiny, blood-smeared body was being passed over the curtain into the arms of its parents. At the sight of what would turn out to be Jacob, Adam had disintegrated into a sobbing mess. There'd been no energy left for joy. Only relief.

Perhaps this time it would be different, less overwhelming. Or perhaps, considering what they'd been through since then, it would be even more overwhelming. Adam sighed. It was a waste of energy trying to predict how either of them would react. And soon enough he would need every ounce of energy he possessed to cope with the endless rounds of nappy changing, bottle-feeding and everything else looking after a newborn entailed.

As if Adam was transmitting his thoughts to her through touch, Ella rested her head back against his chest, drew in a deep breath and said, "Tell me it's going to be alright."

"It's going to be alright." There was a trace of hesitation in Adam's voice, barely noticeable but there nevertheless.

"Who knows, maybe Zara will be just what Henry needs to bring him out of himself?"

Cold fingers seemed to squeeze Adam's stomach at Ella's words. He drew away from her, turning his back so that she wouldn't see the guilty glimmer in his eyes. "I'd better get some writing done."

He returned to his desk and stared at his laptop. His fingers hovered over the keyboard, but no words came. His gaze slid across to a paperback with a silver-framed mirror on the cover. He traced the outline of the spectral face trapped in the glass. Its soft, androgynous contours could have belonged to a young woman or a pre-pubescent boy.

A ripple of disapproval crossed his face. The mirror had originally been blank, open to interpretation like the story within. Yes, Fenton House was haunted, but whether by ghosts of the mind or of the supernatural persuasion was not for him to say. All he'd done was to lay out events as they'd transpired. The rest was beyond his realm of understanding. To imply otherwise would be to lie to his readers. But profits were all his publisher cared about. And judging by the rise in sales since the cover was revised, people didn't want ambiguity. They wanted – needed – to believe there was more to Fenton House's history than a very earthly tale of greed, madness and murder.

He flipped through the book to a photo of a girl who looked to be in her twenties. Short, dyed red hair accentuated her gaunt, chalk-white face. Thick black mascara ringed her sad panda eyes. A caption beneath the photo identified her as 'Faith Gooden'.

Adam flashed back to the moment Faith had materialised out of nowhere in Fenton House's entrance hall, her eyes as blank as those of a sleepwalker, her painfully thin body clothed in nothing but bruises and lacerations.

"Who did this to you?" he murmured as if she was right there in the bedroom with him.

Then he was mentally fast-forwarding through time again to another person – a middle-aged woman with unnervingly direct eyes. Detective Sergeant Penny Holman was presenting him with a sheet of paper headed 'Forensic Biology Laboratory Report. Confidential. Samples submitted. Trace DNA from fingernails.'

Those are the lab results from your son's fingernail scrapings, she was gravely informing him. *Faith Gooden's blood was found under Henry's fingernails.*

Penny's voice was joined by Henry's – *It was an accident, Dad. Honest.*

Their voices babbled back and forth, vying against each other, rising loud enough to make Adam's head pound. He silenced them by clapping the book shut. He tossed it aside as if disgusted by it and focused on the screen again, but still nothing would come.

Abaddon, Adramelech, Asmoday, Azazel, Belphegor, Melchiresa, Ornias, Xaphan, Beelzebub, Belial, Lucifer, Satan... The names spooled through his mind. "If only you *were* real," he said with a heave of his lungs. How simple things would be. No ambiguity. Just good and evil.

Briiing... Briiing...

He sprang to his feet at the ringing of the phone and darted to the door. "I'll answer it," he called downstairs before swerving into the nursery and snatching up the handset. 'Number Unavailable'. There was a jarring inevitability to the sight. He put the phone to his ear. "Hello?"

No reply.

His heart lurched. There it was again. A sobbing so low as to be barely audible.

Tentatively, almost fearfully, Adam asked, "Henry, is that you?"

The sobbing stopped dead. There was a moment of silence, then a tiny, faltering voice said, "Help me... Please help me... I'm scared... Please help me, Daddy."

Adam snatched the phone away from his ear, his face a mask of horrified bewilderment, like someone was playing an incomprehensibly cruel trick on him. He stared at the handset for several long seconds before returning it to his ear. The caller had hung up.

His head bowed in frowning thought, Adam returned to the master bedroom. He took a photo from the top drawer of his bedside table. Jacob and Henry beamed at him from behind a Star Wars birthday cake decorated with ten candles. At a glance, the twins were identical, but to Adam the differences were even more glaring than the similarities. Jacob's hair was a fraction lighter than Henry's. His eyes were not quite as deep set. What always struck Adam, though, was the difference in their smiles. Jacob's was broad and toothy. There was no hint of anything hiding behind it. Henry's smile was thin and showed no teeth. It wasn't insincere, but somehow it wasn't entirely honest either. It gave the impression that he didn't want to be in the photo. Or maybe he wanted to be in the photo, just not with Jacob at his side.

Adam traced a fingertip around Jacob, murmuring, "My beautiful boy, why did it have to be–" He broke off, his dark eyes awash with shame at what he'd almost said. Tears slid down his cheeks and fell onto the photo.

3

Omens

Head down, hands stuffed into his trouser pockets, Henry scuffed his way along the pavement. A group of boys about his age passed him from behind. One shoulder-barged him, shouting, "Freak." The boys ran off, laughing. Henry didn't even bother to look at them. He'd heard it all before – weirdo, ghost boy, psycho, Damien of The Omen. It wasn't the name calling that bothered him. What bothered him was when kids at school started being friendly, because invariably it was only a matter of time before the questions followed – What's Fenton House like? Do you think it really is haunted? Did you see any actual ghosts?

He'd taken to giving different answers every time. *Fenton House is creepy as shit... It's just a big old house, it isn't scary at all... Yeah, it's seriously haunted. I saw loads of ghosts... Ghosts are bullshit.* One time, he told a girl who kept bugging him, *There were ghosts in every room. They talked to me all the time. They said, Where am I? How did I get here? Help me. Please help me. I'm so scared.* The next day he'd been summoned to the headmaster's office. The headmaster had received an angry phone call from the girl's father. She'd woken up in the night screaming that she'd heard her mother's voice. It turned out that her mum had died in a car crash the previous year.

The headmaster had sternly warned Henry to keep his ghost stories to himself.

So now he ignored the questions too. For that matter, questions or no questions, he simply ignored everyone as much as possible. It hadn't taken his classmates long to realise that he wanted to be left alone. Apart from the moronic bullies, they were happy to oblige.

Henry kicked a stone along, his lips pursed like he was sucking on something sour. He couldn't stop thinking about the way his dad had looked at him in the kitchen. It had made him want to yell, *Why do you hate me so much?* But what would have been the point when they both already knew the answer?

"Jacob," murmured Henry. "Jacob." The anger drained from his features as he repeated his brother's name, leaving behind a sort of jaded blankness.

His expression soured again as he lifted his eyes to the groups of kids chatting and laughing at the school gates.

He turned on his heel suddenly and strode back the way he'd come. He went into a café, ordered a coke and took it to an empty table. Someone had spilled sugar on the tabletop. He absentmindedly drew three concentric circles in it with his fingertip. A bluebottle fly landed in the centre circle. He studied its translucent wings, the curved black hairs on its back and spindly legs, the oily red sheen of its disc-like eyes.

"Beelzebub, is that your name?" he asked it.

The fly buzzed into the air briefly before settling on the sugar again.

"Where's Jacob? Where's my brother? Is he at Fenton House?" Henry was momentarily silent as if waiting for an answer, then he added, "Wherever he is, you can't have him." He slammed his palm down on the fly and felt its fat body pop. He lifted his hand, revealing a swirl of greenish-yellow blood in the sugar. The squished insect was stuck to his palm. He flicked it off and wiped his hand with a serviette.

He left the café and mooched along a street lined by small shops. All around was the hustle and bustle of suburban London – shoppers, office workers, street cleaners, dog walkers, joggers, mothers pushing prams – but he appeared oblivious to it. When a spot of rain landed on the back of his neck, he squinted up at a sky mottled with gold-edged grey clouds. If it was going to rain, he would have to find shelter. It was only ten o'clock. There were another five-and-a-half hours to kill before he could return home.

He let his feet carry him past jumbles of Edwardian and Victorian houses, boxy maisonettes and low-rise flats. He knew where he was going without having to look. He came this way most days with Edgar. There were places nearer to home to walk the pug, but they were also nearer to Whipps Cross Hospital. The merest glimpse of the hospital's red brick Gothic towers could bring on flashbacks – Dad running into A&E with Jacob in his arms; Doctors and nurses flocking around Jacob; that last fleeting glimpse of Jacob being rushed away on a trolley bed; Dad asking, *What happened?*

That was the first time he'd seen *that* look in his dad's eyes. The doubting, suspicious, fearful look that said, *Did you do it deliberately? Did you mean to hurt your brother? Did you? Did you?*

Henry became aware of a tingle between his shoulder blades. The unsettling sensation crawled up his neck like static-charged fingers. He glanced over his shoulder. A woman was staring at him from the opposite side of the street. As their eyes connected, Henry's breath stopped in his throat. The woman was dressed head-to-toe in black – black boots, black drainpipes, black leather jacket. She had short, blood-red hair and a pinched, pasty face. Black mascara was daubed around her eyes.

He felt a sudden suffocating sensation, like his ribs were constricting around his lungs. He knew *those* eyes.

An image sprang into his mind – a naked, starved-looking creature, her body a mass of bleeding scratches, her eyes so swollen with fear that they appeared to fill her face.

A wind picked up, blowing rain into Henry's eyes. *Faith,* the wind seemed to whisper. *Faith, Faith...*

He gave a sharp shake of his head. It couldn't be her. It wasn't possible.

The next instant, before he was even really aware of what he was doing, he was running away from the woman. He didn't look to see if she gave chase. He didn't want to know. All he wanted to do was put as much distance as he could between her and himself.

Legs pumping as hard as he could make them go, he swerved into a side street. A few metres further on, he veered onto a footpath that cut between some houses. He still couldn't bring himself to look back. He had the strongest feeling that if he looked into *those* eyes again his heart would stop and he'd drop dead on the spot.

The alleyway passed into the shadows of tall trees that dotted a patch of grass. A church loomed into view. Beyond iron railings, ranks of lichen-spotted gravestones laid siege to the golden stone building. The sun peeping between the clouds sparkled on tall stained-glass windows.

His lungs heaving, Henry ran across a small carpark to a tree-lined avenue of graves and altar tombs. As on most weekdays, the graveyard was deserted. He often wandered aimlessly there with Edgar trailing along at his heels. Occasionally he would lie on the grass at the graveyard's centre, where the noise of the city was like waves murmuring over a shingle beach. And sometimes in those moments, he could almost imagine he was back on the Lizard Peninsula. The cries of gulls, the briny air, the black cliffs, the emerald sea, the granite spires of Fenton House – he could remember it all so clearly, yet at the same time it seemed as unreal as a dream.

A path led past the church's square bell tower to wooden double doors. Heavy-duty iron hinges creaked as Henry opened one half of the doors.

His footsteps slowed as he advanced into the lofty, silent nave. The stained-glass windows were casting a rainbow of light across the whitewashed walls. As he dropped onto a pew, a cloud passed in front of the sun, dousing the room in shadow.

"She won't come in here," he told himself, watching the entrance. "She *can't* come in here."

Minutes crawled by like hours. Rain began to pitter-patter against the windows. He hugged his arms across himself, shivering as his sweat cooled. It was colder in the church than it was outside. He looked more closely at his surroundings. Thick stone pillars and dark-wood pews flanked the central aisle. Carved portraits of serene faces were inlaid into the walls. Tall organ pipes fenced off the rear of the nave. At the front of the nave, several steps led to a wooden altar and an eagle shaped brass lectern.

Henry inhaled the calming scent of old wood and beeswax, but it didn't ease the tension from his face. Had he really seen Faith? Could it simply have been someone that looked like her?

He thought about how the woman's eyes had drilled into him. Why would a stranger have been staring at him like that? And if it wasn't a stranger, then who else could it be but Faith?

A slimy feeling slithered its way through his mind as another possibility occurred to him. "What's your name?" he murmured, laying down and resting his cheek against the cool wood. "What's your name? What's your..."

The question faded on his lips. His eyelids seemed to weigh

a ton. God, he was so tired. He hadn't slept properly in... well, in forever. Sleep draped itself over him like a warm blanket. He felt a brief sinking sensation. Then, as if someone had removed a blindfold from his eyes, he found himself standing in a high-ceilinged room softly lit by logs burning in a stone fireplace. A bearskin rug was splayed out in front of the fire, its massive jaws gaping in a silent roar. A stag's head stared beadily down from above the mantelpiece. The wood-panelled walls were hung with paintings of bizarre creatures – a bearded man with a bare muscular torso and the lower body of a horse; a bird with flames licking its crystal plumage; a bloated, warty toad wearing a crown of leaves. The paintings seemed to pulse and sway in the firelight.

A trio of concentric circles with what looked like a rifle's crosshairs at their centre were chalked on the floorboards. Four words, each lined up with a point of the cross, circumnavigated the outer circle – ADONAI, AZLA, TZABAOTH, TETRAGRAMMATON.

Henry tilted an ear at a closed door. Was that a murmur of sobbing from beyond it? The sound swelled like the moan of a rising storm. There was something gut-wrenchingly familiar about it.

"Jacob." The name floated from his lips and hung almost visibly in the air.

He started towards the door, but it was like he was on a treadmill. No matter how fast he went, the door didn't get any closer. Looking down, he saw that he was in the centre of the inner circle. He stiffened as if he was, indeed, caught in a rifle's crosshairs.

At that instant, the sobbing stopped. A hoarse, disembodied voice took its place, fading in and out of hearing. "In the name of the Father... Eternal and unchanging... Hear me... Reveal... My enemies..."

My enemies... My enemies...

The words echoed in Henry's ears, lifting him out of sleep. His eyelids fluttered open. Squinting at the sunlight that was, once again, splashed across the nave, he sat up. A bespectacled, snowy-bearded vicar in a white surplice and black stole was at the lectern. Spotting Henry, the vicar removed his glasses and said in surprised tone, "Oh hello there."

Henry sprang to his feet to make a run for it, but hesitated as the vicar said, "It's OK. You're not in any trouble."

Despite this assurance, Henry edged towards the double doors.

"You don't have to leave," the vicar continued gently, as if he was talking to a skittish animal. He tapped a notebook on the lectern. "I'm practising a sermon. Perhaps you could let me know what you think of it."

Henry paused by the doors. "I don't know much about the Bible and all that kind of thing."

The vicar smiled. "I'll let you in on a secret. Sometimes I feel like I don't know much about 'all that kind of thing' either."

Henry chewed his upper lip. "Can I ask you something?"

The vicar spread his hands. "Ask away. That's what I'm here for."

"You believe in ghosts, right?"

As if Henry had laid a verbal trap, the vicar chose his words with care. "I believe in an afterlife."

"Well what if when someone dies they don't go to Heaven or Hell? What if their soul or spirit or whatever is trapped here?"

"How do you mean trapped?"

Henry didn't reply for a moment, then gave a sheepish shrug.

"You can speak freely," said the vicar. He gestured to their surroundings. "Whatever you say will go no further than these walls."

"Demons." Henry's voice was a self-conscious mumble, but the nave's acoustics carried it to the lectern.

"Demons?" the vicar said, as if unsure he'd heard correctly.

"Demons want to trap souls, don't they?"

The vicar's smile broadened. "It sounds to me like you've been watching too many horror movies."

Henry's face scrunched in annoyance. "You don't know what you're talking about," he retorted, turning to yank open the doors.

"I'm sorry," said the vicar. "That was patronising."

Henry gave him a sidelong look and waited to see what else he had to say.

The vicar was no longer smiling. "Why are you so interested in demons and..." he paused for the right words, "lost souls?"

Again, Henry replied with a shrug.

The vicar gave a nod of understanding. "I'd be lying if I said I had the answers to your questions. I will say this – the Bible warns us, do not seek out the mysterious and the supernatural. You will only find evil."

His forehead furrowing, Henry lowered his gaze.

"Are you in some sort of trouble?" asked the vicar. "If so, perhaps I can help."

"I have to go now. Thanks. Bye," Henry said quickly.

He was out of the door before the vicar could respond.

Glancing all around like a rabbit emerging from its burrow, he scurried along a footpath flanked by glistening wet graves. Wisps of steam rose from the weathered headstones as they dried in the hot sun.

He looked over his shoulder at the church clock. It was almost three o'clock! He'd only seemed to doze off for minutes, but five hours had passed. The school bell would soon be ringing for home time. Relief swept through him at the realisation that he needn't spend the next few hours on the streets. Not that the walls of a house offered much, if any, protection from Faith or whatever entity was pretending to be her.

Henry put on a spurt of speed at the churchyard gates, racing across a quiet road towards an opposite street corner. The quickest route home was to go back the way he'd come, but he would rather have gone miles out of his way than pass the spot where he'd seen Faith.

The vicar's words kept going through his mind – *the Bible warns us, do not seek out the mysterious and the supernatural. You will only find evil.*

But what if the mysterious and the supernatural sought you out? What then?

To avoid being followed, he took a circuitous route through a warren of streets. He paused at a scrap of grass not far from home, his gaze drawn by a shrill keening sound. Curiosity lit up his eyes. A big ginger cat was tormenting a pigeon, repeatedly pouncing on it, then retreating into a crouch. The pigeon staggered around, calling out in distress and weakly flapping its blood-spotted wings.

Henry's eyes darted up and down the street, as furtive and wary as those of the cat. There was no one to be seen. He took out a smartphone, zoomed its camera in on the grisly little scene and set it recording. The pigeon flopped over in exhaustion. With a kind of lazy pleasure, the cat prowled forwards to lock its jaws around its prey's throat. It remained clamped onto the helpless bird for a minute or two. Then, with a derisive flick of its tail, it padded away.

Henry watched the departing cat with something akin to admiration. His mum said cats were cruel. He didn't agree. Cats were clever, not cruel. They knew when to be still and when to pounce.

He approached the pigeon and squatted down for a closer look. Black-tipped grey feathers were scattered around the motionless bird. Dark red puncture wounds glistened on its throat. Henry selected an intact feather and prodded its quill into the blood. He took an A4 pad from his rucksack, opened it at a blank page and drew a circle in blood. Wetting the quill tip again, he wrote 'ADONAI' outside the circle. He tore out the sheet of paper and placed it on the grass. Like he was creating some surreal work of art, he picked up the pigeon and carefully placed it in the circle.

That tingling sense of being watched stole over him again. Eyes narrowed against what he might see, he turned to the street. A spindly old lady with a Jack Russell at her side was watching him. There was an unmistakable gleam of disapproval in her eyes. Blinking away from her gaze, he rose to his feet and hurried home.

He stopped at a low gate and glanced back along the street. The lady and her dog were gone. Were they apparitions too? He knew what his mum would say – *You're just imagining things and scaring yourself. Stop this or you'll make yourself ill again.* In her own way, she was just as bad as his dad. Always dismissing and belittling him. Always making him feel stupid.

His eyes glimmering with resentment, Henry crossed a postage-stamp of a yard to a windowless door. As quietly as possible, he inserted his key into the lock and opened the door. In the gloomy porch beyond, he hung up his coat and took off his shoes. He didn't linger, not for a second. Another windowless door led to the small square of hallway. Edgar emerged from the living-room, wagging his stubby tail.

"Hello boy," whispered Henry, scooping up the pug, smiling as Edgar's rough tongue licked his face. A murmur of music and a clink of pans came from the kitchen. His mum, he knew, would be humming along to the radio as she cooked tea. He looked towards the top of the stairs, hoping that, as usual, his dad was closeted away writing in the front bedroom. He couldn't face the thought of having to spin him some yarn about his school day.

He padded upstairs with Edgar in his arms. A swishing sound drew his gaze to the nursery. His dad was on his knees varnishing the floorboards. Henry's stomach sank at the sight. His dad always wrote until 6 or 7 pm, unless he couldn't focus for some reason. No doubt he'd been stewing all day over their clash that morning.

As Henry tiptoed into his bedroom, Edgar wriggled out of his clutches and belly-flopped to the carpet. Henry grimaced at the thud. Seconds later, there came a knock at the door and his dad poked his head into the room. Henry held in a sigh, bracing himself for another of his dad's dreaded talks.

Adam smiled at him and Edgar. "Hello you two."

Henry's eyes narrowed a fraction. There was something not entirely convincing about his dad's smile. "Stop pretending you're happy to see me." He regretted the words the instant they left this mouth, not because they erased his dad's smile, but because they were as good as asking for the very thing he wanted to avoid.

Adam's gaze dropped to the floor, only for a heartbeat, but it was enough to bring a sneer of vindication to Henry's face.

When Adam's eyes met Henry's again, there was an appeal for forgiveness in them. "I love you."

"Then why do you make me feel like everything I do is wrong?"

Adam winced as if the words were needles piercing his skin. "I'm sorry if that's how I make you feel, Henry."

Henry resisted the urge to fire off another retort, hoping his dad would get the message and go away. He stared at his feet as his dad continued, "I hate to see you like this and I feel as if it's..." He corrected himself reproachfully. "I *know* it's my fault. I'm the one in the wrong, Henry. Not you."

Henry squinted at his dad as if he suspected a trick.

Adam cleared his throat, obviously working up to something. "These past few months all I've thought about is the baby. I haven't given you any attention. I want us to spend some time together before Zara's born." The forced-looking smile returned to his lips. "We could go shopping for ear plugs. You're going to need them soon enough."

Instead of amusement, the clanging attempt at humour drew a vacant stare from Henry. For a second there, he'd thought his dad was actually going to be honest. He should have known better. *Why don't you just say it? You think I deliberately hurt Jacob. And you're scared shitless I'll do the same to the baby.* The words flashed through his mind, but he wasn't about to open that can of worms. That would be too much like admitting his dad was right.

Silence hung between them like a foul smell. Henry's gaze drifted to Edgar. The pug was curled up on the bed, already snoring. The only thing Edgar seemed to enjoy more than eating was sleeping. Henry often thought how easy life would be if they could swap places – no school, no expectations, no worries. So long as Edgar had a plentiful supply of food and somewhere comfortable to crash out, he was happy.

A deep crease scarred the space between Henry's eyebrows. *Happy.* God, how he hated that word. He'd never really felt happy. Not even when Jacob was alive. Not that anyone seemed to notice back then, because Jacob had been happy enough for both of them. His ever-present grin had made Henry's skin crawl with irritation.

The crease faded. No, that wasn't right. There had been a time when he was truly happy. Seven days that had come and gone like a flash of lightning, yet were more precious to him than all his other memories combined. He could sit lost in his head for hours reliving that cherished week – playing in Fenton House's garden, walking on the cliffs, gazing at the sea, exploring the house, discovering the secret passageways...

"Henry?"

His dad's infuriatingly concerned voice dragged him back to the present. Henry's gaze moved around his messy little bedroom and the narrow landing. How he hated this house too. Sometimes he felt like there wasn't enough air in its cramped interior to breathe properly.

"You looked like you were miles away," said Adam.

Henry shifted uneasily from foot to foot. His dad was staring at him as if he knew only too well where his mind had wandered off to. "I have to do my homework."

The lie had the desired effect. "Oh, OK." Adam started to turn away, then added in an awkward hesitating manner, "If you need anything, if you want any... *help*, just let me know." His gaze lingered on Henry for a few more seconds before he left the room.

Henry quickly closed the door and listened to his dad's footfalls moving away from it. He waited until he heard the creak of the nursery floorboards before turning to sit down at his desk.

He popped in a pair of earbuds and put on some music, shutting out everything except what was right in front of him.

He scrutinised the video of the cat toying with the pigeon as if he was trying to decipher a puzzle.

After several viewings, he took a copy of *Between Worlds* from a bookshelf and flicked through it to a photo of three concentric chalked circles with a cross at their centre. 'ADONAI', 'AZLA', 'TZABAOTH', 'TETRAGRAMMATON' were written along the outer circle. A caption identified the photo as a 'Reconstruction of the symbol of summoning found on the living room floor'. Notes were scrawled in the book's margins – 'Does not conjure demons by name', 'Who was Faith trying to summon?'

He switched on his PC's monitor and Googled 'Adonai'. It brought up the dictionary definition – 'A Hebrew name for God'. A link led him to a page listing the names of God in Judaism. He scrolled through the long list, lingering on any names that caught his interest. 'Tetragrammaton – the name of the biblical God of Israel'. 'Tzabaoth – the God of the armies of Israel'. 'YHWH – the most commonly used name of God in the Hebrew bible.' 'El Shaddai – God Almighty'. 'Baal – my Lord, my Master, my Owner'. He clicked on a bracketed link '(*see also Baal the demon*)'.

A tingle wormed its way through him as he found himself staring at a beautifully grotesque drawing of a three-headed creature. The heads of a cat, a toad and a man were perched atop the hairy legs of a spider. The man wore a jewel-encrusted crown, from beneath which protruded a pair of pointed ears. His brow was furrowed and his eyes looked worried. A nose so long that it overhung his downturned mouth dominated his face. The toad had bulbous eyes and a lipless mouth as wide as its face. The cat had black fur on its head, fading to white on its throat and face. There was a watchful gleam in its eyes.

Henry skimmed over the accompanying text. 'Bael (also Baal or Ba'al) is one of the seven princes of Hell. The Pseudomonarchia Daemonum states that, "Their first king is called Bael who, when he is conjured up, appeareth with three heads; the first, like a tode; the second, like a man; the third, like a cat. He speaketh with a hoarse voice, he maketh a man go invisible (and wise), he hath under his obedience and rule sixtie and six legions of divels."'

Henry broke off from reading, running his suddenly dry tongue over his lips. "He speaketh with a hoarse voice," he said, thinking about the voice from his dream. Or had it been the vicar's voice?

He Googled 'Pseudomonarchia Daemonum'. An occult blog described it as a 'sixteenth century catalogue of demons'. A smile flitted across his face as he pictured a sort of Argos catalogue of demons and the prices they demanded for fulfilling the deepest, darkest desires of those that summoned them.

He thumbed through *Between Worlds* to an underlined passage – '"Call it the Devil. Call it a demonic spirit. Call it a multi-dimensional entity. Call it what you will, but make no mistake, it's out there waiting, always waiting for you to invite it to a banquet where it dines on your greed, lust, hate, envy and anger."' They weren't his dad's words. To his dad, greed, lust, hate, envy and anger *were* the demons. The words belonged to an expert on the supernatural that his dad had turned to in desperation when things started going bump in the night at Fenton House. Supposedly, such 'multi-dimensional entities' lived in the spaces between spaces. No, not *lived*, Henry corrected himself. These entities had never lived. Life was the thing they both hated and hungered for more than anything else.

His thoughts returned to his conversation with the vicar.

You believe in ghosts, right?

I believe in an afterlife.

He flicked forwards a few pages to another highlighted

passage – '"The afterlife is just a label. I'm talking about alternate realities where there are things that are constantly striving to find a way into this world. Walter Lewarne had an overwhelming desire to appease the spirits of the dead. That's dangerous enough in itself. When spirits don't pass on, it's always for a reason. And that reason usually isn't good. Such spirits are angry, lost and confused. They often don't realise they're dead. All they know is they feel wronged and hunger for some sort of resolution."'

Henry shuddered as the expert's words seemed to conjure up a faint echo of the sobbing from his dream. He shook off the sensation and read on. '"Speaking to them can provide that resolution, but I suspect Walter tried to go a step further. I think he was searching for a way to allow spirits to enter the physical plane. For that he would have needed a portal."'

"The mirror," murmured Henry, closing the book. He stared at the mirror on the cover. Walter's mirror. His portal to those parallel dimensions. Was that how Faith had found her way back into this world? Could others do the same?

There was only one way to find out.

He Googled 'How to summon Bael'. The top link took him to a webpage with an illustration of 'Bael's Sigil' – a circle wrapped around a smaller circle. 'B A E L' was written clockwise between the circles, each letter corresponding to a point of the compass. Within the smaller circle was an enigmatic symbol – a leaf-like shape pointing north-south, overlaid by a tube pointing east-west. From either end of the tube flared what looked like triple-headed axes. A pair of stickman legs with circles for feet sprouted from the lowest part of the leaf. Between the legs was an outline drawing of what appeared to be a ram's head with inward curling horns.

The blog instructed Henry to draw the sigil. He dug a protractor out of his pencil case and set about doing so. He took his time, painstakingly ensuring he got the details right. As the sigil took shape, an unsettling sensation that he wasn't alone crept over him. He rose to peek out of the door. There was no sign of his parents or anyone else, but the feeling wouldn't go away. It reminded him of how he felt when he awoke in the dead of night with only his inner demons for company. Now, as at those times, taunting voices seemed to whisper in his ears.

No one likes you. Not even your own parents. Dad hates you. Mum only pretends to like you. You'll see. She'll forget about you as soon as the baby's born. You might as well be dead. At least then you'd be with Jacob. Although Jacob probably hates you even more than Dad for what you did to him. And anyway, he's going up to Heaven and you're going down to Hell. You're going to burn for eternity.

"Leave me alone. Leave me alone," Henry repeated, until the voices retreated to whatever dark corner of his mind they'd crawled out of.

His gaze alternated between the screen and his drawing. Satisfied with his handiwork, he read the rest of the instructions. According to the blog, he didn't need candles, an animal to sacrifice or any of the other stuff he associated with black magic to summon Bael. Apart from the sigil, all he needed was an 'enn'. 'An enn is a chant in a demonic tongue used to invite specific entities into the physical plane.' stated the blog. 'Every demon has its own enn. See below for Bael's. Warning: do not speak the enn out loud unless you are prepared for the consequences.'

Henry committed Bael's enn to memory. *Ayer Secore On Ca Bael. Ayer Secore On Ca Bael…*

He rooted through a jumble of stationary until he found a chunk of white chalk. His gaze returned to the paperback. "I know your name," he said to the spectral face in Walter's mirror. "Now you'll have to show yourself to me."

4

Accusations

Heaving a sigh, Adam pressed the lid onto the tin of varnish. He'd had enough of DIY. Right then, what he needed more than anything was a glass of wine.

He headed downstairs, pausing at the bottom to look into the porch. It was strange. He often thought about demolishing the little wood-and-brick structure, yet knew he would never do so. There was nowhere else where he felt so connected to Jacob, nowhere else where he could picture him so clearly. He saw him right then, lying on a bed of broken glass, drawing his last breaths.

Tears threatened to find their way into Adam's eyes. Blinking them back, he headed through the living room. Ella was stooped over a chopping board in the kitchen. She glanced at him with red-rimmed eyes. Tears were streaming down her flushed cheeks. "Onions," she explained a touch unconvincingly, wiping her eyes with the back of her hand.

Adam ducked into the fridge, took out a bottle of white wine and poured himself a glass. He didn't bother returning the bottle to the fridge. He would need it again soon.

"I wish I could have a glass," said Ella, watching Adam take a tellingly big mouthful of the pale liquid.

He glanced at her enormous belly. “It won't be all that long before you can.”

“Not if I'm breast feeding.”

“I'm sure the odd glass wouldn't do any harm.”

Ella gave an unconvinced, “Hmm.” They both knew there was no way she would touch a drop until Zara was weaned off breast-milk. Just as they were both well aware that if they weren't careful, they would cosset the child into oblivion. Adam lifted his glass to his lips again.

“Did you even taste that?” Ella gently chided.

He glanced at his glass, saw it was empty, then reached for the bottle. “Henry's home.”

“Oh, I didn't hear him come in. Where is he?”

“In his bedroom.” Knowing it would put Ella's mind at ease, he added, “Edgar's with him.”

“Good. He spends too much time on his own up there.”

“Not that Edgar's much company. He must sleep twenty hours a day.”

Ella gave Adam a concerned smile. “You seem tense. Has something happened?”

He made no reply. What was he supposed to say? *I think Henry's seriously ill and I'm not sure there's anything we can do to help him.*

Now it was Ella's turn to sigh heavily. “Sometimes I wonder if it's our fault.”

“If what's our fault?”

“I don't think Henry's ever been happy, except for when we were living at...”

She trailed off, but Adam didn't need to be a mind reader to fill in the blanks. The unspoken words seemed to echo in his ears – *Fenton House, Fenton House...* They had a tacit agreement that they wouldn't mention that place. They'd only lived there for a week, but during that time they'd seen a new side to Henry. It was as if the house had unlocked a door inside him. For those seven days, he'd truly come alive, like a prisoner set free. The day they returned to London was the day the cell door had slammed back shut.

"How can it be our fault?" asked Adam. "We raised him the same as Jacob."

"Did we though? I tried to treat them both the same, but..." Ella closed her eyes briefly like she was confessing to something shameful. "Jacob was so easy to be around, always laughing and joking. With Henry it's..." She struggled to find the words to explain. Her gaze travelled the cramped kitchen. "I often ask myself if this is the best place for–"

Anticipating what she was about to say, Adam interrupted her with a shake of his head. "We've been down that route before, Ella, and look what happened. Besides, this is hardly the right time to be thinking about moving."

"I know, I know," she agreed reluctantly, touching her bump. She rolled her eyes towards the ceiling. "It's just, I want..." She faded off into a melancholy-tinged silence.

Adam pictured Henry in the room above, poring over the list of demons – Satan, Beelzebub, Lucifer, Bel-whatever-he-was-called and the rest of the motley crew. A faint scornful smile touched his lips. Here they were in a city teeming with criminals of every ilk, and there Henry was worrying about make-believe beasties. It was laughable. Or was it? Maybe it was the most natural thing in the world for him to be escaping into fantasies of other worlds and mythical creatures.

He gave Ella's hand a gentle squeeze. "You want what's best for everyone."

She met his gaze for a few heartbeats, then let her head fall forwards onto his chest. Cupping a hand against the back of her head, he kissed her wavy hair.

"What if it *is* our fault?" Ella's voice was a guilt-wracked whisper.

Adam picked his words with care. "Perhaps we have been bad parents." He touched Ella's belly tentatively, almost as if it frightened him. "But now we have a chance to get it right."

She frowned. "What you mean is we should do our best to make sure Zara is nothing like Henry."

Yes, that's exactly what I mean. As the thought passed through his mind, he blinked away from her gaze.

Reading his reaction, Ella drew back from him. A silence heavy with regret hung between them. She flinched at a knock on the front door. "Who could that be?"

"I'll go see."

With the swiftness of someone relieved for an excuse to leave a room, Adam put down his glass and made his way to the door. A stern-faced old lady was standing stiffly on the path. Her grim grey eyes exuded a kind of righteous indignation that made him wonder if she was one of the Jehovah's Witnesses that occasionally came knocking. He dredged up a smile, steeling himself for a doorstep sermon.

"Mr Piper?" she asked as solemnly as someone bringing news of a death.

A tingle of misgiving ran through him. "Yes."

"My name's Doreen Simmons. I live at number fifty-four."

"What can I do for you, Mrs Simmons?"

"I'd like to talk to you about this." Doreen opened a carrier bag, holding it at arm's length as if its contents disgusted her.

Adam peered inside the bag. His forehead wrinkled with

bemusement. "You want to talk to me about a dead pigeon?"

"Your son killed it."

A sharp dropping sensation hit Adam. "Why would Henry kill a pigeon?"

"It would be better if we spoke inside."

As irritated as he was unnerved by Doreen's pompous, grave tone, Adam was half-tempted to close the door in her face. He knew, though, that he needed to hear what she had to say. More than that, he needed Ella to hear it, not in spite of her condition but because of it. The time for making excuses for Henry was almost over. For Zara's sake, no matter how painful it might be, they had to face the future with open eyes.

He gestured for Doreen to come in. Glancing from side to side as if checking whether Henry was lurking nearby, the old lady stepped into the porch. As Adam closed the door and ushered her through to the living room, Ella called to him, "Who was it?"

"It's Doreen Simmons."

"Who?" Ella poked her head into the living room. Her eyebrows lifted at the sight of Doreen. "Oh hello."

"Hello, Mrs Piper," said Doreen, still holding the carrier bag at arm's length. "As I was just saying to your husband, I live at number fifty-four."

Ella glanced at the bag, then gave her a curious smile. "I know. I often see you walking your dog."

"Would you like to sit down, Mrs Simmons?" asked Adam, motioning to an armchair.

"No thank you." Her gaze travelled the room like she was searching for something. "I take it you're not Christians."

Ella's smile faded at the old lady's disapproving tone. "What makes you say that?"

In answer, Doreen put the bag on the coffee-table and pressed its sides down. The pigeon was lying on a bloodstained sheet of paper, its head crooked at an unnatural angle across its plump body. Dried blood speckled its ruff of white neck feathers.

"What the hell is this?" Ella asked with a nauseated swallow.

"Black magic," stated Doreen.

There was a stunned silence, then Ella echoed in confusion, "Black magic?"

"Well what else would you call this?" Doreen lifted the pigeon, revealing a circle drawn in blood alongside a single word.

The plummeting sensation hit Adam again with such force that he sank down onto the sofa.

"Adonai," Ella read out in little more than a whisper.

"Black magic," reiterated Doreen, her voice sharp with accusation. "Your son was doing black magic on that poor bird."

There was another moment of silence. Ella's usually soft features had hardened like cement. "Could you please just tell us what you saw, Mrs Simmons?" Despite the gleam of anger in her eyes, her voice was calm.

Doreen stabbed a bony finger at the circle. "I saw your son draw that *thing* with this pigeon's blood." Her words quivered with revulsion.

"Did you actually see him kill the pigeon?"

"Well, no," Doreen conceded. "But there was no one else around."

Ella flashed Adam a look in which relief merged with a sort of challenge.

Leaning forwards, he scrutinised the pigeon's blood-encrusted neck. "These look like bite marks."

"Maybe he bit it and drank its blood," Doreen suggested.

Ella laughed, arching an eyebrow at Adam that made it clear she thought the old lady wasn't quite right in the head.

"I don't find this funny," bristled Doreen.

"Neither do we, Mrs Simmons," Adam assured her.

Sensing an ally, Doreen spread her hands towards him. "I'm only here out of concern for your son."

Ella let out another brusque laugh. "Really? And here's me thinking it was because you're a meddling old bag with nothing better to do."

"H-how dare you!" spluttered Doreen, so outraged that she could barely get her words out. "If this is your attitude, there's no wonder your son's such a–"

"Such a what?" Ella broke in, her voice laced with warning.

Adam raised his hands in an appeal for calm. "We appreciate your concern, Mrs Simmons."

"Speak for yourself," snapped Ella. "I've heard enough of this nonsense. I want her to leave."

Doreen touched a crucifix pendant at her chest as if drawing resolve from it. "I know this is hard for you to hear, Mrs Piper, but your son is–"

"My son is a perfectly normal boy."

Adam gave Ella a frowning glance. Did she really believe that? Was she so blinkered by love?

Doreen pointed at the pigeon. "*That* is not the work of a normal boy. It's the work of the Devil."

Ella's eyes flared from anger to outright fury. Doreen retreated a step as if fearing the pregnant woman might take a swing at her. Adam was on his feet in a heartbeat. He inserted himself between the women and motioned towards the door. "Thank you for bringing this to our attention, Mrs Simmons."

"The reverend at St Mary's is a wonderful man," she said. "I could arrange for your son to speak–"

Ella was shaking her head before Doreen could finish. "We'll speak to Henry and find out the truth for ourselves."

Doreen eyed her indignantly. "I've told you the truth."

"I'm sure you have," Adam said diplomatically. "But perhaps you didn't see what you thought you saw. You don't know for certain that Henry killed the pigeon." He pointed to the 'black magic' symbol. "Well maybe he didn't draw that either." Self-recrimination jabbed at him. Of course Henry had drawn the fucking thing. Who else could it have been?

"I know what I saw," Doreen insisted. "And I've said what I came here to say. I only hope you have the good sense to listen." She glanced at Ella's belly. "Especially with that little one on the way."

She's right! The words teetered on the tip of Adam's tongue, but looking at Ella's exhausted face he couldn't bring himself to say them.

With that, Doreen turned to head for the front door. She stopped abruptly in the hallway and, with a slow twist of her head, looked towards the top of the stairs. Her lips compressed into severe lines at the sight of Henry. "Come down here and tell your parents what you did," she demanded.

Henry made no reply, engaging her in a staring contest. Irritation prickled through Adam at Henry's well-practised blank look.

Doreen's hand returned to her crucifix. A slight quiver found its way into her strident voice as she repeated, "Come down here."

Ella craned her neck around the doorframe to peer up the stairs. "Go to your room, Henry."

He didn't acknowledge his mum's request either. With slow relish, he mouthed at Doreen, *Fuck you.*

"Henry!" Adam exclaimed in a reprimanding way.

"You little demon," gasped Doreen. "Do you know how God punishes those that needlessly kill His creatures?"

"Yeah, he sends them down there." Henry pointed to the floor. "I hope I do go to Hell. Who wants to spend eternity in Heaven with a bunch of nosey bitches like you?"

"How dare you speak to Mrs Simmons like that," said Adam. "Apologise right now."

Henry's insolent gaze slid across to his dad.

"Apologise." Adam's tone left no room for argument.

Henry turned vacant eyes towards Doreen again. "Sorry." The word was dripping with insincerity. Before she could respond, he stomped into his bedroom and slammed the door behind himself.

Treating Adam and Ella to a pitying look, Doreen said, "I'll pray for you."

"Save your prayers for someone who gives a shit," said Ella.

Doreen stared at her speechlessly for a moment before turning to Adam. "God help you."

With a hiss of breath that indicated she'd reached the end of her tether, Ella turned and strode from view.

Biting down on his own irritation at Doreen's melodramatic words, Adam gestured with an open hand towards the front door. The old lady gave him one last lingering look as if hoping he would see sense. Then, nodding to herself like she was satisfied she'd done her godly duty, she made her way outside.

Ella reappeared clutching the pigeon. She tossed it after Doreen, shouting, "Don't forget your pet."

The pigeon bobbled along the paving stones and came to a rest against the gate. Doreen looked from the bird to Ella, her lips moving silently, perhaps bestowing the promised prayer.

"Can you believe that crap?" Ella ranted as Adam shut the front door. "Who the hell does she think she is, talking to us like that? The sanctimonious old–"

"Please Ella," Adam implored. "You shouldn't be getting yourself worked up like this."

"I need to talk to Henry." She turned towards the stairs.

"Hang on. Let's just take a moment to decide what we want to say to him."

Ella allowed Adam to usher her to the sofa. She sat with her arms crossed defensively over her bump.

With an oddly stiff movement, Adam picked up the bloodstained sheet of paper. *ADONAI.* The word seemed to ring out like an alarm in his mind. Others followed it – *AZLA, TZABAOTH, TETRAGRAMMATON* – conjuring up an image of Faith Gooden and three other figures, all of them dressed head-to-toe in black, gathered around the completed magic symbol in Fenton House's candlelit living room. "So he's summoning demons now, is he?"

"Don't be ridiculous, Adam," retorted Ella. "You don't even believe in any of that."

"It doesn't matter what *I* believe." He glanced at the ceiling. "It's what *he* believes."

Ella accepted his words with a heavy sigh. "So what do you think we should do?"

Adam forced his lips into what he hoped was a comforting

smile. “Maybe this is a good thing.”

“A good thing?” Ella repeated as if doubting her ears.

“It forces us to deal with this situation before…” He trailed off with a *you-know-what* glance at Ella’s bump.

“Yes, but deal with it how?”

Adam was revealingly silent.

Another sigh escaping her, Ella heaved herself to her feet and headed for the hallway. “Henry,” she called up the stairs. “Come down here, please. Your father and I want to talk to you.” She looked at Adam with both a plea and a warning in her eyes. “Don’t be too hard on him.”

Maybe if we’d been harder on him, we wouldn’t be in this situation, Adam resisted the impulse to reply. His stomach knotted at the sound of Henry descending the stairs. He retrieved his glass of wine and took a quick mouthful. The cool liquid eased its way down his throat and loosened the knot.

Like a rat sniffing at a trap, Henry hesitatingly entered the room. He peered at his parents from under his long fringe.

Adam held up the bloodstained sheet of paper and said simply, “Well?”

Treating him to the same dead-eyed look as he’d given Doreen, Henry shrugged his slender shoulders.

“What about the pigeon whose blood you drew this with? Mrs Simmons says you killed it. Is she right?”

Henry lowered his gaze, obstinately maintaining his silence.

“Talk to us, Henry,” implored Ella. “How are we supposed to help you if you don’t tell us what’s going on?”

The anonymous caller’s faltering voice shivered through Adam’s mind. *Help me… Please help me… I’m scared… Please help me, Daddy.*

"I..." Henry nervously picked at a zit on his chin. "I keep dreaming about Fenton House."

"Fenton House." Adam rolled his eyes. "Christ, will we ever hear the last of that bloody house?"

Henry shot his dad an aggrieved look. "This is why I never talk to you about this stuff."

"You never talk to us about *anything*, Henry."

"Oh screw this."

Henry turned to storm off, but Ella caught hold of his hand. "We're sorry you feel you can't talk to us, Henry." Glancing pointedly at Adam, she added, "Aren't we?"

With almost comical indecision, he opened his mouth, closed it, then opened it again and said, "Yes."

Henry cast him a doubting sidelong look.

"Tell us about your dream," urged Ella.

Henry's gaze returned to the floor. After a moment, he began, "I'm in the living room. There's a magic symbol on the floor." He glanced at the sheet of paper. "You know the one." He paused, eyeing his parents as if he was unsure whether to continue.

"Go on," Ella gently prompted.

"Do you know what Adonai means?"

"You know full well that we–" Adam impatiently started to say, but fell silent at a sharp glance from Ella.

"Adonai is a Jewish name for God," she said.

"What about Baal?" asked Henry.

Her forehead furrowed. "Baal?"

"Baal is a name for God too, but it's also another name for

the demon Bael."

"To know the name of a thing is to have power over that thing," said Adam.

The quote drew a glare from Henry. "You've been snooping around my room."

"Hang on, you've lost me," said Ella, looking back and forth between the two of them.

"Henry thinks this Bael is the entity that Walter Lewarne supposedly brought into Fenton House," explained Adam. Looking intently at Henry, he added, "Isn't that right?"

Henry's mouth hung open for a few seconds, then he shut it with a click of his teeth.

Adam nodded as if the response answered his question.

Henry pouted at his feet as his dad continued, "What I don't understand is why you need to know its name. We're never going back to Fenton House, so even if demons exist – which they don't – but even if they do, what does it matter which one haunts Fenton House?"

"Demons don't haunt places, ghosts haunt places," Henry muttered.

"No, Henry, *people* haunt places," Adam corrected him back. "Fenton House isn't haunted. *You* are."

With a soft plea in her voice, Ella shifted the conversation back to the dream. "So you're in Fenton House's living room. What next?"

"Someone's crying," Henry resumed sullenly. "I can't see who, but I know–"

"It's Jacob," Adam pre-empted.

Henry's dark eyes narrowed as if he suspected his dad had been snooping around not only in his room, but in his head.

"Jacob?" Ella echoed, her voice quiet with unease. "Why would Jacob be there? And why would he be crying?"

"He's there because Dad and I called him there," Henry said like it should have been obvious. "We looked into Walter Lewarne's mirror and asked him to come back."

Adam shook his head. "No, no, that's not quite right."

"Yes it is. You looked into the mirror and said, 'I'll never forgive myself for what happened to you, Jacob. I'd give my life to be able to tell you how sorry I am. If you come back to me, I'll never let you down again.'"

"You're misquoting me."

"Did you or didn't you say those words?" Henry demanded to know like a lawyer cross-examining the accused.

"Yes," Adam conceded, wincing as his thoughts returned to the moment of desperate weakness Henry was referring to. "But not in the way you're suggesting."

Henry responded with a dismissive shake of his head. "You tried to bring Jacob back. Admit it. You tried to bring him back. Didn't you? Didn't you?"

Adam's forehead knotted tighter and tighter at Henry's badgering. His mouth opened, but once again he closed it without saying anything. His gaze fell away from Henry.

"And it worked," Henry continued with a little rise of triumph. "And now Jacob's crying because he's trapped there. Bael is holding him prisoner."

His words compelled Ella to ask, "Holding him prisoner? Why?"

Henry flapped a hand back and forth between himself and his parents. "Because of us. Bael wanted our souls, but we escaped. So he's taking revenge on Jacob."

Ella's breath suddenly caught in her diaphragm. She

clutched her belly as Zara dealt her several jolting blows.

Adam moved swiftly to her side. “What is it?”

She wafted him away. “I’m fine.”

“No you’re not. This is upsetting the baby.”

“Bael will never stop torturing Jacob,” said Henry.

Adam glared at him. “That’s enough.”

“That’s why we have to go back to Fenton House,” persisted Henry. “We have to free–”

“I said that’s enough!” Adam exploded.

Henry flinched and said nothing more, but defiantly held his dad’s gaze.

Adam thrust out a hand. “Give me your phone.”

“Why?”

“Give. Me. Your. Phone,” Adam repeated, enunciating each word like Henry was hard of hearing.

Henry’s eyes widened as if something had occurred to him. “I can prove I didn’t kill that pigeon.” He pulled out his phone, tapped at the screen and displayed it to his parents.

Some of the strain faded from Ella’s features as she watched the footage of the cat killing the pigeon. “I knew the old bag was wrong.” She shot Adam a look of vindication. “Henry would never hurt an animal.”

Wrinkles of doubt crept across Adam’s face. Maybe Ella was right. Maybe Henry would never deliberately hurt an animal or, for that matter, anything else.

“Give me your phone,” Adam said for a third time, his tone softer but no less resolute.

Henry grudgingly handed it over.

Adam navigated to ‘Call History’. It was empty. He

frowned at the screen, unsure whether to be relieved or troubled. "Have you cleared your call history today?"

"No."

Adam replayed the anonymous phone calls in his mind – the sobbing that had seemed to reach him from across a vast distance, the gut-wrenching plea for help. He thought about Henry's dream. It couldn't be a coincidence. There was just no way. So either Henry had made the calls or Jacob really was–

He cut off the thought with a shake of his head and lifted his gaze to Henry. "It was you, wasn't it?"

"What was me? I don't know what you're on about."

"You've lost me again as well," said Ella.

Adam looked at her apologetically. "I should have told you about this earlier, Ella, but I didn't want to upset you. Those phone calls weren't wrong numbers. The first call, all I could hear was someone crying. The second call..." He fell silent as the voice clawed at him again.

Help me... Please help me... I'm scared... Please help me, Daddy.

He couldn't bring himself to repeat the heartrending words out loud. Ella looked so brittle that he feared they would shatter her like glass.

"The second call was what?" she prompted.

"Was the same as the first. It sounded like a scared child."

"It wasn't me!" Henry piped up, his recently broken voice lurching from gruff to falsetto.

Adam eyed him intently. "Then who was it? Was it Bael trying to trick me into returning to Fenton House?"

Henry's nostrils flared with annoyance at his dad's sardonic response. "It wasn't me. Honest."

Adam's mind looped back to some other similar words – *It was an accident, Dad. Honest.* "Stop lying," he snapped.

"Why would he be lying?" Ella put in defensively.

Adam threw up his arms in exasperation. "You bloody well know why. He hates it here and he loves *that* house." His eyes daring Henry to deny it, he added, "Don't you?"

Henry pressed his lips into a tight line.

As if his silence was as good as an admission of guilt, Adam jabbed a finger at him. "*He's* the one trying to manipulate us into going back there, not some..." he let out a derisive laugh, "demon."

Ella's caramel brown eyes probed Henry's face. "Did you make those phone calls?" Her tone was tender, not accusing. "I'll understand if you did. It's hard on all of us living here. And I promise you, sweetheart, once the baby's born and everything's settled down, we can talk about moving house." Her gaze shifted to Adam. "Can't we?"

He saw in her eyes that it wasn't a question, it was a demand. With a sigh in his voice, he said, "Yes."

Henry's glowering, uncertain gaze alternated between his parents. He scratched at the spot on his chin again. Wincing, he looked at his finger. A dot of blood glistened on it. As if angered by the sight, he burst out, "This is a waste of time. It doesn't matter what I say. You never listen to me. And even if you did, you wouldn't believe me. All you care about is the baby."

"Ah," said Adam, his eyebrows lifting. "We're finally getting to the nub of it."

"The baby won't change anything," Ella assured Henry.

His lips twisted into an ugly smile. "Now who's lying?"

"Ah, so you admit you're lying about the phone calls?"

Adam triumphantly hurled at him.

"W-what?" stammered Henry. "No, that's not what I–" He broke off, furious red blotches discolouring his cheeks. His fingers flexed like he wanted to punch his dad, but instead he snatched back his phone, whirled away from him and stomped out of the room.

"Henry," Ella called after him imploringly.

"Leave him be," said Adam. "Let him calm down."

Her eyebrows pinched into a sharp V. "You're right about one thing, Adam, you should have told me about the phone calls." Her gaze drifted to a framed photo on the mantelpiece – a school portrait of Jacob taken shortly before his death. She reached out to touch his smiling face. "Did the crying sound like Jacob?"

"It sounded like both him and Henry."

"You'd be able to recognise the difference."

"Would I? It's been so long since I heard Jacob's voice that I'm not sure I would. Anyway, it *wasn't* Jacob." Adam shook his head and gave a despairing little laugh. "I shouldn't even have to say this to you."

"You don't have to say it. I can see what's going on here. My hormones are all over the place right now, but I'm not crazy."

"This is beyond crazy, Ella. It's dangerous."

"You're right. So let's sell Fenton House. Perhaps then Henry will stop looking for excuses to go back there."

"I've told you, I'll never sell that place." Adam's words were set in stone.

"Why? The haunted house stuff is a load of nonsense. Right? So where's the harm? With the money we could live anywhere we want."

"It's not about the house being haunted or not haunted. It's about its history. Some places have a past that draws the wrong people to them."

Ella raised an eyebrow wryly. "You mean people like us."

"Yes, I mean people like us. But also people like Faith Gooden – fragile people, mentally ill people," Adam paused for emphasis before adding, "suicidal people. Are you willing to put anyone else's life at risk?"

"No," Ella somewhat reluctantly accepted. "So what do you think we should do?"

A deep weariness washed over Adam at this repetition of her earlier unanswered question. "Whatever we do, Ella, we can't run away from this. If Fenton House taught us anything, it's that our ghosts will follow us wherever we go."

He illustrated his words by holding up the bloodstained sheet of paper again. Ella stared at it, her face pinched with worry. With a sudden movement, she took it off him. She strode into the kitchen and twisted a knob on the gas hob. A ring of blue-tipped flames whooshed into life. She held a corner of the page to them. It blackened and burst into flame. With a glimmer of satisfaction, she watched the magic symbol burn.

When the flames licked her fingers, she dropped what remained of the paper into the sink and turned on the mixer tap. Ashy water swirled down the plughole. Shooting a defiant glance at Adam, she stole away his wine glass and took a sip. Closing her eyes, she released a long sigh.

She didn't resist as he took back the glass. He rested his forehead against hers and closed his eyes too.

The tiny, frightened voice broke back into his thoughts.

Help me... Please help me... I'm scared... Please help me, Daddy.

It was only Henry imitating his brother. There was no other possibility. But still…

A shuddering breath escaped him. God, how he longed to hear Jacob's voice again. He would have traded everything he had for just a few words.

"Our poor little boy," murmured Ella. "Our poor little boy."

Adam wondered which 'little boy' she was referring to.

5

Journeys

Prowling around his bedroom as restlessly as a caged tiger, Henry muttered, "Why don't they ever believe me?"

You know why, answered a voice in his head. Others joined it, taunting him in unison. *They hate you. They wish it was you who'd died, not Jacob.*

"Shut up," he retorted, pressing his hands over his ears in a vain attempt to block out the voices.

Everyone hates you. Even Jacob wished you weren't his brother.

"That's not true!"

Ayer Secore On Ca Bael.

Henry stopped as if he'd walked smack into a wall.

Ayer Secore On Ca Bael. Ayer Secore On Ca Bael.

His head shrank between his shoulders as if he expected Bael to materialise right there and then. "No." His voice was shaky but determined. "Not here."

He turned to his desk and tapped at the keyboard – 'Trains from London to Cornwall'. There was a train departing

Paddington Station in just over an hour. It was due to arrive in Redruth at 9:57 pm. From there he would have to take a bus to the Lizard Peninsula. He Googled 'Redruth to Lizard bus timetable'. The last bus of the day for The Lizard departed Redruth railway station at 10:15. He could be at Fenton House by tonight. His heart pounding at the prospect, he grabbed a jar of coins and banknotes from under his desk. He emptied it onto the carpet and counted his savings – fifty quid and change.

He blew a disappointed breath through his nostrils. A child's single cost over seventy quid. On top of which he was going to need bus fare. He glanced at an alarm clock on his bedside table. The minutes were ticking away. It took at least half-an-hour to ride the tube from Walthamstow Central into Central London. That would leave him ten or fifteen minutes to buy a train ticket and get to the departure platform. Even if he left at once, it would be a close-run thing.

He shoved the money into one trouser pocket and the drawing of Bael's sigil into the other. As he stood up, his gaze came to land on Edgar. The fat old pug was snoring contentedly.

"Sorry, Edgar." Henry stroked the pug's soft, warm fur. "I'd take you with me if I could."

With a little wrench, he turned to crack open the door. He tiptoed into the master bedroom and looked in the top drawer of his dad's bedside table. As usual, his dad's wallet was nestled amongst a jumble of pens and notebooks. It contained thirty-five quid in notes and a couple of quid's worth of loose change. He pocketed the money along with a bankcard.

A photo of Jacob and himself standing shoulder to shoulder behind a birthday cake caught his eye. The memory of that long-ago moment flooded his mind. Out of camera shot, some of their friends had been sitting around a table laden with party food.

Except they weren't your friends, were they? the sneering voices piped up. *They were Jacob's.*

"Shut up," Henry muttered again, flipping the photo upside down.

He dug deeper into the drawer. Right at the back, he found what he was searching for – a bundle of keys. Gripping them so that they didn't jangle, he crept down the stairs. He paused on the bottom step, craning his neck to squint through the thin gap between the hinges of the living-room door. The room was empty. He caught the muffled sound of his parents talking in the kitchen. A smoky scent tickled his nostrils. Fighting an urge to sneeze, he slunk into the porch, tucked his coat and trainers under an arm and opened the front door. He jammed his feet into his trainers, set off running and stumbled over something. He looked down. The dead pigeon stared sightlessly back. On a sudden whim, he picked it up and wrapped it in his coat.

The streets swept by in a blur as he dodged around fellow pedestrians and darted across busy roads. Soon enough, the square tower of St Mary's Church came into view.

The Bible warns us, do not seek out the mysterious and the supernatural. You will only find evil.

The vicar's warning tolled in his mind. Just for the briefest of moments, his pace faltered. Then he sprinted over a T-junction and veered towards a semi-circular steel-and-glass building with ranks of red double-decker busses parked alongside it. After passing beneath the blue and red circle of the Underground logo, he weaved his way along the station's crowded central aisle.

Pursued by the eerie strains of a busker's violin, he descended a flight of concrete stairs to a white-tiled tunnel. A multi-coloured map of interconnected lines on the wall told him that he needed to take the Victoria Line to Oxford Circus, followed by the Bakerloo Line to Paddington. He joined a queue at a bustling gate-line, shifting impatiently from foot to foot as he waited his turn. He tapped his Oyster Card on the card reader, raced through the barriers and down a long bank of steps flanked by escalators. A broad, arched corridor brought him to the stiflingly warm Victoria Line platform.

A train *swooshed* into view. Its carriages were almost empty. At that time of day, most people were travelling out of Central London.

He dropped onto a seat, breathing hard, the stale air stinging his throat. The doors slid shut and the train accelerated into the blackness of a tunnel, clanking and whining as it picked up speed. After a few minutes, a plummy voice announced, "The next station is Blackhorse Road." The train squealed to a standstill. A handful of people dressed for an evening out got aboard. The carriage gradually filled up as the process was repeated at several more stations.

Out of the corner of an eye, Henry glimpsed a flash of scarlet hair at the far end of the carriage.

His heart suddenly felt like it was trying to jump out of his chest. Was it her? Was it Faith?

He started to rise to his feet for a better look, but hesitated. Did he really want to know? The mere thought of finding himself face-to-face with her again made his legs feel rubbery.

"The next stop is Warren Street," came the announcement as the brakes screeched into action.

Henry checked the list of stations overhead. Warren Street was the last stop before Oxford Circus. Passengers disembarked and boarded. The train surged back into motion.

As a horribly familiar tingling sensation climbed his spine, Henry shrank down onto his seat, covering his face with a hand. He peeked through his fingers, his gaze reluctantly but irresistibly inching towards where he'd seen the red hair.

"The next stop is Oxford Circus. Change for Bakerloo and Central Lines."

A sort of queasy relief flooded through him as the train shuddered to a halt. He was on his feet and out of the doors before they were fully open. He shimmied through the passengers waiting to board, following the 'Bakerloo Line' arrows. A series of identical-looking tunnels brightly illuminated by strip lights gave him the dreamlike impression that he was running without getting anywhere.

Then he was at the Bakerloo Line platform, breathlessly jumping onto another train. As it whooshed into motion, he peered from beneath his fringe at the platform. There was no red hair to be seen.

He glanced at the list of stations. There were only a handful of stops to go. He resumed staring at the floor, listening to the tannoy.

Regents Park... Baker Street...

His shoulders lifted almost to his ears. There was that feeling of being watched again. It was like having pins and needles in his brain.

Don't look, he ordered himself. *Looking makes her real.*

Marylebone... Edgware Road... Paddington.

Once again, he was out of the doors like a sprinter from the starting blocks. He fought his way through another network of white tunnels crammed with commuters, tourists and transport workers. Steep escalators carried him up to the overground station. He emerged into a vast, glass-roofed space bathed in late afternoon sunlight. Endless streams of travellers were making their way to and from the overground platforms. Others were queuing at the ticket office and information desk or milling around coffee stands and fast-food restaurants. Rumbling trains and echoing tannoy announcements provided a soundtrack to the bustling scene.

Henry peered up at the 'Departures' board. His train was due to depart platform two in five minutes. There was no time to queue for a ticket. He took out his phone, navigated to a ticket-booking website and tapped the relevant numbers from his dad's bankcard into the purchase page. Once the transaction was verified, he checked his emails for the digital ticket, hurried to the ticket gates and held his phone over the scanner. The barriers swung open and he ran along a walkway divided by steel pillars. A long, sleek blue train was waiting with its engine ticking over on the tracks.

A sudden urge – more than that, a compulsion – to look over his shoulder gripped Henry. He turned and his breath froze in his throat. The crimson-haired woman was staring at him from beyond the ticket gates. A man dragging a suitcase dashed through the gates. The woman followed him onto the platform. Wide-eyed, Henry watched her walking towards him. Or perhaps she only appeared to be walking. Perhaps she was actually floating across the flagstones.

The peep of a whistle alerted him to the train's imminent departure. He whirled and flung himself through the doors as they were sliding shut. Turning again, he found himself divided from his stalker by a pane of glass. Her chillingly familiar brown eyes made him feel like his legs might give out under him.

It *was* her. It *was* Faith

"What do you want?" he mouthed.

I want you, her eyes seemed to answer.

The train accelerated away from the platform. Like lovers, Henry and Faith's eyes remained locked together until they lost sight of each other. As the train emerged from beneath the vaulted glass roof, Henry rested his forehead against the window and let out a shaky breath. For a long moment, all he could do was watch the tracks blurring by as the train gathered speed.

"Welcome aboard this Great Western railway service to Penzance," a pleasantly calm voice announced over the tannoy.

Henry lifted his eyes to the grey high-rises bordering the tracks. His face wrinkled in revulsion. He hated London – the noise, the dirt, the stink. But most of all, he hated the people. Everywhere people, relentlessly hurrying and jostling. Sometimes it seemed that the entire city was just one mad rush of people.

An image took shape in his mind – sun-bleached fields, wildflower-speckled hedges, rolling waves, towering cliffs, gulls wheeling in the wake of fishing-boats. He drew in a deep breath. He could almost smell the salt and seaweed of Treworder Cove. He could practically hear the murmur of the sea. The wrinkles faded from his face.

He swayed along the aisle in search of a seat. The train was packed with well-heeled city workers also escaping the city. Not wanting to risk conversation, he chose a seat next to a snoozing man.

Henry closed his eyes too. As the muffled clanking of the tracks lulled him towards sleep, Faith's pale face found its way into his thoughts. What did she want from him?

Who cares what she wants? he told himself. *You've outrun her twice and you can do it again.*

Idiot, countered the choir of whispering voices. *You can't outrun a ghost.*

His eyes snapped open to scour the carriage. There was no island of red amidst the sea of salt-and-pepper hair.

He slid a hand into the pocket containing Bael's sigil. Whatever Faith's intention was, he would make her regret coming after him. Soon he would be the one with the power.

6

Revelations

Concern and consternation played across Adam's features as he watched Ella pacing between the kitchen and the living room. His gaze lifted towards the sound of Henry walking back and forth overhead, almost in sync with his mum.

"Do you ever feel as if Fenton House still has some strange hold over us?" asked Ella. She stretched out an arm and made a pulling motion. "Like it's trying to drag us back there."

"I try not to feel anything at all when I think about that place." Adam sighed wearily. "But it's impossible not to feel some measure of regret." A laugh of self-contempt threatened to burst out of him. Who was he kidding? *'Some measure'* didn't even begin to describe the depth of his feeling.

Ella looked searchingly at him. Her voice dropped to a murmur. "When you said you love Henry, did you mean it?"

He gave a startled blink at the question. "Of course I did. How can you even ask me that?"

She stared at him for a moment more before heaving a sigh of her own. "I'm sorry, Adam."

He shook his head. "There's no need to apologise. I don't

blame you for doubting me. Sometimes I doubt myself."

A little grimace tugged at her face. She cupped a hand under her belly. "She's kicking again. I think she's going to be a martial arts champion."

Adam smiled. "Take the weight off your feet. I'll make us a cuppa."

Ella slowly lowered herself onto a chair at the kitchen table. Adam gritted his teeth against an all too familiar stabbing sensation in his chest. There used to be four chairs crowded around the little table. Now there were only three. Jacob's chair was gathering dust in the loft. Adam couldn't stand the sight of it, but neither could he bring himself to part with it. Not that putting it out of sight made any real difference. Everything in the house – every nook and cranny, every ornament and item of furniture reminded him of Jacob. Even the air seemed to be indelibly infused with his essence. Occasionally, out of nowhere, Jacob's smell – a sugary mixture of strawberry jam and ginger biscuits – would hit him hard enough to bring tears to his eyes.

Adam's gaze travelled into the living room. God, how he loved and loathed this place, just as he loved and loathed Henry.

"Henry scares me," he admitted, his voice weighed down by shame.

Ella treated him to a look that suggested she'd never heard anything so absurd.

"I'm not scared for myself," he added, glancing meaningfully at her bump.

"What are you suggesting?" Her tone wavered between disbelief and accusation. "That Henry could hurt the baby?"

Adam looked away, unable to bear her eyes.

"This is about Jacob, isn't it?" she continued. "You still

think his death wasn't an accident."

"No I–" Adam automatically began to deny, but cut himself off. His gaze slid to the sink. The plughole was clogged with soggy, blood-smeared paper. He thought about Jacob's blood spreading across the porch floor like an oil spill. Henry and Penny Holman's voices competed again for ascendency in his mind. *It was an accident, Dad. Honest... Faith's blood was under Henry's fingernails... It was an accident... Faith's blood... Faith's blood...* Penny's voice won the battle.

Adam briefly squeezed his eyes shut. "There's something else I haven't told you." He drew in a full breath like someone about to dive off the deep end. "Do you remember that detective who came to Fenton House the night Faith died?"

"Of course I do – Detective Sergeant Holman." Ella's reply was as impatient as it was anxious.

"And do you remember that the police took scrapings from under Henry's fingernails?"

"Yes, yes." Ella made a circular motion with her hand for him to get on with it.

"Well Detective Holman turned up at a book signing a year or so after we left Fenton House." Adam's voice was suddenly a whisper. "She told me they found Faith's blood under Henry's fingernails."

Deep furrows ploughed themselves into Ella's forehead. "Faith's blood under Henry's fingernails," she repeated as if struggling to understand what that meant. "Why didn't this come out during the investigation?"

"Apparently the lab results were misplaced."

Ella's eyes narrowed sceptically. "How do you *misplace* something like that?"

"I've no idea, but why would Penny lie?"

"Because..." Ella falteringly searched for a reason. Failing to find one, she changed tack. "I can just imagine how you reacted when *Penny*," she said the name with a cynical twist of her lips, "gave you the good news. I'll bet you wanted to shout *I told you so* from the rooftops."

A small hurt look crossed Adam's face. "Do you want to know what I did? I told her Henry got Faith's blood on his hands when he put a blanket around her."

Ella's eyes grew distant. Adam could almost see the moment in question replaying in her caramel irises – Faith shuffling into Fenton House's entrance hall looking like she'd been dragged naked through a thorn bush, Ella dashing off with Henry in tow to find something to wrap her in.

"I fetched the blanket," she recalled in a vague tone. "But it was you who put it around..." She trailed off momentarily. "Or maybe I'm remembering wrong." There was a kind of helpless plea in her voice.

"No you're not," Adam said gently.

Both of them lapsed into silence, avoiding each other's eyes as if ashamed of their thoughts. Finally, her voice somehow both resentful and tender, Ella asked, "Why did you keep this from me?"

"For the same reason I'm telling you now – I was trying to protect my family."

Ella looked down at her bump, her anger curdling into self-loathing. "*Family*," she repeated in a disdainful hiss. "What type of family are we bringing this child into?"

"A loving one," Adam said with sudden conviction. "We've been through so much, Ella, and yet here we are, still together. If that's not love, then I don't know what is?"

The acidic cynicism burned its way back into Ella's voice. "You suspect your own son of being..." she sought the right words, "some sort of monster. That's a strange kind of love."

"Is it? I honestly don't know anymore what's strange and what isn't. I'll tell you what I do know, Ella – I will not allow any harm to come to you and the baby."

"Even if that means hurting Henry? Because if he finds out how you feel about him, it will–" Ella fell silent, unable to bring herself to put into words what it would do.

Adam finished the sentence for her. "It will make him hate me even more than he already does." He heaved a sigh before adding, "And I'd deserve it."

"We'd both deserve it for taking him to Fenton House." Ella stabbed a finger at herself and Adam. "It was us, not him, that put our family at risk." She repeated emphatically, "*Us, not him.*"

"And what about what happened before we went there?"

"What about it?" The question was a challenge and a warning.

Adam's eyes pleaded for understanding. "We can't dance around this anymore, Ella. We have to be honest with each other."

"Fine. You want honesty, Adam, how about this – if you breathe one word of this conversation to Henry, I'll leave you and…" Ella faltered at the shock she saw in Adam's eyes, but quickly recovered her resolve. "I'll do everything I can to make sure you don't have access to him."

He stared at her in stunned silence, his face twitching like a bad poker player trying to read an opponent.

She returned his gaze impassively, giving nothing away.

"You're serious, aren't you?" He spoke in a tone of leaden realisation.

"I love you, Adam. Really I do. But Henry's welfare has to be my priority."

He was silent for another moment, his face haunted by uncertainty. His eyes returned to the ceiling. "It's gone very quiet up there."

Ella tilted her head to listen. Adam and she glanced at each other with the same thought in their eyes. Simultaneously, they headed for the hallway. The porch door was ajar. Henry's coat and shoes were gone.

They exchanged another like-minded look. "Henry," Adam called, knowing in his heart that he wouldn't get a response. He raced up to Henry's bedroom. It was empty, except for the sleeping pug.

Lumbering up the stairs behind him, Ella stated the obvious, "He must have sneaked out." She took out her mobile phone and speed-dialled Henry. "It's gone to the answering service," she told Adam. "Where do you think he is?"

He didn't reply, neither wanting nor daring to speculate. His ears caught the whirr of Henry's PC. He clicked the mouse and brought the monitor out of standby. There was a tired inevitability to his voice as he read out the words on-screen. "Paddington Station."

Ella's gaze darted to the monitor. She grabbed the mouse off Adam and clicked onto the Redruth-Helston-Lizard bus timetable. "Oh God," she gasped. "Oh God, oh God..."

Adam placed what he hoped was a calming hand on her arm. "Even if Henry left the house right after Mrs Simmons, he'd be lucky to make the five o'clock train."

"Then let's get to Paddington."

Ella started to move away from him, but he gently stopped her. "You're in no condition to be running around. Besides, someone needs to stay here in case Henry changes his mind."

"What if he *does* make the train?"

Adam grimaced at the possibility. "All the more reason why you should stay here." His meaning was clear – if he had to chase Henry all the way to Cornwall, he didn't want Ella with him.

She eyed him uncertainly. "What will you do when you find him?" The question was tinged with wariness.

"There's no time for this now, Ella."

Adam brushed past her and hurried down the stairs.

"What will you do?" she persisted, following him.

He paused at the front door and looked at her. His eyes pleaded for her trust. "What do you think I'll do? I'll bring him home."

Ella bit her upper lip, not looking entirely convinced.

Adam grabbed his coat and stepped out of the front door. He hesitated again and turned to press his lips against Ella's before murmuring in her ear, "Everything will be alright. I promise."

Giving him a worried smile, she nodded.

"Bye for now, Zara," Adam cooed at the bump, then he ran to a small car parked alongside the kerb. He glanced skywards as a spot of rain hit his cheek. The sun was shimmering behind grey clouds. The air was muggy, like a storm was brewing.

With a wave, he accelerated away from the house. The shortest route to Paddington was south east through Hackney Marshes, but at this time of day the traffic would be a nightmare. Although it added five or six miles to the journey, it would be quicker to head north east through New Southgate, then cut back south through East Finchley and Hampstead.

After emerging from the tangle of residential streets, he raced in spurts along a busy dual-carriageway. He took a slip road into East Finchley, grinding his teeth as he hit bumper-to-bumper traffic. Vehicles nudged dangerously close. Horns blared. Stressed drivers glared and gesticulated at each other.

His gaze alternated between the road and the dashboard clock – 4:37… 4:40… 4:44…

"Shit," he muttered. At this rate, he wouldn't make it to Paddington in time. He just had to hope Henry was having as much difficulty getting to the station.

He escaped East Finchley for the quieter streets of Hampstead. The traffic slowed to a crawl again as it passed the white Georgian houses of Warwick Avenue. Then he was navigating a glinting forest of mirrored-glass towers. The sun broke through the clouds as the caterpillar domes of Paddington Station came into view.

4:58…

He edged along a road clogged with black cabs and red buses. Ignoring the 'No Parking' signs, he pulled over in front of the Hilton's imposing stone facade. He jumped out of the car, dodged and weaved his way through a throng of travellers into the station and peered up at the departures board.

"Shit," he swore again. The train had left on time.

He ran to the platform gates. A few people were milling around. Henry wasn't amongst them.

A flash of bright red hair caught his eye before being obscured by passengers streaming from an adjacent platform. A tingle of recognition ran through him. The feeling was cast aside as he turned his attention to his phone. According to AA Route Planner, it took 4 hours 48 minutes to drive from Paddington to Redruth. By train it took 4 hours 45 minutes. And the train had a head-start.

He sprinted back to the car and tapped his destination into the Sat Nav. The instant the directions flashed up on-screen, he pulled a U-turn.

The drive west through Notting Hill and Ealing was a whirl of overtaking that provoked a barrage of beeping from fellow motorists. He battled his way to the edge of the city where the landscape changed to six lanes of steady traffic flanked by flat fields. He heaved a breath of relief, like a claustrophobia sufferer escaping a cave.

Uncertainty clouded his eyes at a sign for Reading – the train's first stop. He glanced at the train timetable on his phone. The train was due to depart Reading at 5:29. It was already too late for him to intercept it there, but what about at one of the other stations it stopped at along the route? If he tried and failed, it would scupper any possibility of outrunning the train to Redruth. No, it was too big a risk. He would just have to bite the bullet and do the full journey.

As the vehicles around him came together like a coiling spring, he braked sharply and spat out a stream of swearwords. Regardless of what he did, he wouldn't win the race if this sodding traffic didn't ease up.

He took the opportunity to phone home. Ella answered on the first ring and asked, "Have you found him?"

"I think he caught the train," Adam told her, bracing himself for her reaction. "I'm on my way to Redruth."

She made a distressed little sound. "Can you beat the train?"

"Depends on the traffic."

"Oh Jesus. I can't believe this is happening. What if you miss him again?"

"Let's be logical about this, Ella. Even if the worst comes to the worst and he makes it to Fenton House, there's nothing there that can hurt him." Adam's attempt at reassurance rang hollow in his own ears.

Help me... Please help me... I'm scared... Please help me,

Daddy

The voice that was Jacob's, and yet could not possibly be Jacob's, tormented him again. Grief glazed his eyes. How could Henry do this to them? How could he be so cruel?

His temples pounded as anger took over. Maybe Henry and Fenton House were made for each other. Perhaps the little shit would be better off living there than with his family. At least in that remote place, he wouldn't be able to do any harm to anyone except himself.

Now guilt took a turn to jab at Adam. What sort of father was he to even entertain such thoughts? "I promise you, Ella, I'm going to break whatever insane hold that house has over him, even if I have to burn the fucking place to the ground."

Ella was silent a moment, then said uneasily, "Perhaps I should follow you down there."

Adam responded with a forceful, "No."

"Why not? What's the point in me waiting around here?"

"The point is you're eight-and-a-half months pregnant and–" He broke off, fearing any words he might say would do more harm than good.

"And what?" That accusatory edge was back in Ella's voice. "What are you afraid of? Go on, Adam, say it."

"Let's not do this again, Ella," he sighed. "I'm only trying to look after you."

"It's not *me* that needs looking after."

"All of us," he corrected himself. "I'm trying to look after all of us."

"Was that what you were doing when you insisted on moving to Fenton House?" Ella retorted with such venom that Adam winced. "It's a miracle none of us were killed. But, hey, at least you got a bestseller out of it."

"That's not fair, Ella," he protested, but he was speaking to an empty line. She'd hung up.

Hurt glimmering in his eyes, he dialled home again. The call went through to voicemail. He gave another heavy sigh. "I'm sorry, Ella. You're right, I..." He paused as the traffic-jam began to break up. Then he continued, "We can talk about this when I get back. For now, please just stay put. Speak soon."

As he sped south west through gently undulating farmland, his gaze was never far from the clock. Second by second, he was clawing back the time he'd lost on the congested city streets. Farnborough, Basingstoke... The place names prodded a tender part of his mind. He hadn't been out this way since leaving Fenton House two years ago.

A grim smile flickered across his lips. *Leaving* was the wrong word. *Fleeing* would be more accurate.

A dislocating sense of dizziness nibbled at him. Sometimes he wondered whether he'd ever really left Fenton House. Perhaps the past few years were just a dream and, one day, he would wake to find himself living back there with only his 'little demon' of a son and the ghosts of his memories for company.

He lowered his window and cleared his head with a deep breath. The sky was a perfect pastel blue, but there was a smell of rain in the air. Fields of thirsty-looking wheat swayed as if in anticipation.

Andover, Yeovil, Exeter...

He did a quick calculation. It was 8:19. If the train was running on time, it had departed Exeter at 7:23. From there, the train took two hours thirty-four minutes to reach Redruth. Whereas by road it only took around one hour thirty-eight minutes – if, that is, he stuck to the speed limits. At his current speed, he would not only catch the train up but overtake it before Redruth.

Beyond Exeter, the road skirted the edge of Dartmoor. To the south, dark clouds clustered over blunt brown hills. The bleakly beautiful landscape that would normally have elicited a sigh of pleasure swept by unappreciated.

Oakhampton, Launceston...

The road climbed into the peatlands of Bodmin Moor. Cloud shadows flitted across deep-looking tarns and rocky tors. Squinting into the setting sun, Adam overtook lumbering RVs and caravans hooked up to cars.

He felt a flutter of triumph at a sign for Truro. It was 9:21. The train was due to depart Truro at 9:47. Ten minutes after that it would arrive at Redruth. By his reckoning, he was on track to reach Redruth station almost ten minutes before Henry.

A gust of wind rocked the car. Adam flicked on the wipers as rain speckled the windscreen. The screeches of gulls drew his gaze skywards. A huge flock passed overhead, chased by mountains of black cloud. There was an instant of stillness, like a held breath, then the road disappeared behind a curtain of lashing rain.

He didn't ease off the accelerator. He raced along as if winged demons were chasing him. An HGV fired off an extended *PAAARP* as he blindly overtook it. An oncoming van seemed to jump out of the rain at him.

"Shit," he exclaimed, yanking at the steering-wheel. Wheels screeching, the car lurched back into its lane. The van whooshed by, horn blaring, tyres kicking up spray.

"Shit!" repeated Adam as the car aquaplaned across the tarmac onto a grass verge. He slammed on the brakes, bringing the car to a juddering stop. His heart hammering against his ribcage, he released a long shaky breath.

It's the house. It's trying to prevent you from reaching Redruth before Henry.

A humourless laugh trickled between his lips at the absurd notion. The house was just a house. Just bricks and mortar, slate and wood, plaster and glass. Nothing more. None of this was its doing.

No, it's your doing, he could almost hear Ella saying bitterly.

He shook off the thought. There would be plenty of time later for reflection and recrimination. He looked in the rearview mirror. The road was clear. He restarted the engine. The wheels spun and spun, tearing up the turf before finding something to bite into. He pulled back onto the tarmac, grimacing at the sight of the clock. He'd lost his ten minute breathing space. Even though the race between him and the train was neck and neck, he resisted the temptation to floor the accelerator. He would be of no use to anyone if he ended up splattered across the road.

It was dark and the downpour had eased off to drizzle by the time Adam reached Redruth. The Sat Nav directed him through quiet streets of terraced stone houses. Black railings came into view. Beyond them, a snub-nosed train sat on its tracks. Disembarked passengers were filing over a footbridge. He couldn't see Henry amongst them.

He swerved into a small carpark, jumped out and ran inside the station's single-storey brick building. A roller blind with 'POSITION CLOSED' on it covered the ticket office window. At the far side of a waiting area, a door led to the platforms. He headed for the footbridge, craning his neck to peer into the carriages. Empty. Empty. All fucking empty!

Spotting a station guard, he asked a touch breathlessly, "Excuse me, have you seen this boy?" He displayed a photo of Henry on his phone.

The guard squinted behind his spectacles. "Can I ask who you are?"

His cautious manner set Adam's heart beating even faster. "I'm his dad. You've seen him, haven't you?"

"Yes," the guard informed him gravely. "I'm afraid I have."

7

Twins

The room materialised before Henry's eyes as if someone had turned on a projector. Once again, flames danced in the cavernous fireplace. Their flickering light lent life to the scraggly bearskin rug he was standing on.

Henry became aware that his lips were moving of their own accord, rapidly repeating the same words. His voice rose to a whisper, then fell, rose, then fell, rose, then fell... Each time climbing higher like an incoming tide.

"Ayer Secore On Ca Bael. Ayer Secore ON CA BAEL..."

He threw his head back as his chanting reached a crescendo.

"AYER SECORE ON CA BAEL!"

The words reverberated away into silence. His chin dropped to his chest. For a minute, he was motionless, his eyelids drooping as if he was fighting off sleep. He lifted his head as a noise caught his ear.

Schlop.

It sounded like someone slapping the floorboards with a wet fish. He peered around, trying to pierce the shadows beyond the firelight.

Schlop, schlop.

His gaze fixed on a squat black outline in a doorway.

Schlop, schlop, schlop.

With jerky little movements, the bulky shape moved closer. The firelight revealed glistening brownish-yellow skin mottled with warty bumps. A pair of wide-spaced golden eyes stared inscrutably at Henry from above a broad, downturned mouth.

He felt no surprise at the sight of the monstrous toad. Indeed, he felt nothing at all.

Razor sharp looking claws curved from the creature's four bony toes. It tapped a claw against the floorboards as if contemplating what to do. With a whistling inrush of air, it inflated the underside of its throat into a bulbous sack. Its mouth dropped open and a Waaaaah, like the scream of a distressed baby, exploded from it with such force that Henry clapped his hands over his ears.

A pink tongue, thick at the root, tapering to a point, darted out of the yawning mouth and whiplashed around Henry's waist. Before he could even cry out, the sticky tongue was snapping back whence it came with him in its grip. For an instant, he found himself staring into a seemingly bottomless void. Then moist, hot, bitter-smelling darkness enveloped him.

Henry jerked awake, gulping air. He turned his head to look past the man snoring beside him. His breathing slowed as he took in an expanse of golden-brown wheat bathed in soft evening sunlight.

He glanced at his phone. Not long now until the train reached Redruth. Unsurprisingly there was a string of missed calls, voicemails and texts from 'Home' and 'Mum's moby'. He skimmed through the texts – 'Where are you?', 'Call me.', 'Sorry if we upset you.', 'Please call or message. Your dad and I are really worried.'

Henry gave a doubtful little snort. *Dad worried? Yeah right.*

More like he's happy to get rid of me, he was half-tempted to reply.

He returned the phone to his pocket without listening to the voicemails. It didn't matter what Mum had to say. He wasn't going back to London. Not now. Not ever.

"Bloody hell, look at that," said the man next to him, blinking to full wakefulness and staring out of the window.

Vast black clouds were racing in from the south. The stalks of wheat bowed down before them like loyal subjects.

With howling intensity, the storm slammed into the train. Fear fluttered in Henry's chest as the carriage rocked on the tracks. He shut his eyes, but the instant he did so he was back in the repulsively spongy, wet cave of the toad's mouth. Eyes snapping open, he clutched the armrests as if to stop himself from falling out of his seat.

For what felt like hours, the train hurtled down the throat of the storm. Sometimes he seemed to hear a voice on the wind, screaming and wailing, *Waaaaah. Waaaaah...*

When the train emerged from the gale, Henry uncurled his aching fingers and rested back against the seat. He watched heathery hills fading into darkness. The scattered lights of farms and villages twinkled into life. The world beyond the rain-streaked window seemed distant and muted. The gentle *swoosh-swoosh* of the train threatened to lull him back off to sleep.

The drowsiness was dispelled by the tannoy announcing that they would soon be arriving at Redruth station. The train entered a built-up area of gleaming wet roofs and roads. After passing through a short tunnel, it slowed to a stop at a small station.

Henry rose to hurry to the nearest door. The storm had added several minutes to the journey. He needed to move fast if he was to have any chance of catching the connecting bus to The Lizard. The doors swished open. He leaped onto the platform and sprinted to the footbridge. Drizzle tickled his face as he raced over the tracks. A 'Way Out' sign directed him through a waiting room to a car park in front of the station.

"Henry."

The voice stopped him in his tracks. Something about it set his ears thrumming like a guitar string twanged too hard. He turned on his heels, wide-eyed. A noose seemed to cinch around his neck at the sight that greeted him.

Faith's hair looked like blood in the lamplight. Her cartoonishly big eyes met his gaze and held it fast.

Waves of horror crashed over Henry, snatching his legs from under him. He sank to his knees as Faith approached. Her black fingernails shone like obsidian as she reached for him.

He went rigid as her fingers encircled his wrist. He could *feel* her hand on him. How was that possible? He'd watched a Coastguard helicopter winch her body from the base of the sea cliffs by Fenton House. Had she somehow survived the fall? No. No way. She would have been smashed to pieces on the boulders at the foot of the dizzyingly high cliffs.

Faith was dead. And ghosts couldn't touch you. They couldn't dig their nails into your skin and drag you to your feet. So if this woman wasn't Faith's ghost, who was she?

Sister.

The word rang out in Henry's head. Did Faith have a sister?

Hooking an arm around his back, the woman steered him towards a little red car. He weakly tried to pull away from her. Now that he knew she was something solid, something he could fight with his hands, the paralysing fear was draining away.

She opened the front passenger door and manoeuvred him

into the seat.

His eyes rolled towards a train guard looking in his direction from the station's entrance. His lips trembled in an effort to speak, but all that came out was a strangled murmur.

The woman shut the door in his face and, as if nothing untoward was occurring, calmly made her way around the bonnet to the driver's seat. She started the engine and pulled away from the station. The road descended a short slope before passing under a railway bridge.

Henry reached to open his door, but the woman warned him, "Don't. I may not look like much, but believe me I'm more than capable of dealing with you."

His voice strengthening with each word, he asked, "What are you?"

A cheerless smile played on the woman's glossy red lips. "Well, as you've probably worked out, I'm not a ghost. So the question you should be asking is *who,* not *what,* are you. Shall I give you a clue? You and I have a lot in common. For starters, we're both twins."

"Sister," Henry exclaimed as his suspicion was all but confirmed. "You're Faith's twin sister."

"Got it in one. Clever boy. I'm Grace Gooden. And you're the little psycho that drove my sister to suicide."

Henry shook his head vehemently. "No I didn't."

"Yes you did," Grace countered flatly, like she was stating a fact. "Penny told me everything."

Henry's brow creased as if he was searching his memory. "Who?"

Grace shot him a look that said, *Don't even try to play dumb with me.*

She turned at a junction, leaving behind the town centre

for a leafy suburb.

"Where are you taking me?" Henry demanded to know, his voice undermined by a telltale tremor.

"I'm taking you where you want to go."

"Fenton House?"

"Got it in one again."

Henry eyed Grace as if unsure what to make of the reply. "Why would you want to go there?"

"Hmm, now let me think." Her voice was full of mock sincerity. "Could it be to find out why you tortured Faith until she lost her mind and jumped off a cliff?"

"I didn't–" Henry started to deny again, but thought better of it as Grace flashed him another razor-edged glance.

A slip road off a roundabout led to an empty dual-carriageway. Henry watched Grace out of the sides of his eyes, his face pale and tense, his hands clenched into fists on his lap.

"Don't worry," she said. "I won't hurt you unless you force me to. I'm not a psychopath."

"Neither am I," he retorted.

Grace arched a doubting eyebrow.

Biting down on his anger, Henry sat silent. He flinched as Grace jerked a thumb at a carrier bag on the backseat. "Are you hungry?" she asked. "There's a sandwich in there. It's only a crappy pre-packed thing, but it's better than nothing."

Her offer made Henry aware that his stomach was indeed grumbling. He eyed the bag suspiciously.

A smile lifted one corner of Grace's lips. "Not very trusting, are you?"

"Why would I trust you? You're kidnapping me," Henry pointed out belligerently.

Grace gave an exclamation of laughter, taken aback by his statement of the obvious. “Yes, I suppose I am.”

“They’ll put you in prison.”

Grace was thoughtfully silent for a minute, then she asked, “Were you and Jacob close?”

Henry greeted the question with a silence of his own.

She nodded as if that was the response she’d expected. “Twins are supposed to be close, aren’t they? But Faith and I weren’t close when she died. We hadn’t been close for years. It was different when we were kids. We shared everything – a bedroom, clothes, toys, books, CDs. We were identical in almost every way. Even our parents struggled to tell us apart. Did you ever pretend to be Jacob?” Without waiting for an answer, she continued, “Faith and I used to pretend to be each other all the time. Sometimes we did it to get out of doing things we didn’t enjoy – lessons, chores and stuff like that. Other times we did it just for fun.”

“Fun?” Henry muttered as if the word was alien to him. “Where’s the fun in pretending to be someone else?”

“Looking back on it, I don’t suppose it was all that much fun. But it gave us one-up on everyone else.” A slight tightness came into Grace’s voice. “When we hit our teens, everything changed. It was... It was like someone had flipped a switch in Faith. One day we were inseparable, the next she didn’t want to know me. She started dying her hair and refusing to wear anything but black. Then she started sneaking out of the house without me. I followed her and found that she was hanging around with some goth kids. Do you want to know what she did when she saw me?”

“Not really.”

Grace smiled crookedly again. “That’s exactly what Faith would have said. I’m surprised you two didn’t get on.”

"Maybe we would have if we'd ever spoken to each other."

"How come you didn't speak? Did you gag her? Or was she just too scared to talk?"

Henry compressed his lips into a thin line at the goading questions.

Seeing that he wasn't going to take the bait, Grace picked up her story from where she'd left off. "When Faith saw me, she told me to fuck off and leave her alone." A trace of a wince crossed her face as she relived the incident. "I asked what I'd done wrong, but she just laughed at me. I ran home in tears. We didn't speak for days afterwards. Sometimes I'd catch her glaring at me. I thought she was angry because I'd embarrassed her in front of her new friends. You see, I was still in my little princess phase – hair down to my waist, sparkly nails, pretty in pink. All that crap. So I dyed my hair like hers and got dressed up all in black. When Faith saw what I'd done, she..." A more pronounced grimace twisted at her features. "She completely lost the plot. She flew at me, punching and scratching and screaming about how much she hated me."

Grace drew a finger along her cheek, wiping off a streak of foundation to expose a sliver of a scar. "I didn't fight back. I just let her beat the crap out of me. I didn't care if I died. I felt like my world had ended. Eventually she ran out of steam and stopped hitting me. She said something then that I've never forgotten. She said, *I am not you and you are not me*."

Softly and slowly, Grace repeated the words to herself before lapsing into silence.

Henry thought about how his parents had often dressed Jacob and him in matching clothes. He'd used to trail around after Jacob like... His forehead knotted as he struggled to find the right description. His gaze drifted from Grace to the windscreen. They were speeding between grassy embankments illuminated by pools of harsh halogen light. *A shadow*. He nodded to himself. Yes, that was it, he'd felt like his brother's shadow.

At a roundabout, Grace followed a sign for Helston. After passing through Hayle – a pretty town built on an estuary of glistening mudflats – they plunged into dark countryside.

Grace broke the stretch of silence. "Penny showed me the coroner's report. Faith was covered in hundreds of cuts and bruises. Is that what you get your kicks out of? Hurting people? Watching them suffer?"

"I didn't make your sister come to Fenton House," said Henry, his voice low and controlled. "I didn't make her try to summon a demon. I didn't make her disappear and I didn't make her reappear. I didn't do anything to her. Not one thing."

Grace cast a narrow glance at him. "I've been reading about people like you – psychopaths, sociopaths or whatever you want to call them. Have you ever tortured an animal?"

All of a sudden, Henry was acutely aware of the pigeon beneath his coat. Its beak seemed to stab into his ribs like an accusing finger. He furtively shifted position to ease the discomfort.

"Cruelty to animals is one of the childhood warning signs," continued Grace. A taunting tone came into her voice. "I bet you take great pleasure in killing daddy longlegs, don't you? I can just picture you pulling off their legs one by one."

"Fuck off and leave me alone," Henry muttered at her out of the side of his mouth.

Grace stiffened as if a hand had reached out of the past to hit her. The words that Faith had flung at her all those years ago seemed to linger in the air. *Fuck off and leave me alone. Fuck off and leave me alone.*

With a visible effort, Grace arranged her lips into a slender smile. "Oh you're a very clever boy, Henry. But you know what happens to clever boys, don't you? Sooner or later, they mess with the wrong person and then..." She breathed a soft laugh. "Well then they come to a nasty end."

"You don't scare me. You're the one who should be scared."

"Oh really? Why's that? What are you going to do to me?"

Now Henry smiled thinly. "I don't need to do anything. The house will do it for me."

"Ah, I see." Grace smacked her forehead in a pantomime of realisation. "Now I get it. Now it all makes sense. It was the house that tortured Faith. The bricks and floorboards came alive and beat her half to death."

Henry's eyes glimmered sullenly at the comeback. "Don't say I didn't warn you."

"Alright, Henry." There was a cool, derisive note in Grace's voice. "I'll play your game. Fenton House killed Faith, and if I go there it'll kill me too. But what about you? Why won't it hurt you?"

"Because it chose me to live there."

"And why did it choose you?"

"Duh. Because I'm evil. Obviously."

Grace chuckled grimly at the sardonic reply. "Evil attracts evil. Isn't that what they say?"

Henry gave a shrug of calculated indifference. "If you say so." A rumble of thunder drew his gaze skywards.

Grace flicked on the wipers as globs of rain burst against the windscreen.

They sped through sleepy villages. With every passing mile, the gleam of anticipation in Henry's eyes intensified. "Helston," he said with an eager tremor as the road dipped past houses lining a wooded valley.

A sign for The Lizard directed them to the opposite side of the town. Beyond a chain-link fence at the roadside, strips of tarmac crisscrossed a flat expanse of floodlit grass. A carved stone sign identified a cluster of aircraft hangars and brick buildings as RNAS CULDROSE.

"This is where the Coastguard brought Faith's body," said Grace.

Once again, Henry knew better than to reply.

The airbase gave way to more hedgerows and fields. A shudder ran through Henry as the floodlights faded from view. He had the sudden sense that the world he knew and loathed was behind him. The world he'd been hankering after for the last two years was almost within touching distance. He inhaled deeply, savouring the feeling.

"How can you be so happy to be returning to Fenton House after everything that happened there?" asked Grace. "I mean, how many lives has that house taken? Five? Six? More?"

"So you *do* believe Fenton House has killed people?" Henry said with a sly curl of his lips.

"I never said what I believe. I'll tell you what I don't believe," Grace paused for effect before continuing, "*you*. I don't believe a word you've said about my sister or anything else for that matter."

Henry let slip a snort. "Join the club."

Grace subjected him to a searching sidelong look. "Does that mean you feel the same way about me? Or that I'm not the only one who thinks you're a liar?"

He sucked his lips tight against his teeth, annoyed with himself for not keeping his mouth shut in the first place. He reached into the pocket containing Bael's sigil. From some murky recess of his mind, the whispering voices struck up, *Ayer Secore On Ca Bael. Ayer Secore On Ca Bael...*

They came to a flooded dip in the road. Grace forged through water that was up to the headlights. "This road will soon be impassable if it continues raining like this."

"So turn back before you get stuck out here," suggested Henry. "Let me out. I can walk the rest of the way."

"Thanks for the advice," Grace said dryly, "but I'll take my chances."

The further they progressed onto the peninsula, the harder the rain fell, drawing a veil over everything except for a few metres of the road ahead. Henry's heart leapt when he spotted a sign for 'Treworder'. He fidgeted in his seat, barely able to contain his excitement. Not far now.

"The Entity," Grace said out of nowhere.

Henry looked at her like he had no idea what she was talking about.

"Give the blank looks a rest, will you?" she said. "I've read your dad's book. Ghost stories aren't my cup of tea, but I have to admit, it had me gripped. Especially all that stuff about the Entity. Although I don't really understand what the Entity is." She paused as if waiting for Henry to enlighten her. When he remained stonily silent, she went on, "It seems to me that it can be read in two ways. Either Walter accidentally let a demon into his house. Or the Entity is us. By that I mean it's everything that's bad about us. It's our worst emotions – fear, anger–"

"It's the Devil." Henry's words were a simple statement of fact.

Grace treated him to another probing look. "The Devil made me do it. Is that your excuse? Kind of pathetic, don't you think?"

Henry stared at the slashing rain for a moment. He turned to her, his pupils so dilated from looking into the darkness that they almost filled his eyes. "You'll find out soon enough."

"Is that a threat?"

Henry shrugged and yawned, exaggeratedly signalling his boredom with the conversation.

"You say you're not scared of me," said Grace. "Well I'm not scared of you either. Or of Fenton House. Or of the Entity. There's only one thing that really scares me – the thought of living the rest of my life without knowing the truth about what happened to Faith."

Henry showed no sign of having heard her. He leaned forward, peering out of the windows as if afraid of missing something. "There!" He pointed to a left-hand turn barely visible between the sheets of rain.

The tyres squealed as Grace braked hard and took the turn. The road narrowed to a single lane flanked by overflowing drainage ditches.

"There's a right turn you need to take about a mile up ahead." Henry's voice fizzed with nervous excitement. He rocked back and forth, chewing his lips.

The road swung around a blind bend. A short distance further on, Grace braked again at a lane that squeezed its way between shaggy hedges. "Is this it?"

"Yes, yes." Henry was almost frantic with eagerness. His rocking quickened, keeping time with the drumming of the rain. The hedges danced wildly in the wind howling off the sea.

"Fuck," Grace exclaimed as a branch hit the windscreen and became snarled up in the wipers. She stopped the car, wrestled her door open and reached around to free the branch.

A flurry of movement drew her attention to the far side of the car. Before she could make a move to stop him, Henry was out of his door and running. Swearing again, she ducked back into the car and hit the accelerator. Seconds later, she was doing the same to the brakes. The bumper jerked to a stop centimetres from Henry's heels. He was standing stock-still, his gaze fixed on a pair of iron gates that thrust their spear-tipped bars at the sky.

Grace flipped open the glovebox and took out a rectangular black object with a gun-handle grip. She pressed a button and a bolt of blue light crackled between parallel prongs. Stun gun raised and ready, she got out of the car and approached Henry. Seeing his face, though, she lowered the weapon. His eyes had the glazed, faraway look of someone lost between fear and wonder. His lips moved, but if he said anything it was drowned out by the waves pounding the nearby cliffs.

Grace leaned in closer. "What?"

"Home," said Henry. "I'm home."

8

Betrayal

One hour earlier…

The BMW crunched its way along the broad gravel driveway, passing between twin rows of swaying sycamores. In their witch, ghost and devil masks, the car's three occupants could have been heading to a Halloween party. However, their tense, watchful postures spoke of an altogether more serious purpose.

The driveway flared into a circle. At its centre, a column of stone lions rose from a large bowl. Instead of water, the lions spouted ivy from their fanged mouths.

"Be alert and of sober mind," said Natalie. "Your enemy the devil prowls around like a roaring lion looking for someone to devour."

Leon threw her a glance. "What are you gibbering about now?"

"It just popped into my head."

"Sounds like something from the Bible," said Jamie.

"I think it is."

"I didn't know you were religious."

Leon snorted. "She's about as religious as a handjob."

As the car pulled around the fountain, its headlights swept over the vaulted glass roof of an orangery, ivy-clad walls of dark stone and shuttered bay windows before coming to land on an arched porch. Within the porch, a wooden door studded with iron rivets waited to repel any invader. Above it, a tall stained-glass window depicted roots spreading wide and deep from a gnarled tree trunk.

"Fenton House," Natalie breathed in a hushed voice. "The most haunted house in Cornwall."

As if on cue, a whining gust of wind stirred up a swirl of fallen leaves in the porch.

"Looks creepy as fuck," said Jamie.

"Stop talking bollocks and get your game heads on," said Leon. "If I can't pick the lock, it'll take a battering ram to get through that door."

"There are French doors at the back of the house." Natalie tapped the dog-eared paperback. "Remember, we're not the first ones to break into this place."

"I've been thinking about that," Jamie said with a touch of unease. "Why would anyone want to summon a demon?"

"Who gives a toss?" said Leon. "We need to get this car out of sight."

They followed the driveway around the side of the house to a cluster of brick outhouses that were well on their way to being reclaimed by nature. Leon pointed to a garage half-hidden by tangles of ivy and brambles. "That'll do nicely."

He got out of the car and set to work on jimmying the garage's lock with a crowbar. Rotten wood crumbled beneath his fingers as he dragged the double doors open. The headlights illuminated an oil-stained concrete floor occupied by a sit-on mower, a lawn-roller, a few rusty oil cans and about a century's worth of cobwebs.

Drawing aside a curtain of foliage, Leon beckoned the car forwards. Natalie shifted into the driver's seat, eased the BMW into the garage and cut the engine. The acrid tang of petrol and motor oil irritated her nostrils as she got out of the car.

Jamie followed suit, handing Natalie and Leon each a pocket-sized torch from a black holdall before slinging it over his shoulder. The three of them slunk from the garage.

"Do we have to wear these things?" Natalie grumbled, adjusting her hook-nosed witch mask. "I can't see properly and it's making me sweat. You know I get hives when I sweat."

"You'll wear it until I say otherwise." Leon's voice whistled through the saw-toothed mouth of his devil mask.

"I swear you're doing this to get me back for making you come down here. If you really thought there was someone in the house, you wouldn't have driven up to it with your headlights on."

"Yeah, the place looks empty," conceded Leon. "But I'm not taking any chances on anyone seeing our faces. Now stop whinging and show us these French doors."

They skulked across a lawn of knee-high grass towards the looming black outline of the house. The wind swirled around them, dampening their cheeks with sea fret. The darkness pulsed with the rhythmic whoosh and boom of waves breaking over rocks. A handful of steps led up to a patio enclosed by a mossy stone balustrade. Natalie pointed her torch at a pair of shutterless French doors.

Water spattered off Leon's mask. He looked up at the eaves. Tufts of grass and slipped ridge tiles blocked a leaky gutter. Winged gargoyles thrust forked tongues out at him from the corners of the eaves.

"No motion sensor lights, no cameras, no alarm system,"

he observed with a mixture of wonder and disdain. "Total Mickey Mouse security."

"I told you," said Natalie. "Adam Piper's not worried about break-ins. He's worried about what the house might do to anyone breaking in."

"Nice to know he cares," scoffed Leon, turning his attention to the French doors. The frame next to the lock was splintered and secured with screws. He depressed the brass handle and pushed at the doors. With creaking resistance, they moved a centimetre inwards. He peered through the glass. "Looks like they're only held shut by a few screws. Give me a hand here, Jamie."

The brothers leaned their weight against the doors. There was a sharp crack of wood giving way and the doors popped open. The three masked figures stood motionless, listening for noises from inside the house. There were none – at least, none that could be heard over the relentless crashing of the waves.

"Well that was easy," said Jamie.

Leon responded with a sceptical *mmm.* "You'd think this Adam bloke wants to be robbed."

He parted a pair of thick floor-length curtains and padded into the house. Jamie followed, his nose wrinkling at a musty perfume of dust and damp. Natalie hesitated by the threshold with a look of wonder verging on disbelief in her eyes.

Jamie turned to her. "What's wrong?"

"Nothing. It's just that I've wanted to come here for so long. I can't believe I'm actually doing this."

"Shh," hissed Leon, motioning for her to come inside.

Natalie closed the damaged doors as best she could. She advanced into the high-ceilinged room, avidly surveying her surrounds – threadbare three-piece suite, grandfather clock in a corner, tapestries and paintings on the walls, stag's head peering down from above a sooty stone fireplace, brown bearskin rug by the hearth, dark floorboards. Her eyes gleamed with approval in the torchlight. It was exactly as Adam Piper described, except for the dust coating everything.

"I bet they're worth a pretty penny," said Leon, sweeping his torch over a trio of oil paintings adjacent to the fireplace. There was a muscular man with the lower body of a horse, then came a long-necked bird with flaming feathers, and lastly a fat toad wearing a crown of leaves at a jaunty angle.

"What are they supposed to be?" asked Jamie.

Natalie pointed at the man. "That's a centaur." Her finger moved to the bird. "That's a phoenix." Then the toad. "I'm not sure what that is. I don't think it was in the book."

Jamie squinted through the ghost mask's black-ringed eyeholes at the warty creature. "King Toad."

"King Toad," repeated Natalie. Her tone deadpan, she said to Leon, "That'd make a good nickname for you."

"Maybe it's a queen," he countered. "It's got your eyes."

Natalie gave him the middle finger.

He blew her a kiss before turning to flick a brass light-switch. "No electricity."

"That's because no one lives here."

"Don't start with that again."

Easing open a panelled door, Leon poked his head into a dining room furnished with a long oak table and sixteen matching chairs. Tapestries of mythical creatures shrouded the walls. A pair of porcelain King Charles spaniels bookended a marble mantelpiece. He picked up one dog and inspected its base. With a murmur of approval at the sight of a small hole, he returned the ornament to the mantelpiece. "This stuff looks kosher."

"So even if there's no gold, it won't be a wasted trip," said Jamie.

Natalie stooped to run her fingers over the floorboards by the bearskin. "This is where Faith and her friends performed the summoning ritual."

"Did it work?" asked Jamie.

"Of course it worked," Leon put in, returning to the living room. "The Devil himself appeared in a puff of smoke right where you're standing." He gave a long-suffering sigh and cuffed Jamie on the back of the head. "Sometimes I wonder if Mum brought the wrong baby home from the hospital."

His cheeks burning behind his mask, Jamie stared at the floor like a scolded child.

Leon turned to Natalie. "This is your show, babe, so what's our next move?"

"I suppose we should retrace my great grandma's footsteps."

Leon motioned for Natalie to lead the way. She headed over to a door at the far side of the room. It led to a wide L-shaped hallway. Straight ahead were several more doors. To the left, the hallway passed a broad, cantilevered wooden staircase with an ornate banister. The unsupported steps appeared almost to float up the wall. A pair of cobwebby black iron chandeliers dangled from the lofty ceiling. The iron-rivet reinforced front door occupied a stone archway at the entrance hall's far end.

Natalie approached the staircase, her footfalls cushioned by thick gold and red rugs that complemented the baroque floral wallpaper. The aroma of mildew hung heavy.

Leon glanced over his shoulder. Jamie was staring at the toad again with an uneasy glimmer in his eyes.

"Oi," hissed Leon.

Jamie blinked away from the painting. "I swear I can feel that ugly thing watching me," he whispered, hurrying towards the hallway.

"Yeah? Well you'll feel my boot up your arse if you don't keep your mind on the job."

The brothers made their way to Natalie. She was looking up at a portrait of a woman in a lavish gold-leaf frame. An ankle length black dress clung elegantly to the woman's slender frame. Strings of pearls gleamed on her swan-like neck. Dark eyes stared piercingly out of a pale, sharp-featured face framed by a raven-black bob. She seemed to peer down at the intruders with a calculated disinterest.

"That's Winifred Trehearne," murmured Natalie.

"Who?" asked Jamie.

"She lived here a long time ago. She died here too. Of natural causes. Even here, people sometimes die of natural causes." Natalie chuckled as if she'd made a joke. "Her ghost is supposed to haunt these hallways, always lonely and searching."

"Searching for what?"

"For someone alive to keep her company."

Jamie's eyes flitted around as if he expected to see Winifred floating nearby. "I thought some bloke called Lewarne used to live here."

"Walter Lewarne built this place and lived here until he committed suicide in 1920-something."

"He topped himself? How?"

Natalie pointed upwards. "He hanged himself from the highest window. A local man called Anthony James bought the house. Winifred was his daughter. Anthony James was killed in World War Two–"

"Save the history lesson for later," interrupted Leon.

Natalie stuck her tongue out at him through her mask's withered, black lips. They ascended the creaking stairs, padding past moth-eaten tapestries to a rectangular central landing. The beams of their torches shimmered on a stained-glass window in the rear wall that depicted a storm-tossed sea. The sound of the actual sea raging outside gave the turquoise waves an uncannily lifelike quality. Rain began to drum against the glass.

A long door-lined hallway traversed the first floor, extending away from either side of the landing. "Which is the east wing?" asked Leon.

"Why?" asked Jamie.

Leon jabbed a finger at his brother's head. "Hello, Jamie, anyone in?" he jeered, his voice rising carelessly. "The diary. There are two-way mirrors in the east wing's bedrooms."

This time, instead of dropping his gaze, Jamie swatted Leon's hand away and glared at him.

Leon chuckled. "Don't look at me like that, little brother. You know you love me really." He hooked a hand proprietorially around the back of Jamie's neck. "Say it."

Jamie exuded silence.

"Say it," repeated Leon, flexing his thick fingers. "Tell me you love me."

Jamie twisted free. "Piss off, Leon."

Leon squared up to him, amusement and menace playing in his blue eyes. Jamie held his ground, even though Leon loomed half-a-head over him. Leon's fingers curled into mallet-sized fists. "Maybe there is something weird going on in this house. Something must be messing with your head for you to think you can talk to me like that."

"You're the only thing messing with my head, Leon."

"Now, now, boys, play nice," Natalie purred huskily, inserting herself between the brothers. She lifted her mask a few centimetres, drew one of Leon's fists to her heart-shaped lips and kissed their scarred knuckles.

Jamie's eyes shifted around uncomfortably.

Natalie shone her torch at the hallway behind Leon. Its beam passed over six doors – three in one wall, two in the other and one at the far end. "The door at the end of the hallway must lead to the attic."

Interlacing her fingers with Leon's, she drew him along the hallway. He trailed after her like a puppy eager to please. Jamie followed, glowering at the back of his brother's head. When they reached the door, Leon protectively pulled Natalie behind him and opened it. A narrow wooden staircase rose into fusty darkness. Black mould stippled the staircase's bare plaster walls.

"If that's the way to Emily's bedroom, one of these must be Walter's bedroom," said Jamie, motioning to two doors that faced each other at the foot of the stairs.

Leon opened one of the doors. Dustsheets were draped over bulky furniture in the room beyond. He lifted the nearest sheet, revealing a dark-wood wardrobe.

"Doesn't look like Walter Lewarne's bedroom," said Natalie, eyeing a smooth stone fireplace.

Jamie opened the opposite door. "This does."

He stepped into a bedroom that extended outwards from the back of the house. Arched, stone-casement windows were recessed into all three walls at the rear of the room. A four-poster bed with a tatty crimson canopy was oddly positioned in the centre of the floor. Wooden crucifixes decorated each corner of the canopy. Stone pillars adorned with chubby, bow-wielding cherubs flanked a tall fireplace.

Natalie approached the bed as quietly as if someone was sleeping in it. She feathered her fingers over the letters 'WL' embossed on the bedhead.

"Which pillar was it that Emily said is really a secret doorway?" asked Jamie, rapping his knuckles on the pillars.

"The right-hand one, birdbrain," Leon chided, elbowing him aside. He pushed and prodded at the said pillar to no effect. "So how do we open this thing, Nat?"

Seemingly not hearing him, Natalie stroked the mattress. "This is where–" she broke off, pressing her lips together as if she'd been about to let something slip.

"Where what?" asked Jamie.

Before she could answer, Leon repeated impatiently, "I said how do we open this thing?"

"No idea," admitted Natalie, moving to examine the pillars. She traced the fleshy outlines of the cherubs. "Look at these. So cute."

Leon gave Jamie an eye roll that said, *See what I have to put up with?* He ran a finger down the inner side of a pillar. "There's a join here. You can't see it, but you can feel it. Pass me the crowbar."

Jamie took the crowbar out of the holdall and handed it to him.

"What are you doing?" Natalie exclaimed as Leon readied himself to stab the crowbar into the invisible join.

He looked at her like she was soft in the head "What does it look like I'm doing? I'm going to force it open."

"What about the noise? Someone might hear."

"Like who? You were right, there's no one living here."

"Then we can get rid of these," said Jamie, taking off his mask.

Natalie rested her hand tenderly on a cherub. "I hate the thought of damaging the little darlings."

"What do you care if I damage them?" asked Leon.

She put on her husky voice again. "Please, Leon. There must be a hidden button or something. Just give me a minute to find it."

His lips spread into a lecherous smile. "You know I can't say no when you use that voice." He lifted her mask onto the top of her head and slid a thumb across her lips. "I'm gonna go look for those two-way mirrors." He glanced at Jamie. "Stay here and keep an eye out, just in case we're not the only ones here after all."

With a nod, Jamie took up a lookout position by the door.

Leon returned to the hallway and slunk towards the opposite wing of the house.

Natalie resumed her examination of the cherubs, searching in vain for moveable parts. She stiffened as hands encircled her waist and a whisper warmed her ear, "I want you."

"Jamie!" she hissed, digging an elbow into his ribs. "Are you insane?"

He kissed her neck. "Christ, you smell so good."

She cringed away from his lips. "Leon could return at any–"

"Fuck Leon," Jamie snarled, jealousy flashing in his eyes. "Seeing that bastard's hands all over you makes me want to do murder." He flexed his fingers as if imagining them around Leon's neck.

"You're not ready for that yet, Jamie."

"Are you saying I won't do it?" he bristled.

"No. I'm saying we have to stick to the plan. First we find the gold, then we deal with Leon." Natalie took Jamie's hand and raised it to her lips. "OK babe?"

He snatched his hand away as if a forked tongue had touched it. "Don't do that. Don't sweet talk me like you do him."

"I'm not." Natalie caught hold of his hand again. "I don't mean the things I say to him. With you it's different."

Jamie hooked an arm around her hourglass waist and pressed her to him. "Prove it." The words were both a demand and a plea. He slid a hand inside her leggings, sinking his fingers into the firm flesh of her buttocks.

"No, Jamie," she gasped, stumbling and losing her balance as he pushed her backwards. Her breath whistled between her lips as she landed on the mattress. Dust and something else, a scent that was somehow as irresistibly sweet as it was nauseatingly bitter, flew up her nostrils, igniting an almost feverish light in her eyes.

She didn't resist any longer as he pulled down her leggings. With eager fingers, she unbuttoned his jeans and thrust them and his boxer shorts down to his knees. She drew him between her legs, biting down on a moan as he slid inside her. Stretching out her arms like the crucifixes adorning the bedframe, she dug her fingernails into the mattress. More of the pungent perfume was released as she tore through the threadbare material. She filled her lungs with it, thrusting her hips upwards.

Jamie crushed his lips against hers. She twisted her head away, not wanting his breath to taint the mattress's intoxicating aroma. The bitter-sweet scent seemed to seep into every pore of her being, hurling her senses into a tailspin. Eyes twitching shut, she felt herself not soaring, but sinking towards an orgasm. Sinking, sinking, down, down, down into a fathomless sea of pleasure.

A voice floated into her mind. *Emily,* it moaned.

Then, as if her senses had pierced an invisible membrane, she was no longer alone with Jamie. The mattress was writhing with naked bodies. The air was thick with their musky sweat and breathless moans. Their hands were all over her, stroking, squeezing, driving her into a frenzy. Her nails darted to Jamie's buttocks. He tried to pull away as she raked at his flesh, but she clung on like a limpet, jerking her head up to bite his neck.

Emily! Emily!

"Walter," a voice gasped back. Was it her voice? She couldn't tell. Her mind was whirling. Everything was blurring together, bodies melting into each other like hot wax. Faster, faster, panting, groaning, pinching, clawing, pleasure tipping into pain...

As suddenly as a conductor silencing an orchestra, it all stopped. For a lurching heartbeat, deathlike darkness consumed her. Then Jamie's flushed, sweat-streaked face swam into view.

"Jesus Christ," he said breathlessly, rolling off her onto his back. "That was..." he trailed off, at a loss for words.

Natalie sat up on her elbows, looking around as if she was struggling to make sense of her surroundings. There was a salty, metallic taste on her lips. She touched a finger to them and saw blood. Her gaze shifted to Jamie. Beads of blood glistened on his throat where her teeth had broken the skin.

"You're bleeding," she told him.

He felt at the bite mark, then reached behind his back. "You've scratched my arse to shreds." With a shake of his head, he made another attempt to articulate his feelings. "That was the most mind-blowing fuck I've ever had, but I'm not sure I could survive many more like it." The comment was tongue-in-cheek and serious at the same time.

Natalie's gaze did another circuit of the room. "He was right about this place."

"Who?"

"Adam Piper. This isn't just a house, it's... something else. A doorway."

"A doorway?" echoed Jamie.

Their eyes jerked to the hallway at a faint creak. They exchanged a panicked glance, then they were on their feet, frantically yanking their clothes into place and wiping the sweat from their faces. Jamie flipped up the collar of his polo shirt to hide the bite mark. Letting the mask hang at the back of her neck, Natalie smoothed her hair down and felt for smears of lipstick around her mouth. They stared at the doorway, neither of them daring to breathe. A moment passed. Leon didn't reappear.

Natalie puffed her cheeks. "My heart feels like it's about to burst out of my chest."

"Mine too. Fuck, I hate creaky old houses." Jamie poked his head into the hallway. "Leon's been gone ages."

"Has he?" It occurred to Natalie that she had no idea how long he'd been gone. In the throes of their demented lovemaking, time had dissolved into a hazy nothing.

Torchlight suddenly sliced through the darkness of the hallway. "It's him," said Jamie, stooping to take the snub-nosed pistol out of the holdall.

"What the hell, Jamie?" Natalie hissed as he took aim at the doorway. "The plan. Stick to the plan."

He nodded, echoing his brother's cautionary words. "Just in case."

Natalie drew in a steadying breath and composed her face into its usual pouty expression.

The dazzling torchlight dipped to the hallway's crimson carpet, revealing Leon's rugged face. The devil mask was perched atop his head like a strange red hat. He grinned approvingly at the pistol, then growled, "Get that thing out of my face."

"Where have you been?" asked Jamie, obediently lowering the gun. "We were getting worried."

"What are you going on about?" said Leon. "I was only gone a few minutes."

Jamie's forehead wrinkled into perplexed lines, but he said nothing more.

Leon's grin widened at the sight of Natalie. "Something's put colour in your cheeks." Scanning over her hungrily, like someone about to tuck into a fillet steak, he asked Jamie, "Have you ever seen anything more fuckable?"

Jamie pursed his lips as if he suspected Leon was trying to lure him into saying something incriminating. His fingers tightened on the pistol's grip as Leon stepped forwards to plant his hands on Natalie's waist. Leaning in close, Leon breathed into her ear, "God, you make me horny. How about we find ourselves a room?"

Spotting the perilous glint in Jamie's eyes, Natalie quickly changed the subject. "I can't work out how to get into the secret passage."

"No shit," Leon replied with a smug chuckle. He took her hand and drew her towards the hallway.

She resisted his pull. "I'm not in the mood, Leon."

"You will be when I show you what I've found."

"Why? What–"

"You'll see, you'll see."

She allowed him to lead her from the room. Jamie hoisted the holdall over a shoulder, wincing as it rubbed against the bite mark. His eyes as dark as the windows, he followed Natalie and Leon towards the opposite wing of the house. They headed into the first room beyond the central staircase. Jamie flinched to a halt as his torchlight glinted in the beady eyes of a peacock perched on a stone mantelpiece.

Sniggering at his brother's reaction, Leon prodded the bird's shimmering blue and turquoise feathers. "Relax. It's stuffed."

"Yeah, I know. I'm not stupid," Jamie snapped.

Leon held up his hands in mock innocence. "I didn't say you were."

As Natalie eyeballed him, Jamie bit down on the urge to fire back another retort. He took in the rest of the room – four-poster bed, dirty white duvet and pillows, black velvet chaise longue, antique rocking-horse with an equally old looking teddy bear astride it, dressing table, wardrobe, French doors that opened onto a stone balcony.

Leon wafted his hand at the dozens of amateurishly competent water-colours of robins, gulls, ravens, hares, mice, badgers and other wild animals cluttering the walls. "Worthless load of crap."

Natalie stared into a full-length wall-mounted mirror in an alcove beside the fireplace. She touched the glass as tentatively as if her hand might disappear through it.

"What do you see?" Jamie felt a sudden compulsion to ask.

"A doorway," Leon answered for her.

Jamie's heart skipped as he thought about what Natalie had said to him in the other room. Had Leon somehow overheard? No, he couldn't have. He'd been too far away.

Seemingly too distracted to notice or care about the coincidence, Natalie slid her fingers across to the mirror's gilded frame. The wood was cracked and splintered. A chunk of plaster was missing from the adjoining wall. "Did you do this?" she asked Leon.

He frowned at her disapproving tone. "So what if I did? Fucking hell, anyone would think you actually liked this place."

"I kind of do," she admitted. "It's like…" She strove to find the right words. "This house feels so far away from everywhere. It's like the rest of the world doesn't exist."

"I know what you mean," agreed Jamie. "Time seems strange here. Distorted somehow."

"Distorted?" laughed Leon. "I'm impressed, little brother. I didn't realise you knew such big words."

Jamie ground his teeth again at the condescending remark.

Leon moved Natalie aside with a sweep of one hand and prised the fingers of his other into the gap between the mirror and the broken plaster. The mirror swung outwards on silent hinges. Behind it was a long red curtain. "Ta-daaah," Leon exclaimed, swishing the curtain aside to reveal a narrow passageway.

"Yay," said Natalie, giving a delighted clap.

Leon held his arms out wide like a performer accepting applause. She leaned in as if to kiss him, but instead skipped past him into the passageway. He looked at her with a sort of grinning frown, unsure whether to be annoyed or amused by her tease. She pulled aside a second curtain on the opposite wall, exposing another two-way mirror that faced into an almost pitch-black empty room.

"Bloody hell," said Jamie. "It's just like Emily said."

"Of course it is," Natalie responded with a hint of indignation. "My great grandma wouldn't lie."

She shone her torch all around, illuminating cobweb-draped brick walls, a crumbling plaster-lath ceiling and wormhole-riddled joists. A few metres to her left, a staircase rose steeply into darkness. To her right, there was a staircase going down.

Following in Emily's footsteps, Natalie descended the stairs to a passageway squeezed into a dark space between the ground floor rooms. Her torchlight landed on a wooden panel. She pulled the brass handle at its centre. The small panel came loose and she squinted through the peephole behind it. As her eyes adjusted to the darkness, she made out the vague shapes of the living room's sofa and armchairs. Leon and Jamie came down the stairs, their footsteps echoing hollowly. She stepped aside so that they could take turns peeking through the peephole.

"I have to admit, Granny was telling the truth so far," said Leon. A quiver of anticipation found its way into his voice as he eyed the stairs. "Let's see if she can make it three out of three."

He ran his fingers along the angles where the steps met the walls. Unlike in the diary, there wasn't even a hair's width between the wood and the bricks. Triceps flexing, he tried to move the staircase sideways. There was no give in it. He withdrew the crowbar from his belt and stabbed at the wood until the blade found purchase between a tread and a riser. With levering motions, accompanied by the squeak of nails coming loose, he pried the tread upwards. He shone his torch into the gap. A hiss of disappointment escaped him. There was only a flagstone floor to be seen in the triangular cavity behind the staircase.

"Where's the trapdoor?" Natalie wondered out loud.

"You tell me."

"Maybe this isn't the right place."

"This is *exactly* the place described in the diary."

"What if Walter blocked up the trapdoor because Emily knew where it was?" suggested Jamie.

"Yes, that must be it," said Natalie.

Leon made a dubious rumble in his throat. He resumed stabbing and levering at the staircase. After a few minutes, a pile of splintered wood lay at his feet. Sweat dripping from his forehead, he ducked through the enlarged gap. He tapped the crowbar against the flagstones, producing a dull, solid *thunk.* The squares of smooth stone were tightly fitted together. Like a surgeon at an operating table, he held out a hand and said, "Hammer and chisel."

Jamie passed him the requested tools. Angling the chisel against a join, Leon brought the hammer down hard. Chips of stone ricocheted off the walls. A clang loud enough to wake the dead should there be any sleeping nearby reverberated along the passageway. He hit the chisel again, traversing the joins, searching for weaknesses.

After a dozen hammer blows, he flung down the tools. "No way are we breaking through this without a pneumatic drill."

Natalie squeezed into the hollow alongside him. "There must be a way to open it," she said, running her fingers over the flagstones and the walls, searching for anything that might be an opening mechanism.

Leon slammed the side of his fist against the floor. "Either Great Granny was talking out of her arse or that Walter prick was taking no chances of anyone else getting into his vault."

"If he blocked up this entrance, there has to be another way in," said Jamie.

Faint lines marred Natalie's unblemished forehead. "Yeah, but where could it be?"

Several silent seconds passed.

"Well?" pressed Leon.

"Give her a chance to think," said Jamie. Leon threw him a scowl, but Jamie was turning away and cocking an ear to the passageway. "Can you hear that?"

"Hear what?" asked Natalie.

"It sounds like running water."

Her eyes widening as a sudden thought hit her, Natalie clambered out of the aperture.

"Where are you going?" Leon called after her as she swept past Jamie and set off at a run along the passageway.

"Adam Piper heard running water the first time he came here," Natalie answered without looking back. "He thought there was a burst pipe."

"So what?" Receiving no reply, Leon snatched up his tools and muttered, "I don't know who's crazier – her or us for following her."

After ten or fifteen metres, Natalie came to a flight of stone steps leading downwards. Goose pimples prickled her skin as she descended into a pool of cold, damp air. A corridor with granite block walls stretched away from the bottom step. The left-hand wall was streaked with what looked to be slimy orange and green algae. Water seeped between the joins of the lower blocks, forming rivulets on mossy flagstones before draining away through the opposite wall.

Natalie silently recited a few words from *Between Worlds*, 'The corridor passed beneath what I judged to be the entrance hall. A second stone stairway led upwards to another passageway.'

Her heart gave a little leap as the second set of steps came into view. They brought her to a brick-walled passageway. She dropped to her haunches by a wooden panel recessed in the bricks.

A length of wood was wedged across the panel as if to hold it shut. Jamie arrived at her side, slightly out of breath. "Jesus, Nat, I thought I'd lost you for a second there."

Leon wasn't far behind. "Go haring off like that again and I'll put you over my knee."

"This is the secret panel Adam Piper first used to get into these passageways," Natalie told them. "His son Henry found it by *accident*." She emphasised the word as if she considered it to have been anything but an accident.

She tried in vain to pull the length of wood away from the panel. With the exaggerated patience of a parent dealing with a clueless child, Leon said, "Out of my way." Whipping out the crowbar again, he effortlessly levered the length of wood free. As if it was being pushed by an invisible hand, the panel swung inwards on hidden hinges.

Leon put on an eerie voice. "Ooh. Spooky."

"Must be spring-loaded," said Jamie.

Leon tilted an eyebrow at him that said, *Duh, you think so?*

They ducked through the opening. Natalie swept her torch over the long rectangular room beyond – red fleur de lis patterned floor tiles, matching embossed wallpaper, two silver candelabra with red candlesticks atop a pair of glittering stone pedestals, red velvet sofa and armchair facing each other in front of a gaping fireplace.

"The Lewarne Room," she said, her voice almost reverently hushed. "No one was allowed in here without Walter's permission."

Her torch lingered on oil paintings in the alcoves that flanked the fireplace. A knot formed between her eyebrows.

In one painting, a rosy-cheeked baby was puckering its lips in anticipation of suckling at its mother's milk-swollen breast. The woman was looking down at her child with heavy-lidded, sleep-deprived eyes. In the painting that occupied the other alcove, the same woman's eyes were saucers of horror. A bare-chested man whose chiselled muscles made Natalie think of Leon was tearing the baby from its mother's arms. The man's calm, determined expression as he thrust a dagger into the child's neck made the gruesome scene even more disturbing.

Turning at the click of a latch, Natalie saw that the secret panel had swung shut of its own accord.

"That thing's got a mind of its own," said Jamie.

Natalie's gaze returned to the baby's strangely bloodless wound. Her golden eyes glistened with something that might have been tears. A spasm of irritation pulled at her face as Leon weighed a candelabra in his hands and said, "This is solid silver. It has to be worth a couple of thousand at least."

"Is that all you give a shit about?" Natalie muttered.

"What's got your knickers in a–" he started to ask but broke off, his eyebrows lifting in comprehension as he noticed the paintings. He swiftly returned to his previous musings. "Who just leaves stuff like this lying around for the taking?" He frowned as if troubled by the question.

"Not everyone's as obsessed with material possessions as you, Leon."

"Said the girl who spends half her life shopping."

"Yeah well maybe my priorities have changed."

Leon gave a doubtful, "*Pfft*!"

Jamie ran his fingers over one of the glittering green and black spotted pedestals. "This feels…" he searched for the right word, "scaly. I wonder what it's made of."

"Serpentine," Natalie told him. "It's a type of rock found around here."

"Is that why they call it Lizard Peninsula?"

The question received no answer. Natalie was staring at the baby again, fixated by the dagger plunging into its pale flesh.

Jamie eyed the grisly painting too. "You couldn't pay me to put that on my wall."

"You just don't know how to appreciate good art," said Leon.

"You call *that* good art?"

Leon chuckled. "I call that a fortnight in the Bahamas."

"They are no more," murmured Natalie, reading out the words embossed on a wooden panel above the mantelpiece.

"Kindermond," said Jamie.

"The murder of children," Natalie added grimly.

"So Walter put up these paintings to remind himself of what his guns did to the Krauts." Jamie puffed air between his lips. "Imagine having that shit on your conscience. Poor bastard."

"Oh yeah, it's a wonder the poor, filthy rich bastard could look himself in the mirror," Leon said sarcastically.

The words prompted Natalie's eyes to dart around the room. "The mirror. Where's the mirror?"

"What mirror?" asked Jamie.

She moved to pick up a black-and-white photo from one of the pedestals. 'Walter Lewarne. 1915' was engraved into a brass plaque on the frame. The man himself was standing rigidly in the centre of the photo, looking every inch the lord of the manor in a three-piece-suit. Walter's short dark hair was centre-parted. His eyes stared intensely out of deep hollows. He was facing his reflection in a tall arched mirror flanked by curtains. The downwards curl of his thin lips seemed to suggest that he didn't like what he saw.

"*That* mirror," said Natalie.

"That doesn't look like this room," observed Jamie.

"It's not. The photo was taken in a secret basement below this room. That's where the sound of running water's coming from."

Jamie clicked a finger and pointed at Natalie. "Which is how Adam Piper found the basement. Am I right?"

"Pretty much. The basement was flooded, so he moved the mirror to up here."

"What's so special about that mirror?" asked Leon.

"Walter used it as a portal."

"A what?"

"A doorway."

"Walter was trying to talk to dead soldiers, wasn't he?" said Jamie.

The comment drew a reassessing glance from Natalie, as if it had occurred to her that perhaps Jamie was more perceptive than she'd thought. "Yes, he wanted to ask for their forgiveness, but instead he opened the door for something else to get into this world."

"Let me take a wild guess what that 'something else' was," sneered Leon, tapping the devil mask meaningfully.

Natalie fetched a framed photo from the second pedestal. The faded colour image was a family portrait of a middle-aged man, a younger woman and a girl on the cusp of adolescence. The girl was seated between the man and woman on The

Lewarne Room's sofa. She and the woman were straight-backed and solemn-faced. Conversely, the man was slouched against the cushions, exuding an air of louche boredom. All three were dressed in their Sunday best – grey suit and open-necked white shirt for the man, knee-length black dress for the woman, frilly red Alice dress for the girl. The girl appeared to have inherited her delicate facial features from the woman and her owlishly big eyes from the man, whilst the mousey brown hair fanned over her shoulders was all her own. A wavy blonde bob framed the woman's demurely made-up face. The man's greying black hair was slicked back like a movie villain.

"That's George and Sofia and their daughter Heloise," said Natalie.

"And who in the name of fuck are George, Sofia and Louise?" Leon asked in a tone that made it abundantly clear he couldn't care less about the answer.

"*Heloise*," corrected Natalie. "They lived here in the mid-nineties. Then one day they just disappeared into thin air. Or so it seemed." Her gaze fell to the tiled floor. "Adam Piper found George and Sofia's skeletons in the basement. They starved to death after Heloise trapped them down there."

"Jesus, she killed her parents," said Jamie. "Why?"

"Some think it was because her dad was going to sell Fenton House to pay his gambling debts. Others think it was because of the Entity. That's what Adam Piper calls the demon Walter let into the house."

"Oh I get it," laughed Leon. "Louise was–"

"Heloise," Natalie corrected him again.

"*Louise*," he repeated with taunting relish, "was possessed."

Jamie looked askance at his brother. "Possessed?"

"Yeah, you know, like in The Exorcist."

"Take the mickey all you want, Leon, but how do you know she wasn't possessed?" said Natalie.

He gave a bark of laughter. "How do I know? Cos this is the biggest load of horseshit I've ever heard. That's how I know. I swear to God, if I have to listen to one more word of this shit I'm going to start banging heads together. All I want to do is finish this job and get the hell out of here."

Natalie pointed at the floor. "Then we need to get into the basement."

"And how are we supposed to do that?"

"There's a trapdoor."

"Oh isn't that just wonderful, another trapdoor," Leon groaned sarcastically.

Natalie got onto her hands and knees. She crawled around the room, scrutinising the tiles. Her fingers lingered on a cracked tile. She pushed a long fingernail into the crack. Her nail travelled along it to a paper-thin fissure in the black grouting. She traced out a four-by-four square of tiles.

"This is it." Her voice was an excited whisper. She rose and hurried to the fireplace.

"What are you doing?" Jamie asked as she traced her fingers over the wooden panel's raised lettering.

"It says in the book that these letters open the trapdoor."

"What book?"

"Adam Piper's fucking book," Natalie snapped. "Stop asking stupid questions and let me think." She was silent for a few seconds, then she recited from memory, "The letters were smoothly varnished with no joins between them and the wooden back plate." Pushing and prodding at the letters, she added, "Nothing seemed to move, but suddenly there was a sound like a spring being released."

She looked expectantly at the cracked tiles, but there was no 'sound like a spring being released'.

The brothers exchanged a glance as she resumed fiddling with the letters. Leon twirled a finger next to his temple, then said, "Sod this for a game of soldiers." He grabbed the holdall from Jamie, took out the hammer and brought it down with all his force on the cracked tile.

Jamie shielded his eyes as shards of ceramic flew everywhere.

"Wait," Natalie exclaimed as Leon raised the hammer for another blow. She pointed at the floor. "Look."

An edge of the four-by-four square of tiles had risen a centimetre. Dropping to one knee, Leon hovered his palms over it. He gave a little shudder as icy fingers of air tickled him. "There's a draught coming from under the floor."

Jamie swapped the pistol for a screwdriver. He worked its flat head into the thin gap between the ridge and the adjacent tiles and put his weight on it. Leon did the same with the crowbar. There was a moment of creaking resistance. Then, as if a spring had indeed been released, the trapdoor pinged upright. The basement exhaled a dank breath into the brothers' faces. Jamie pinched his nose to stop himself from sneezing.

Leon peered into the opening. He ran his torch's beam down stone steps to flagstones submerged beneath a shallow layer of clear water. A soft gurgle of running water reached their ears.

As wary as a cat, Natalie approached the trapdoor. A crucifix crisscrossed by scratches was engraved into its underside. "St Michael the Archangel, be our defence against the wickedness and snares of the Devil," she murmured, reaching towards the crucifix but stopping just short of it.

"What did you say?" asked Jamie.

She repeated the words, adding, "They're for protection from evil spirits."

"Is that what the cross is for?"

Natalie nodded. "It's supposed to stop anything evil from escaping the basement." Her gaze shifted to the top step. "That's where George and Sofia were found. Imagine dying like that."

Jamie shuddered at the thought of it. "At least they had each other."

"I'm surprised one of them didn't eat the other," said Leon. "That's what I'd do." He patted Natalie's bum. "There's enough meat on there to keep me going for weeks."

She afforded him a thin smile of tolerance.

"That's sick, Leon," said Jamie. "Even you wouldn't do something like that."

"You wanna bet? If it came down to it, I'd do whatever it takes to survive. I'd even chow down on your ugly mug." Leon thrust his face towards Jamie, sucking his teeth like Hannibal Lecter.

Natalie heaved a sigh. "God, you're such a dickhead, Leon."

He grinned at her. "Yeah, but you love me anyway." He lowered his foot onto the top step, hesitated and gave the trapdoor an uneasy look. "You sure you didn't bring me here to bump me off like George and whatshername?"

"Don't put ideas in my head," Natalie said with a wry twist of her lips.

He chuckled and blew her a kiss before continuing his descent. Dapples of light played off the flooded flagstones onto granite block walls. The basement was the same dimensions as the room above. A pair of long, tatty black curtains hung on one of the interior walls.

"This isn't the vault," Leon called up to his companions, his voice sharp with disappointment.

"I never said it was," replied Natalie. "I thought there might be a way into the vault down there."

"Well there's no door that I can see. There are just some manky old curtains and a hole in the wall."

"A hole in the wall?" Jamie parroted.

"Yeah, part of the wall's collapsed. That's where the water's coming in."

"Is the mirror there?" Natalie asked eagerly.

Leon gave a growl of irritation. "I told you, I don't want to hear one more word about mirrors or portals or–"

"Oh give it a rest yourself, Leon," countered Natalie, descending into the basement. A shiver crawled up her legs. With every step closer to the water, the temperature plummeted. Part of the wall to her left had collapsed inwards, scattering granite blocks and chunks of mortar across the floor. A steady stream of water was flowing from a gaping circular hole at about chest height. The hole's interior looked like it had been worn smooth by a thousand years of erosion.

Her attention shifted to the floor-length velvet curtains. They swayed ever so slightly in the water that nibbled at their frayed hems.

She tentatively stepped into the water, stirring up puffs of pale sediment. It came up to the ankle of her low-heeled boots. Even through the leather, the cold was enough to make her breath whistle between her teeth. "This water's freezing!"

Leon dipped a hand into the glassy pool. He quickly withdrew it. "Christ, it's so cold it burns. No way is that coming from a burst pipe."

"Must be from deep underground," said Jamie, squatting down at the top of the steps.

"The house is built on a natural spring," said Natalie, edging towards the curtains. "That's where the name Fenton comes from. It's a variant of venton, the Cornish word for a spring. There's supposed to be a connection between natural springs and paranormal activity. Something to do with the energy generated by running water. It makes it easier for ghosts to manifest."

Leon shook his head, blowing out a resigned sigh.

Natalie stood silently in front of the curtains for a moment, like someone paying their respects at a grave. She slid her long fingers between them. The material had a slimy texture. As she parted the curtains, her eyebrows knitted together.

Leon let out a laugh heavy with irony at the sight of the bare wall behind the curtains. "You gotta love this place."

Natalie touched the rusty hook the mirror had once hung on, murmuring, "Where are you?"

"So what now, babe?" There was a jeering edge to Leon's question. "Any more bright ideas?"

"Leave off, Leon," said Jamie.

Leon glared up at him, his pupils contracting to pinpoints in the beam of Jamie's torch. "You're really pushing your luck, little brother."

Natalie nibbled at her nails, musing, "There must be another way." Her eyes returned to the circular hole in the opposite wall. "I wonder where that goes."

"If you think I'm going to crawl in there to find out, you can think again," said Leon.

"You wouldn't fit in there anyway," Jamie pointed out.

"You would though," said Natalie, eyeing up Jamie's lean frame.

Leon burst out laughing so hard that he clutched his stomach. "You're priceless, Natalie. Why do something yourself when you can have your little admirer do it for you, eh?"

A tremor ran through her at the word 'admirer', but she kept her expression deadpan. No way did he suspect the truth. The bastard was too arrogant to ever suspect she would cheat on him, especially with Jamie. "Oh go fuck–" she started to retort, but broke off as a movement from above caught her eye. "Jamie, look out!"

As the warning rang in Jamie's ears, something that felt like a sledgehammer slammed into his back. With a winded, "Oof," he plunged down the steps into the icy water. White lights flashed in front of his eyes as his forehead hit a flagstone. He reared up groggily, coughing, spluttering and clutching his head.

Leon was scrambling up the steps.

Natalie rushed to help Jamie to his feet, calling after Leon, "Please tell me you can open it."

Her words made Jamie's heart thump even harder than it already was doing. Surely they could only mean one thing. He looked at the top of the steps. A groan escaped his lips, partly because of the pain that crackled down his spine, but mainly because he saw that his suspicion was correct – the trapdoor was shut.

Leon shoved at the trapdoor. It didn't budge. Thud after thud boomed around the basement as he futilely tried to force the trapdoor open. Changing tack, he braced his broad back against the crucifix. Veins swelled on his neck as he thrust upwards. Nothing. Not even a creak of movement.

Leon's gaze jerked to Jamie. "Where's the bag?"

Pointing to the ceiling, Jamie croaked, "Up there."

"Shit!" Leon squinted at his phone. "I've got no service. Anyone got service?"

Jamie and Natalie looked at their phones. "No," they answered.

"Shit! Shit! Shit!" Leon slammed a fist into the trapdoor and stated the obvious. "We're trapped."

Natalie started up the steps. "Move out of the way. Let me have a look."

"And just what do you think you'll be able to do?" Leon retorted. "You said it yourself, that Lewarne bloke wanted to make sure nothing could get out of here. Why do you think this trapdoor's so thick?"

Jamie gingerly felt at a lump on his forehead before running his fingers over the throbbing knuckles of his spine. "My back hurts like a bastard."

"Good, you useless prick," said Leon. "Why weren't you keeping an eye on the trapdoor?"

"How was I to know it would close like that?" protested Jamie, his trainers squelching as he climbed to the trapdoor. He touched the crucifix as if afraid it might burst into flame. "What the hell even made it do that?"

"It was probably a draught."

"That trapdoor's too heavy for a draught to–" Natalie began, but fell silent as Leon cast a dark look at her.

"Maybe there *is* someone else in the house," said Jamie. "What happened to that girl who trapped her parents down here?"

"Heloise is dead," said Natalie. "She hanged herself from

the same window as Walter."

"Why?"

Natalie shrugged. "She'd been hiding out in the secret passages since killing her parents."

"But you said they lived here in the nineties."

"They did. Somehow, she survived in the passages for over twenty years. She killed herself the day Adam Piper and his family left here. Perhaps she couldn't handle the thought of being alone anymore."

Leon let out a slow hiss, pressing his palms to his head as if to keep it from splitting apart.

Natalie and Jamie exchanged a glance. They'd seen that look on his face before, usually preceding a violent outburst. They watched him tensely, waiting to see what he would do.

He sprang up suddenly, ran down the steps and sloshed through the water. Bending over, he clamped his hands onto a microwave oven-sized granite block. With a grunt, he hoisted it upwards. He managed a few stuttering steps before losing his grip. The block hit the floor with a resounding *thunk!*

"The sodding thing's covered in slime," he said, displaying globs of translucent gunk on his palms. "What is this crap?"

"Looks like frog spawn," said Natalie.

Leon beckoned to Jamie. "Give me a hand here."

"My back isn't up to it," said Jamie.

"Fuck your back!" exploded Leon.

A curious gleam flickered in Jamie's eyes as he glimpsed something unfamiliar lurking behind Leon's anger – was it desperation or even fear? He'd always thought of his brother as fearless, someone that thrived on danger. A sort of electrical tingle coursed through Jamie at the realisation that perhaps, just perhaps, he'd stumbled across a weakness in Leon.

He descended the steps, stiffening as he entered the icy water. The brothers clasped either end of the block. Jamie drew back his hands, his nose wrinkling in revulsion at the snotty strings of slime dangling from his fingers.

"Hey, I know what this is," said Leon, recovering his sneer. "It's demon vomit, like in–"

"The Exorcist," cut in Natalie. "You've already told that joke."

Leon flashed her a clench-toothed grin.

Jamie took hold of the block again and tried to lift his end. His breath whistled out as pain flared in his spine. The block splashed back into the water. He straightened tentatively, massaging his back. "Just give me a minute."

Leon dipped his hand into the water. "Hey, I think this water's rising."

Natalie tested the depth with her foot. The water almost reached the top of her boot. "You're right. It's a good couple of centimetres deeper. It must be all the rain."

"What if it keeps raining all night?" said Jamie. "Do you think the water could get as high as the ceiling?"

"If it does, at least we won't have to worry about starving to death," Leon said with dry fatalism. He glared at the granite block as if it offended him. Blowing out his cheeks, he heaved it into his arms again. Like a strongman undergoing a trial of strength, he fought his way up the steps. Upon reaching the top, he swung the block like a battering ram. The entire basement seemed to tremble as the block slammed into the trapdoor. He lost his grip on it, springing aside to avoid his toes being crushed. It thundered down the steps and splashed into the water.

Leon examined the trapdoor. The only trace of damage

was a small dent where the block had struck the crucifix. "What the actual fuck?" he exclaimed. "This is... It's..." Words failed him. He plonked himself down on a step and pressed his hands to his head again.

Jamie stared at his brother with a disbelief of his own. He'd never seen him like this before. Sitting hunched up on the steps, Leon looked smaller, shrunken somehow. Their entire life, Leon had made him feel about two feet tall. Nothing, not even screwing Natalie, had ever changed that – nothing, that is, until now. He could practically feel himself growing taller, like some kind of parasite that fed on fear. It was the most incredible, wonderful sensation. In that instant, he didn't care about the gold or even about Natalie. All he wanted was to find a way – any possible way – to hold on to the feeling.

He turned to slosh across to the hole in the wall. He shone his torch into the aperture. A throat-like tunnel curved upwards into inky darkness. He ran a finger over the thick layer of slime that coated the tunnel's slightly rippled surface. He sniffed his finger and said with a choke in his voice, "It smells like bad eggs."

"Hydrogen sulphide gas," said Natalie. "It's produced by sulphur bacteria in groundwater." As both brothers treated her to a look of astonishment, she approached the hole and scooped up a fingernail's worth of the gelatinous gunk. "That's what this stuff probably is – bacterial slime."

Leon's eyes narrowed as if he was suddenly wondering how well he knew her. "Hydrogen sulphide gas? Sulphur bacteria? My, my, aren't you the little fount of knowledge. Did you read about that in Adam Piper's book too?"

"Yes. Walter's mirror was covered in the stuff."

"Is it dangerous?" asked Jamie.

"I'm not sure. It might be."

Leon gave a mirthless laugh. "So if we don't drown or starve, we'll be gassed to death. This just gets better and better."

"At least it's not demon vomit," Jamie said dryly. He rubbed the slime between his fingers. "It's as slippery as lube. Dangerous or not, it'll help me slide through the hole."

"Are you seriously going in there?" asked Leon.

"What other option do we have? Like you keep saying, Leon, it's about time I manned up."

There was a newfound steel in Jamie's voice. Leon frowned faintly, unsure what to make of it. He looked at Natalie. "By rights, it should be you going in there."

Before she could reply, Jamie said adamantly, "No. I'm going." The exhilarating feeling of strength swelled inside him with each word. As he stooped to peer into the hole again, though, doubt threatened to steal it away. Could he really do this?

Would you rather spend the rest of your life kissing Leon's arse? responded another part of him.

The question didn't need answering. Dredging up a smile, he glanced at Leon. "See you soon."

"Be careful," Leon said, his voice so full of concern that shame stabbed at Jamie.

Fuck you, Leon, he thought resentfully. *Fuck you for acting like a brother for once.*

He looked at Natalie and wished he hadn't. Soft shadows highlighted her full lips, high cheekbones and feline eyes. Christ, she so was beautiful. The urge to kiss her threatened to overwhelm him. He wrenched his gaze to the hole. It seemed to stare back, wide open, waiting...

Sucking in his breath like someone about to dive into

unknown depths, Jamie ducked into the hole. His shoulders rubbed against its sides as, arms outstretched, he wormed his way forwards. A shudder ran through him, not because of the bitterly cold water, but because he suddenly had the strongest impression that he was crawling into the mouth of a living thing.

He wriggled along the slippery tunnel, ascending towards… Towards what? With every metre he progressed, the substance coating the walls was coagulating into a gluey white mass. He wiped clumps of it from his eyes. The sulphurous stench was nauseatingly strong. What had Natalie called the gas this gunk gave off? Hydrogen-something-or-other. He couldn't think straight. His head was spinning. He breathed as shallowly as possible.

The tunnel plateaued. His torch illuminated a flat stretch of rock with a couple of centimetres of water sitting on it. He squirmed onwards. Without warning, the tunnel contracted around him like a swallowing throat. Panicked gasps surged from his lungs. He couldn't move. *You're trapped!* his mind screamed. Now not only his head was spinning. The tunnel itself seemed to rotate like a washing machine in front of his eyes. Faster, faster, whirling, blurring. The gooey walls were pulsing, squeezing the air out of him. *You're going to die!*

He scrunched his eyes shut as waves of terror crashed over him. In his mind, he saw his entombed corpse decomposing until it was indistinguishable from the white sludge.

St Michael the Archangel, be our defence against the wickedness and snares of the Devil.

Somehow, from somewhere, the words found their way to him. Fighting for enough breath, he spoke them out loud. "St Michael the Archangel, be our defence against the wickedness and snares of the Devil."

Too late for prayers, another internal voice sneered with a kind of malignant pleasure. *After what you've done, you deserve to die here. What sort of scumbag screws their brother's fiancée?*

"Fuck you!" Jamie's retort was a strangled shriek. He pounded his fists against the rock. "It's my turn. *My* turn!"

As if flinching away from the blows, the walls loosened their grip, only a fraction, but it was enough to spur him to renewed effort. He sucked in his abdomen and held his breath. Striving to keep his movements calm and methodical, he pulled with his hands and pushed with his feet. A whimper of relief escaped him as he edged forwards centimetre by centimetre. The tunnel abruptly sloped downwards. Like a tapeworm, he burrowed deeper into the bowels of the house. Then, just as suddenly as he'd become stuck, he was sliding with gathering speed down a water chute.

He juddered to a stop as the tunnel levelled out again. A few metres further on, the water dwindled to a trickle and the slime dried to a yellow-green crust. The tunnel was now big enough for him to crawl commando-style on his elbows.

He squinted blearily. Was that an opening up ahead?

Numb with cold and fatigue, he continued crawling. Another sob of relief trembled from his lips as his fingers curled over the lip of a circular hole. The torch slipped from his grasp and clattered against a hard surface. As slimy as a newborn baby, he slithered out of the tunnel onto dry flagstones. For a long moment, all he could do was lie there, gulping down cold, salt-tainted air. When sufficient strength had seeped back into his limbs, he sat up and retrieved the torch. His eyes bulged like King Toad's. A bubble of faintly hysterical laughter burst on his lips.

He clambered to his feet and staggered to the centre of the square room. The walls and ceiling were solid rock shot through with veins of green and red serpentine. Apart from a rusty iron-bar door, thick wooden shelves occupied every bit of wall space. Likewise, gold bars occupied every bit of shelf space.

Time and salty air hadn't tarnished the gold. The neat stacks of rectangular bullion glowed in the torchlight as if illuminated from within.

Jamie picked up a bar. His tired arms trembled at its weight. Its smooth surface was swirled like fingerprints. He rubbed it, then put his fingers to his nose. There was no brassy smell. In fact, there was no smell at all. '999.9 FINE GOLD' was stamped into the centre of the bar. To either side was 'THE ROYAL MINT REFINERY R.M.R' and '400 oz.'. What was that in kilos? He hefted the bar. It had to be ten or eleven kilos. So that meant this one bar was worth what? Six hundred thousand quid? Maybe more.

"Six hundred thousand." A quiver of laughter ran through his words. His eyes gleaming with feverish excitement, he counted the bars. Ten, twenty, thirty, forty, fifty… More. Many, many more.

His torch cast crazed shadows as, breaking into a jig, he chanted in a singsong voice, "Fuck you, Leon. I don't need you anymore. Fuck all of you. I don't need anyone anymore." No, that wasn't true. He ran his tongue over his lips. He could still taste Natalie's sweet lipstick. He needed her. What's more, he needed her to be his and his alone. The thought of Leon putting his hands on her burned through him like acid.

A tauntingly soft voice broke into his thoughts. *So what are you going to do about it?*

"I'll… I'll…" he stammered, trembling with impotent rage.

You'll what? You'll do the same as always – fuck all.

"I'm not scared of him."

A slither of laughter tickled his mind. *Prove it.*

"I will!" he bellowed, spittle flecking his lips. "I'll make sure he never touches her again."

You'll need a weapon. The voice had taken on an encouraging tone.

"I've got a gun."

Then what are you waiting for? Leon could be fucking her right now.

Jamie's breath hissed through his teeth at the possibility. A solid *clunk* rang out as he returned the gold bar to its shelf. He turned to the door. The briny air had corroded the iron bars to a finger's width in places. He rattled the door, dislodging a shower of rust flakes. The lock held firm. He braced a foot against one bar and strained at its neighbour with his hands. Gradually, creaking and cracking, the bars bent. Arms as taut as high-tension wire, he threw his head back and gave it all he had left.

With a loud *ping*, one bar fractured. Jamie reeled backwards against a shelf. Dizzy and breathless, he rested his forehead on the gold. Lovingly, like he was caressing Natalie, he ran his fingers over the silky metal.

A moment passed before he could bring himself to relinquish his touch and turn his attention to the door again. The lower half of the broken bar was lying on the floor. He waggled the upper half free from its socket and levered at a neighbouring bar with it until the gap was wide enough to squeeze through.

As Emily had described, a passageway with walls of solid rock rose away from the vault. After a minute or two, his torchlight landed on stone steps that climbed to a horizontal grey slab. A rust-speckled iron ring dangled from a chain on the right-hand wall.

He pulled the ring. A muffled *clunk-click* was followed by what sounded like rusty gears grinding into motion. Slowly, steadily, a hidden counter-weight lifted the stone trapdoor. He poked his head into the triangular cavity behind the damaged staircase. The stairs had shifted sideways into a recess in the wall, leaving a gap just wide enough for a slim man like himself or Walter Lewarne to sidle through.

There was another *clunk-click* and the trapdoor began to close. He snatched up a broken stair tread and braced it between the thick granite slab and floor. The wood bowed slightly, then the trapdoor shuddered to a halt.

He wedged another length of wood into place before heading into the passageways. Although it was warmer above ground, a fresh bout of shivering racked his body. Could he really point a gun at Leon and pull the trigger? He shook his head. Who was he trying to kid?

You're pathetic. The soft voice was back, dripping with derision. *I knew you'd pussy out.*

Jamie hung his head. He was all talk, a load of hot air with nothing to back it up. Leon knew it. And soon Natalie would too. *You're not ready for that yet, Jamie.* Her earlier words turned like a knife in his gut. Perhaps she already suspected that he wasn't the man he made himself out to be. He could just picture the scorn in her eyes when she realised he would never break free of his brother. The thought stole the strength from his legs. He staggered and stuck out a hand to steady himself. His palm slapped against cold wood, then the pressure vanished and he was passing through the wall like...

Like a ghost.

The words echoed in his head as he toppled sideways and landed on something soft and shaggy. A musty animal scent tickled his nostrils. Rolling onto his back, he saw a section of wood-panelled wall swinging shut. The secret door clicked seamlessly back into place. He swept his torch over his surroundings. The big old bearskin rug had cushioned his fall.

Goosebumps prickled his flesh as a cold, wet wind billowed through the curtains.

He stood up and took several somewhat unsteady steps towards the hallway before coming to an abrupt halt. The torchlight lingered on the oil painting of the fat toad. For a second – just a second – the gold-speckled black eyes seemed to gleam and bulge with life.

Jamie blinked. Was he hallucinating? Perhaps the hydrogen-something-or-other gas was messing with his head. The wind rattled through the French doors again. He cleaned his lungs out with several deep breaths.

The voice slunk through his mind, prompting, urging – *The gun, the gun, the gun.*

He hurried into the hallway. His eyes darted around before settling on a door under the staircase. 'The Lewarne Room' was engraved into a brass plaque. As he opened the door, deep creases gathered on his forehead at the sight of the holdall. He'd half hoped it wouldn't be there. His feet dragging like wet sand was sucking at them, he approached the bag. He took out the stubby starter pistol, his expression a cocktail of anxiety and excitement.

He flipped open the cylinder and counted off the six bullets. In the car, he'd told Natalie the bullets were blanks. They both knew that was a lie. The gun had been converted to fire live ammo. You couldn't hit a thing with it from more than a few metres, but up close it was nastily effective. He took aim, picturing Leon's infuriatingly handsome face.

"Bang," he mouthed.

He approached the embossed wooden panel above the fireplace. "They are no more," he murmured, tracing his fingers over the eerie message. "Was it worth it?" he wondered out loud. He stood silent for a moment, as if hoping the air would answer him. Closing his eyes, he sucked in a breath and muttered to himself, “Man up, Jamie. Man up. It’s now or never.”

His eyes snapped open at a faint click. He’d barely been touching the letters, but somehow he’d tripped the opening mechanism. The trapdoor had nudged upwards a finger’s width.

“Jamie, is that you?”

At the sound of Natalie’s voice, a rush of longing washed away his lingering doubts. “Yes, it’s me,” he called back, running to pick up the chisel.

Leon let out a muffled whoop. “I never thought I’d be so happy to hear your voice, little brother!”

Jamie smiled crookedly. *Thanks for being your usual dickhead self, Leon,* he felt like replying. *It makes this so much easier.* He stabbed the chisel into the front edge of the trapdoor and levered it upwards.

With enough force to throw him backwards and send the chisel flying, the trapdoor sprang open. Concealing the pistol behind his back, he scrambled to his feet and peered into the basement. Leon and Natalie were huddled together shivering on the steps. The water had risen to cover the bottom two steps. Jamie’s nose wrinkled as he caught a whiff of the sulphurous fumes.

Leon broke into a broad grin. “You did it, Jamie. You fucking did it,” he exclaimed with a sort of disbelieving half laugh. “I didn’t think you had it in you.”

“You do surprise me.” Jamie’s reply was grimly deadpan.

Leon’s grin faltered. An uncertain light flickered in his eyes as if he sensed but didn’t yet understand that some balance had shifted. “What happened?”

“What do you think happened? I crawled through that stinking slime until I found a way out.”

"What was it like?" asked Natalie. There was a sort of ghoulish curiosity in the question.

"It was..." Jamie lapsed into thoughtful silence for a second. "It was like being reborn."

A smile spread across Natalie's face as if that was the answer she'd been hoping for. "*Now* you're ready, Jamie."

"Ready for what?" asked Leon.

In answer, she twisted away from him and shoved him in the chest. His mouth gaping in mute shock, he flung his arms out, desperately trying to keep his balance. Another shove sent him toppling backwards into the water. Then Natalie was leaping towards the trapdoor.

For a few hammering heartbeats, Jamie was too taken aback to react. Leon resurfaced with a choking roar. Flinching into action, Jamie caught hold of Natalie's outstretched hand and hauled her into The Lewarne Room.

Leon clambered to his feet, spluttering, "What the fuck?"

Jamie's mouth was suddenly bone dry. How many times had he fantasised about this moment? How many nights had he lain awake inwardly rehearsing what he wanted to say? He swallowed hard, working up enough spit to speak. "How does it feel, brother?" His voice sounded strange in his ears – too calm, too self-assured.

"How do you think it feels? It's freezing."

"He's not talking about the water," Natalie said with a scornful twist of her lips. "He's talking about–"

Jamie silenced her with a hiss. This was *his* moment, no one else's. Slowly, relishing each word, he said, "Nat and me have been fucking for months."

Leon's lips worked soundlessly for a moment before he retorted, "Bullshit!"

An ugly smile lifted Jamie's lips. "Oh yeah it must be bullshit, right? Because how could anyone ever cheat on you? God's gift to women." He glanced at Natalie. "Tell him."

"It's true." Her tone was mercilessly matter-of-fact. It crushed Leon's face into an almost comical gurning grimace.

An irresistible peal of laughter surged up Jamie's throat. "How does it feel?" he demanded triumphantly. "How does it feel? Eh? Eh?"

Another roar exploding from him, Leon lurched up the steps. He stopped dead as Jamie whipped the pistol out from behind his back.

"What you gonna do with that?" growled Leon. "It fires blanks, you moron."

"Does it?" Jamie did his best imitation of his brother's trademark smirk. "Shall we find out?"

Leon eyeballed him uncertainly, gnashing his teeth in frustration. "Keep pointing that thing at me and you'd better be willing to use it."

Jamie cocked the pistol's hammer as if to say, *Try me.*

Leon's gaze flitted between the gun and his brother's taunting eyes. "I'll kill you for this, Jamie."

"Not if I kill you first." Jamie's grin widened. "Who knows? Maybe your ghost will be haunting this dump while Nat and me are sunning it up on a Caribbean beach wondering how to spend the gold."

"Gold?" Natalie and Leon parroted in unison.

"Oh didn't I say?" Jamie paused, milking the moment for all it was worth. "Emily *was* telling the truth. There's enough gold beneath this house to buy a Caribbean island."

"More bullshit," said Leon.

"Well you'll never know, will you?"

"You haven't got the balls to shoot me, little brother."

Jamie's smile wavered at the goading remark. "Don't tempt me, Leon. I swear I'll put a bullet in you."

"So do it." Rediscovering his own grin, Leon spread his arms wide. "Pull the trigger!"

"Let's just shut him in down there," urged Natalie, reaching for the trapdoor.

"No," Jamie exclaimed so vehemently that she snatched her hand back.

The brothers glared at each other, locked in a silent battle. Jamie's knuckles paled on the pistol's grip as Leon said, "I've always wondered whether there's something wrong with you, Jamie." He tapped his temple. "Something up there."

"If there is, it's your fault."

Leon's grin climbed higher. "It's always someone else's fault, isn't it Jamie? Well not this time. This time I'm going to teach you what it means to take responsibility for your own actions." His gaze slid across to Natalie. "And when I'm finished with him, I'll deal with you. No man will ever want to stick his dick in you again by the time I'm done. What will you do without your pretty face, eh?" He sneeringly harked back to their conversation in the car. "Can't read maps. Can't drive. Can't make a decent sarnie." He paused a breath before adding, "Can't even make a baby."

Natalie's lips thinned into a bloodless line of rage. "You bastard."

Leon directed his smirk at Jamie again. "I bet you didn't know that, did you? Her womb's all messed up. I was never actually going to marry her. What use is a woman who can't give you a baby? Think about that, little brother. Is she worth it?"

"Fucking bastard!" Her eyes flaring like golden flames, Natalie yanked the diamond engagement ring off her finger and flung it at Leon. It flew past his face and plopped into the water.

He laughed. "Another one to add to the list – can't throw to save her life."

Natalie snatched up the crowbar. "You're always talking the talk, Leon. Let's see if you can walk the walk."

His fingers curled into fists, but his feet remained frozen in place.

Natalie's lips peeled away from her perfect white teeth. "You're the one who's full of shit, Leon." She reached out to fondle Jamie's groin. "Jamie's ten times the man you'll ever be."

Gurning with rage again, Leon launched himself at the trapdoor. The pistol's muzzle flashed white and orange in the gloom. An ear-splitting *boom* tore through the room. Leon's hands darted to his head. Blood streamed from under them into his eyes. For a second, he teetered back and forth, mouth hanging open in a silent scream. Then his eyes rolled white and he collapsed like a puppet whose strings had been cut.

Jamie gawped down at him like he couldn't believe his eyes. Was Leon dead? Could he really be dead? He blinked out of his reverie as Natalie kicked the trapdoor. It dropped shut with a thud of finality. She prised at it with the crowbar to no effect. Satisfied it was secure, she turned to Jamie.

The pistol was shaking in his hand. She gently removed it from his grip. Lacing her arms around his neck, she kissed him so deeply that the tension melted from his body. When she drew away, he said with a tremulous sigh, "I love you." He blinked again, surprised by himself. Something akin to fear flickered in his eyes as he waited for Natalie to respond.

Smiling, she traced a finger along his jaw. "Good."

"I want you to know that..." He stumbled clumsily over his words. "Well, that it makes no difference to me."

"What doesn't?"

"Whether or not you can have a baby. I don't want children anyway. I mean, who wants to bring a kid into this fucked up world?"

Natalie's smile faltered. "Let's not talk about that." Her reply was flat, gouged of emotion.

"That's fine by me. We never have to talk about it again if you don't want to."

Summoning up a small smile, Natalie leaned in to press her lips against Jamie's again. As they were kissing, his eyes drifted to the trapdoor. He parted his lips from hers and asked, "Do you think he's dead?"

"If he isn't, he will be soon enough." She tugged at his arm. "Show me the gold."

Jamie bent to pick up the holdall. The ghost mask peeked up at him from between the open zipper. An uneasy frown creased his forehead. "And what about Leon's ghost? Do you think it will haunt this place?"

"Yes," Natalie said without hesitation.

A shudder snaked through Jamie. "Will he haunt us too for what we've done?"

"His spirit will be bound to this house, so not unless we live here."

"Live here?" Jamie echoed incredulously. "I'd rather live in a cardboard box."

"Then let's do what we came here to do," urged Natalie.

Jamie returned the tools to the bag and slung it over his shoulder. He gave the trapdoor a last glance. "Goodbye brother," he murmured before approaching the secret panel. It offered no resistance as he pushed it inwards. He stooped into the passageway and led Natalie down the steps to the mossy corridor beneath the entrance hall.

He placed a palm against the algae-slimed granite wall as if trying to sense what was happening in the basement.

Not a sound – not even the faintest burble of running water – reached his ears.

"*Is* there something wrong with me?" he wondered out loud.

Natalie took his hand. "Well you just shot your brother in the head, so..." she trailed off with a meaningful click of her tongue.

Jamie pulled his hand away. "You think this is funny?"

Natalie sighed. "Sometimes, Jamie, you have to dance with the Devil to get what you want."

"Meaning?"

"Meaning don't freak out on me now." She held her thumb and forefinger a centimetre apart. "We're this close."

Jamie took a deep breath and gave a nod of resolve. She caught hold of his hand again and drew him swiftly up the next set of steps. As they neared the living room, King Toad hopped into in his mind, its eyes like gold coins, its skin like serpentine. From somewhere nearby he seemed to hear a guttural *croak!* He pulled up, his eyes darting around like he expected to see King Toad staring back at him.

Natalie looked over her shoulder. "What is it?"

"It's..." He hesitated, feeling foolish at the thought of telling her. *It's only the house creaking in the wind,* he said to himself.

She placed her petal-soft palms against either side of his

face. "Just think about that Caribbean beach. We can have that. We can have it all. We just need to stay focused. OK?"

Jamie nodded. He took the lead, turning sideways to slip through the space between the staircase and the wall. He was relieved to see that the wooden props hadn't given way under the pressure of the trapdoor.

"So the staircase *does* move," Natalie said in a vindicated tone. She ran her fingers along the edge of the stone slab. "Walter must have put this in after Emily found the vault."

"I don't blame him, considering what's down there."

Her eyes shining with excitement, Natalie descended the steps. She stopped suddenly and whispered, "It's her!"

"Who?"

"Emily."

Jamie's eyes flitted around like moths circling a lightbulb. "I don't see anything."

Natalie looked at the ceiling. She reached up to stroke the seams of serpentine. "Of course," she murmured to herself as if coming to an obvious realisation. "Psychic ether."

"Psychic what?"

"Some rocks can store psychic energy." Natalie pressed Jamie's hand to the serpentine. "Do you feel it vibrating?"

"No."

"That's because you're blocked. Open yourself up, Jamie. Allow yourself to feel the unseen."

"Feel the unseen? What does that mean?"

"Sometimes when things happen, they leave behind an invisible mark." Natalie tried to put it in terms Jamie would understand. "Think of it like a UV marker pen. You need to look with more than just your eyes to see what's there. Does that make sense?"

"Not really, but nothing about this place makes sense to me." Wrinkles of thought spread from the outer corners of Jamie's eyes. "Do you remember the first time we met?"

"Yeah, it was in that crappy nightclub on Lambeth Road."

"Leon was showing you off like a trophy. I thought you were just another one of his bimbos. Didn't take me long to realise there was a lot more to you than the fake tan and hair extensions, but...." Jamie trailed off as if worried his words would cause offence.

"But you didn't think I was such a weirdo." Natalie filled in the blanks with a twinkle of amusement in her eyes.

He smiled faintly. "Something like that."

"Don't you know it's OK to be crazy if you're rich? So let's go get rich." With a wink, Natalie drew Jamie along the passageway.

Goosebumps prickled his flesh, partly because the temperature was dropping, but mainly at the thought of seeing the gold again, of touching it, of feeling the cool smoothness of its glowing surface.

"There's a light up ahead," said Natalie.

Jamie squinted at the tunnel. It was pitch-black beyond the reach of the torchlight.

Natalie turned an ear towards the darkness. "There's a voice. Do you hear it?"

"No." With the hesitancy of someone who didn't really want to know the answer, Jamie asked, "What's it saying?"

"Kindermond."

Kindermond.

The word seemed to echo in Jamie's ears as the vault's

rusty door came into view. The bent iron bars pushed Natalie's breasts to one side as she squeezed between them. Her torchlight glanced off the gold, throwing a warm glow across the cold room.

"It's *him*!" she gasped. "It's Walter."

"What's he doing?" There was little interest in Jamie's voice. His gaze was fixed on the gold.

"He's scratching himself to bits. There's blood all over him."

Jamie didn't appear to hear Natalie. He touched the gold as if needing to reassure himself, once again, that it was real. God, it was so beautiful. Nothing could taint it. Not rust. Not time. Not even psychic... whatever it was called.

A self-congratulatory voice whispered through his mind, *Now this, this is truly worth it.*

"It's here!"

Natalie's ecstatic exclamation drew his gaze. She was staring wide-eyed at something on the floor near the hole in the wall. She got down on her knees as if to pray. The flagstones in front of her shimmered like molten gold. She stretched out a hand, immersing it in the pool of light.

Approaching her, Jamie saw that a long mirror in an arched silver frame was lying on the floor. "That wasn't here before."

Natalie cast him a sidelong glance. "Are you sure?"

"Yes. Someone else must have been in here after me." His eyes nervously searched the shadows. He squinted into the hole. "Do you think Leon could have–"

"No," Natalie interrupted, anticipating the question. "Leon's dead. And even if he isn't, he wouldn't fit through that hole."

Jamie's eyebrows knitted together. "Maybe the mirror was here and I just didn't notice it." His gaze returned to the gold. The sight smoothed the lines from his brow. "My attention was on other things."

With exaggerated care, Natalie slid her fingers under the mirror, lifted it upright and stood it against a shelf. "Look in the mirror. Look as closely as you can and tell me what you see," she murmured, leaning towards the glass until her breath misted it.

"What did you say?" Jamie asked absently, not taking his eyes off the gold.

"Nothing, just something someone I admire once said."

Jamie unzipped and upended the holdall. The ghost mask fell to the flagstones, followed by a jumble of house-breaking tools. He picked up a gold bar, cradling it in his hands like a newborn baby. "I reckon the BMW can handle about five hundred kilos. So we can only take fifty bars with us today. We'll have to make at least one more trip down here for the rest." He placed the gold bar in the bag and reached for another. There was a soft clink as he packed it alongside the first. "I hate to leave even one bar here, but–"

"Jamie."

Natalie's voice was low, but there was something about it, a solemnity that made him glance at her. He did a startled double take.

Her clothes and underwear lay at her feet. The mirror's glimmering light danced over her toned body. Her nipples stood out like bullets of flesh in the cold air. Faint networks of blue-green veins flared outwards from their dark areolas. It wasn't only her nakedness that etched deep lines into his forehead again. She'd pulled the witch mask down over her face. The wrinkled, warty visage contrasted jarringly with her smooth skin. One of her hands was tucked behind her back as if she was concealing a present.

"I want you to love me, Jamie." An undertone of quietly desperate need permeated her voice.

"I do love you. I told you that. Now will you take off that mask and stop this... whatever it is you're doing."

"I have taken my mask off."

In quick succession, Jamie's eyes narrowed in bemusement, then widened in comprehension. "Are you saying this is the real you?"

Natalie motioned to the mirror. "This is what I see in there."

"No. This isn't you at all, Nat. You're..." Jamie fumbled for the words to express himself. "You're the most beautiful woman I've ever seen."

A laugh shuddered through the mask. "Beautiful? I saw nothing beautiful in the mirror. I only saw the truth. Ever since I first read my great grandma's diary when I was a teenager, I've wanted to come here. But something always held me back. Then I read Adam Piper's book and it was like a voice calling out to me, telling me it was time to take what's mine. I'm not only talking about that." Natalie flicked her chin dismissively at the gold. "I'm talking about this house and everything in it."

"You're not making any sense, Nat."

"You're wrong. For the first time in my life, I'm making complete sense." She pointed at the ceiling. "Out there I'm nothing, but here..." She heaved in the briny air as if it was the best she'd ever tasted. "Here I can be anything I want to be." Her hand dropped to her belly. "Even a mother."

Sadness and sympathy mingled in Jamie's brown eyes. "I told you, I don't care about having kids," he said softly. "But if it means that much to you, we can get you help. There must be a doctor out there that can–"

"It's not a doctor that I need," broke in Natalie. "I've already seen half the doctors in London and they all say the same thing – the endometriosis has done too much damage."

Jamie swept a hand at the gold. "Yeah but now you can afford the best money can buy. I'll bet there's some new treatment–"

"Stop," Natalie cut him off again. With her middle finger, she traced out a triangle beneath her belly button. "You see these scars?"

Bending his head to look closely, Jamie saw that each point of the triangle was marked by a scar so small and faint that he hadn't noticed them before.

"They already tried to cut out the cysts," Natalie continued. "It didn't work. It just left me in pain." Her voice was a hollow murmur. "So much pain that nothing ever really took it away. Not painkillers. Not alcohol. It never stopped, day or night." A tremor of awe filled the hollowness. "Until I came here. When I stepped inside this house, it was like..." She struggled to describe what she'd felt. "It was like something reached inside me and pulled it all out – the cysts, the pain, all of it *gone*." The last word came out in a sigh of relief as deep as the sea.

Jamie winced a little as if his brain hurt from trying to make sense of what Natalie had said. "How's that possible?"

She stretched her long fingers towards the mirror. "Look and you'll see."

Slowly, his gaze followed her hand. Something like relief flickered in his eyes. "All I see is my reflection."

Natalie repeated her earlier entreaty. "Open yourself up, Jamie." This time, she added, "Open up and let Him in."

"Him?" he echoed. "Who's Him?"

She smiled, seemingly amused by the question. "Do you

know why Leon laughed at you your whole life?" Before Jamie could answer, she continued, "I'll tell you why – because you let him. It's as simple as that."

Jamie greeted her words with a scowling grin. "Yeah, well now he's dead. So who had the last laugh, eh?"

"He's dead," Natalie agreed. "But he's not gone."

Jamie's gaze darted around the vault again. They were still alone. His unease turned into irritation. "OK, Nat, enough of the bullshit. Take that mask off."

She was silent for a moment as if mulling over his request. Then she began, "I have this recurring dream. I'm looking around a house. It's this house, but not this house. There are mirrors everywhere. Tall mirrors, small mirrors, rectangular mirrors, round mirrors, oval mirrors. Every kind of mirror you can think of. The strange thing is, when I look in them, I see nothing. No reflection. It's like looking into a deep well. Then I hear the crying." She swallowed as if trying to loosen her throat. "It sounds like a baby screaming for milk. It gives me this feeling." She clenched her hand. "Like the air is being squeezed out of me. I try to find out where the crying is coming from, but no matter where I look it doesn't get any closer. It's always there, but just out of reach."

Sympathy flickered back into in Jamie's eyes. "I..." He searched for some words of comfort, but lapsed into the silence of someone out of their depth.

"There's no need to feel sorry for me," said Natalie. "I know I'll be a mother one day soon. He took the pain away. And now He's going to give me a baby. Maybe it was Him that brought us together upstairs." She placed her palm against her belly. "Maybe there's already a life growing inside me."

Jamie stared at Natalie's stomach as if wishing he had x-ray vision. What if she was right? What if he was going to be a dad? Something stirred in him at the thought, a longing he hadn't realised was there.

"We can raise a family here, Jamie." Natalie's voice took on a dreamy quality. "Imagine what it could be like – the house, the garden, the sea, just you, me and our baby."

He found himself picturing just that. Fresh air, space, privacy, all the things he'd yearned for as a child growing up in a Tower Hamlet's high-rise. Could they make it work? Could this be their paradise?

His uncertainty hardened into grim certainty as Natalie added with a chillingly gleeful edge, "Oh and let's not forget Leon. His ghost will get to see what we have and what he will never have. He'll know pain like we knew pain. He'll know hopelessness and despair and–"

"Stop this," Jamie said again. He pleadingly held out his hands. "Let's load up the car and get out of here. If you really are pregnant, we can bring up our child anywhere in the world." He put a hand over his heart. "I'm not Leon. You don't have to worry about me hurting you." Taking himself by surprise, he dropped to one knee. "Leon didn't want to marry you, but I do. I want to spend my life with you."

Natalie looked down at him, her eyes as unreadable as the mask. "Yes, I'll be your wife, Jamie." Rather than a joyous acceptance of his proposal, it was an impassive statement. "But it *has* to be here."

Jamie closed his eyes. "This is the last time I'll ask. Take that thing off and help me load up the car." He gave Natalie a moment, then opened his eyes one at a time like a child peeking at a scary movie.

She stared back at him at him through the mask's repulsively shrivelled eyeholes.

He heaved a sigh. "OK, Nat, have it your way. You do what you want, but I'm out of here." He turned to resume packing gold bars into the holdall. "I'm only taking my share."

"No gold leaves this house."

Jamie cocked an eye at Natalie. "What?"

"No gold leaves this house," she repeated. "Not now, not ever. It's what he wanted."

"Who's *he*?" snapped Jamie, losing his patience. "The Entity? The Devil? The Ghost of Christmas fucking Past?"

"My great grandad, Walter Lewarne."

Jamie's eyebrows bunched. "Your great grandad, Walter–" He broke off with a burst of incredulous laughter. "You know what? You're right." He pointed to the mask. "This *is* the real you. An insane witch. That's what you are. Well good luck to you. I hope you're happy here with Great Grandad and Grandma." He held up a gold bar. "This is all I need for company."

"You didn't kill Leon for *gold*." Natalie's lips curled contemptuously on the word. "You killed him for *me*."

Jamie wrinkled his nose as if he'd caught another whiff of the eggy fumes. "Maybe my first impression of you was right after all. You make out like you're different, but you're just as full of yourself as Leon. Sorry to burst your bubble, Nat, but if it's a choice between you and thirty million quid's worth of gold, then you lose."

"What about the baby?"

"What baby? There is no baby. There's no Entity. No ghosts. It's all a load of bullshit you tell yourself so you don't have to face up to the reality that you'll never be a mother."

"You're wrong." The tremor in Natalie's reply betrayed how deep Jamie's words had cut.

"I don't think so, but I'm not gonna hang around to find out either way." He slotted the gold bar into the bag.

"So you're nothing but a thief?"

Jamie shrugged. "I suppose so. Maybe the mirror showed me who I really am after all."

"Nothing shall be removed from this house," Natalie intoned like a priest reciting scripture. "Not one bar of gold, not one painting, not one book. Nothing bought with the blood of innocents shall leave this house."

Jamie let out a laugh that sounded more sad than amused. "Is Great Grandad still here with us? Is he telling you what to say?"

"Don't you see, Jamie? You can be so much more than you are. You *must* accept this chance."

He was motionless for a moment, unnerved by the pleading look in her big golden eyes. Then he wrenched his gaze from hers and put a couple more gold bars into the bag. He tested the bag's weight. The material creaked under the strain. "I reckon that'll do for now."

"I'm warning you." Natalie's voice rang with finality.

"You're warning me?" Jamie laughed again. "What are you going to do? Cast a spell on me?"

A metallic click came from behind Natalie's back. Jamie retreated a step as she moved her hand into view. Her slender fingers were wrapped around the pistol grip. The hammer was cocked. She levelled the stubby barrel at his face. Her pupils gleamed like wet glass. Was she crying? The mask made it difficult to tell.

A single lethally soft word slid from her lips, "Kindermond."

In that instant, Jamie knew he was a dead man and the clearest thought came to him – *I hope you're wrong about what comes after this, Nat. I hope there's nothing on the other side.* He opened his mouth to give voice to it, but there was no time. His last words had already been spoken.

The muzzle flash blinded him. The gunshot deafened him. The bullet penetrated below his left eye, shattering his cheekbone, tunnelling through his brain and exiting the back of his head. Tears of blood rolled down his cheek from a hole big enough to slot a finger into.

As if performing a parody of Leon's final moment, Jamie swayed on his feet before his legs concertinaed and he collapsed in a heap. His limbs twitched, his mouth worked like a fish out of water, then a sudden stillness stole over him. A halo of blood formed around his head, looking almost luminous against the grey of the floor.

Natalie picked up the ghost mask and placed it over Jamie's face. She dipped her fingers into the steaming crimson liquid. Like a hunter blooding herself, she slathered it over her stomach.

She turned to the mirror, her voice rising in supplication. "Master, help me. I put myself into your hands. I acknowledge you as my God. The one true God." Throwing her head back, she cried out, "Master, I call to thee! I summon thee from the other side. Come forth so that I may commune with thee. Come to this mirror and see how I praise thee." She closed her eyes, flexing her fingers against her tummy and chanting, "Grant me thy dark gifts, my master. Grant me thy dark gifts..."

9

Home

"I'm home." Henry's voice was so thick with emotion that the words struggled to free themselves from his throat.

"Home?" Grace echoed dubiously, blinking as rain lashed her face. "You only lived here for a week."

Henry looked at her as if he'd forgotten she was there. "It didn't feel like only a week."

"So what did it feel like?"

He wrinkled his forehead. "It's difficult to explain. Time is different here. Minutes can feel like hours."

"Then those two days Faith was missing for must have felt like weeks to her." Grace squinted into the wind whistling over the cliffs. Tears of mascara streaked her pale cheeks. "She died over there, didn't she?"

"Yes," Henry said with a wary glance at the stun gun in her hand. "But I didn't see it happen."

Her probing gaze returned to him. "What exactly did you see?"

Henry pointed through the bars of the gates. "I was over there with my mum. Faith ran past us and out of the gates."

"Like the Devil himself was chasing her," Grace quoted from *Between Worlds*. She'd read the chapter where Faith died so many times that its every word was branded into her mind. "What then?"

"Dad ran after her. That's all I saw."

Grace closed her eyes as the wind whipped around her. The scene from the book played out in her head – Faith running towards the cliffs, naked, bleeding, out of her mind with fear; Adam close behind, but not close enough to prevent her from plummeting to her death.

For a second, Grace seemed to hear a scream carried on the wind. Her eyes snapped open. "How do we get through these gates?"

Henry pulled a bunch of keys out of his coat pocket. He took hold of the padlock. "Oh," he exclaimed in surprise when the chain the padlock was attached to slithered free and clattered to the ground. He pushed the gates. They swung inwards, gouging at the gravel.

"What does that mean?" wondered Grace.

"There's probably been another break-in."

Grace's eyebrows lifted at Henry's casual tone. "Another break-in?"

"For months after Dad's book came out, the police were calling us all the time about people like you trespassing in the grounds. One or two even got into the house and filmed themselves looking for paranormal activity."

"I'm not a ghost hunter."

Henry scanned over Grace's black clothes, vampy makeup and scarlet hair. "You look like one."

Before she could reply, a blast of wind almost buffeted her off her feet. She grabbed Henry's arm and pulled him to the car.

As she got behind the steering wheel, the storm slammed the door shut. Pushing a hand through her wet hair, she said, "I look like this because every time I see my reflection it reminds of what I need to do."

Henry hugged his arms across his chest as if suddenly realising just how drenched and cold he was.

Grace grabbed a blanket from the backseat. "Here, dry yourself off with this."

He accepted it with a grudging, "Thanks."

As Henry rubbed at his mop of hair, Grace nudged the gates fully open with the front bumper and accelerated along the avenue of sycamores. The tall trees waved their branches and moaned as if simultaneously welcoming and warning the newcomers. Flurries of leaves swirled in the headlights. Grace manoeuvred around a fallen branch, mounting one wheel onto the lawn. As the car swung back onto the driveway, the lion-headed fountain came into view. Henry rocked back and forth, giddy with excitement.

Grace slid him a curious look. "What is it about this house? What makes it so special?"

"You'll see," he replied in a quick whisper. He inhaled sharply as the headlights revealed the granite walls of Fenton House. His eyes hungrily took in the stained-glass window that could have graced any cathedral, the gargoyles spouting water from their fanged mouths, the central tower stabbing up into darkness.

"You're right. Now I see why Faith was so obsessed with this place," conceded Grace. "It would have fitted perfectly into her fantasies of ghosts and demons."

"They aren't fantasies," Henry retorted, tossing the blanket into her face. He sprang out of the moving car, staggered for several steps, recovered his balance and ran towards the porch.

Swearing at herself for allowing him to pull the same trick twice, Grace cut the engine, flung open her door and went in pursuit. She caught up with him in the deeper darkness of the arched porch.

"Get off me!" he yelled as she grabbed his arm.

"Shh," she hissed. "What if someone *has* broken in? Do you want them to know we're here?"

"I don't care."

"Well I do. Now pipe down." She reached into the pocket containing the stun gun.

Taking the hint, Henry angrily bit his lips.

Grace shone the pale circle of her mobile phone's torch at the bolt-studded front door. There was no sign of forced entry. Henry's keys were dangling from the lock.

He yanked his arm free, throwing her off balance. The torchlight darted around wildly as she lurched after him and fell to her knees. There came the clunk of the key turning in the lock, followed by the squeak of hinges. Scrambling upright, she saw that the heavy door was open just enough for Henry to slide through. She shoved it wide open. The wind pursued her into the house. She came to a shuddering halt. There was that voice in the storm again. She seemed to catch words amidst the wails.

Help me. Help me...

Was it Henry? Was the little psycho playing mind games? She whipped out the stun gun, muttering, "OK, Henry, if you want to find out the painful way that you can't scare me off, that's fine by me."

She closed the door and shone her phone around the entrance hall – arched doors, black chandeliers, red and gold floral wallpaper, broad staircase, marble fireplace. The light lingered on a portrait of a strikingly pale woman in a long black dress with a white fur stole draped over her shoulders. There was something aloof, even haughty about the woman, yet at the same time her dark eyes had a sad beauty.

A similar sadness seeped into Grace's eyes. Haunted houses, witchcraft – Faith had believed in those things with all her heart. Grace had tried to believe in them too, if only in the hope it would bring the two of them closer together, but she could never get past the feeling that it was superstitious nonsense.

She fought back the tears that threatened to fill her eyes. She couldn't allow her emotions to get the better of her. Not here. Not now. The torchlight moved away from the portrait, climbing the staircase, passing over paintings and tapestries.

Henry was nowhere to be seen.

"Where are you, you little shit?" she said under her breath.

She peered through an open door into a dining room furnished with a dusty table, chairs and sideboard. Porcelain spaniels bookended a mantelpiece at the far end of the room. Fantastical creatures decorated the panelled walls – a winged lion, a unicorn, a bird with cloven-hooves.

Her gaze jerked towards the rear of the hallway at a noise. Not a noise carried on the wind, but one revealed by a momentary lull in it – the gurgle of running water, as if a tap had been left on. Holding the stun gun out in front of her, she advanced along the hallway, ready for Henry, ghost hunters or anything else that might be lying in wait.

The hazy beam of torchlight stopped on a brass plaque next to a door beneath the stairs – 'The Lewarne Room'. An image of Faith shuffling towards her, arms outstretched, zombie-eyed and bleeding from too many scratches to count overwhelmed her consciousness. From somewhere – she couldn't tell where – the agonised plea floated to her ears again.

Help me. Help me...

Faith drew closer. So close that Grace could see the ranks of old self-harm scars on her wrists. Like a blind person wanting to feel what someone looked like, Faith stretched her fingers towards Grace's face. Closer. Closer...

Grace felt a scream pushing up her throat, but before it could break free the apparition dissolved into the air. She heaved a shaky breath. Had she just seen a ghost?

A whisper of sardonic laughter passed her lips. If ghosts were manifestations of every shitty emotion there was to feel, then yes, she'd just seen one.

She opened the door and cautiously entered The Lewarne Room. Her torchlight fixed upon a figure at the centre of the tiled floor. Henry was kneeling between the serpentine pedestals, head bowed.

Relief and anger – primarily anger – swept through Grace at the sight of him. "Right, this is your last chance," she snapped, striding forwards. She pressed the stun gun's trigger and waved the crackling zigzag of electricity in front of Henry. "You see this? Pull anymore disappearing tricks and I'll hit you with a thousand volts. Do you hear me?"

He didn't lift his gaze from the tiles. "The mirror's gone."

His voice was so desolate that Grace couldn't help but soften her tone. "Walter's mirror?"

Henry nodded. "I need it to–" He broke off as if he'd been about to say something he shouldn't.

"To do what?"

He didn't respond.

Grace's anger took over again. "No more games, Henry. It's time for you to tell me the truth about what happened to

Faith."

He sprang upright as if she had indeed zapped him with the stun gun. "I'm not a liar!" His voice was indignantly shrill. "I don't know what happened to your sister. Maybe the house did it to her, maybe it was Heloise or maybe she did it to herself."

Did it to herself. The words reverberated in Grace's ears. She winced as she thought about Faith's scarred wrists.

Henry's eyes narrowed a fraction, like a chess player who'd spotted a weakness in an opponent's strategy. "My dad got hold of your sister's medical records when he was researching his book. She'd tried to kill herself before." He made a slashing motion across his wrists.

"That was years ago. She'd been through a ton of therapy since then. She was better than she had been in a long time."

"How could you know that? You said you hadn't seen her in forever."

Uncertainty glimmered in Grace's eyes. Was Henry right? Had Faith's wounds been self-inflicted? Sounding like she was trying to convince herself of her words, she said, "Her depression was under control."

"How could you know that?" Henry repeated, his voice almost tauntingly soft.

"Because her psychiatrist told me. So did her GP and her boyfriend," countered Grace, recovering more of her icy assurance with each word. "*That's* how I know she didn't do it to herself. And I *know* this house didn't do it to her. Which leaves only three possibilities – either Heloise or you or both of you did it. Penny Holman told me something else." She leaned in closer, scrutinising every movement of Henry's features, clearly readying herself to unleash some damning revelation. "Faith's blood was under your fingernails, but it wasn't under

Heloise's."

His mouth opened and closed, but no words came out. Shock and bewilderment vied for position on his face.

Grace imitated his soft tone. "You didn't know that, did you? I bet your mum doesn't know either. Your dad knows, though. He's known for years what you really are."

Henry's surprise flipped into wide-eyed realisation, as if something that had long been troubling him suddenly made sense. His gaze drifted back towards the floor.

Grace ducked her head, refusing to relinquish eye contact. "How did Faith's blood get under your fingernails?"

He shook his head like he didn't understand the question. "The mirror–"

"Screw the mirror and all the other bullshit," cut in Grace. Like a detective pressing a suspect, she demanded, "Answer the question. Answer the question!"

"Fuck off and leave me alone," retorted Henry.

Grace smiled grimly. "That won't work this time. Neither will your little trick with the voice."

"Trick with the voice?" Henry echoed as if he didn't have a clue what she was talking about.

Grace mimicked the disembodied voice. "Help me. Help me." Her smile crawled higher. "Is this what you did to Faith? Gaslighted her until she lost her mind?"

A fresh wave of realisation rolled across Henry's face. "You've heard her, haven't you? Faith's spoken to you."

"I'm warning you, Henry." Grace tapped a finger meaningfully against the stun gun's trigger.

"What did she say?" he persisted, seemingly unconcerned by the prospect of being blasted with a thousand volts.

"She didn't say anything," snapped Grace, her mask of calm slipping. "Because she's dead and the dead can't fucking talk."

"Yes they can," Henry shot back, his words going up and down like a squeaky seesaw. He blushed, more mortified by his breaking voice than by Grace's threats. He cleared his throat and continued, "A megaphone for the dead – that's what paranormal experts say this house is."

"*Paranormal experts*," scoffed Grace. "The only thing fraudsters like that are expert at is scamming anyone stupid enough to believe them."

"You'll find out soon enough just how wrong you are."

"That sounds like a threat."

Henry turned away from Grace's glare and stared morosely at the cracked tiles that marked out the trapdoor. "You're the liar, not me," he muttered. "It's written all over your face. You know Faith's still here. Just like J-Jacob's here."

Catching the slight stumble in his voice, Grace said, "You don't like talking about your brother, do you?"

Henry pressed his lips together, emanating a silence that spoke louder than any words.

"I can't imagine how terrible it must have been watching him bleed to death." Grace paused a beat before adding mercilessly, "Especially as he died because of you."

Her words blanched the colour from Henry's face. "It was an accident." His voice was almost inaudible.

Grace's blue eyes shone with satisfaction at his reaction. "I can't be the only one to have wondered whether you meant to hurt Jacob. The thought must have crossed your dad's mind after Penny told him about the blood."

"It was an accident!" exploded Henry, jerking around to

eyeball her. He towered a full head over her. "Everyone knows that, just like everyone knows your crazy drug addict sister killed herself."

She held her ground, returning his stare. "The only drugs found in Faith's blood were her medication. Do you know that she'd moved in with her boyfriend a few weeks before she died? Or that she was working in a café and studying graphic design? Of course you don't, because your dad left all that out of his book. And I'll tell you why he left it out." She jabbed a finger into Henry's chest hard enough to make him take a step backwards. "He was hiding the truth that my sister's death was no more of an accident than your brother's."

Henry shook his head hard. "I didn't mean to hurt Jacob, and I don't know how your sister's blood got under my nails. But it doesn't matter what I say, because you'll never believe me. The only person you'd believe is Faith, so let's talk to her."

Grace's face creased in puzzlement. "Talk to her?"

"Last time I was here, I tried to use Walter Lewarne's mirror to talk to Jacob. I..." Henry faltered as if ashamed. "I wanted to say sorry to him."

"Like Walter wanted to ask for forgiveness from the German soldiers that died because of him?"

"Yes." Henry quickly corrected himself. "I mean no." His eyes flashed with irritation. "Are you just going to keep trying to catch me out with stupid questions or do you want to hear what I've got to say?"

One corner of her lips crooking up, Grace motioned for him to go on.

He eyed her guardedly for a moment, then resumed, "I didn't think Jacob had heard me, but I was wrong."

"How do you know?"

"Because I've been hearing his voice for weeks." Henry

grimaced at the thought of it. “I called Jacob here. He’s trapped in this house because of me. He came through the mirror and he can leave through it too. So can Faith.” He gave Grace an almost pleading look. “We can set them free. We just need to find the mirror.”

She responded with a sarcastic clap. “I have to hand it to you, Henry, that was an Oscar-worthy performance.”

His face instantly reverted to an unreadable mask. “I’m going to find Walter’s mirror and set my brother free.” He glanced at the stun gun. “If you want to stop me, you’ll have to use that thing.”

Grace eyed him thoughtfully. “OK, I’ll play along. Where do we look for the mirror?”

“Someone could have put it back where it came from.”

“You mean the basement?”

“You know that’s what I mean. You’ve read my dad’s book.” Henry dropped to his haunches by the broken tiles. He ran his fingers over the cracks. “These tiles are way more badly damaged than I remember.”

Grace’s gaze moved warily around the room. “Maybe whoever opened the front gates also tried to open the trapdoor.”

Henry pushed his fingers into the jagged fissures and attempted to prise the trapdoor open. His thin arms trembled with the effort. He snatched his hand back and examined it. Blood was seeping from under a fingernail. He sucked it clean, rising to approach the fireplace. He prodded and twisted at the letters on the wooden plaque to no effect.

He expelled a sharp breath. “Why is nothing happening?”

The question was directed at the room rather than at Grace, but she answered regardless. “Perhaps the house doesn’t want to let us into the basement.”

Henry greeted the dry comment with an unamused smile.

"Why would the mirror be down there anyway?" asked Grace. "Seems more likely to me that the police took it away as evidence."

"Evidence of what?" Henry slid her a sardonic glance. "Paranormal activity?"

"I could ring Penny and ask," she suggested with a provocative gleam in her eyes.

Henry gave an unfazed shrug. "You won't get a signal here."

Grace looked at her phone. "You're right again. No service."

Henry stood in frowning silence for a few seconds before hastening towards the hallway. Grace blocked his way. Another flash of annoyance crossed his features. "I want to search the other rooms."

"Slowly," she warned him. "No disappearing or else you know what'll happen."

Huffing through his nostrils, he resumed walking at a marginally slower pace. Grace stuck to his heels as he headed into the dining room. No mirror. He poked his head through a doorway beside the fireplace. His phone lit up two stiff-backed, sea-green sofas flanked a matching marble coffee-table. Wind and rain battered the shuttered window, providing an apt soundtrack for oil paintings of storm-wracked seas and shipwrecks.

No mirror.

Henry turned to open a door in the dining room's rear wall. As he stepped into the room beyond, he lowered his gaze as if looking for something he'd dropped. He stiffened like a startled deer as wind billowed through the curtains at the far side of the room.

With her stun gun poised for action, Grace swiftly moved to swish open the curtains. She reeled backwards as a powerful gust thrust the French doors at her. Regaining her balance, she caught hold of the doors and held them shut. "These doors have been forced," she said, examining the splintered wood around the lock.

"That's where Faith and her friends broke in."

Grace picked away a shard of wood. "This looks more recent."

Henry was no longer listening to her. He was staring at the floor again. He stooped to draw a circle with his finger on the dark floorboards. "This is where they tried to summon him."

"Summon who?"

Henry either didn't hear or chose not to. He started to straighten but froze, his gaze fixed on a painting of a hump-backed toad with a crown of leaves perched jauntily on its head. It stared back at him, its gold-speckled eyes glittering in amusement.

"God, what an ugly creature," commented Grace.

Henry shushed her as if afraid the toad would take offence.

She cast a curious glance at him. "Does this painting mean something to you?"

"No," he answered a touch too quickly to be convincing. "It's just that it didn't used to be here."

"Are you sure?"

He reached out to touch the painting, but his hand stopped short. "No," he admitted. "Sometimes when I think back it's..." He groped for the right description. "It's like I'm looking through a dirty window."

"I know what you mean."

The likeminded words drew a surprised look from Henry. "You do?"

Grace nodded. "Sometimes I struggle to picture Faith's face. How's that even possible when we were identical?" She shook her head at the absurdity of it. With a hint of hesitation, as if admitting to a shameful secret, she continued, "My flat's full of mirrors. And I mean *full*. The walls are covered in them. I keep telling myself I'm going to get rid of them, but when I'm in the flat I see Faith everywhere I look. It's almost like she's still alive." She heaved a sigh. "I don't know why I'm talking about this to you of all people. Perhaps it's because you're the only person who might really understand what I'm talking about."

Grace fell expectantly silent.

Henry returned her stare, his face as inscrutable as the Sphinx.

She gave a shake of her head that was part frustration, part annoyance. "Of course you don't understand. How could someone like you possibly understand?"

"Someone like me?" Henry's reply was flat with contempt. "You mean a psycho?"

Grace spread her hands in a gesture that said, *Your words, not mine.* "Right, where shall we look next?" Her tone was as light-hearted as if they were hunting for Easter eggs. "The study? The games room? Or how about the library? Who knows, we might find a book about how to speak to the dead. Then we wouldn't even need a magic mirror."

Henry glowered at her. "Don't make fun of me."

"Faith had loads of books like that," she went on. "The Lesser Key of Solomon. The Grand Grimoire–"

"Shut up."

"The Arbatel of Magick. The Magus. The–"

"Shut up!" yelled Henry, his voice breaking. "Shut up or I'll–" He snapped his mouth closed, regaining his self-control as quickly as he'd lost it.

Grace's faux-nonchalance changed into something genuine, yet no less cynical. "Or you'll what, hmm? What will you do to me, Henry?"

Jaw muscles clenched, he held his silence.

Slowly, calculatingly, Grace resumed listing the books. "The Picatrix. The Pseudo… The Pseudomona…" She faltered, struggling to remember the full title.

"The Pseudomonarchia Daemonum." Henry filled in the blanks, his voice rising again, but this time in excitement not anger. "You're right, we might not need the mirror."

"How do you know about that book? Did Faith tell you about it?"

Without answering, Henry headed for the hallway. Shadows flared across the walls as Grace followed him along a corridor that branched off from the rear of the hallway. After passing several doors, he went into a kitchen as big as the entire downstairs of the house in Walthamstow. He crossed the worn flagstone floor, skirting around a farmhouse table surrounded by mismatched chairs. A door next to a sooty old Rayburn led to a laundry room with a twin-tub and a ceiling-mounted clothes rack. Tangles of pipes sprouted from an iron monster of a boiler and snaked across the ceiling.

Logs, kindling and yellowed newspapers were stacked against a wall. He started filling a wicker basket with them. "We need a fire," he explained in reply to Grace's questioning look.

"What for?"

"You want to speak to your sister, don't you?"

Hugging the basket to his chest, Henry returned to the

kitchen. He set it down on the table, then rifled through drawers of cutlery, cloths and various odds and ends. Grace watched him closely, resting her finger on the stun gun's trigger lest he pull out a knife. With a triumphant flourish, he held up a box of matches. He retrieved the basket and lugged it to the living room.

Grace looked on as he lined the fireplace with screwed up newspaper. He struck a match and held it to the paper. As flames crackled into life, he chucked on the kindling and logs. When the fire had properly taken hold, he took a folded sheet of paper and a piece of chalk from his pockets. He smoothed out the paper on the floorboards.

"What's that?" asked Grace, eyeing the drawing of a circle within a circle.

Henry peered up at her through his fringe. "Someone hasn't been doing their homework."

"Don't get clever. Just tell me."

"It's a sigil. A magic symbol."

Grace read out the letters between the circles. "L-E-A-B."

"You've got it back to front. It's B-A-E-L."

"Bael?"

"He's one of the seven princes of Hell." Henry lapsed into silence for a moment, then recited from memory, "Their first king is called Bael who, when he is conjured up, appeareth with three heads – the first, like a toad; the second, like a man; the third, like a cat. He…" He paused again, striving to recall the words before continuing decisively, "He speaketh with a hoarse voice, he maketh a man go invisible and wise."

Grace glanced at the painting of the toad. A glint of realisation came into her eyes. "That's a quote from the Pseudomonarchia Daemonum, isn't it?"

"Yes." By the gathering glow of the fire, Henry moved aside the rug and chalked out a large circle on the floorboards. "The Entity is Bael."

Grace's forehead rippled with confusion. "I thought you said the Entity was the Devil."

Henry sighed sharply. "Could you be quiet? I'm trying to concentrate."

Grace's own irritation showed as she sucked her lips into a thin line.

After completing the concentric circles, Henry inserted the four letters between them, evenly spaced like the points of a compass. He painstakingly set to work on drawing a symbol within the inner circle. A stickman wielding a pair of three-headed axes took shape – or at least that's what it appeared to be to Grace. Between the stickman's legs was something that might have been disproportionately large genitals or perhaps a ram's head with inward curving horns.

A withering smile played on Grace's lips. "So now you're going to summon Bael, are you?"

"Yes."

Her grin wavered at Henry's straight-faced reply. "And what will you do if the Lord of Hell actually answers your summons?"

"Prince of Hell," corrected Henry. "I'll make him do as I say."

"How?"

"To know the name of a thing is to have power over that thing."

"And how did you find out the Entity's name?"

Henry shot Grace a narrow look. "Why should I tell you when you'll just laugh at me?" With a flick of his hand, he motioned for her to step away from the sigil.

She moved towards the fireplace, folding her arms. "Get on with it then. I can't wait to meet the Prince of Hell."

Not rising to the taunt, Henry inhaled deeply. He held his breath for one second... two... three... His heart was pounding against his ribcage. Four seconds... five... six... His breath didn't want to come out. Seven seconds... eight... nine... Suddenly he was exhaling and Bael's enn was rushing from his lips. "Ayer secore on ca Bael. Ayer secore on ca Bael."

His face fearful and expectant, Henry stared at the sigil. It seemed to shimmer in the firelight.

"Ayer secore on ca Bael. Ayer secore on ca Bael."

"Nothing's happening," Grace pointed out dryly.

Henry raised his voice as if that would help Bael to hear him. "Ayer secore on ca Bael."

"Perhaps he's not taking any calls today."

Henry's face spasmed in annoyance. Composing himself with another deep breath, he looked at the toad, taking in every detail – the bumpy skin, the stubby legs, the curved claws, the saucer eyes, the lipless mouth. Holding the image in his mind, he returned his gaze to the sigil and resumed chanting, "Ayer secore on ca Bael." He enunciated each word as clearly as possible, pouring all his concentration, all his willpower, all his desperate desire to talk to Jacob into the enn.

Still nothing happened.

A heat that had nothing to do with the fire burned Henry's cheeks. Why wasn't it working?

Because it's a joke, his inner voices gloated. *You're a joke. You're just one big stupid joke.*

"Perhaps Bael wants some kind of offering," suggested Grace. She arched an eyebrow meaningfully at Henry. "Do you know any virgins we could sacrifice?"

Anger scorched through him like wildfire. *Fuck you,* he silently shouted at her. *How about I cut out your tongue and offer it to Bael?*

Grace's eyelids hooded her shrewd blue eyes. "You want to hurt me, don't you?" The words were spoken like an invitation. "You'd like to do to me what you did to Faith." With an impulsive movement, she reversed the stun gun and offered the handle to Henry. "Take it. Use it on me. You could knock me out, even kill me. No one would ever know. And even if someone found out what you'd done, they wouldn't blame you for it. After all, I kidnapped you."

He eyed the stun gun, chewing his lips nervously. "As soon as I try to take it, you'll use it on me."

"No I won't. I promise." Her voice seductively soft, Grace repeated, "Take it. I can see you want to."

Henry's fingers twitched. She was right. He did want to take it. Then he would be the one in control.

Don't fall for it, warned his inner voices. *She's playing with you like that cat with the pigeon.*

Henry's eyes lit up as an idea popped into his head. Like a magician producing an animal from nowhere, he put a hand inside his coat and whipped out the pigeon.

"What is *that*?" Grace exclaimed.

"What does it look like?" Henry replied, dropping to his haunches.

Grace peered over his shoulder at the blood-encrusted bird. "Where did you get it?"

"I didn't kill it."

"That's not what I asked."

"Walthamstow."

"You've been carrying that thing since London." Grace's voice swayed between revulsion and curiosity. "What the hell for?"

Henry shrugged. "Maybe Bael wanted me to."

Grace squinted at him as if trying to figure out whether he was having her on. "Oh yeah right, maybe he fancies a nice bit of pigeon for tea."

Ignoring her mocking words, Henry placed the pigeon in the centre circle. Once again, he sucked in a breath and chanted, "Ayer secore on ca Bael. Ayer secore on ca Bael."

Grace glanced towards the French doors, suddenly aware that the wind had dropped to a whisper. A heavy stillness draped itself over the room. She turned in a slow circle, scanning the dusty furniture, the lifeless grandfather clock, the blazing hearth. The hairs on her arms prickled as she was struck by the impression that the house was listening, and not just listening, but watching in anticipation.

"Ayer secore on ca Bael."

Grace's gaze returned to Henry. His eyes were half closed. His voice was quieter, yet deeper, more rhythmic and resonant. Over and over he repeated the chant, not slowing, not speeding up, steady as a ticking clock.

The storm continued to hold its breath.

Logs crackled in the hearth, providing an incongruously pleasant background track. As Grace inhaled sweet pine smoke, she found herself wondering what it would be like to live in Fenton House. Silence, privacy, space – there would be an abundance of all the things she'd lacked as a child sharing a bedroom with Faith. Even now, as an adult, paying the rent on her one-bedroom flat was a constant struggle. Moving from one low-paid job and grotty property to another, those were the rhythms of her life. There was never time to stop, take a step back and think about who she was and who she wanted to be. Here she could do that. Here she could indulge in whatever whim took her fancy – reading, gardening, hiking, swimming or simply doing nothing.

"Ayer secore on ca Bael."

She closed her eyes and saw a procession of long, lazy days stretching out in front of her – afternoons sipping wine in the sun, evenings dozing by the fire. No more dragging her aching bones out of bed in the morning and hustling her way through crowded streets to some mind-numbing job. No more neighbours arguing and playing loud music all night on the other side of paper-thin walls. No more watching those same walls close in, feeling her life slip away minute by minute. She could be one of the lucky few to escape, to be truly free to live.

The thought of it was almost enough to bring tears to her eyes.

A sound on the periphery of hearing brought her back to the moment. "Do you hear that?" she asked in a hushed voice.

"Yes."

"It sounds like someone in pain."

Henry gestured towards the hallway. "It's coming from over there."

Their shadows looming ahead of them, they padded to the hallway. "It's getting louder," said Henry, approaching The Lewarne Room. There was a shudder in his voice that matched the shudders running up and down Grace's spine.

"It's probably just the wind."

"That doesn't sound like the wind," Henry disagreed as another moan trembled in the air.

Grace put a hand on his shoulder to halt him. She called

through The Lewarne Room's doorway, "If anyone's in there, come out."

The only reply was more moaning.

"I don't care what you're doing here," she tried again. "I won't report you to the police so long as you leave this house right away."

The tortured sound briefly fell below hearing level before rising again.

"I'm armed," warned Grace. Her palm slippery with sweat against the stun gun's grip, she edged into the room. Her gaze darted over the pedestals, sofa and armchair. There was no one to be seen.

Henry struck a match and moved between the candelabras, lighting their red candles. Each flame that flickered into life chased away more of the darkness. Another burst of moaning drew his eyes to the floor. Grace was already on her knees, pressing an ear to the tiles.

"There's *something* down there," she whispered.

"Do you think it's–" Henry started to say.

"No, I don't think it's the sodding Prince of Hell," Grace cut in. "It must be whoever opened the gates." Her fingers probed the cracked tiles. "The question is – how did they get down there?"

Henry approached the fireplace and reached for the embossed lettering again.

"Good idea," said Grace, her voice dripping with sarcasm. "Let's see if the house has changed its mind about letting us into the basement."

He ran his fingers over the letters. Grace gave a little start as, with a click, the front edge of the trapdoor lifted a centimetre. Suspicion swirled in her eyes. "You knew how to open it all along, didn't you?"

He treated her to a look that said there was no point in answering her question. With a conflicting mixture of eagerness and apprehension, he moved to prise at the raised edge.

"Wait," said Grace.

The word was barely out of her mouth when the trapdoor flew upright like the lid of Jack-in-the-box. Henry reeled backwards. Grace threw out a hand to catch him.

As if a mute button had been pressed, the moaning stopped dead. Henry and Grace stared at the opening, seemingly frozen in place by the icy air flowing out of it. One second passed, two, three...

Schlop.

Henry's whole body went rigid. The wet slapping sound was straight out of his nightmare. Hideous images swirled through his mind – the giant toad crawling into view, its cavernous mouth dropping open, its pink tongue darting out to coil around him and pull him down into hot, moist darkness.

Schlop, schlop.

Something was climbing the basement's steps. *Something.* He exchanged a glance with Grace, mouthing, "It's *him.*"

She shook her head, but her big blue eyes asked what she would not, or dared not, say, *Could it really be him? Could it be Bael?*

Schlop.

Henry took a step backwards as a grinning crimson face crowned by black horns emerged from the opening.

Grace backed away too, but then exclaimed, "It's a mask." There was a distinct quiver of relief in her voice.

Henry saw at once that she was right. It was a plastic devil mask. Bloodshot eyes squinted through the eyeholes. Clumps of bloody brown hair were pasted to the mask's forehead. More blood was streaked over the masked figure's tree trunk neck and muscular tattooed arms. Black chest hair curled over the open collar of a dripping wet polo shirt. The man's thigh muscles flexed against skin tight jeans as he clambered into the room. He swayed on the lip of the trapdoor, looking around as if trying to work out where he was.

"Who–" Henry's voice caught in his throat. He swallowed and tried again. "Who are you?"

"Who are you?" the man parroted slowly like he didn't understand the question. Trainers squelching, he took several unsteady steps before staggering against one of the pedestals. Shadows leapt all over the place as the candelabra toppled to the tiles.

Henry and Grace retreated in unison towards the doorway.

"Stay where you are," Grace warned the man. She shook the stun gun at him. "Do you know what this is?"

He gave it a perfunctory glance, then continued to wobble towards Henry and her.

A blue thread crackled between the electrodes. "Don't make me hurt you."

The man stopped and teetered back and forth like a drunk almost unconscious on his feet.

"What are you doing here?" Grace demanded to know. "How did you get in the basement? What happened to your head?"

"What... How..." stammered the man, bewildered by the quick-fire questions.

"Is there a mirror in the basement?" asked Henry.

"Mirror?" As if his brain had short-circuited, the man's chin dropped onto his chest. A string of bloody saliva dangled from the mask's mouth-hole.

"What do we do?" Henry asked Grace out of the side of his mouth.

Before she could reply, the man jerked his head up and bellowed, "Where the fuck are you? You're dead. Do you hear me? Dead!"

Henry and Grace dodged aside as, seemingly oblivious to their presence, the man charged towards the hallway. Grace made to zap him with the stun gun, but Henry caught hold of her wrist. "Don't," he whispered. "Let's see what he does."

Throwing him a sharp glance, she pulled her arm free. They ran into the hallway in time to see the man disappearing into the dining room. Like a child playing hide and seek, he called out in a sing-song voice, "Come out, come out wherever you are."

They slowed down to peek into the room. The man was peering under the table. He snatched up a chair and hurled it at the fireplace, shattering one of the ceramic dogs. "Bitch!" he roared. "When I get my hands on you, I'm gonna make you eat that fucking gold." He lurched towards the living room door and barged it open.

Grace glanced askance at Henry. "Gold?"

With a shrug, he headed for the living-room. He poked his head around the door frame, intrigued to see what, if any, reaction the masked man had to the sigil. The bizarre bloodstained figure was standing at the centre of the concentric circles. A strange, hopeful light shone in Henry's eyes as the man bent to pick up the pigeon.

"What's he doing?" wondered Grace as the man turned the bird this way and that like he was examining its wounds. Her puzzlement was joined by revulsion as he parted the pigeon's beak and put it to his mouth. He puffed several breaths into the bird before rapidly compressing its chest. "This guy's off his rocker," she murmured as he continued giving CPR to the pigeon – five breaths, ten compressions, five breaths, ten compressions...

Grace stepped into the room, stun gun raised. "Put that down."

She might as well have been talking to a brick wall. Five breaths, ten compressions, five breaths...

"Put that–" she began to repeat more loudly, but broke off.

"Look," Henry gasped. "Did you see that?"

Furrows ploughed their way across Grace's brow. She shook her head in denial of her own eyes.

The man balanced the pigeon in his dinner plate of a palm. For a moment, it lay motionless, then its grey-and-white spotted wings twitched again. Its yellow beak opened, stretching wide and emitting a series of distressed-sounding grunts.

"That's impossible," Grace murmured, blinking as if to clear her vision. "It was dead."

"Yes," said Henry. "It was."

The pigeon popped up onto its clawed feet. It flapped its wings, trying to take flight, its grunts rising to a high-pitched scream. Henry hunched his shoulders as the sound went through him like a knife scraping glass.

The man stared blankly at the bird, seeing yet not seeing. Its flapping grew more frantic as he turned his palm over. It hooked its scaly red toes around his fingers, hanging upside down like a bat. With a final piercing scream, it spread its wings to full extension, released its grip and flapped off in a swirl of feathers.

Henry's gaze followed it to the darkest corner of the room. "Where is it? I can't see it."

Grace swept her phone's torchlight across the ceiling and located the pigeon perched atop the grandfather clock. Startled, the bird took flight again, swooping into the hallway.

Grace and Henry stared after it in stunned silence. A heavy thud yanked their attention back to the masked man. He was lying face down in the sigil, as deathly still as the pigeon had been before its apparent resurrection.

Grace warily prodded him with her foot. Nothing. Not a twitch. Stun gun at the ready lest he was playing dead, she felt for a pulse in his wrist.

"Is he alive?" asked Henry.

"Yes. Help me move him to the sofa."

Taking hold of an arm each, they lifted the man. He sagged between them like a sack of grain. "God, he weighs a ton," grunted Grace, quivering with strain as they manoeuvred the man onto the cushions.

They rolled him onto his back, propping his head against the arm of the sofa. Grace carefully parted his blood-matted hair, exposing a penny-sized hole in the centre of his forehead just below his hairline. The swollen rim of the wound was as blackened as a bomb crater. Glimpses of bone were visible through a film of congealing blood.

"It looks like he's been shot," she said.

"By who?"

Grace responded with a *how-should-I-know* shrug. "We need to get him to a hospital."

"No."

"What do you mean no? He'll die if we don't."

"You can't die if you're not alive."

Grace frowned at the cryptic words, then scoffed, "Oh of course, silly me. This isn't just some dickhead in a Halloween mask, it's Bael the Prince of Hell."

"You saw what he did to the pigeon."

Grace's eyebrows knitted into a perplexed knot. "I'm not sure what I saw."

Henry's voice grew shrill with exasperation. "You said it yourself, the pigeon was dead."

"I thought it was, but..." Grace groped for a credible explanation. "Maybe it was in a coma."

"A coma?" Henry sneered at the suggestion. "I watched a cat almost bite off its head. It was as dead as... as Jacob and Faith." He nodded as if that was the final word on the matter.

"OK, so explain this to me. If this guy really is a demon, how come he can be hurt like anyone else?"

Henry sighed like he was dealing with an idiot. "Demons can't take on physical form in this world. They need a body to possess."

Now Grace's face contracted into a sneer. "You're saying he's possessed?"

As she spoke, a shriek of wind flung the French doors open with enough force to shatter a pane of glass. She ran to wrestle them shut and set about pushing a heavy sideboard across them.

A smile teased Henry's lips. "We can't go outside in this weather. It's too dangerous."

His pleased tone sent a little shudder through Grace, although she had to admit that he was right. The nearest hospital was at least ten miles away. They'd be lucky to make it halfway there before the wind drove them off the road or speared a branch through the windscreen.

A pale glow lit up Grace's face as she checked her phone's signal. Heaving a sigh, she pushed the phone back into her pocket.

Henry's smile climbed higher. "Still no service?"

Ignoring the smug remark, Grace looked uncertainly at the unconscious man. Fresh blood was seeping from his wound. Henry dug out a crumpled tissue. It instantly turned into bloody mush as he pressed it to the ragged hole. The man stirred and let out a low groan, but didn't open his eyes.

"Stop touching the wound," said Grace. "You could do more harm than good."

She eyed the dining room and hallway doors. With sudden urgency, she closed the dining room door and pushed an armchair up against it.

"You're wasting your time," Henry said as she turned to the other door. "Whoever did this to him, you can't keep them out of here. There are secret doors everywhere."

Grace ran a despairing hand through her hair. "So what you're saying is, we're totally fucked."

"The house will protect us." Henry was calm with certainty.

Grace let out a sharp laugh. "The house will protect us? Have you listened to yourself?" Indecision glimmered in her eyes as they alternated between the French doors and the bleeding man. Shouldn't she at least try to get him to a hospital? Was the truth about Faith worth more than his life? "He's not your responsibility," she told herself out loud, trying to sound as if she believed it. "You're not going anywhere until you know the truth."

Henry pointed at the man. "He'll tell you the truth. I'll make him."

"And just how the hell do you intend to do that when he's–" Grace broke off, shaking her head. "You know what? This isn't a haunted house, it's a madhouse. I thought I was crazy buying all those mirrors, but this–"

"The mirror," Henry exclaimed, his eyes springing wide open.

He raced towards the hallway. He was halfway to the door before Grace could even react. She glanced at the wounded stranger. He clearly wasn't going anywhere anytime soon. "A madhouse," she muttered again as she set off in pursuit of Henry. It wasn't difficult to guess where he was going. She entered The Lewarne Room in time to see him descending into the basement. She scanned the shadows. Satisfied no one was lurking in them, she ran to the trapdoor.

Henry was halfway down the steps. He lifted his crestfallen gaze to Grace. "The mirror isn't down here."

"Why is the mirror so important?"

"Why do you ask so many stupid questions?" Henry snapped, swinging from disappointment to irritation.

As he ran up the steps and dodged past Grace, she called after him, "I'm just trying to understand."

He slowed at her genuine sounding words, peering sceptically over his shoulder. "The mirror's like... it's like a phone that can Facetime the dead." He nodded, pleased with his analogy. "Without it, there's only one way to find out why Jacob and Faith called us here."

"Faith didn't call me here."

"Yes she did," Henry replied in a tone that left no room for debate. He turned to continue on his way to the living room. He dropped to his haunches beside the comatose man.

Grace came up behind Henry. "So how do we make him tell us what we want to know?"

"Demons never just tell the truth. Not even if you summon them by name." His voice took on the solemnity of a reverend delivering a sermon. "When He lies, He speaks His native language, for He is a liar and the Father of Lies."

"Are you talking about Bael or yourself?"

Mouthing a sarcastic laugh, Henry reached for the blood-spattered mask. His fingers hovered over it for a moment, trembling ever so slightly, before curling under the lower rim. His voice sank to a murmur. "Bael." He started to lift the mask, breaking a crust of blood. "Bael, I have summoned you and now you must answer me."

His eyes flinched towards the hallway at a sound like a door slamming. Grace whirled around, stun gun raised. Wind screamed along the hallway, sweeping leaves ahead of it.

"That was the front door," Grace whispered.

Henry and she glanced at each other with the same question in their eyes – had the door been opened by someone entering or leaving the house?

10

Father

Adam hunched over the steering wheel, squinting into the rain-drenched night. The wind kept trying to push the car into the hedges that flanked the road. He drove as fast as he dared, weaving around fallen branches and splashing through deep puddles. The storm could have been a manifestation of his state of mind. Round and round in his head whirled the words of the Redruth train station guard.

Your son was with a young woman. He didn't look very well. She had an arm around him like she was holding him up. She put him in a red car and drove off. I didn't see the make or reg.

The revelation that a stranger had bundled Henry into a car was upsetting enough, but what the guard had said next set Adam's head reeling.

I was too far away to get a good look at the woman, but I'd say she's in her twenties. Skinny. Nothing to her. Very pale. Dressed head to toe in black. Short, bright red hair.

The description had dredged up a vision of a painfully thin woman whose mascara-ringed eyes stared out of a milk white face topped by a shock of crimson hair.

The guard had continued speaking, but Adam was too dazed to listen. Numbly, he'd returned to his car. Numbly, he'd battled his way through the storm to Helston and beyond.

Even now, his eyes were glazed over like he'd been punched in the head. A name kept whispering through the darkest corners of his mind – *Faith, Faith, Faith...*

He knew it couldn't be her. He'd seen her plummet from the cliffs near Fenton House. He'd stared down at her broken body on the wave-washed rocks. And yet the whispering wouldn't stop – *Faith, Faith...*

Sweat shimmered on his upper lip. It wasn't far now. Soon he would set eyes on the dour grey walls and staring windows that haunted his dreams. He'd hoped this day would never come, yet somehow he wasn't surprised that it had.

A sign materialised from the rain – 'Treworder'. He left the main road behind for a flooded lane. Leaving plumes of spray in his wake, he raced towards the coast. The lane was as deserted as the moon. The first time he'd come out here, the isolation had felt like a breath of fresh air. Now it pressed in on him like a suffocating embrace.

Who was the red-haired stranger? Maybe she had nothing to do with Faith or Fenton House. Perhaps she was just a Good Samaritan. Or was there an even simpler explanation? What if the bus service to The Lizard had been cancelled because of the storm? Henry would have had to call for a taxi to take him to Fenton House.

A grim smile touched Adam's lips. A twenty-something goth girl taxi driver. He hadn't come across many of them.

The lane curved sharply to the left. Beads of sweat merged to trickle down his face. Fenton House was so close now that he could almost feel its presence lurking in the blackness beyond the headlights.

Not for the first time since Redruth, the thought passed through his mind, *Perhaps you should call the police.*

Once again, he dismissed the idea. What if Penny Holman caught wind of the situation? She'd be out here in a flash with her questions and suspicions. No way in hell was he chancing that. Besides, at this point the question was moot. The storm had wiped out his phone's signal even before he passed into the dead zone of the peninsula.

Another turn took him onto a lane so narrow that the wind-tossed hedges lashed the windows. As the car climbed a short slope, the *whoosh* and *boom* of waves pummelling cliffs drew his gaze to the impenetrable darkness on his left. The sound was like a hypnotic suggestion taking control of his consciousness, bombarding him with images of himself chasing after Faith, diving to catch hold of her, losing his grip and watching her disappear over the cliffs.

Spear-topped iron gates loomed into view. He wasn't surprised to see that they were open. The wind seethed in the sycamores as he crunched along the gravel driveway. A particularly violent gust was followed by an explosive *crack!* He flung his hands up to shield his eyes as a tree trunk smashed into the bonnet. A branch speared through the windscreen, skewering the passenger seat. The impact hurled him forwards. The seatbelt locked, jerking him backwards. The wheels spun helplessly for a few seconds, spitting gravel, then the engine cut out and the headlights died.

For a moment, Adam sat too stunned to move. Grimacing at a sharp pain in his neck, he looked at the branch embedded in the passenger seat. Half a metre to the right and it would have impaled him instead.

It's the house.

The words that had rung out in his head after skidding off the road to Redruth resurfaced. Only this time, he couldn't laugh them off.

A sudden protective feeling surged up in him so

powerfully that he retorted out loud, "It doesn't matter what it is. He's my son. I won't let any harm come to him."

Rain swirled into his face as he shoved the door open. Smoke billowed from the car's crushed bonnet, stinging his eyes as he clambered over the fallen tree. Almost bent double into the wind, he fought his way forwards. Once, twice, he was buffeted off his feet. Each time, his face set like concrete, he got up and pressed on.

Nothing was going to stop him from reaching Henry. Nothing!

Strands of ivy whipped him as he passed the lion-headed fountain. Then he saw it – the house. He ground to a standstill as his phone's torch revealed snapshots of weathered stone and shuttered windows. Apart from the proliferation of ivy growing up the walls, the place looked the same as the last time he'd seen it. The only thing missing was Heloise dangling at the end of a rope from the tower's uppermost window.

Something whooshed past his face and thwacked into the gravel. He looked down at the shattered remnants of a slate roof tile. An ominous creaking drew his gaze up to the vague, tapering outline of the tower. It sounded like the granite blocks were shifting and grinding against each other under the storm's assault.

An even greater sense of urgency gripped him. Forget ghosts, demons and mysterious women. If the very real storm brought the tower crashing down on their heads, they'd be lucky to escape with their lives.

He forged onwards, slowing warily at the sight of a little red car. He squinted through its windows. Nothing marked it out as a taxi. So who was the goth girl? Was she one of the paranormal fanatics that occasionally came to his book signings in search of answers he didn't have? Or perhaps Henry had met her through social media. He hoped to God it was something so simple.

A shudder that ran all the way down to his toes brought him to a halt again as he entered the porch. He stared at the bolt-studded door, shivering cold yet with sweat seeping from every pore.

"It's nonsense," he remonstrated with himself. "All of it. Total fucking nonsense."

He reached to twist the door knob. A surge of wind wrenched it from his grasp, slamming the door into the hallway wall. Bracing one hand against the wall, he thrust the door shut.

Swiping his sleeve across his face, he turned to survey the entrance hall. An orange glow was flickering from beneath the staircase. He knew only too well what doorway lurked in the shadow of the stairs. The Lewarne Room would doubtless have been Henry's first port of call. His gaze paused on a portrait of a wisp of a woman. She stared back, neither welcoming nor hostile, merely watching.

Winifred Trehearne. Just one of the ghosts said to haunt the house. Anger burned in Adam's chest. Not at Henry, but at himself. How could he have brought his family here? How could he have been so blinded by his need to escape his grief over Jacob's death?

Craning his neck around a stone pillar, he saw that the door to The Lewarne Room was open. Five red candles were burning. Melted wax was dripping off the candelabra like spilled blood. Henry was nowhere to be seen. Adam's heart lurched as his gaze landed on the open trapdoor.

Was Henry in the basement? Was he calling to Jacob in Walter's mirror? Perhaps he was already talking to his brother, lost forever to the same insanity that had blighted the lives of the house's former inhabitants.

Adam jerked around at the sound of footsteps – stealthy footsteps betrayed by creaky floorboards. A soft orange glow was seeping from the living room too.

Faith, Faith, his mind whispered again, returning him to the night he'd discovered her and three of her friends performing a magic ritual in that room. "Adonai," he murmured the word that had been chalked at her feet. *Adonai. God.* Faith hadn't been trying to talk to God, though. Quite the opposite.

A slender shadow emerged from the living room, stretching across the hallway floor. Adam glanced from side to side, instinctively looking for somewhere to hide. With a shake of his head, he remained where he was. No hiding. Whatever the house had to throw at him, he would face it head on.

The shadow's owner stepped into view. Adam's mouth opened and closed mutely, like he was trying to speak in a vacuum. Another bout of shuddering took hold of him. The short red hair. The delicate, gaunt face. The mascara-ringed blue eyes. The pale skin made to seem even paler by black clothing. It *was* her. It was Faith back from the grave!

A gangly boy with a familiar way of hunching his head between his shoulders joined the apparition. "Henry!" Adam's voice breathlessly combined relief and incomprehension.

"You shouldn't have come here," Henry replied in an emotionless monotone. "Is Mum with you?"

"Of course she isn't."

"Stay where you are," the apparition warned, pointing a gun-like thing at Adam. A thread of electricity crackled between metal prongs.

Instead of fear, he felt an almost overpowering urge to laugh out loud at himself. A stun gun. Not exactly standard issue for ghosts. "Who are you?"

"Her name's Grace," Henry answered for her. "She's Faith's sister."

Adam nodded as if he should have known. "You're here to find out what happened to Faith."

"I'm here for the truth," said Grace.

"You already know the truth."

"I know that you're a liar."

"I don't know what–"

"Yes you do," Grace cut him off.

Adam opened his mouth to reiterate his denial, but seeing the warning in Grace's eyes he held his tongue.

"She's spoken to Penny Holman," Henry told him.

"Penny Holman," Adam echoed with a heavy sigh of comprehension.

"I bet you wish she'd just shut up and go away, don't you?" said Grace. "Well she's not going anywhere and neither am I. Not until I find out why my sister's blood was–" She broke off with a gasp of surprise as Henry snatched the stun gun from her hand. There was another crackle of electricity. She shrank away from Henry, but he lurched past her to press the prongs against his dad's chest.

With a guttural cry, face contorting, limbs twitching and tying themselves into knots, Adam collapsed to the floor. His convulsions quickly subsided and he attempted to sit up.

Crackle! Crackle!

Adam's spine stiffened ramrod straight as Henry zapped him again. When Henry released the trigger, Adam's head banged back against the floor.

Henry impassively watched his dad's eyes roll upwards into his skull, then he turned to Grace.

She met his gaze with a hard stare. “Try that on me and I’ll smash your face–” She gave another sharp inhalation as he tossed the stun gun to her.

“Help me,” he said, stooping to grab one of his dad’s limp arms.

“Help you do what?”

“We have to lock him in the basement.”

Grace squinted at Henry like she was studying some repulsively fascinating creature. “You really are a little–”

“Yeah, yeah, I know, I’m a little psycho. Now, are you going to help? Or do you want to deal with my dad when he wakes up?”

A strangled groan from Adam prompted Grace into action. She shoved the stun gun into her pocket and took hold of his other arm. They dragged him towards the upright trapdoor.

“Wha… What…” he slurred, his head lolling against the tiles.

“I’m not going to let you ruin everything,” Henry told him. “Not this time.”

Catching sight of the trapdoor, Adam’s eyes swelled in horrified comprehension. “No… Please, no.”

He threw Grace a glassy-eyed look of appeal. Avoiding his gaze, she continued dragging him. She shivered at a bitterly cold draught from the basement.

Rearing up as if he’d been slapped awake, Adam tried to twist his arms free. Grace obliged by letting go and grabbing his feet instead. She jerked them upwards, upending him over the rim of the opening. He toppled backwards, tumbling and slithering down the steep steps. He clawed at the stone, halting his fall halfway down.

“No!” he cried out one last time as Henry reached for the

trapdoor.

Without affording his dad a glance, Henry tipped over the slab of wood and ceramic. It thudded shut, plunging the basement into darkness. Adam blindly scrambled up the steps and thrust at the trapdoor. It didn't budge. "Let me out, Henry! Let me out right now!"

His demand met with silence.

His fingers moved over the wood, reading the braille of scratches. His mind conjured up an image of George and Sofia Trehearne clawing at the trapdoor after Heloise slammed it on their heads, condemning them to a slow death from starvation.

Would Henry really do that to him? A sob forced its way up his throat, not at the prospect of starving to death, but at the fact that he was asking himself such a question.

11

Mother

Blinking as if she was emerging from a deep sleep, Natalie turned away from the mirror. She looked at Jamie's corpse. The ghost mask was an island in a lake of blood. She dipped a toe into the glossy liquid like a swimmer testing the water. It was cold. How long had she been standing there? Minutes? Hours? Not that it mattered. Time was an irrelevance. The Master had given her an eternity to enjoy the house. All she needed now was someone to share her happiness with.

Touching her bloodstained stomach, she murmured, "Grant me thy dark gifts."

She tilted her head and listened for a moment before peering into the hole in the wall. On the periphery of hearing, she caught a sound. What was it? Shouting? Banging? The voice of the storm? Her gaze fell to the pistol in her hand. She swung open the cylinder. There were three rounds left. Snapping the cylinder shut, she headed for the barred door. She squeezed between the bent bars and unhurriedly made her way along the tunnel. There was no rush. She would never need to rush again.

She paused several times to feather her fingertips over veins of serpentine, her eyes heavy-lidded, breath sighing between her plump lips. They were all around her – Great Grandma Emily, Great Grandad Walter, Winifred Trehearne and the others. So many nameless others. She could feel their loneliness, confusion and fear.

"It's OK," she told them as tenderly as a mother soothing a scared child. "I'm here now."

She ascended the steps and slid through the gap between the wall and the staircase. She stopped and stood listening again. It wasn't the storm. Someone else was in the house. Someone alive. At a murmur of voices from the living room, she quietly removed the rectangle of wood and squinted through the peephole.

The room was bathed in the warm radiance of flames from the hearth. Her gaze glided across the floorboards to where the bearskin rug should have been. A faint smile touched her lips at the sight of the sigil. Apparently she wasn't the only one communing with demons this night. She would enjoy watching whoever it was do whatever they'd come here to do, just so long as they left afterwards.

Her smile vanished as she saw a familiar figure on the sofa. Leon appeared to be unconscious or dead. One of his arms dangled limply against the floor. His hair was clotted with blood where the bullet must have hit home. Was that what the banging had been – Leon trying to escape from the basement? Had he somehow managed to break out? Or had the owners of the voices she'd heard let him out? If so, where were his rescuers? Had they run away? She ground her teeth as another possibility occurred to her – perhaps they'd gone for help. Not that the arrival of police and paramedics would be anything more than an inconvenience. She would simply retreat to the vault and wait for them to leave. They would never find her. The Master would make sure of that.

The thought was thrust from her mind by a female voice with a Cornish accent. "Is that why you tortured Faith –

because she was ruining everything for you?" The accent was soft, but the tone was harsh with accusation.

Faith. The name brought to mind the goth girl whose sad eyes looked out from the pages of *Between Worlds*.

"OK, Grace, I admit it," came an exasperated retort. "I tortured your sister."

Natalie's eye widened against the peephole as a teenage boy slouched into view. He had an awkward, hunched gait. His clothes hung on him like a scarecrow's. A scattering of pimples dotted his cheeks. His eyes peered sullenly through a loose fringe.

"Henry," Natalie murmured to herself.

He was taller and thinner than in the book, but she had no doubt that it *was* him. He radiated an air of hard-done-by petulance and me-against-the-world injustice that his dad had described with merciless accuracy.

A waifish woman was following close behind Henry. Natalie's eye grew even wider. Physically Grace was identical to Faith, but that was as deep as the resemblance went. Grace's eyes exuded an angry sadness, not the helpless sadness of Faith.

What were Henry and Grace doing here? Was it a coincidence? Natalie's smile returned. Of course it wasn't.

"I told you, no more games," warned Grace, pursuing Henry to the sofa.

"I'm not playing games." Henry's goading tone contradicted his words. "I was angry with Faith because she made my mum want to move back to London. So I kept her prisoner in the secret passageways and tortured her until she begged to be put out of her misery."

Her eyes burning with rage, Grace grabbed Henry by the arm and jerked him around to face her.

He met her glare with a challenge in his eyes. "That's what you wanted to hear, isn't it? You've been looking for an excuse to hurt me. Well now you've got one. So what are you waiting for?"

Grace's face twitched with uncertainty. For a breathless moment, her fingers and eyes remained locked on Henry. Then she released his arm and lowered her head in apparent shame, like she'd failed some crucial test.

With a contemptuous snort, Henry turned away from her and sank to his haunches. He lifted Leon's hand and dropped it. The knuckles clunked against the floorboards.

"Dead," Natalie whispered as if saying it made it so.

Grace stooped to press two forefingers against the underside of Leon's wrist. "I can't find a pulse," she said with a grim shake of her head.

"He's not dead." There was no alarm in Henry's reply, just cold certainty.

"How can you be so sure?"

He sighed like a teacher tired of explaining the same thing over and over. "Demons aren't alive or dead."

Demons? Natalie's eyebrows pinched together behind her mask. Did Henry think Leon was some sort of demon?

"Then what are they?" asked Grace.

Henry was silent for a moment. He signalled his failure to find a satisfactory answer with a shrug. "They're something else. Something not physical. That's why they need a vessel to interact with our world."

"But surely a vessel of flesh and blood can still die, even if it's possessed by a demon."

"Yes, the vessel can die," conceded Henry.

"Then what happens to the demon?"

"It has to find a new body to possess." Henry eyed the sigil, chewing his lips in thought. He straightened and stepped into the centre circle, then beckoned Grace to join him.

"Is it supposed to be safe in there?"

"Not safe, but safer."

"Thanks, but I'll take my chance out here." Grace smiled wryly. "I've never been possessed before. Who knows, it might be good for a laugh."

Natalie let slip a murmur of laughter at the bravado in Grace's voice. *Who are you trying to kid, bitch? I can smell your fear.*

Henry gave a *suit yourself* shrug. His eyes narrowing to intense slits, he spread his arms towards Leon. "I call to you again from this circle. Bael, Prince of Hell, I ask–" He hesitated and changed his words. "I command you to do as I say."

A louder snigger escaped Natalie. She clapped a hand over her mask's mouth-hole. Oh this was good. No amount of gold could buy entertainment like this.

Leon showed no sign of responding to Henry. Indeed, he showed no sign of anything beyond being dead.

"Where's the mirror?" Henry demanded to know. "I need to speak to my brother." He pointed to Grace. "And she needs to speak to her sister. If the mirror isn't here, then you must speak to them for us. Ask them why they've called us here. What do they want from us? If you do this, we will pay whatever price you want."

"Will we?" said Grace. "That's news to me."

"Shh," Henry hissed at her.

Natalie clamped her lips together, just barely containing her laughter.

Henry's face scrunched into a constipated expression. "Bael!" he cried. "Bael!"

That was too much for Natalie. A guffaw forced its way out.

"Did you hear that?" Grace spun on her heels, her eyes probing the shadowy extremities of the room.

"Hear what?" asked Henry.

"I thought I heard laughter."

Henry turned in a slow circle. Natalie's amusement evaporated as his eyes came to rest on the peephole. She stared straight back at him as unblinking as a statue. A shuddery tingle coursed through her, like a current of connection was flowing between their gazes. She couldn't be certain, but Henry seemed to shudder too.

She felt a powerful compulsion to direct her thoughts towards him. *Hi Henry. I want to tell you that it doesn't matter if you hurt Faith. She was nothing. You're special. I know what it's like to be different, to feel like you don't fit in. You never have to feel that way again. Not here. Not with me.*

Henry's gaze fell away from the peephole. "What am I not doing?" he wondered out loud.

"Maybe Bael wants another offering," suggested Grace. "Have you got any more pigeons for him to resurrect?"

Natalie frowned against the mask. *Pigeons to resurrect? What the fuck was she going on about?*

Henry's nose wrinkled in irritation at Grace's bone-dry tone. "You can't deny what you saw."

"Can't I? Like I keep saying, there's only one thing I'm sure of – you're a liar."

He greeted the accusation with a defiant smile. "Liar, psycho, freak – I've been called it all a thousand times before. It used to bother me, but then I started to kind of like it. Do you know why? Because it means I'm different. I'm special."

Different. Special. Natalie's heart fluttered at the words. There *had* been a connection. Henry might not be consciously aware of it, but their minds had touched.

"Oh yeah, you're definitely *special,*" sneered Grace.

Henry betrayed no outward reaction to the taunt, but another electric frisson thrummed through Natalie. He scuffed a foot at the sigil, lowered himself into a cross-legged position, planted his chin on his knuckles and stared at Leon like he was waiting for some sort of sign.

Natalie stroked the wall as if it was his face. *Poor Henry. I feel your pain.* Her sympathy curdled into hate as her gaze shifted to Grace. "I'm going to make you understand just how special he is." Her voice was an acid whisper.

Grace moved to peer between the curtains. She shielded her eyes as wind whipped through a broken windowpane. "When is this storm going to let up?"

"How should I know?" muttered Henry.

"It was a rhetorical question." Grace tilted her head contemplatively at him. "Perhaps I was wrong about you. I'd convinced myself that you drove Faith to suicide, but now I'm wondering if you're capable of such a thing. I don't mean morally, I mean mentally. Psychopaths are supposed to be highly intelligent, but you... well, let's be honest, Henry, you're not the sharpest tool in the box."

Natalie dug her long fingernails into the crumbling mortar between the bricks, imagining that she was clawing Grace's face. Oh how she was going to enjoy making this worthless bitch realise she wasn't fit to lick the dirt off Henry's shoes. Her anger turned to amusement again as Henry said coolly, "Is that all you've got?"

Grace and he eyeballed each other as if testing who would blink first. They looked at the ceiling as a tremor vibrated down the walls. Natalie glanced upwards too, frowning as the house creaked like a ship in heavy seas.

"Sounds like this place is getting ready to fall down," said Grace. Her eyes darted back to the French doors as the floor began to shake like a mini-earthquake.

"You should leave while you still can," said Henry, reading her body-language.

She slitted her eyes at him. "Is that a threat?"

He shook his head. "You still don't get it, do you? You're in danger here, but not from me."

"You're right about that," murmured Natalie, her words spiked with malicious intent.

"And what if the house *does* fall down?" asked Grace.

Henry gave an unconcerned shrug. "I don't want to die, but nothing will ever make me leave this house again."

Grace's eyebrows knotted as she struggled to wrap her head around his words. "Why would you want to live here alone?"

"I won't be alone."

"Right again," mouthed Natalie.

Grace laughed incredulously. "You're living in cloud cuckoo land. You're fourteen. How would you survive? You can't drive. You don't have any money."

"Yes I do," said Henry. "Or I will have when I find the gold."

"What are you talking about? What–" Grace broke off, her confused expression fading as Henry glanced at Leon.

Natalie stabbed her fingernails deeper into the mortar. Had the stupid bastard told them about the gold? If so, she would hunt down his ghost and inflict all the tortures of Hell upon it.

"That poor sod's brain is scrambled eggs," said Grace. "He didn't know what he was saying."

"Yes he did. There's gold hidden somewhere in this house. A *lot* of gold. Why else would someone have shot him?"

Natalie's fingers relaxed. Leon clearly hadn't mentioned the vault.

Unable to dispute Henry's logic, Grace changed tack. "What about your dad? As soon as you let him out of the basement, he's going to take you back to London. Or are you planning to do to him what Heloise did to her parents?"

Natalie's tongue emerged from the mask's mouth-hole, licking the withered black lips as if anticipating a delicious feast. Adam Piper was here too? Oh this night just got better and better.

Henry's silence made it clear he didn't have an answer to Grace's question. She pointed at Leon. "And what about him?"

"I'll look after him." There was something akin to pleading in Henry's voice. "You can just go."

"How many times do I have to tell you, Henry? I'm not going anywhere until I find out what happened to Faith."

He slapped a palm against the floorboards. "Now I know why your sister wanted to get away from you so badly. Why can't you just leave me alone?"

Grace's eyes flashed at the mention of Faith, but she bit down on her anger. "Tell me the truth and I'll do just that."

"Whatever I say, you won't believe me," Henry replied with a sigh, tired of repeating himself.

"OK, well why don't I tell you what I think happened? And if I'm right, you don't even have to say a word, all you have to do is nod."

Henry eyed her as warily as a wild animal being offered food.

"I think you found out about Heloise shortly after moving here," Grace continued. "And I think you two got on like a house on fire. When Faith broke in and almost ruined things, the pair of you decided to make an example of her. But things didn't go as planned. She escaped from wherever you were keeping her prisoner. Luckily for you, the damage had already been done, her mind was broken and she finished what you'd started."

Henry stared at Grace, silent, inscrutable.

"I'm right, aren't I?" she said. "Just nod and I'll do as you want. I'll leave this house and you'll never see me again."

"You want to know what I think?" Henry's tone was surly with self-pity. "I think you'll only leave me alone when I'm lying dead at the bottom of the cliffs like your stupid bitch of a sister."

Grace's voice dropped menacingly low. "Say that again and I might just prove you right.

Henry's lips quivered as if he wanted to goad her further, but couldn't quite work up the nerve.

Natalie tickled the pistol's trigger. *I'm not going to shoot you in the head,* she silently told Grace. *I'm going to shoot you in the stomach and enjoy watching you slowly bleed to death.*

Henry's gaze returned to the floorboards. He traced a finger along the sigil, searching for some inaccuracy that might explain the ritual's failure. As far as he could tell, he'd reproduced the symbol without error.

Grace looked at him with a cleft between her eyebrows, as unsure as him what to do next.

A flicker of movement at the far side of the room caught Natalie's eye. A grey shape sailed soundlessly through the air and landed on the grandfather clock. As her eyes adjusted to the deeper gloom, she made out a small head atop a plump feathered chest.

Was this the pigeon Leon had supposedly resurrected?

Suddenly her mind was racing with questions. What if Leon really had brought the pigeon back to life? Or rather, what if something else working through him had done so? Maybe that *something else* was now inside the bird, on the lookout for a more suitable vessel.

Neither Henry nor Grace appeared to notice the pigeon. Grace approached Leon, removing something from her pocket. Firelight gleamed on glass as she flipped open a small mirror. She held it over the devil mask's mouth-hole for several seconds before displaying its clear surface to Henry. "Well we don't need to worry about getting him to a hospital anymore." She put away the mirror and started searching Leon's pockets.

Natalie knew Grace would find nothing. Leon was always careful not to carry any form of ID when he was on a job.

Grace pulled a car key out of his jeans. "BMW," she said, displaying the logo on the key to Henry.

"Idiot," Natalie muttered at herself for not having thought to retrieve the key.

"I didn't see any other cars outside," said Henry.

"Must be hidden somewhere nearby." Grace put the key in her pocket, then turned her attention to the mask. "It's time we had a look at your face," she said to Leon.

"Don't do that," Henry exclaimed as she made to lift the mask.

"Why not? You were about to take it off before your dad showed up."

“What if Bael needs the mask to be taken off so he can jump into a new body?”

Natalie wasn’t surprised by Henry so closely echoing her thoughts again. They were almost perfectly in tune with each other. She could feel it. “He is yours, as I am yours, Master,” she said softly.

Grace’s hands hesitated over the mask, but then she shook her head, reproaching herself for even considering Henry’s words. She took hold of the horns and started to lift them. Henry sprang towards her, reaching out to pull her away from Leon. He stopped abruptly at the sigil’s outer circle, his arms wind-milling like someone on the brink of a cliff.

Grace watched him fighting to keep his balance. He reeled backwards as if he’d been hit by a blast of wind, landing heavily on his backside. A broad grin split Grace’s lips. Laughter whistled through her teeth.

Henry sprang to his feet, red faced. “Stop laughing!”

She shook her head, letting him know that she either wouldn’t or couldn’t stop.

“Stop fucking laughing at me.” The words jumped from him in a screech.

Grace’s laughter only intensified at his breaking voice. She clutched her sides, tears spilling from her eyes.

Sniffing the air, Natalie caught a whiff of something almost indescribable. A fresh-foul odour, faint enough that she might have imagined it, yet pungent enough to scorch her senses.

Henry stamped his feet like a toddler throwing a tantrum. He lashed out with balled fists, but couldn’t reach Grace from within the sigil. Spittle flew from his mouth as his speech degenerated into incoherent shrieks.

Natalie drew in a deep breath, running her hands over

her breasts, caressing their erect nipples. She bit her lower lip, stifling a moan. "I smell you, Master," she murmured. "I smell you everywhere. I feel you everywhere. I am yours. Tell me what I must do. Give me a sign."

Her gaze was drawn to the pigeon again as, beadily eyeing Grace, it spread its wings like it was about to swoop at her. Natalie nodded as if acknowledging a command. It was time to put an end to Grace's sanctimonious goading and baiting. A permanent end.

Finally reigning in her laughter, Grace stepped within reach of Henry. "Hit me." She spread her arms, inviting him to take his best shot.

His clenched fists trembled at his sides, caught between rage and wariness.

"Hit me," Grace repeated forcefully. "Show me who you really are. Come on, you little freak. Show me!"

Seemingly caving in to her demand, Henry jerked up his fists.

Natalie tensed in readiness to run to his aid, but at that instant a howl of wind sent leaves billowing through the hallway door. The storm raged around the house, slamming doors and rattling chandeliers before being shut out again.

"Adam?" a tremulous voice called from the hallway. "Henry?"

Henry's eyes sprang wide. "Mum!" The look on his face suggested he didn't know whether to be horrified, happy or annoyed.

"Well, well," Natalie said with a chuckle. "The whole gang's here."

Grace's eyes shone with apprehension at the sound of approaching footsteps.

A figure strode, or rather waddled, into view. Ella's wet hair clung to her puffy, flushed face. Water dripped from the hem of her long coat. Her tired eyes took in Henry, Grace and Leon. Her mouth fell open but nothing came out, as if so many questions were whirring through her mind that she couldn't decide which to ask first.

Natalie wasn't looking at Ella's face. Her huge golden eyes were fixed on the bump that looked ready to burst out of Ella's coat.

"Pregnant," she breathed.

From the looks of it, Ella wasn't far off full-term. Indeed, her cheeks were puffing in and out like she might go into labour at any second.

A sob of joy forced its way out of Natalie. "Oh Master, now I see. Now I truly understand your power. This gift is worth more to me than all the gold in the world. I don't know how I'll ever repay you. Thank you, my master. Thank you. Thank you."

12

Jacob

Ella's mind somersaulted from relief to confusion and horror as she absorbed the scene in front of her eyes. The sight of Adam's crushed car had already thrown her into panic-mode. Now she found herself confronted by this nightmare. She couldn't make sense of it. Why was there a man on the sofa wearing a Halloween mask? Why was there a woman here who looked like Faith Gooden? Why? How? Why?

Her ears caught a muffled banging from somewhere behind her, like the wind was demanding to be let back in. She started to glance over her shoulder, but then pressed a hand to her bump and clenched her teeth against a wince. Zara had been mercifully inactive throughout the long drive, but the moment they'd passed through Fenton House's gates she'd begun kicking and squirming. Ella felt another spasm of movement beneath her palm. Christ, it was like there was a nest of angry snakes inside her.

"Are you OK, Mum?" asked Henry, starting towards her but stopping once again at the border of the sigil.

Ella wafted away his concern. She pointed to Leon. "Is he..." She faltered, reluctant to say what she was thinking.

"He's dead," Grace informed her.

Ella stared straight ahead at Henry, not acknowledging Grace, perhaps hoping she would simply go away. "*Please, please* tell me you have nothing to do with this, Henry."

Grace's eyebrows lifted at the question. What did it say if Henry's own mother thought him capable of killing?

"Of course I don't," he replied indignantly, his face a picture of injured innocence.

"Neither of us does," said Grace.

Ella shot her a sharp glance. "I'm talking to my son, not–" Her words were cut short as Zara's wriggling pushed a loud burp up her throat. Massaging her belly in an attempt to soothe the hyperactive foetus, she asked Henry, "Where's your dad?"

His tongue darted across his lips. "I... I..." he stammered.

Ella frowned at Henry's guilty manner. "Where's your dad?" she repeated firmly.

Blinking away from her probing gaze, he threw a desperate look at Grace. A grateful glimmer came into his eyes as she said, "I realise how this must look, Mrs Piper–"

"Do you?" Ella interrupted. "Do you really? Because from where I'm standing you look like an insane person."

"I'm sure I'd be thinking the same thing if I were you. Perhaps you'll see things differently when I tell you my name is–"

"Right this moment, I don't care what your name is," Ella cut her off. "I just–" A gasp whistled through her teeth as Zara dealt out a vicious kick. She composed herself with a deep breath. "I just want to know where my husband is."

"Dad's fine," Henry told her.

A flicker of relief passed over Ella's face, then her expression hardened again. "That's not what I asked, Henry."

His gaze fell away from her. Seeing that one of his feet had strayed beyond the outer circle, he jerked it backwards.

The sudden movement drew Ella's eyes. A line like a knife cut appeared between her eyebrows as she saw the sigil. "What have you done?" Her voice was a fearful whisper.

Henry stared mutely at the floor, fidgeting his feet along the inner curve of the circle.

"What have you done?" repeated Ella, this time not asking but demanding. "Tell me or–"

"Or what?" interjected Henry, suddenly meeting her gaze. "What are you going to do? Ground me?"

She pursed her lips, uncertain how to respond to his challenge.

His lips curved into a sour smile that was part triumph, part accusation. "You haven't even asked if I'm OK. All you care about is Dad."

As if angered by Henry's words, Zara lashed out again. With another gasp, Ella bent forwards and put out a hand to steady herself against the doorframe. "That's not true, Henry," she said between slow breaths. "I love you. So does your dad."

"Yeah right, sure he does," scoffed Henry. "Even you don't believe what you're saying. If you did, you wouldn't be here."

A corner of Grace's lips crooked upwards. "He has a point there."

"No one asked for your opinion," snapped Ella. "I'm not interested in anything you have to say, unless you can tell me where my husband is."

"He's locked in the basement."

"The basement," Ella echoed in quiet horror. She cast Henry a look that was more sad than angry. "How could you?"

He blinked away from her gaze and glowered at Grace as if she'd betrayed him. His expression shifted to surprise as she said, "It was my idea to put him down there."

"Oh, it was your idea, was it?" Ella's reply was loaded with scepticism. She pointed at the sigil. "I suppose that was your idea too?"

"I drew it," said Henry. "I have to speak to Jacob–"

"Don't!" Ella shouted with sudden fury. "Don't you dare mention your brother's name in this god-forsaken place."

A sound as ominous as a cracking glacier drew their gazes to the ceiling.

"You should be careful what you say about the house, Mum," cautioned Henry.

"Why? Have I hurt its feelings?" Her tone anything but sincere, Ella said to the ceiling, "Please accept my sincerest apology. Don't worry, you won't have to put up with me for much longer." A trace of vindictive satisfaction found its way into her voice as she added, "Or anyone else."

"What does that mean?"

"It means I'm going to do what I should have done a long time ago. I'm going to have this place demolished."

Henry's eyes sprang wide. "You can't do that!"

"Yes I can. It's my house. I can do what I want with it."

"But... But..." spluttered Henry, unable to express the depth of his dismay.

"But nothing." There was a ring of finality to Ella's words. She beckoned to him. "Come on, we're leaving."

He stared at her, his lips sucked in like a toothless old man. His feet didn't move from the inner curve of the circle. "It's not safe to go out in the storm."

One arm clasped across her belly as if to restrain its occupant, Ella stabbed a finger at the floor by her feet. Enunciating each word forcefully, she said, "Get over here. We are leaving right now."

Her voice pulled Henry forwards. His trainers breached the sigil.

"I'm sorry," said Grace. "But I can't let you leave."

Ella threw her a look that was both an appeal and a warning. "How are you going to stop us?" She glanced down at her bump. "Are you going to hurt my baby?"

"I'm not here to hurt anyone. I'm here to–" Grace's voice died on her lips. The dining room door was scraping open, pushing aside the armchair. She took several steps backwards, her eyes bulging as the gap between door and frame widened.

At the same instant, a strange shuddering cry burst from Ella. She stared open-mouthed at something behind Henry.

Curiosity competed with apprehension in his eyes as he turned towards whatever had forced its way into the room.

His pale lips trembling in search of words that wouldn't come, he swiftly backtracked into the sigil.

A naked woman was sliding into view. She had the type of body he'd recently started to fantasise about – long legs, athletically curvy thighs and hips, flat stomach, large breasts. But her face... Her face was the stuff of nightmarish fairy tales – warty green skin, thin black lips, hooked nose. What was she? A witch? A ghost?

As she advanced into the firelight, he saw that she was neither. She was just a woman wearing a plastic mask.

Bitch! When I get my hands on you, I'm gonna make you eat that fucking gold.

The dead man's words echoed back to Henry. Surely this

was who they'd been aimed at. His suspicion was all but confirmed as he spotted the pistol in the masked woman's hand. His head shrank down between his shoulders at the sight.

She sashayed towards him on the balls of her feet, chin held high like a model working a catwalk. A sensuously soft voice emerged from the mask. "Hello Henry. It's an honour to meet you."

Uncertainty clouded his expression, not only because she knew his name, but because of her admiring words. "Who are you?" he asked, his Adam's apple bobbing in his scrawny neck.

"I'm Natalie, of course," she said, sounding surprised that he didn't know the answer.

"Natalie?"

"There's no need to pretend, Henry. I know you feel the same connection I do."

"What connection?" asked Grace, curiosity overcoming her shock. She retreated another step as Natalie hissed at her like an angry cat.

Natalie's gaze returned to Henry. "You don't have to be afraid," she assured him. "I'm here to protect you."

Through trembling lips, he murmured, "Bael?"

"Do I look like a demon?" chuckled Natalie.

Henry scanned up and down her blood-smeared body. "Yes."

She laughed again. "I'm just someone like you." She proffered a hand, palm upwards. "Someone who's looking for–"

"Get away from him!" The hoarse shout came from Ella. She staggered towards Henry, stooped from the weight of her belly, her face scrunched in agony.

Henry let out a cry as Natalie aimed the gun at his mum.

Ella came to an abrupt stop, her cheeks blowing like she'd sprinted a hundred metres. Her usually mellow brown eyes blazed with protective fervour. "If you hurt my son, I'll kill you."

"Why would I hurt him?" Natalie asked. "We're going to be family."

"*Family?*" Ella's lips twisted as if the word tasted bitter. "You sound like her."

"Who?"

"Heloise. That's what she wanted – a new family to replace the one she murdered."

"Heloise was willing to do whatever it took to protect her home. So am I. And so too is Henry." Natalie glanced at him. "Isn't that right?"

His gaze danced between her and his mum. Guiltily lowering his eyes, he nodded.

"So you see, Ella," continued Natalie, "If I hurt Henry, I'd only be hurting myself."

The twisted logic did nothing to ease the tension from Ella's features. "This isn't Henry's home."

"Yes it is," he stated, lifting his head to look his mum in the eyes. "And it always will be."

Ella's lips parted, but she could find nothing to counter the simple truth in Henry's words.

Natalie swung the pistol towards Grace. "Get down on your knees."

Grace thrust her chin out, almost daring Natalie to pull the trigger. "Whoever you are, I'm not afraid of you."

Another malevolent hiss seethed from the witch mask.

Grace flinched, but still didn't get down on her knees. Natalie cocked the gun's hammer.

"Why are you here?" Henry asked quickly, seeking to draw her attention away from Grace.

Natalie looked at him, but kept the gun aimed at Grace. "The same reason you're here."

He frowned bemusedly. "Jacob?"

The velvety amusement returned to Natalie's voice. "You belong to your father, the Devil, and you're compelled to carry out his desires. He was a murderer from the beginning, not holding to the truth, for there is no truth in him. When he lies, he speaks his native language–"

"For he is a liar and the father of lies," Grace interrupted in a tone of revelation. Her eyes stabbed at Henry. "I was right. You murdered my sister."

He shook his head in denial yet again. "No I didn't."

"Liar!"

Grace took a couple of steps towards Henry, heedless of the gun. Natalie's finger tightened on the trigger. Quickly, almost fearfully, she lowered the gun as Ella stepped in front of it.

"Faith was your sister?" Ella said to Grace.

"Twin sister."

"Twins." Grief floated through Ella's voice. She gave a nod of understanding. "It makes me sick to admit it, but there have been times when I've wondered if…" she faltered, looking as if she was indeed about to vomit.

"If Henry was a murderer," Grace finished for her.

Anger and injury rolled across Henry's face as Ella nodded. She sought out his gaze, her eyes swimming with shame, pleading for forgiveness. "But I was wrong."

"No you weren't," put in Natalie.

Ella glared at her as if she herself was contemplating murder. She reigned in her emotions with a slow breath. "You don't know anything about my son."

"Don't I?" Looking at Henry, Natalie spoke with motherly tenderness. "I know you've always felt like you don't fit in. And that no one's ever really understood you. Not even Jacob. I'm right, aren't I?"

"Don't answer her, Henry," said Ella. "Don't play her sick game."

His gaze jerked back and forth between her and Natalie like he was the rope in a tug-o-war.

"You never have to feel that way again," Natalie continued. "Live here with me and I promise you'll never be ridiculed or judged. You can be who you truly are. We can be a happy family."

A pained yearning filled Henry's eyes. He blinked as if he'd been wrenched out of a daydream as Grace scoffed, "A family of crazed murderers. How wonderful." Pity mingled with her scorn. "It'd be funny if it wasn't so tragic."

Natalie sidestepped so that she had a clear line of sight to Grace. "Just nod," she said to Henry. "Nod and I'll shut her up permanently."

"Yes, go on, Henry," taunted Grace. "Nod and prove once and for all that you're the killer we know you are."

"Stop it." Ella's words were more of a plea than a demand. "This is not how to get justice for your sister."

"Then how *is* Faith going to get justice?"

"I don't know," Ella admitted. "Maybe it isn't possible. Maybe you just have to accept that your sister's death was no one's fault."

"No one's fault?" A bitter laugh burst from Grace. "Nice try, but we both know that's not true."

Ella's voice jumped in frustration. "My son is not a murd–" She broke off with a grimace, hunching forwards, her teeth clenched against the wild flurry of movement within her bump.

"Mum," exclaimed Henry, his eyes darting in an agony of indecision between her and the outer chalk circle.

"I know about the blood under Henry's nails," said Grace.

Ella shook her head to show that, as far as she was concerned, the blood proved nothing. "You weren't there," she gasped, struggling to control her breathing. "You don't know what it was like. Nothing made any sense."

"It makes perfect sense. Your son tortured Faith because–"

Grace was interrupted by a loud, affected yawn from Natalie. "Boooring," she groaned. "Henry, will you please just nod so I can put this lame bitch out of her misery."

His tongue flickered his across lips. His eyes flew all over the place, searching for something, anything to land on that wasn't Natalie.

"Don't be scared," she coaxed. "Have you ever killed a fly?"

Henry thought about the bluebottle he'd crushed in the café back in Walthamstow. Had it really just been that morning? It seemed like another lifetime ago now. "Yes."

"Well that's all she is – an annoying fly that needs to be squashed. We're the only ones that matter here. You, me and..." Natalie fell silent, casting a furtive glance at Ella's belly.

"Henry." Ella said his name like she was gently rousing him from sleep. "Look at me."

He somewhat reluctantly turned towards her.

She dredged up a smile. “It doesn’t matter that Faith’s blood was on your hands.”

“Honestly, Mum, I don’t know how it got there.”

Ella waved away his protestation of innocence. She spoke with little gasps between her words. “It doesn’t matter. I love you. You’re my best boy.”

“Best boy?” Henry’s voice ached with the need to believe her.

“Wow, she’s an even better liar than you, Henry,” said Natalie.

“Shut your mouth!” Ella spat at her.

A chuckle slithered through the mask. “Did I hit a nerve?”

Henry’s eyes thinned at Natalie. “Why should I listen to you?”

“Don’t listen to me.” She made a sweeping gesture. “Listen to *them.* Listen to Walter, Winifred, Heloise and all the others. They have chosen us.”

“For what? What do they want from me?”

“What do we all want?” Her tone suggested the answer was blindingly obvious. “To be loved.”

Grace motioned at the body on the sofa and said with a grimly mocking curl of her upper lip, “Oh yeah, just look at all that love.”

As if in reply, a gurgling groan slipped past the man’s lips.

“Bael!” gasped Henry.

“No, just Leon,” said Natalie, moving to snatch up the iron poker from the hearth.

A rattling cough convulsed Leon. Saliva shot through with blood bubbled out of his mask’s mouth hole.

"Tell her," Henry urged him. "Tell her who you are."

Natalie placed the tip of the poker to her lips like a silencing finger, padding to the sofa as soundlessly as a cat.

"Who... who..." croaked Leon.

"It's me," soothed Natalie.

"Nat?" There was no recrimination in the reply, only confusion. Leon dragged in enough breath to ask, "What's going on? Where am I?"

"You're dreaming."

"Dreaming?" Leon's voice was a ragged whisper. He lifted a trembling hand to wipe at his eyes. He snatched his hand back with a sharp exhalation. "There's something wrong with my face." Panic clawed at his words. "I'm bleeding!"

Natalie shushed him. "It's a dream, remember? Just a dream."

Blinking at the blood in his eyes, Leon twisted his head towards Natalie. He gave another gasp. "Your face... What happened to your face?"

She shrugged. "You tell me, babe. It's your dream not mine."

"This isn't a dream, Leon," interjected Grace. "You've been shot."

With a venomous, "*Sss!*" Natalie whirled and strode towards her, levelling the pistol at her face. Grace skittered backwards, tripping over her own feet and falling to the floor.

"Shot?" exclaimed Leon. He feebly felt at his forehead. A hoarse cry burst from him as his fingers found the bullet wound.

"Bael," Henry tried again. "I have summoned you and now you must do my bidding."

"Oh Jesus. Oh Jesus Christ." Whimpers punctuated Leon's words. "Jamie... I remember now. This... isn't... a dream."

Raising the poker overhead, Natalie ran back to Leon. He had just enough time to let out a rasping scream before the head of the poker smashed into the devil mask.

"No!" Henry cried as she lifted the poker again.

Leon's second scream was little more than a grotesquely wet whistle. The poker hurtled downwards with sufficient force to cave in his nose. Its hook tore away a chunk of cartilage as Natalie yanked it free. Leon convulsed and gagged as a third blow smashed his teeth down his throat. A fourth split his skull open like a watermelon. Blood spouted spasmodically from the fracture, spray-painting her abdomen. Leon's eyes rolled back and a deathly stillness took hold of him, but Natalie wasn't done. Unhurriedly, almost languidly, as if extracting maximum pleasure from every blow, she pummelled his face into tatters of bone and flesh.

She made to stab the poker into his eyes, but hesitated. "No, I want you to see me," she breathlessly told the corpse. "I want you to see my happiness."

"Oh no, please no, please no."

The gasped words came from Ella. She was feeling around under her coat. She withdrew her hand. Seeing the straw-coloured liquid glistening on her palm, she gave a rapid shake of her head. "No, no, no..."

Natalie dropped the poker like a child who'd lost interest in a new toy. With a giddy tremor, she said, "Your waters have broken, haven't they?"

Still shaking her head, refusing to believe it was true, Ella sank to the floor and rolled onto her side. A pool of liquid spread across the floorboards from under her.

Grace half rose and started towards her. "Oh fuck you!" she

yelled, stopping in her tracks as Natalie took aim at her once more.

Pressing a hand to the small of her back, Ella puffed her cheeks and blew out a long moan.

"Is the baby coming?" Henry asked anxiously, starting towards her.

Natalie ticked a finger at him. "Ah, ah, don't break the circle."

He hesitated, one foot hovering next to the outermost curve of chalk, his face screwed up with indecision.

Natalie squatted down beside Ella. She dipped her fingers into the amniotic fluid, sniffed them, then gave a, "Mmm," like it was sweet perfume. "It's happening." Her voice was tinged with disbelief. "It's really happening."

"No it isn't," Ella retorted through clenched teeth.

"Why deny it? Let it happen." Natalie spread her arms in exultation. "Where better for a new life to be brought into the world?"

"My baby will not be born in *this* house," Ella insisted fiercely, as if by sheer force of will she could make her words a reality. Battling to keep her breathing steady, she clambered onto her hands and knees.

Natalie placed a hand on Ella's back. "You should lie still."

"Don't fucking touch me," exploded Ella, trying to elbow her away.

Natalie swatted the blow aside, prompting Henry to add his voice to the fray. "You better not hurt my mum!"

She looked at him as if she couldn't understand how he could say such a thing. "I wouldn't hurt your mum any more than I would hurt you, Henry."

As if to prove she was telling the truth, Natalie pulled the bearskin rug across to Ella. She put her hand on Ella again, firmly manoeuvring her onto the thick brown fur. Ella rolled onto her back, pale and sweaty.

"Have the contractions started?" asked Grace.

"Yes, the sodding contractions have started," retorted Ella, arching her back. "Christ," she gasped. "It feels like I'm having one long contraction." She threw Natalie a panic-stricken look. "This isn't right. It's happening too fast."

"No, it's happening exactly as it should," said Natalie. "I have given Him two souls and now He is giving me my reward."

Two souls. Henry's eyebrow lifted curiously. Who had the second soul belonged to? The question was driven from his mind as his mum let out a discordant burst of laughter.

"You're insane," she shrieked at Natalie. "Totally insane." She turned her head towards Grace, crying out wordlessly, *Please don't let this happen.*

In response, Grace furtively slid a hand into her pocket. Natalie was too fixated on Ella to notice.

"Leave her alone!" Henry demanded as Natalie reached under Ella's knee-length coat.

"It's going to be OK, Henry," Natalie told him, pulling down Ella's maternity leggings.

"No it's not," groaned Ella, no longer resisting. Indeed, lifting her feet to make it easier for Natalie to drag the stretchy material over her trainers. "I already feel like I have to push. It was hours before I felt like this with Jacob and–" She broke off, her breath whistling through pursed lips. Wriggling frantically, she dragged up her coat and splayed her legs.

At the sight of his mum's dilated vagina, an urge to vomit hit Henry hard. Pressing a hand to his mouth, he spoke through his fingers. "Don't push, Mum."

"I *have* to!" she yelled, hunching her head forwards and scrunching her features.

"That's it." Natalie breathed encouragement. "Push, push."

Ella squeezed her eyes tight shut. "Oh go away, please go away." Her voice snagged on a sob. She jerked her head back against the bearskin, her cheeks blowing like bellows. "Slow down Zara! You're going to tear me apart."

"Don't resist it," said Natalie, her eyes wide and glittering.

With each spasm that gripped Ella, more of the viscous straw-coloured fluid gushed onto the rug. Natalie pushed her fingers through the sopping wet fur and massaged the sticky discharge into her own belly. She glanced upwards at a rumble like an approaching landslide. "I hear you!" she cried out. Her gaze returned to Ella. "The house wants to help. Open yourself up to it. Let it take the pain away."

"No." Ella's voice rose to a scream. "It's *my* pain. It's *my* baby." Her eyes snapped open and she glared at the room. "Are you listening? Do you hear me? I will give you nothing. Nothing!"

"Then it will take what it wants."

Ella confronted Natalie with an unblinking, immovable stare. "I'll die before I let you touch my baby."

Natalie nodded as if to say, *I would expect no less.*

"Don't talk like that, Mum," Henry pleaded. "You're not going to die."

"We're all going to die," said Natalie. "The only question is when."

"Shut up," he shouted at her. "Shut up or I swear to God–"

"God?" she interrupted with a snort. "Which God do you mean?"

An ear-shattering scream erupted from Ella. "She's coming out! She's coming out!" Her face sort of folded in on itself as she braced her palms against the floor. "*Gnnn... gnnnnnn...*"

"I can see the head," exclaimed Natalie, springing up and jigging from foot to foot.

Henry glanced towards the hallway as, from seemingly far away, he heard a rapid banging. Was it his dad hammering to be let out of the basement? Or was the house dancing around as excitedly as Natalie?

Ella wrenched her head from side to side, her eyes almost popping out of their sockets. "This isn't right. There's..." She strove to catch her breath. "There's something wrong. Oh Christ, the pain!"

Henry clapped his hands to his ears as another of his mum's screams tore into him. Out of the corner of his eye, he spotted Grace edging towards Natalie. The stun gun was halfway out of her pocket. In a couple of seconds, she would be within striking distance. A second after that, Natalie would be keeling over stiff with convulsions.

He gnawed his lips, torn by the sight. In his mind's eye, he saw his dad being released from the basement, he saw them battling through the storm to find a hospital, he saw himself having to endure hours of police interrogation. Infinitely worse than that, though, he saw himself returning to his life in London – the claustrophobic house, the crowded streets, the drab buildings, the airless classrooms. Every day the same. Rinse repeat. Rinse repeat. He saw it all in a blink. The future flashing before his eyes. A vision of hell on earth.

Grace was almost at Natalie's shoulder.

"Keep pushing," urged Natalie, breathing almost as rapidly as Ella.

"It's too painful," sobbed Ella. "Please make it–" She

clenched her teeth and let out a guttural groan.

The stun gun was out of Grace's pocket.

Sounding incredulous at the words coming from his own mouth, Henry yelled, "Watch out."

Natalie's eyes jerked away from the emerging baby and flew wide at the sight of Grace. Fast as a striking snake, she whipped the butt of the pistol into Grace's jaw. Grace dropped the stun gun and staggered backwards, blood coursing from her mouth. To a soundtrack of Ella's shrieks and gasps, Natalie leapt after Grace, shoved her to the floor and thrust a knee into her stomach. Grace's breath whooshed from her lungs. She futilely tried to buck off the bigger woman. Clamping her muscular thighs to Grace's narrow waist, Natalie lashed at her with the pistol. Grace flung up her hands. The wood and metal grip clattered off her forearms.

Falling into the same strangely unhurried rhythm as when she'd beaten Leon to death, Natalie slammed the pistol into Grace over and over again. Grace cried out at the crack of a breaking bone. Her right arm dropped limply onto her stomach. Natalie mercilessly lifted the pistol for another blow.

"Stop, please stop!" implored Henry.

Natalie cast him a glance. The pistol hovered over Grace for a moment longer, then Natalie lowered it and picked up the stun gun. She pressed its trigger, staring past the crackling electrodes at Grace. "Don't move a muscle or I'll stick this in your mouth and fry your insides," she warned before rising and stepping backwards.

Grace held herself as motionless as the corpse on the sofa.

Natalie gave Henry a nod of thanks as she turned towards Ella.

Cringing away from her unwanted gratitude, he looked sheepishly at Grace. He wished he hadn't when he saw the stare she was directing back at him. *Now I know,* her eyes said with cold certainty. *Now I know.*

Anxiety chased away all other emotions as Henry's gaze returned to his mum. She appeared to be too overwhelmed by labour pains to notice what was going on around her. Her eyes were glassy and unfocused. Tears and sweat glazed her face, gluing her hair to her cheeks. She was panting like an exhausted dog. The baby's excruciatingly large head was halfway out. A halo of fine blonde hair clotted with blood and mucus ringed its pale, wrinkled scalp.

"It's coming, it's coming," said Natalie, dropping to her knees between Ella's legs like a worshipper at an altar.

Ella reared up on her elbows suddenly, screaming, "I can't do this!"

"You don't need to suffer like this, Ella. Ask for my master's help. Offer yourself to Him."

"God help me."

"Your God won't help you. All your God offers is pain in this world and the next. Only my master can take this pain from you. Let Him fill you with His mercy."

Ella's head dropped back, then jerked up again. "Take your hands off me," she screeched at Natalie.

"I'm not touching you. That's your baby's head. It's almost out."

Ella's lips formed into a hyperventilating O. For a second, she seemed to bring the pain under control, then she began slamming her head against the rug as if trying to knock herself unconscious. Hollow thuds resonated around the room.

Now Henry cried, "Stop, please stop," at his mum.

She gave no sign of having heard. Scream after scream ripped from her gaping mouth. As if mimicking her, the wind leapt up to a frenzied crescendo that rattled the French doors like maracas.

Shouting to make herself heard, Natalie said, "Repeat after me – Master, help me. I put myself into your hands."

Ella pulled her knees towards her stomach, veins pulsing on her neck and forehead. She blew out a series of wheezing grunts, her face turning a suffocated purple.

"Breathe," urged Henry, tears spilling down his cheeks. "Breathe, breathe."

Pursing her lips, Ella attempted to regulate her breathing. Again, she only managed to do so for a brief moment. A spasm of agony twisting her face, she resumed banging her head against the floor.

"Say it," demanded Natalie. "Ask for His help!"

This time, Ella cried out in a breaking voice, "Master, help–"

"Don't!" broke in Grace. She repeated Ella's earlier words. "Don't play her sick game."

Natalie levelled the pistol at her. "One more word and you die."

Grace glared back at Natalie as if debating whether to put her threat to the test.

Both women's gazes returned to Ella, drawn not by a scream but by a sudden silence. Ella's entire body was rigid with strain. The muscles of her clenched jaw looked like knotted wood. She lashed out as if the pain was something she could fight off with her fists. Another guttural scream surged from her, rising and rising until it seemed almost to tear apart the air.

The baby's mucus-slimed head inched its way out, facing upwards. Frothy, bright red blood flooded from under it.

Henry gasped in horror. Was it the baby's blood or his mum's?

"No," cried Natalie, dropping the pistol and the stun gun. She supported the baby's head with one hand, frantically fumbling at its neck with the other. "No, no, no."

"Wha... what is it?" Ella slurred, drunk on agony.

"Push!"

"The baby... Is the baby..." Ella felt between her legs. She snatched her hand back with a choking sob.

"Push as hard as you can." Natalie's voice was cracking with desperation. "Push or I'll cut you open from one end to the other!"

The threat was needless. Ella was already pushing with everything she had left. Pushing, gasping, pushing, gasping, wringing every last drop of energy out of herself. Her heart was sputtering like an engine running out of fuel. She felt as if she was being split in two. None of that mattered now, though. All that mattered was pushing, pushing, down, down, harder, harder...

As Ella pushed, Natalie pulled, angling the oxygen-starved blue body upwards. A face as wrinkled as an overripe plum came into view, eyes glued shut, ears flattened, lips crusted together. A sob scraped out of Ella's dry throat as she saw what her fingers had felt – the umbilical cord was wrapped like a noose around the baby's neck.

The baby's disproportionately big head dropped forwards onto Ella's stomach. The thin, blood-slathered arms and legs flopped around as Natalie rotated the newborn, disentangling the umbilical.

Freed from its snare, the baby remained sickeningly silent and still.

"Is she..." Henry could barely bring himself to ask the

question. “Is she dead?”

“It isn’t a she.” Natalie raised one of the baby legs, exposing a shrivelled scrotum and penis. Her eyes flickering like golden flames, she hissed at Ella, “Look what you’ve done! Why couldn’t you just ask for His help? Why? Why?”

Ella was no longer listening. Her eyes were closed. One side of her mouth was drooping as if she’d suffered a stroke. Her legs had fallen so wide apart that her knees were nearly touching the floor. Blood as thick as gravy and speckled with glistening black clots was haemorrhaging from her vagina. The pearly umbilical cord snaked from the baby’s naval to the unborn placenta. The baby looked dead. Ella looked dead.

Like an astronaut taking their first steps on a new planet, Henry tentatively moved beyond the outer circle. “Mum.” His voice was toneless, uncomprehending. “Mum, open your eyes.”

Grace got to her feet and approached Ella too, keeping a wary eye on Natalie. Cradling the floppy-headed baby in the crook of her arm, Natalie retrieved the pistol and pointed it at Grace. Hands raised, palms facing outwards, Grace continued to advance.

“Mum,” persisted Henry. “Why won’t you open your eyes?”

“Because she’s dead,” sneered Natalie. Tears found their way out of her mask’s eyeholes as she spoke to the air. “I hope you can hear me, you selfish bitch. I hope you’re tortured for eternity by the knowledge that you killed your baby.”

“She’s not dead.” Henry’s voice was a monotone of denial. “She’s just tired. She’s sleeping. That’s all.”

Grace bent to feel for a pulse in Ella’s wrist. She looked up at Henry, her eyes somehow angry and sympathetic at the same time. “She’s not sleeping.”

Henry shook his head. “Mum, Mum, Mum.” His tone degenerated into a whine, like a child badgering for attention.

"Mum, Mum," Natalie mimicked contemptuously. "I thought you were special, but you're just like the rest of them. *Pathetic*." She spat the word out like an obscenity. "You don't deserve to live here. You're not worthy of this house."

She tenderly placed the baby on the rug. Her hand lingered on it for a moment, then she rose to grab Henry's shirt collar and drag him towards the billowing curtains.

He tried to twist free. "Let go of me!"

"You're not worthy," Natalie repeated, her voice booming like a fire and brimstone preacher. "You must leave this house."

Henry recoiled from her words, staggering and falling to one knee. "I am worthy. I am!"

"Then prove it." Natalie hauled him upright and thrust the pistol at him handle first.

Henry gawped at it, his expression shifting from surprise to confusion and finally, as Natalie glanced at Grace, understanding.

"Prove it." Natalie reiterated her challenge in a voice as hard as the rock the house was built on.

Slowly, hesitantly, then suddenly Henry reached out to accept the pistol.

"That's it." Natalie's tone softened encouragingly as Henry took trembling aim. "Good boy."

Finding herself staring down the barrel of the gun yet again, Grace lifted her chin and faced Henry in defiant silence.

"A soul for a soul," continued Natalie, returning to the baby. She dropped to her haunches and ever so gently cupped a hand around its head. She looked at Henry, her eyes urging, imploring, yearning. "Repeat after me – Master, help me."

A perverse smile flickered on Grace's lips as Henry said, "Master, help me."

"I put myself into your hands," went on Natalie. "I acknowledge you as my God. The one true God."

Again, Henry parroted her words.

Natalie's voice rose. "Master, I call to thee." She lowered her gaze to the baby. "A soul for a soul. That is my bargain."

Silence stretched away from her words. The pistol shook like a leaf in the wind.

"What are you waiting for?" Grace asked Henry, her voice jarringly calm. "Call to your master."

"Master, I call to thee," he obliged, discovering a sudden calm of his own. "A soul for a soul. That is my bargain."

The boom of a gunshot ricocheted around the room, somehow seeming to linger even after it had faded away.

Grace's eyes flinched down to her chest, wide with the expectation of seeing a bullet wound. Her brow knotted more in surprise than relief. There was no blood. A wet wheezing sound drew her gaze to Natalie.

A crimson line stretched from dead centre between Natalie's breasts down to her groin. With each gurgling exhalation, a fresh pulse of blood bubbled from a small hole. She gawped at Henry, her eyes shimmering with disbelief. She slowly rose to her feet and advanced towards him on legs as stiff as concrete bollards. One, two, three steps... Each movement seemed to take every ounce of will she possessed. Blood cascaded down her legs and trailed across the floorboards.

Henry held his ground, squinting at Natalie along the barrel of the pistol. His hand was steady.

Four, five, six steps...

Wheeze, gurgle, wheeze, gurgle...

Veins squirmed like green worms on Natalie's neck as she

lifted her hands.

Seven steps...

She was almost within touching distance of Henry. Her fingers flexed as if she was summoning the last of her strength to throttle him. He remained motionless, his expression unreadable. Her feet stuttered to a halt. Spreading her arms like a crucifix, she clawed in enough air to form three faltering words, "You... are... worthy."

She pitched forwards at his feet. Blood burst from her nose as her face hit the floor. The last of her breath dribbled from her, then she was silent. Henry nudged her with his foot. Nothing.

He stepped over Natalie and hurried to his mum. Blood was still oozing from her torn vagina. It reminded him of the red reservoir that had flowed from Jacob's lacerated wrists. His gaze traversed the rippled umbilical cord to the baby. His new brother's crumpled face was as ugly and beautiful as the creatures that stared out of the oil paintings.

Henry's inscrutable mask slipped and his lips wobbled. He shook his head as if annoyed with himself. "I kept my part of the bargain," he said to the walls. "Now it's your turn."

"It seems like your master isn't listening." Grace's voice was a strange brew of sadness and derision.

Paying her no heed, Henry called out, "Give me what you owe me." There was a moment of silence. "Give it me," he repeated with a petulant twist of his lips. "Give it me! You fucker, you arsehole, you wanker, you–"

He broke off from the roll call of obscenities, squinting into a gloomy corner of the room. The sound that had caught his attention came again. It was something between a squawk and a grunt. His eyes climbed the grandfather clock and fixed on a flutter of movement amidst the darkness.

The pigeon!

With a gasp of realisation, Henry sank to his knees and set aside the pistol. A stomach-churning metallic, faintly fishy, wet dog stench assaulted his nostrils as he bent over the blood-soaked rug. The baby's head lolled lifelessly as he picked it up by the shoulders. Adjusting his grip so that one hand cradled the back of its head, he parted its blue lips.

He put his lips around the baby's, pinching its nostrils shut. His cheeks puffed as he blew into its mouth. The baby's chest inflated and deflated. He blew four more breaths into it before rapidly compressing its chest ten times. He paused, searching for the slightest sign of life. The baby's limbs hung as limp as cooked spaghetti.

"That won't work," Grace said as Henry blew into the baby's mouth again. "It's been too long."

Ignoring her, he filled the baby's lungs with four more breaths before resuming the compressions.

"Henry." There was no contempt in Grace's voice now, only pity. "He's gone."

Four breaths, ten compressions, four breaths...

"That's enough." Grace reached out and tried to draw him away from the baby. His eyes flared with such fury that her hand flinched back as if she'd touched a boiling kettle.

With a sort of repulsed fascination, she watched him administer another round of CPR. The baby still showed no sign of life. Two more rounds... Three... Henry's actions were becoming increasingly forceful. With each chest compression, the baby's limbs danced about convulsively.

"That's enough," Grace repeated. "Enough!"

Hurling a cry of frustration at the baby, Henry hammered his fist against its chest with what seemed enough force to shatter its ribs. The baby's head jumped up, then dropped back.

A small clot of mucus marbled with blood slithered down its chin. As Henry lifted his fist to deliver another blow, Grace shoved him sideways. He caught her hand and dragged her to the floor with him. They rolled into the sigil in a tangle of straining limbs.

Pain seared through Grace's injured arm as she attempted to pin Henry's wrists. He wrenched a hand free and lashed it into her face. She returned the favour, clawing four bloody lines along his cheek.

"That's for my sister!" she spat. "So is this. And this. And this."

He shielded his face with his forearms as blows rained down. It was as if a dam had burst inside Grace, unleashing a torrent of rage.

Henry spotted the pistol just inside the outer circle. Grace was so lost in anger that she didn't notice him reaching for it. His hand closed around the grip. His index finger slid through the trigger guard. A punch landed flush on his nose, bouncing his head off the floorboards. For an instant he lay stunned, tears blurring his vision. Then he jerked the muzzle towards her face.

As if someone had pressed pause, Henry and Grace froze mid movement. Incredulity swirled in Grace's opal blue eyes. She made no move to stop Henry as he squirmed out from underneath her. The sound that had cut through her anger came again, rising from a low mewling to a high warbling.

She shook her head, unable to accept what her eyes were seeing even as the baby's tiny tongue vibrated between its wide-open lips. Eyes scrunched shut, the newborn kicked out legs that were already turning from blue to pink.

Henry scrambled to his brother's side. With jerky, uncoordinated movements, the baby stretched his hands out as if he wanted to be picked up. Henry took off his coat and swaddled the newborn in it. Taking care to support his brother's bobbling head, he scooped him up and cradled him against his chest.

"Hello," he murmured, stroking the baby's cheek. It had a rough, slightly scaly texture.

The baby let out another shrill cry.

Henry shushed him. "It's OK. Don't be frightened. I'm your big brother Henry."

Rediscovering her voice, Grace said, "No, do be frightened."

As if to shield his brother from her words, Henry turned his back on her. "Take no notice of her, Jacob."

"Jacob?" Grace parroted, struggling to believe her ears.

"Yes, that's his name." Henry's slow, deliberate reply dared her to say otherwise.

Her lips lifted into an uneven smile. "Oh I get it. You and your master did a swapsie." She motioned to Natalie's corpse. "You gave him her soul and he gave you back Jacob's."

Eyeing Grace coldly, Henry cuddled the baby closer. "Me and Jacob are the only ones that matter here." He repeated Natalie's words. "You're just a fly that needs to be squashed."

Grace drew in a breath, sucking back her anger. "Look, we need to put aside our feelings and get your brother to a hospital." She glanced at the umbilical cord that tethered the baby to his dead mother. "Or find some way to call for an ambulance."

"No. No hospitals. No ambulances." Henry's gaze swept around the room. "The house will look after us."

"The house?" Grace let out a burst of scathing laughter. "Is the house going to cut the umbilical cord? Will it provide milk for the baby?"

"His name's Jacob."

"OK, his name's Jacob," Grace accepted in an exasperated tone. "What about nappies? What about clothes? What about the thousand other things you need to look after Jacob? I suppose the house is just going to magic them up out of thin air, is it?"

As if her words weren't worth a moment's consideration, Henry peered down at Jacob's bawling face and soothed him in a sing-song voice, "Squashed like a fly, squashed, squashed, squashed..." He rested his cheek against his brother's forehead. Comforted by the feel of skin on skin, Jacob's cries faded to a tremulous mewling.

With a sighing shake of her head, Grace rose to her feet. "I don't know whether to feel sorry for you or to hate you. I know this, though – I'm not going to let you hurt anyone else. This insanity ends now."

She started towards the hallway, but stopped as Henry aimed the pistol at her. This time, she didn't even blink. "Do it. Pull the trigger. Add my soul to the total. It might buy you a bit of time, but that's all." Her gaze travelled over the trio of corpses. "Sooner or later, people will come looking for them and for me. And when they do, they'll take Jacob away and put you where you belong – in a padded cell."

Henry lowered the pistol and spoke with quiet certainty. "You're not going anywhere. You had your chance to leave, but now it's too late. After everything you've seen, the house can't let you go."

Laughing again, Grace rolled her eyes towards the ceiling. "Is that right? Are you going to stop me from leaving?" She spread her hands like someone inviting God to strike them down. "Go on then, stop me."

Her challenge went unanswered. Flashing Henry a look of joyless victory, she continued on her way.

"Squashed like a fly," he resumed singing, whilst playing with Jacob's tiny fingers. "Squashed, squashed, squashed..."

13

Endings

"Henry! Henry!"

Adam yelled and hammered at the trapdoor until his voice was hoarse and his knuckles were bleeding. He slumped to the cold stone steps, resting his forehead on his hand. His teeth rattled as the dank air cooled his sweat. He turned on his phone's torch and looked dazedly around himself. *Am I really here?* his eyes seemed to ask as he took in the algae-slimed walls and flooded flagstones.

Yes, answered the throbbing lump where the back of his head had slammed into the steps, *you're really here.*

At least Walter Lewarne's mirror wasn't here too. Although if it had been, he would have derived great pleasure from smashing the fucking thing into a million pieces. Hopefully someone had already taken it upon themselves to do the job for him.

His gaze came to rest on the collapsed section of wall. The hole looked bigger than he remembered. Clear water was flowing from it. The water level wasn't far from its lower rim. What if the storm didn't abate soon? What if it worsened? Would the water eventually rise high enough to drown him?

His heart squeezed, not at the possibility of drowning,

but at the thought that he might not live to see his baby girl come into the world. "Zara," he murmured. His new beginning. His second chance at getting fatherhood right. No one and nothing was going to take that away from him. Not Henry. And definitely not this bastard house.

With renewed vigour, heedless of his skinned knuckles, he pounded his fists against the trapdoor. After a futile explosion of energy, his arms gave up on him again. He threw himself down and lay sprawled across the steps like a boxer out for the count.

Minutes, or maybe hours, crawled by. You could never quite tell with this house. It had a way of distorting time. In fact, it had a way of distorting just about everything, like a hallucinogen that could open the door to Heaven or Hell. His mind spooled back to the first time Ella and he had visited the house, their wild lovemaking on Walter Lewarne's bed after months of grief-stricken celibacy. He'd been convinced at the time that Fenton House was the new beginning they so desperately needed. He couldn't have been more wrong. This wasn't a place for new beginnings. It was a graveyard for the living.

"Adam! Henry!"

The shout from above snapped him out of his reverie. He jerked upright, his heart palpitating at the muffled yet horrifyingly recognisable voice.

"Ella?" he croaked. He shook his head. No, his mind must be playing tricks on him. It couldn't possibly be her. Could it?

Maybe I should follow you down there.

Her words from the last time they'd spoken came back to him. He shook his head harder. *She wouldn't drive all this way, not in this weather, not in her condition,* he sought to reassure himself, but he knew full well what she was capable of when it came to Henry. She'd go to any lengths to protect him, even if it meant putting herself and Zara in danger.

"Ella," he shouted as loud as his raspy voice would permit.

No response. He beat his fists against the trapdoor again before despairingly turning them against his forehead. Why was Henry doing this? What had made him so cruel? Was it something to do with the way they'd raised him? He shook his head again. They'd always been careful to treat Henry and Jacob the same, yet the twins had been as different as night and day. He simply couldn't bring himself to believe that this would be happening if it had been Henry not Jacob who'd bled to death in his arms.

Why couldn't it have been Henry? Why? Why?

He shutdown his thoughts with a hard rap of his knuckles against his head. His words struggled past a lump of shame. "I'm sorry, Henry." More pleading than demanding, he called out, "Open the trapdoor. I'm not angry with you anymore. I don't blame you for hating me. All I'm asking for is a chance. Just one more chance to... to..."

He trailed off into resigned silence. What was the point? No matter how many chances Henry gave him, things wouldn't change between them. He'd tried to convince himself otherwise, but Ella's pregnancy had exposed the bitter truth. Upon learning that he was going to be a father again, six words had rung out in his head, the same six words that had haunted him since Jacob's death – *It was an accident, Dad. Honest.* He'd realised right then that he would never be able to trust Henry around the baby. He'd put on a happy face when they sat Henry down to tell him they were expecting a new addition to the family, but inside he'd never hated anyone as much as he hated himself at that moment.

"Zara," he breathed, lowering his head. The name rang hollow in his ears. Ella was right, it didn't fit. The baby didn't represent a new beginning, she represented an ending.

He closed his eyes, listening to the water gushing into the basement. He heaved a sigh as heavy as his heart. Maybe it would be for the best if he died down here. Perhaps then, without all his baggage holding her back, Zara *would* have a chance to live up to her name.

Grief, anger, guilt, shame, grief, anger… His emotions were like a wheel of fortune. Where would it stop next?

An image popped into his mind of Henry and Grace prancing around a chalk circle whilst chanting, *Adonai, Azla, Tzaboth, Tetragrammaton.*

The sound of his own laughter bouncing off the walls startled him. How did anyone take that nonsense seriously?

He sprang up, banging his head on the trapdoor as a blood-curdling scream penetrated the floorboards. "Ella!" he cried out as scream followed scream. He knew with sickening certainty that it was her. He'd heard her like that once before – the day the twins were born. Panic injected fresh strength into him. He attacked the trapdoor with his hands, elbows and shoulders.

Waves of screams assaulted his eardrums, rising and falling, rising and falling, then only rising until it sounded like Ella was being tortured to death.

Feverish with desperation, he raked his fingernails along the gouges George and Sofia Trehearne had inflicted on the trapdoor. "Let me out!" he bellowed, oblivious to his fingernails breaking and peeling back. "Let me out!"

His shouts degenerated into helpless, gasping sobs. He wanted to clamp his palms to his ears and shut out the terrible cacophony. At the same time, he clung to the screams because silence could mean something even worse.

Almost incoherent with rage, he bellowed, "Henry, open this trapdoor or I'll break every bone in your body. I swear it on your brother's grave!"

The basement flung his threat back at him like a mocking impression. With a roar, he launched himself at the trapdoor. His head crunched into it hard enough to set his ears ringing. He staggered backwards. The next thing he knew, he was tumbling down the steps and splashing into the icy water. The shock of it washed away his panic. He clambered back onto the steps and hauled in a shaky yet calmer breath.

Think! he commanded himself. *There are secret passageways, false walls and hidden doors all over this place. Maybe there's more than one way out of here.*

His gaze returned to the water gurgling from the hole. If it was rainwater draining through the foundations, maybe the tunnel led up through some structural fault to the surface. A tingle of claustrophobia crawled over him at the thought of trying to find out if that was the case. He lowered himself back into the waist-high water and sloshed around the basement, rapping his knuckles against the walls. One after another, the granite blocks produced a solid *thunk*.

No false walls. No hidden doorways. Just the immovable trapdoor and... He peered into the hole. The tunnel did indeed slope upwards. He measured its width against his shoulders. It would be a tight fit.

He ran a finger over the smooth, slightly rippled tunnel walls. His nose wrinkled at the sticky slime on his fingertip. What was it? Some sort of bacteria? Ectoplasm? He'd explored both possibilities in his book, speculating tongue-in-cheek that the spring water acted as a 'supernatural energy drink' for the house. The slime was thus a waste product – a sort of 'ectoplasmic piss'.

He'd given more serious consideration to the possibility that the slime was a bacterium that fed on the nutrients in running water. After publication, he'd soon come to realise the futility of trying to inject logic into the narrative. No one wanted to hear about something as banal as bacteria or Sick

Building Syndrome. They wanted ectoplasm, evil spirits and all the rest of that crap.

With trembling fingers, he took off his coat and dropped it into the water. He ducked into the hole, his arms outstretched in front of him. He angled his phone to illuminate the tunnel, keeping it above the water with difficulty. The throat of stone stretched away into impenetrable blackness. Another bout of screaming propelled him forwards. He spluttered and blinked as water bubbled up into his face.

The strangely spongy walls tightened and loosened against him as if they were part of a living entity. A strong sulphurous smell stung his throat. Fighting an urge to retch, he wriggled and writhed his way onwards.

How far had he come? Ten metres? Fifteen? It was difficult to tell. There wasn't enough room to look back. The tunnel was still rising with no end in sight. The water flowing under him was glacially cold. He gritted his teeth, futilely trying to keep them from chattering. His hands were so numb he could barely hold the phone.

A few metres further on, the tunnel levelled out. Was this the top of the incline? Like a tapeworm inching into its host's intestines, he squirmed onto the flat stretch of rock. After a short distance, the tunnel angled downwards. He swept his phone's pale light along the roof. Water dripped from the rock like milk being strained through muslin. There were no visible cracks or fissures.

He lay shivering with uncertainty. Did he really want to go deeper into... into wherever the tunnel was leading him? What if it was a dead end? Would he be able to crawl backwards up the slope? His stomach clenched into a sick knot at the possibility of getting stuck. But what option was there other than to press on? Returning to the basement would be as good as abandoning Ella to her fate. He closed his eyes, picturing her loose brown curls, her soft caramel-eyes, her quirky lopsided smile. Holding onto the image, he edged towards the downward slope.

He gasped as, with convulsive suddenness, the slimy walls contracted around him. His heart thundered against his ribs. He was stuck like a lump of half-chewed meat in a throat. The walls seemed to pinch tighter and tighter. He couldn't breathe! Was the tunnel collapsing under the weight of all the rain? Oh Christ, he was being crushed alive!

He twisted his body, frantically attempting to corkscrew himself free. Sharp nodules of rock tore his t-shirt and the skin underneath. The pain barely registered. Greenish-white blobs were flashing in front of his eyes. He fumbled his grip on the phone. It skittered away from him to the brink of the downward slope. He reached for it, his blood pounding like storm waves in his ears. The foul air was burning his lungs. The blobs of light were bleeding into each other. He blindly stretched and stretched. His ears popped. Suddenly they weren't pounding anymore, they were ringing. Or was the sound coming from outside his head? Was it some sort of high-pitched mechanical whine? Crushing, burning, ringing – it was an orchestra of agony. Water filled his mouth as he screamed. There was an instant, like a sharp intake of breath, then it was as if he was being lifted and carried away by the water. The sickly glow was all around him. Everything was rushing by, colour and noise, blurring and mixing. Faster, faster, faster...

Then, with equally jarring suddenness, it was over and he wasn't in the tunnel anymore. There was no more ringing in his ears or pain in his lungs. The light was still there, but now it was the white glow of a computer screen.

He sat blinking for a moment before lowering his eyes to a keyboard. He pressed a key as if afraid his finger would pass through it. A 'q' appeared onscreen. His gaze moved around the room – his room, his little study in Walthamstow with its old filing cabinet and flat-pack desk. He looked down at himself.

He was wearing faded blue jeans and a striped polo-shirt. He shook his head at the impossibility of it. He'd binned those clothes along with everything else he'd been wearing on the day Jacob died.

There was a sudden thundering of feet. The door flew open and Jacob ran into the study with his brother in hot pursuit. Jacob was flushed and breathless with laughter. Henry had on his usual serious face. He pulled at Jacob's arm, saying, "You're not allowed."

Jacob pushed him away. "Yes I am." His dark chocolate eyes swung towards Adam. "Aren't I, Dad?"

Adam's mouth opened. All that came out was a stuttering, "I-I..."

"Aye! Aye!" laughed Jacob. "You sound like a pirate."

"Dad said he wouldn't be finished until six o'clock," said Henry.

"It *is* six o'clock."

"No it's not."

"Yeah it is. Can't you even tell the time yet?" teased Jacob, jabbing his brother in the ribs.

Henry screwed his face into an exaggerated grimace. "Ow, that hurt." He looked at his dad, obviously wanting him to reprimand Jacob. When he got no response, his wince turned to an aggrieved pout.

Jacob playfully poked him again.

"Right, you're dead meat," yelled Henry, making a grab for his brother. Evading him with a squeal of delight, Jacob darted from the room. Henry gave chase. Jacob did a sharp left into their bedroom. He tried to shut the door in his brother's face, but Henry squeezed into the room.

Very slowly, Adam stood up. Not feeling his feet beneath

him, he moved onto the landing. Laughter, shouting and banging came from the twins' room. Another sound attracted his attention – someone was humming in the master-bedroom. He tentatively pushed the door open. Ella was putting on earrings at a dressing-table by the window. A black dress hugged her hourglass curves. Her face was made up for a night out. She smiled at him – a smile untainted by grief and regret. The smile he'd fallen in love with.

"How do I look?" she asked.

Again, he struggled to find his voice. He touched two fingers to his throat, searching for a pulse.

Ella frowned faintly. "Are you alright?" She rose to approach him. He stiffened as she put her hand on his. The lines between her eyes intensified. "Your hand's like ice."

He suddenly pulled her into a tight embrace, pressing his face against her neck, inhaling her scent like it was oxygen.

"What's the matter?" she asked in a tone of soft concern. She tried to look at his face, but he buried it deeper into her shoulder. "You're starting to worry me, Adam. What's going on?"

His forehead crumpled like a confused child's. How could he explain? How could anyone hope to explain this... this... whatever was happening here? He flinched at the sound of the twins crashing out of their bedroom. They charged into the master bedroom. Jacob was chasing Henry now.

"Calm down, you two," Ella admonished as Henry led his brother around the bed, hurdled over it and raced out of the room. The twins thundered down the stairs. "Someone's going to get hurt," Ella called after them.

Someone's going to get hurt. The words echoed in Adam's mind. For a heartbeat, his vision rippled like a pond in the wind. Finger by finger, he let go of Ella. He returned to the landing.

"Adam." Ella's voice was caught between puzzlement and concern.

He showed no sign of having heard her. His pupils shrinking to pin points, he peeked over the banister. He gave a start at the touch of Ella's hand on his shoulder.

"Bloody hell," she said. "You've gone as white as... well, as a sheet."

He stared mutely at her. The house was silent too. There was a charged feeling in the air, like static electricity gathering before a thunder storm. It made the hairs on his arms stand on end.

Ella seemed to feel it too. Shuddering, she said with an uneasy chuckle, "I think someone just walked over my gra–"

She broke off as a shout rang out downstairs. "I'll get you for that!"

Recovering his voice, Adam breathed, "*Jacob*."

As if a starter pistol had gone off, he lurched towards the stairway. In a single, wild bound, he leapt halfway down it. Henry hurtled across the hallway and flung the plate-glass porch door shut behind himself. Once again, Jacob was in close pursuit. He tried to pull up, but it was too late. All he could do was throw his hands up in front of his face. A split second before Jacob hit the glass, Adam crashed into him. Both of them thudded to the floor and lay in a stunned heap.

Ella dashed downstairs. "Anyone hurt?"

"I don't think so," said Adam, getting to his feet and lifting a shell-shocked Jacob with him. Ella yanked open the porch door. "What the hell are you trying to do?" she yelled at Henry. "You could have killed your brother."

He blinked shamefacedly, looking ready to burst into tears.

"Well, what have you got to say for–" Ella continued, but Adam cut her short.

"It's OK, Ella. He just wasn't thinking."

"He never bloody thinks."

"Let's just be thankful no one got hurt."

With a sigh, Ella nodded. "You're right." She treated Adam to a smile that swiftly morphed into a quizzical frown. "How did you know what was going to happen?"

"I–" Adam's voice failed him again. A burning pressure was building in his lungs. He pressed a hand to his chest, trying to exhale away the discomfort.

Jacob peered up at him with big, worried eyes. "Dad?"

His voice sounded garbled, like he was speaking under water. Adam's vision wobbled woozily. He swayed and grabbed hold of Jacob's arm.

"You're hurting me," said Jacob, trying to pull himself free.

Adam held on as if he was clinging to a cliff face. Splodges of darkness seeped in from the edges of his vision like ink on blotting paper, until all he could see was Jacob's heartbreakingly beautiful face. Then the splodges bled into each other and only blackness remained.

Adam's ears popped. There was a sensation of fluid running out of them. A barrage of choking, spluttering and gasping rushed in. It took him a moment to realise that it was the sound of his own lungs clawing at the air.

He cracked open his eyes, blinking away a blindfold of slime. Palely illuminated rock shot through with glittering serpentine swam into view a couple of metres overhead. He was lying on his back at the base of a rock wall. A thread of glutinous gunk dribbled from a hole halfway up the wall. Had the tunnel spat him out like a ball of phlegm?

He lay unable to do anything except breathe. His lungs were raw, his throat was raw, but nothing was rawer than his mind. It was as if his brain had been turned inside out and every thought was an open wound.

It had seemed so real – Ella's untainted smile, Jacob and Henry thundering around the house, himself tackling Jacob to the floor. For a moment back there, he'd almost come to believe that he'd woken from a nightmare after dozing off at his computer; that Fenton House was nothing but a phantom conjured by his unconscious mind; that Ella, the twins and he could be a complete family again.

A sob trembled from him. *Why couldn't it have been real? Why? Why?*

He sniffed back his tears. *Pack in the self-pity,* he scolded himself. *Move. Get up. Ella needs you.*

Flexing life back into his numb limbs, he twisted his head to get a better look around. His phone was lying on the floor beside him, its torchlight shimmering through a film of slime. A gasp rasped from his throat as he found himself staring into a snow-white face with empty black-ringed eyes.

A ghost! Oh Christ! It's a ghost! cried out his dazed mind. Then he saw that the unearthly face was attached to a decidedly earthly-looking body. If indeed it was a ghost, it was one that liked to dress in fashionable clothes. Neither was there anything particularly spooky about the pool of blood the body was lying in.

He shakily reached out to prod the face. Plastic. It was a mask. He lifted it away, revealing the blood-streaked face of a man in his twenties or thirties. He swallowed convulsively at the sight of the reddish-black hole in the man's cheek. Was it a bullet hole? What else could it be? But who'd shot him?

As if seeking answers, Adam's eyes darted around the rock chamber – a little pile of tools; a bulging black holdall. His mouth fell open as his gaze swept over shelf after shelf of gold bars. Surely this must be the proceeds of Walter's grim business. How many lives had it cost to amass such a fortune? Ten thousand? A hundred thousand?

The gold shone like soft sunlight. Its warm glow seemed to seep into him, chasing away his shivers. Another question inserted itself into his mind – what did it matter how many had died? The gold held no guilt for him. It only held out the possibility of freedom – freedom from work, freedom from need, the freedom to do just about anything.

His eyes eagerly roved around the rest of the vault, skipping over the iron door, interested in only one thing – counting the gold bars. Ten, twenty, thirty, forty, fifty... More than he could spend in a dozen lifetimes. He let out an oddly shrill laugh that died on his lips as his gaze landed on Walter's mirror. A different kind of icy feeling shuddered through him.

The words he'd spoken the last time he looked into the mirror rose to the surface of his mind. *I'll never forgive myself for what happened to you, Jacob. I'd give my life to be able to tell you how sorry I am. I want to say sorry to you too, Ella. From now on things will be different. I'll never let you down again.*

"I'll never let you down again," he echoed. Yet here he was making the same old mistakes, allowing himself to be seduced by visions of wealth whilst the woman he loved was in God knew what danger.

Hatred powering his limbs, he clambered to his feet and grabbed a gold bar. Raising it overhead, he staggered towards the mirror. He brought it arcing down towards his reflection.

Midway along its journey, the gold bar seemed to hit an invisible barrier. Adam whirled towards the door. There was nothing beyond its rusty bars other than a few metres of dark rock. He snatched up his phone and directed its light into the passageway. Once again, there was a look in his eyes like he was questioning whether he was awake.

He'd seen Ella. He'd seen her in the mirror, staring at him from outside the door, her face strangely devoid of expression. He'd seen her. He'd– Wrinkles of doubt spread across his forehead. Had he though? Had he really seen her? Where was she now? She couldn't have disappeared in the space of time it took him to turn towards her. She was hardly in any condition to be running around. Besides, why would she have run off? And why had she looked like she was in a trance?

He dropped the gold bar as if it was a worthless rock. "Ella," he called out, dashing to the door. The only reply was the echo of his own voice. He squeezed between the bent bars, heedless of the blood that welled from deep scratches on his chest.

Shouting for Ella, he set off at a staggering run. It occurred to him that he should be relieved to know she was alive and, despite her screams, apparently unharmed. Yet he was gripped by a fear so intense that the very air seemed to be clotted with it. He paddled wildly with his hands, feeling like he was wading through chest-high mud.

By the time he reached the trapdoor, he was gasping as if he'd run up a mountain. Step by laborious step, he dragged himself through the opening. Recognition flickered in his eyes as he peered through the hole in the staircase. He recalled the excitement he'd felt upon discovering that the house was riddled with secret passageways. It had all seemed like a big adventure at first...

He slid through the gap at the side of the staircase. The secret panel to the drawing room was open a sliver.

A burst of sharp laughter came from the direction of the living room, followed by a woman's voice. "Is that right?" The words had a ring of challenge. "Are you going to stop me from leaving? Go on then, stop me."

Was it Grace? Who was she talking to? Ella? Henry?

Fuelled by a fresh surge of adrenaline, Adam ran through the drawing room. He hurdled a fallen chair in the dining room and skirted along the table to the half-open living room door.

Wariness slowing his footsteps, he eased through the doorway. A devilish glow danced on a scene that might indeed have sprung from the bowels of Hell.

Blood. For an instant, that was all he could see. Just blood, blood and more blood. The room was a grisly rainbow of it, ranging from the lightest scarlet to the darkest burgundy.

Much of the blood had clearly originated from the man on the sofa. It looked like someone had frenziedly attacked him with a hammer. Whoever had done the deed hadn't been satisfied with merely killing him. It was as if they'd tried to obliterate every trace of who their victim had been. The hatred evident in the destroyed landscape of flesh and bone was almost palpable.

Horror and puzzlement played in Adam's eyes. Fragments of what looked to be red plastic were embedded in what was left of the man's face. Had this man worn a mask too? Had he and the man in the vault been accomplices? Had they been killed over the gold? If so, who killed them?

Oh God, please don't let it be anything to do with Henry.

As the thought stabbed at Adam, his gaze shifted to a woman sprawled on the floorboards. A pool of blood glistened in the deep valley of her bare breasts. A green witch mask covered her face.

Ghost. Witch. What next? Vampire? Mummy? And why was the woman naked? What insanity had possessed her? His thoughts returned to the vault. In some unknowable way, he could feel it throbbing away down there, deep under the house, like a ship's engine room.

His aghast eyes travelled onwards to a body spread-eagled

on the bearskin rug.

"Ella?" he murmured, taking in the waxy pale face streaked with sweaty hair.

No, it couldn't be her. It wasn't possible. He'd seen her only minutes ago at the door of the vault.

You saw her reflection, corrected a voice in his mind.

His face scrunched into a scowl. What was the difference? Mirrors only showed what was there. Right? Yes. Fucking right!

Like someone lost in darkness, he felt his way forwards with his feet. Ella's eyes were as blank as the bear's. Except it wasn't Ella lying there. It wasn't! It wasn't!

There was something between the imposter's thighs, something that sprouted like a tentacle from her bloody, torn vagina. He knew what it was. He knew and wished he didn't.

His gaze followed the pale blue, spiralling cord. It disappeared into a bundle of black material. As if he'd poked his head above water, he became aware of a plaintive mewling. A little hand encrusted with blood emerged from the bundle.

Adam closed and opened his eyes, perhaps hoping to dispel the sight. *It's not Zara,* he told himself, his face a portrait of pitiful desperation. *It's a doll. Yes, that's what it is. A doll.*

A pair of hands were cradling the doll. He recognised those hands. He'd watched them grow from being as small as the doll's hands. If he looked closer, he knew he would see a brown mole on the left hand. With infinite reluctance, his gaze climbed to Henry's face. Bleeding scratches zigzagged across Henry's cheeks. Blood was trickling from his nostrils too. Their gazes met. For once, Henry's eyes were swirling with emotion. Indeed, there were too many emotions to make sense of – surprise, fear, remorse, sadness, happiness. Anger pulsed in Adam's temples. What was there to be happy about? He clenched his fists, trembling with the urge to pummel the happiness out of Henry.

Adam shook his head. It wasn't Henry. Granted, every feature of his face was as it should be, right down to the smallest detail, but it couldn't be him. It was another imposter or an actor or... Or something... Anything... But not Henry.

Adam's voice crawled out. "Who are you?"

The boy's face creased in confusion. "I'm Henry."

"No you're not."

"Yes I am. I'm Henry."

"Stop saying that!" exploded Adam, spittle flying from his mouth.

"Please, Dad–"

"One more word." Adam raised a fist. "Say one more word and I'll shut your lying mouth."

"He's telling the truth." The voice came from over by the hallway door. It added sardonically, "For once."

Adam's eyes darted to the speaker. He let out a bleak laugh at the sight of Faith's doppelganger of a sister. She too looked like she'd been in a fight. Her lips were swollen and split. A cut straddled the bridge of her nose.

"And why should I believe you either?" he demanded to know.

"I'm the only one here who isn't a liar."

Adam resisted an urge to lower his gaze at the flat accusation in Grace's reply.

A warbling cry drew her attention to the reddish-pink hand poking out of the bundle. Her eyes returned to Adam. "I suggest you get a grip on reality because you have a baby to look after."

With a jerky movement, the tiny hand pushed aside the

folds of material. A tonsure of blood-matted blonde hair came into view followed by a squished-looking face. Granite grey eyes stared at Adam from between puffy eyelids. Saliva glistened on the baby's burbling lips.

The sight crushed Adam to his knees.

It wasn't a doll. Oh Jesus Christ, it *wasn't* a doll.

Bewilderment filled his eyes as the baby kicked its body into view. "A boy," he murmured. Almost giddy with relief, he repeated, "A boy. It's a boy!" He flashed Grace a look of wild triumph. "Ella's pregnant with a girl, so this *thing* can't be my child."

"The doctors got it wrong," said the boy who claimed to be Henry. He held the baby up in the firelight. "Look at him. He looks just like Mum."

Adam blinked as if trying to clear his vision. Splodges of white light were bobbing like will-o'-the-wisps in front of his eyes again, but they didn't obscure the fact that the baby had Ella's almond eyes and rosebud lips.

A movement from off to one side drew Adam's gaze to the painting of the toad. He fell backwards with a gasp, landing on his elbows. The grotesque creature was flexing its clawed feet as if it was about to hop right out of the gold-leaf frame.

"Dad?"

Adam's bloodshot eyes swung back to the boy. "I'm not your dad. Where are my wife and son? Tell me or I'll..." he faltered before continuing in a rasp like a saw scraping across bone, "I'll kill you."

"You don't mean that," the boy exclaimed, his voice high-pitched with shock.

"Don't I? Try me."

The boy withdrew a pistol from his trouser pocket. His

eyes apologetic and pleading, he took aim at Adam's chest. "Don't make me hurt you, Dad."

The warning fell on deaf ears. Adam was staring at the toad again. Its mouth was opening wider and wider, until its cavernous black interior filled his vision. He rose to his feet and took several steps towards the mouth as if it was sucking him in.

"Get a grip," Grace said again.

He turned to her, squinting like someone moving from darkness into light.

She pointed at the boy and the baby. "They *are* your sons." Then at the dead woman on the rug. "And *that* is your wife. How could this be faked? How? It's not possible. Even if it was, why would anyone do such a thing? Think about it. You're a writer. What's the motivation?"

"What's the motivation?" echoed Adam. His face crumpling, he repeated, "What's the motivation? What's the motivation?" A painfully pathetic rise of hope came into his voice. "You're punishing me."

"You're right," admitted Grace. "I wanted to punish you for hiding the truth. I wanted it so badly it almost drove me crazy. But not anymore." She glanced at the spread-eagled corpse. "You've been punished enough."

He shook his head again. "Ella's in London. She's waiting to hear from me. I should... I should call..." He stumbled over his words, his face twitching with the strain of holding reality at bay.

An exasperated breath whistling through her teeth, Grace marched over to Adam and grabbed his hand. He resisted, but only weakly, as she dragged him to his so-called wife. She pushed his face towards the dead woman. A cocktail of scents pummelled his senses. First there was coppery blood and sour sweat, then there was floral perfume, but underneath them all there was something musky-sweet. His throat closed around a sob. He knew that scent better than he knew his own.

"Ella." His voice was a tortured whisper. Sobs convulsing his body, he buried his face in her hair. He breathed in her scent and held it inside him for as long as his lungs would allow. Kissing her face all over, he pleaded, "Ella, can you hear me? Ella, it's me. It's Adam. Ella. Get up. Ella. Ella..." He twisted his fingers into her hair, his knuckles whitening. His head snapped up.

"Murderer," he hissed at Henry, his eyes awash with tears of rage.

Henry shook his head vehemently. "I didn't do this. Honest I didn't."

A shuddering sense of déjà vu hit Adam. The all too familiar avowal of innocence felt like nails clawing at exposed nerve endings. With a tormented cry, he lurched forwards. Grace sidestepped, barring his path to Henry and the baby. They didn't need her protection, though. Adam charged past them, crossing Bael's sigil on his way to tear the toad painting off its hook. The gold leaf frame came apart at the corners as he slammed it against the floorboards.

"Don't," cried Henry.

Ignoring him, Adam flung the broken frame into the fire. He snatched up the canvas and consigned it too to the flames. The thickly textured oil paint ignited into a fizzing, bluish-green blaze.

Clutching the bawling baby to his chest, Henry darted fearful looks around the room as if he expected Bael to exact some sort of instant revenge for the painting's destruction.

Adam's wild eyes searched for another target. An almost gleeful light flared in them as they homed in on the grandfather clock.

Rocking the baby, Henry shouted, "You're upsetting Jacob."

Adam swivelled towards him. "Jacob?"

Henry glanced at the baby. "Yes, Jacob."

Adam's eyes widened in realisation. A fit of laughter seized him. "Jacob," he repeated, his voice crackling with hysteria.

He ran to the grandfather clock, braced a foot against the wall and toppled it over. A plump grey shape took flight from behind the clock's crown of carved vines. The antique timepiece hit the floor with a clanging crash, scattering broken glass.

Adam was no longer laughing. He was watching the pigeon flap around the room. His jaw hung as slack as Ella's. That look was back in his eyes – the trapped-in-the-headlights look of someone questioning the reality of what they were seeing.

The pigeon's wings shimmered like an oily rainbow as it circled above the sigil. The fire highlighted the streaks of blood on its white neck feathers. Adam drifted towards the sigil, passing absently through the slick of blood by the sofa. Leaving a trail of tarry-looking footprints, he entered the chalk circles. "Is that the pigeon from Walthamstow?"

"Yes," said Henry.

Adam's gaze followed the pigeon as it flapped into the hallway and was swallowed by darkness. His pupils were glassy and unfocused as if he was asleep with his eyes open. "But it was dead," he mumbled as much to himself as to Henry.

"And now it's alive again." There was a certain satisfaction in Henry's reply.

"How?"

"My master brought it back to life."

Adam frowned at him. "Your master?"

"That's not true," said Grace.

"Yes it is," asserted Henry. "My master breathed life into the pigeon, the same way He breathed life into Jacob." He took hold of the umbilical cord. "This was wrapped around Jacob's neck. He wasn't breathing. Or do you deny that as well?"

"No but–"

"A soul for a soul. That was the deal."

"What deal?" asked Adam, glancing back and forth between Henry and Grace as if he couldn't decide who to believe.

Henry pointed to the masked woman. "I gave Him her and He gave us Jacob."

Adam looked at the pistol in Henry's hand, seemingly noticing it for the first time. "You killed her?"

"I *had* to." Henry's tone implored for understanding.

"Oh bullshit," Grace countered. "You're just looking for anything to blame but yourself. Faith was the same. She only saw what she wanted to see. She never took responsibility for the mess she'd made of her life."

"It's true," Adam said in apparent agreement.

Grace threw her hands wide. "Finally, you're speaking sense."

"Am I?" Adam hesitated uncertainly, then added, "Yes, I believe I am." As the last word left his mouth, he sprang forwards and snatched the pistol from Henry.

Henry let out a surprised cry. A different kind of astonishment took hold as his dad asked, "How did you do it? How did you make the..." he paused for the right word, "deal?"

"What are you doing?" asked Grace, her eyes narrowing

warily. A sour laugh slid between her lips as Adam took aim at her. "Oh you've got to be kidding me."

"Tell me how," said Adam, staring at Grace but speaking to Henry.

Silence settled over the room, disturbed only by the crackle of the fire. At long last, the storm seemed to have passed. Jacob's crying had stopped too. His broad almond eyes were closed. Saliva bubbled between his lips as his chest rose and fell steadily.

In a small, strangely hollow voice, Henry began, "Repeat after me – Master, help me."

"Master, help me," said Adam.

"I put myself into your hands. I acknowledge you as my God. The one true God."

Once again, Adam parroted the words.

Grace jerked her chin at Ella's corpse. "This won't bring her back."

"I can't know that unless I try," said Adam, his expression a muddle of apology and threat.

"Master, I call to thee," said Henry. "A soul for a soul. That is my bargain."

"Master, I call to thee," resumed Adam.

"You're going to lose everything you have left," said Grace, a tremor edging into her voice.

"A soul for a soul!" Adam shouted her down. The pistol was shaking in his hand. He tried to steady it with his other hand, but the shaking only intensified. His teeth were chattering like he was back in the icy water of the basement. One by one, he forced the required words between them. "That. Is. My. Bargain."

On the final word, Grace flung up her hands as if they could stop a bullet. When the gunshot didn't come, she slowly lowered her hands.

Adam's face was frozen into a rigor-mortis-like grimace. A sob built in his chest and trembled up his throat before bursting from him. "I'm sorry, Ella." He sank to his knees. "I can't do it."

Grace subjected him to a look that was part pity, part contempt. She motioned to Henry. "That's because you're not a psychopath like him. You're just a coward."

"You're right." Adam's voice was drowning in self-loathing. "I'm a coward. I'm weak. I'm–"

He broke off as, extending a hand, Henry said, "Give me the gun, Dad."

Adam shuddered at his son's calm request. Torn with indecision, he looked back and forth between Henry and Grace.

"You know, don't you, that it's not my soul the Devil wants, it's yours?" she said. "Give him the gun and he's got you. He'll use you until he doesn't need you anymore and then..." Her eyes travelled meaningfully over the corpses littering the room.

"She's talking rubbish, Dad," said Henry. "I love you, and I love Jacob, and I love Mum. I want us all to be happy here. We can still be happy here. You just have to trust me." Holding his dad's gaze, he added like an accusation, "*For once*."

"Trust you?" Adam repeated as if trying to work out what that meant. Shame dragged his eyes down as he slid the pistol into his trouser pocket. "I'm sorry, Henry."

"Don't be." There was no hint of annoyance in Henry's reply. "It makes no difference anyway. The house won't let her leave." He looked searchingly at Grace. "You know I'm right. I can see it in your eyes."

She returned his stare. "You know what I see in *your* eyes, Henry? Lies, lies and more lies."

The baby mewled and kicked out in his sleep. Henry softly shushed him, then said to Grace, "You should stay with us." He gestured towards the French doors. "What have you got to go back to out there that's so great?" A sarcastic edge came into his voice. "Oh yeah, I know, a flat full of mirrors."

"Not for much longer," she fired back. "I'm getting rid of them." With a crooked smile, she added, "Tell you what, Henry, you can have them. You could dress up like your mum and make-believe she's still alive."

Henry shook his head to show that her taunts had lost their power. "Jacob needs a real mum, not a make-believe one."

"Are you seriously suggesting I could be his mum?" Grace asked with a gasp of incredulous laughter. "Now I *know* you're insane."

"You should listen to him," said Adam. "He knows what he's talking about." His voice dropped as if he didn't want the walls to overhear him. "*It* won't let you leave."

Grace gave him another look of pitying contempt. "So a pigeon comes back to life like a shitty magic trick, and now you're ready to believe anything Henry tells you?"

"It's not only the pigeon." Adam pointed at the floor. "I saw Ella *down there.*"

"Down where?" scoffed Grace. "In Hell?"

"Laugh all you want, but I'm telling you, I saw her in the mirror."

"You mean Walter's mirror?" Henry asked eagerly.

"Yes."

Henry drew in a deep breath, closing his eyes and enjoying a moment of quiet celebration. Then, motioning to Grace, he said to his dad, "That means we don't need her. The mirror is..." He searched for the right description. "It's our doorway to Mum."

"Doorway to a living hell, more like," said Grace.

Henry glanced at her as if to say, *Are you still here?*

Grace's gaze lingered on Adam, but his face remained grimly resolute. With a sighing shake of her head, she turned her back on him. "Enjoy your madhouse," she threw over her shoulder as she headed for the front door.

"Stay with Jacob," Adam told Henry, setting off in pursuit of her.

Henry nuzzled the baby's head. "Did you hear that? He called you Jacob."

His eyes sleepy slits, Jacob gurgled as if in approval.

"What are you going to do?" Adam asked as Grace opened the bolt-studded door. A jolt of surprise went through him at the steely blue light that slunk into the hallway. Somehow it didn't seem right that the night was coming to an end. Or indeed that, after everything he'd witnessed, it could ever be day again.

"What you mean is, am I going to the police?" she replied, rustling through a drift of leaves in the porch. "You'll just have to wait and see, won't you? Perhaps I'll write a book of my own about Fenton House. I reckon it would be a bestseller and I could do with the money."

Adam's face was a mass of ticks and twitches as he tried to work out if Grace was being serious. "Gold," he spluttered. "There's a room full of gold under this house. You can take as much as you want."

She stopped and looked at him. For a second, she seemed to mull over his offer, then a small smile played across her lips. "Thanks, but you can keep your gold and I'll keep my soul."

With an exaggerated movement, she stepped one foot out of the porch, then the other. She arched an eyebrow at Adam as if to say, *Well, I'm still alive.*

She continued on her way towards her car, crunching wet gravel underfoot. Adam blinked as a salty breeze stung his eyes. A thread of pink was splitting the horizon. The cloudless sky looked washed clean. Leaves and branches were strewn across the garden. The grass was glistening like a newborn baby.

With her face bathed in watery light, Grace too looked oddly renewed. Inhaling a lungful of the crisp air, she eyed the brightening sky. "Looks like it's going to be a beautiful day." Her gaze strayed over Adam's shoulder into the house. "Good luck with keeping your master happy. You're going to need–"

She broke off, her eyes springing wide. A blur of grey whooshed past Adam, skimming his head as it arrowed towards Grace. She flung up her hands, but she wasn't fast enough to prevent the pigeon from crashing into her face. She staggered backwards, crying out as the bird sank its claws into her cheeks and stabbed its beak at her eyes. Flailing at the frenziedly flapping creature, she managed to knock it away. Amidst a swirl of feathers, it dive bombed her. Its flashing beak found its mark. She screamed as blood streamed from one of her eyes.

Horrified, entranced, Adam watched the pigeon gouge deeper into Grace's eyeball. She tore it off her face and hurled it away from her. It righted itself mid-air, spreading its wings for another swooping attack. Half-blinded, she thrust her hands out to keep it at bay. For a heartbeat, the bizarre combatants were framed, like a painting, against the backdrop of rolling cliffs and choppy sea. Then a thunderous *CRACK* split the air. Adam's gaze jerked towards the sky as if he expected to see it shattering into pieces.

A rumbling tremor raced down the walls. A heartbeat

later, a deluge of stone blocks and slate tiles blotted out the sky. Grace let rip a scream that was silenced in the same instant it left her mouth as falling debris enveloped her. One second she was there, the next, like a vanishing act, she was gone.

Squinting against the dust kicked up by the thunderous impact, Adam edged out of the porch and tilted his head back. Where the tower had once been, there was only a jagged stub. Chunks of granite teetered at seemingly impossible angles, ready to come crashing down at the slightest provocation. There was a gaping hole in the roof below the broken tower.

His gaze returned to the mound of rubble. "Grace?" he said without enthusiasm, like someone fulfilling an unwanted obligation.

Silence.

There was no sign of the pigeon either. Was it entombed with her? Did it matter?

"Dad," Henry shouted to him. "What happened?"

Adam didn't reply. He stared at the grim cairn for a moment more. Nothing moved except the settling dust. He turned to go back into the house. The entrance hall's ceiling was cracked in several places. Plaster dust frosted the stairs.

Instead of returning to the living room, he headed into the secret passageways and descended through the trapdoor. Seams of serpentine sparkled like strip lights illuminating a path to... To what? Heaven? Hell?

Upon reaching the vault, he didn't afford the gold or the corpse a glance. The only thing he had eyes for was the mirror. His fingers trailing over its shining surface, he filled his lungs with the faintly sulphurous air emanating from the hole in the wall. "Come back to me, Ella," he murmured. "Come back and haunt me. Haunt me. Haunt me. Haunt me..."

14

Beginnings

Ranks of empty chairs marched along either side of a central aisle. A couple of metres beyond the front row, a simple pine coffin rested atop a plinth. Red roses festooned the coffin, perfuming the air with their sweet scent. Within a stone arch, long rippled curtains partitioned the chapel from the furnace that the coffin would soon slide into. A tall crucifix and wall-mounted speakers flanked the arch. Sunlight flooded through rectangular windows that ran the length of the chapel. Outside, a lawn mown into perfect stripes sloped down towards a wooded valley.

A vicar in a black cassock and white surplice with a purple stole draped over his shoulders was addressing the chapel from a lectern. The vicar's bald head and puffy pink face gave him the look of an overgrown baby. His softly spoken voice was on the verge of being drowned out by the wails that relentlessly echoed around the room.

The vicar's gaze alternated between his sermon notes and his small audience. To the left-hand side of the aisle only two chairs were occupied – one by a skinny, po-faced teenager in baggy black trousers and an equally ill-fitting white shirt; the other by a black-suited man cradling a baby that was showing off an ear-shatteringly healthy pair of lungs.

Adam's eyes exhibited the broken veins and thousand-yard stare of someone who hadn't slept properly in days. He was attempting to insert an ice-blue teething-ring between Jacob's quivering lips. In response, the baby kept twisting his head from side to side. With each warbling cry, Jacob's lips peeled back from swollen gums, revealing several teeth cutting through at once.

Catching the teenager's gaze, the vicar spoke in a reassuringly gentle tone. "Death will be no more. Mourning and crying and pain will be no more, for the first things have passed away."

Henry greeted the words with a surly stare.

The vicar blinked away from him to the opposite side of the aisle, where once again only two of the front chairs were occupied. Ella's parents also looked as if sleep had been a stranger to them for days. Linda's frazzled grey hair and haggard face painted a portrait of crippling loss. She was wiping her eyes with a tear-drenched tissue. Richard's rigid posture and clenched features spoke of someone just about keeping their emotions in check. His cheeks were as angrily red as Jacob's. He was doling out a steady supply of tissues to his distraught wife.

As if enthused by their display of grief, the vicar lifted up his voice. "And the one who was seated on the throne said, 'See, I am making all things new.' Also he said, 'Write this, for these words are trustworthy and true.' Then he said to me, 'It is done! I am the Alpha and the Omega, the beginning and the end.'"

End. The vicar emphasised the word, wrenching a sob from Linda. She buried her face in a handful of tissues. Seemingly not knowing what else to do, Richard attempted to press another tissue into her hands. Like the baby with its teething-ring, she turned her face away and sobbed all the louder.

The vicar's benevolent gaze shifted to a forty-something woman with dark, bobbed hair sitting on her own in the back row. He frowned faintly. The woman was scrutinising the other funeral-goers. She had the air of a predator sizing up her prey. How had she come to be here? This was a closed funeral. The deceased's husband had issued strict instructions that, besides the children and himself, only her parents were to be admitted to the service.

"To the thirsty I will give water as a gift from the spring of the water of life," the vicar continued, his gaze circling back to the teenager's unblinking eyes. "Those who conquer will inherit these things, and I… I…" He stumbled over his words. Why was the boy staring at him like that? It made him feel oddly naked.

Jacob's wails ratcheted up to a volume that seemed loud enough to wake the coffin's occupant. Adam yawned. Even with the baby howling in his face, he looked ready to nod off.

Catching her sobs in her throat, Linda rose to cross the aisle.

"What are you doing?" Richard said in a disapproving whisper.

Paying him no notice, she held out her hands towards Jacob. "Give him to me. I'll take him outside."

Adam looked at her blearily. She kept her eyes on Jacob, unable to bring herself to meet Adam's gaze. An uncomfortable moment passed. Her voice trembling with pained eagerness, she repeated, "I'll take him outside."

"You won't be able to stop him crying, Grandma," Henry informed her.

She dredged up a thin smile and said with a touch of sarcasm, "It might surprise you to know that I've had a lot of experience with settling babies, yourself included."

"It won't make any difference." There was a certainty bordering on arrogance in Henry's reply.

"He's right," Adam backed him up, releasing a weary sigh.

Linda remained where she was, her hands stubbornly outstretched. Her eyes somehow pleading and aggrieved at the same time, she forced herself to look at Adam. He stared back, his own eyes devoid of grief, devoid of guilt, devoid of sympathy, devoid of anything except exhaustion.

The vicar cleared his throat.

"Linda," Richard said insistently, half-rising to catch hold of her arm. As he drew her back to her seat, his gaze passed over Adam. For a second, his mask of control threatened to slip. His lips tightened into trembling lines and something that could only be hate flickered in his watery eyes.

Too tired to notice or care, Adam resumed rocking Jacob.

"Those who conquer will inherit these things," repeated the vicar, his rapid speech betraying an eagerness to get the ceremony over with, "and I will be their God and they will be my children." He paused a breath to let the words sink in before continuing, "It is now almost time for us to leave this place, but before we do Ella's eldest son, Henry, would like to say a few words."

Adam threw Henry a surprised look. It was news to him that Henry had made any such arrangement. His eyes fixed on his shoes, Henry unfolded his gangly limbs from his chair and approached the lectern. Smiling sympathetically, the vicar stepped aside. Henry took a scrunched-up piece of paper from his trouser pocket and smoothed it out on the lectern. He stared at it for an extended moment, red splotches mottling his cheeks as he worked up the courage to speak.

The woman in the back row leaned forwards, listening intently as Henry began in a low, nervous voice, "Now we see things imperfectly, like puzzling reflections in a mirror, but then we will see everything with perfect clarity. All that I know now is partial and incomplete, but then I will know everything completely, just as my *master*…" The word jumped with jarring shrillness from his mouth. The red on his cheeks intensified. He stood silent for another moment, shifting awkwardly from foot to foot, before regaining enough composure to finish the reading. "My master now knows me completely."

The woman settled back in her chair, her forehead puckered, quietly repeating Henry's words to herself like someone trying to solve a riddle. Richard and Linda were frowning too, clearly unsure what to make of the reading. Something closer to relief was flickering in Adam's eyes.

Doggedly staring at the floor, Henry shoved the sheet of paper into his pocket and slouched back to his seat.

The vicar took up his position behind the lectern again. "Erm, yes. Thank you for that, erm, poignant reading from Corinthians," he said unconvincingly. "Forgive me for splitting hairs, but the correct quote is, 'Just as *God* now knows me completely.' It is indeed an apt message to finish on. For those of us bound to this physical life, the mirror shows only our own reflection. For Ella the veil has dropped away. She is with God now. At peace."

Bowing his head, the vicar solemnly approached the coffin. Tinny organ music blared from the wall-mounted speakers. With an electronic whirr, a pair of curtains slowly closed in front of the coffin. A hoarse sob escaped Richard as he finally lost his self-control. Even before the coffin was hidden from view, Adam was rising to his feet. Cushioning Jacob's head against his shoulder, he headed for double doors at the opposite end of the chapel.

Casting a sheepish glance at his grandparents, Henry trailed after his dad. Linda was weeping into a tissue again, so immersed in her grief that she didn't notice the slightly premature departure of Adam and her grandsons. Richard glared after Adam, scowling so fiercely that he appeared to be on the brink of attacking him. His anger turned to anguished longing as he caught sight of Jacob's chubby, tear-stained face.

The woman in the rear row also watched Adam and Henry as if waiting for the right moment to pounce, but there was no anger in her eyes, only curiosity. "Sorry for your loss," she said in a soft Cornish brogue. Her perfunctory, yet somehow deeply personal manner seemed to suggest that she was either confused or trying to confuse them about her intentions.

Adam stared straight ahead, refusing to acknowledge her presence. Henry's gaze was locked on his feet again.

Adam's step faltered as the curtains met behind him with a click. He made to look over his shoulder, but stopped mid-motion. For several seconds, he stood stock-still, stooped as if the baby was weighing him down. Then, with a sudden urgency, he pushed through the doors onto a veranda shadowed by a vaulted roof. Exhaling like he was clearing something noxious from his lungs, he made for a small carpark.

Henry followed close behind again, but turned at the sound of voices. His grandparents and the dark-haired woman were emerging from the chapel. The woman reached to lay a commiserating hand on Linda's arm. Richard was several paces ahead of them, his expression as ominous as a black cloud. Henry sucked his upper lip uneasily. From the way all three of them were looking at his dad and Jacob, it didn't take a genius to guess what they were talking about.

Richard broke away from the women, striding towards the carpark.

"Please, Richard, don't, not here," Linda called after him.

His shoes slapping the block-paved driveway, Richard homed in on his son-in-law.

“Dad,” said Henry.

Adam looked over his shoulder at the warning in Henry’s voice. Seeing Richard, he heaved a sigh and passed Jacob to Henry.

“Shh,” soothed Henry, cuddling the bawling baby.

“I want a word with you,” barked Richard.

Adam stepped forwards to meet him. “There’s nothing left to say, Richard.”

“Nothing left to say? Nothing left to bloody say?” he spluttered. “My daughter is dead!”

Adam gave another heavy sigh at this statement of the obvious.

Richard’s face quivered, caught between horror and bewilderment. “Soulless. That’s what you are.” He threw a glance at Henry. “No wonder Henry’s like he is.”

Adam pursed his lips, holding in his own anger as Richard continued to rant, “If you really loved Ella, you’d have had her laid to rest in Walthamstow with all her family and friends there to say goodbye.”

“I love Ella more than you’ll ever know.” Adam’s voice was calm, but with an undercurrent of barely contained emotion.

“Oh do you now,” Richard retorted dismissively. He jabbed a finger at Adam. “You were never good enough for her.”

An ironic smile touched Adam’s lips. “On that we both agree.”

Richard glanced at Henry and Jacob. “You don’t deserve these kids either. You’re not fit to be a father.”

“You promised you wouldn’t do this today, Richard,” remonstrated Linda, coming up behind him with the uninvited woman.

Richard looked apologetically at his wife. "I know, love, but when I think about what he's done–"

"And what exactly have I done?" interrupted Adam.

Richard squinted at him as if wondering whether he was for real. "You know damn well. If it wasn't for you, Ella would never have stepped foot inside that bloody house and she'd still... she'd still be–" His voice cracked at the thought of what might have been.

Seizing on the gap in conversation, the keen-eyed woman extended a hand to Adam. "Hello, Mr Piper."

He glanced at her hand, but made no move to accept it. "Hello, Detective Sergeant Holman." The dryness of his tone seemed to suggest that he wasn't fooled for a second by the policewoman's polite manner. "I didn't expect to see you here. Thank you for coming."

Penny raised an eyebrow, obviously about as convinced of his sincerity as he was of hers. "I wanted to offer my condolences and pay my final respects. Your wife was a lovely woman."

"Yes, she was." Adam's words were carefully chosen.

Like old enemies trying to psych each other out, their gazes remained locked for a moment. Penny looked past Adam. "Hello Henry. I'm sorry for your loss." For the first time, her voice betrayed a forced note.

Henry avoided eye contact.

Undeterred by his pouting silence, Penny continued, "That was an *interesting* reading you gave."

The ambiguous remark elicited an indifferent grunt from Henry. He scuffed a foot at the tarmac in apparent boredom.

She stooped to catch his eye. "'My master,'" she quoted. "Who's your master?"

Before Henry could reply, Adam put in, "I'm sorry, but we have to get going. Jacob's tired out."

"Jacob." Penny's lips curved into what looked to be a genuine smile. "I heard that's what you'd named him. Was it Ella's idea?"

"It was mine," Henry said with a challenge in his voice. He eyeballed her through his fringe, daring her to doubt him.

"Well I think it's a great idea. It's important not to forget the past."

Henry's eyes narrowed at the loaded words.

Penny reached a finger towards Jacob's rosy face, cooing, "Hello, Jacob."

Very deliberately, Henry took a step backwards beyond her reach.

Her smile took on a fixed quality. "You've shot up since I last saw you, Henry. How old are you now?"

"He's fourteen," Adam answered for him.

"Fourteen," echoed Penny, pushing her lips out in thought. "I remember being that age. So many changes happening so fast. It's difficult enough to deal with all that stuff, never mind everything else you've been through. I honestly don't think I'd have been able to cope, but you..." She gave an ambiguous shake of her head. "You just seem to take it all in your stride."

"OK, enough." All pretence of politeness had deserted Adam's voice. "No more games. Frankly, Detective Holman, you can stick your insinuations where the sun don't shine."

Penny responded with a wry nod that said, *Fair enough.* "Before you go, Mr Piper, I'd appreciate it if we could have a brief word in private."

"You never give up, do you?" Adam said with a jaded laugh. He jutted his chin at Penny. "Get this through your thick skull, my son and I have nothing more to say to you. From now on, any contact you have with us will be through a solicitor. Do I make myself–"

He broke off, his forehead knotting as Penny held up a photo.

"Do you know who this is?" she asked.

"Don't answer that," Adam said to Henry. He glowered at Penny. "More games?"

Shaking her head, she traced a nail around the young woman in the photo. "Take a good look, please."

Adam exhaled sharply, then scrutinised the photo. A glimmer of uncertainty crossed his features. He looked at Penny as if he suspected a trick. She stared back, pokerfaced. "OK," he said, gesturing to the far side of the carpark.

Taking his meaning, the policewoman started towards the indicated spot.

Adam's gaze moved over Richard and Linda before landing on Henry. "Will you be OK?"

Henry nodded.

Adam followed Penny. When they were out of earshot of the others, he said, "You've got one minute."

She held up the photo again.

"That isn't Faith Gooden," said Adam.

Her eyes tracking every movement of his face, Penny asked, "How can you tell?"

"Just something about her expression. It isn't as…" He paused, trying to find the word he wanted.

"Haunted?" offered Penny.

The provocative suggestion drew a soft laugh from Adam. "Who is she?"

"Isn't it obvious? She's Faith's twin sister. Her name's Grace Gooden."

Adam was careful to lift his eyebrows a little, but not too much. "I didn't know Faith had a twin."

Her business-like tone giving no indication as to whether she believed him, Penny said, "On the night your wife died, traffic cameras captured Grace's car travelling west on the A30 near Redruth. Where do you think she was going?"

"How should I know?" Adam's gaze strayed beyond the policewoman. Richard and Linda were moving in to flank Henry. Linda stooped towards Jacob. A note of impatience came into his voice. "Get to the point."

"Neither Grace nor her car have been seen since then. I just wondered–"

"Wondered what?" cut in Adam, watching Linda lift Jacob from Henry's arms. "Whether she was on her way to Fenton House?"

"You have to admit, it's a hell of a coincidence."

"So what? They say life's full of coincidences, but who knows, perhaps there's no such thing."

"Meaning?"

"Meaning I don't have an answer for you. That was also the night of the worst storm to hit Cornwall in years. Grace Gooden's car is probably in a ditch somewhere with her inside it."

"We've been searching the area where she was last seen. Nothing so far."

Penny's last few words were spoken to Adam's back as he strode towards Linda and Jacob. Linda was pacing back and forth, rocking her grandson in her arms. Her attempt to settle him down was having the opposite effect. Jacob's screams cut through Adam like a wire through cheese. Richard stepped in front of Adam.

"Get out of my way." Adam's voice was a low growl.

Holding his ground, Richard called to Penny, "Detective Sergeant Holman, this child is in severe distress." He gestured to Jacob. "For his safety, I demand that you remove him from the care of this *person*," he spat the last word at Adam.

"Jacob's distressed because you're upsetting him," retorted Adam. "Now move or I'll call the police."

Blanking him, Richard looked expectantly at Penny.

"I suggest you do as he says," she told him.

"Do as he says? Do as he bloody says?" exclaimed Richard, not budging an inch. "That bastard killed my daughter and now he's taking our grandchildren away from us."

"A major obstetric haemorrhage," countered Adam. "That's what the coroner said killed Ella."

Richard snorted. "I couldn't care less what the coroner said."

Adam threw up his hands in exasperation. "Why would I hurt Ella? I need her. The children need her."

"*You* killed her," Richard said intractably. "Maybe you didn't strangle the life out of her with your own hands, but you might as well have. Go on, deny it." He made a bitterly triumphant sound as Adam's eyes fell away from his. He glanced at Henry, wrinkling his nose as if his grandson was some repulsive insect. "You two can live in that vile house till it falls down around your ears for all I care, but I won't let you put Jacob in danger."

Fury sparked in Adam's eyes. He opened his mouth to fire off a retort, but thought better of it as Penny stepped into his field of vision.

"I understand how you feel," she said to Richard. "But the fact is, without proof that Jacob's welfare is at risk there's nothing I can do."

Richard's florid jowls trembled as tears threatened to escape his eyes again. Adam dodged around him suddenly and strode towards Linda. She hugged Jacob tightly to herself, eyeing Adam like he was about to mug her. He stretched out his hands and made a gentle appeal. "Please, Linda, I need to get Jacob home."

Her eyes shone with reluctance. "Home where?"

"You know where."

"But why?" Linda shook her head in bewilderment. "Why does it have to be there? How can you stand to even set eyes on that house after everything that's happened there?"

Adam glanced meaningfully at Henry. "It's not the only house with bad memories."

Linda had no reply to that, other than distraught silence. She looked at Jacob as if trying to memorise his face down to the smallest detail. She kissed his head and nuzzled his fine blonde hair. Then, ever so slowly, she proffered him to Adam, asking in a pitifully hopeful tone, "Will you let us see him?"

"Of course." He took Jacob into his arms. "I would never keep Jacob from his grandparents. There's plenty of room at the house if you want to visit."

Richard let out another snort. "You must be joking. That place is pure evil."

"Oh shut up, Richard," snapped Linda. Taken aback, he stared at her open-mouthed as she added, "It makes no difference to me whether it's at Fenton House or on the moon, *I* will be seeing my grandchildren." Her eyes returned to Jacob, misted by sorrow and joy. "Grandma will see you soon, little angel."

In reply, the baby peeled back his lips and let out such a fierce cry that he brought up a blob of milky sick. Adam dabbed it away with the bib around Jacob's neck. He glanced at Henry. "Say goodbye to Grandma and Grandad."

"Bye Grandma, bye Grandad," Henry said in a dour, dutiful tone.

Richard pressed his lips together and shifted his eyes off to the side, refusing to acknowledge his grandson. Linda mouthed a silent *Bye,* too full of tears to speak.

Without affording Penny a glance, Adam turned to head for the boxy people carrier that Ella and he had bought in preparation for the baby's arrival. As he opened the nearside rear door, the policewoman piped up at his shoulder. "'Why would I hurt Ella? I need her. The children need her.'"

A tremor of annoyance passed over Adam's face. "Is there some reason why you're repeating my words back to me or are you just trying to antagonise me?"

"You talk about Ella as if she's alive."

"So what?"

"So nothing. I'm just making an observation."

"Are you deaf or just stupid?" sneered Henry. "My dad's already told you where you can stick your observations."

A sharp glance from Adam warned him against saying more.

Adam gave Penny a smile of deathly politeness. "Was there anything else?"

Penny shook her head. "That's all, for now."

Adam's eyes seemed to sink even deeper into their sockets. "*For now,*" he echoed with a resigned sigh. "Can I give you a piece of advice?" His voice limped out as if he barely had the energy to speak. "Get on with your own life and stay out of ours. That way we'll all be happier."

"I hope you're right." Penny emphasised her words with a meaningful look at Jacob.

The faintest flicker of a wince pulled at Adam's face, but it was enough to betray that Penny had touched a nerve.

Seemingly on an impulse, she reached inside the collar of her blouse and lifted a delicate silver chain over her head. "I'd like Jacob to have this."

Henry eyed the little crucifix attached to the chain. "He could choke to death on that."

"I realise he's too young to wear it. I just thought..." Penny faltered, flustered by Henry's almost accusing stare. "My mother gave me this when I was a little girl. I used to keep it under my pillow. I suppose it made me feel safe. Perhaps you could hang it by Jacob's cot."

Adam smiled, not coldly, just indifferently. "I'm afraid I can't accept it."

He turned to strap Jacob into his seat. Henry moved around the car to duck into the backseat alongside the baby. Dodging Penny's gaze, Adam got behind the steering-wheel. As he started the engine and pulled away, Linda raised her hand in a half-hearted wave. Neither Adam nor Henry waved back.

Adam drew in a deep breath through his nose. The car's interior still smelt so strongly of Ella that, if he closed his eyes, he knew it would be like she was right there beside him.

A long driveway wound its way past a memorial garden of marble plaques to a lane hemmed in by hedgerows.

"Would you really let Grandma come to stay?" asked Henry.

Adam was tellingly silent for a moment. He grimaced as the close confines of the car amplified Jacob's relentless wailing. "Check his nappy, will you?"

Henry unbuttoned Jacob's pastel blue romper suit and peered into his nappy. "It's dry."

"See if he wants his bottle."

Henry lifted his eyebrows as if to say, *Really?*

"Just do it," said Adam, flashing him an impatient glance.

Henry dug a baby bottle of milk out of a bag overflowing with wet wipes and nappies. He tried to insert the teat into Jacob's mouth, but his brother clamped his gums together and swivelled his head from side to side.

Henry gave his dad an *I-told-you-so* look.

The wails palpitated against Adam's eardrums, scattering his thoughts like leaves in the wind. Only one other noise had ever affected him like that – the combined cries of the twins as babies. Their simultaneous bouts of colic had rendered him unable to write for months on end.

He pressed down harder on the accelerator, accepting what he already knew – only one thing would stop the tears.

"His cheeks are bright red," said Henry. He tickled under Jacob's chin. "You just need a pair of horns and you'd look like a proper little devil."

"Save the jokes," snapped Adam. "I'm not in the mood."

They sped south through villages of stone cottages clustered around market squares. At the centre of one such village, he pulled over. "I'll just be a minute," he said, jumping out of the car. He hurried into a little shop with a sign over the door that read simply 'ANTIQUES'. Furniture, paintings and ceramics jostled for space alongside a tall gilt-framed mirror in the window.

A man with spectacles balanced on his head appeared at the window to lift the mirror from view. A moment later,

Adam emerged from the shop with the mirror cocooned in bubble-wrap. He slid it into the boot, then got back behind the steering wheel.

As he pulled away from the kerb, he said, "I spotted the mirror on the drive out and I thought..." He lapsed into silence as if too ashamed to admit what he'd thought.

"You don't need to explain it to me, Dad."

"No, but maybe I need to explain it to myself."

"Don't feel bad about what happened, Dad. Nothing you could have done would have changed anything."

Adam's forehead twitched at Henry's matter-of-fact tone. "What about you? Could you have changed anything?"

"No," Henry answered without hesitation. "It wasn't my fault. None of it was my fault."

A sick lump formed in Adam's throat. With a hard swallow, he forced it down like bitter medicine. "I don't suppose it matters whose fault it is."

They drove on, not speaking or looking at each other. Jacob's incessant wailing made the rest of the journey seem torturously long. At last, they came to the turn for Treworder.

Despite the racket, Henry heaved a sigh of pleasure. Somehow the sun suddenly seemed brighter, the sky bluer, the grass greener. He opened a window to let in the coconut-scent of gorse flowers. His shining eyes followed gulls riding thermals high overhead.

"We're almost home, Jacob," he informed his brother.

"Yes, we're almost home," Adam echoed, his voice as empty as Henry's was excited.

A mile or two further on, they turned off the narrow lane to Treworder onto the even narrower lane to Fenton House. The creased carpet of the sea rolled out in front of them.

Beyond the wind-sculpted hedges, fat honey-brown cows munched grass. Butterflies and bees swirled around the car like confetti celebrating their return.

Henry rocked forwards in his seat, greedily drinking in the scene. He let out a giddy little whoop as the rusty iron gates came into view. Adam stopped the car, got out and opened the gates, straining against their sagging hinges. He returned to his seat, pulled through the gates, then closed them. Faintly flushed from exertion, he reached for a pen and pad of paper. He flipped open the pad, revealing a long list topped by 'three-piece-suite'. 'French doors', 'carpets', 'floor tiles', and many more items followed. Several had already been ticked off the list. He added 'front gates'.

The car passed along the avenue of sycamores. There was a conspicuous gap where one of their number had been chainsawed down to a stump. Sawdust frosted the lawn where a tree surgeon had mulched the fallen tree. Wheel ruts in the gravel showed where the crushed car had been hauled onto the back of a truck to be taken away for scrap.

Beyond the lion-headed fountain, the mound of rubble and its grim contents were gone too. In their place, stone blocks were piled alongside bags of mortar, stacks of lumber and pallets of slate tiles.

"Look, Jacob, look at what busy bees the builders have been," said Henry, pointing to the latticework of scaffolding that covered the house's walls. "Our house will soon be as good as new."

A ladder crossed the pristine repaired roof and scaled the tower. The scaffolding-encased finger of stone was also well on its way to being restored to its former glory. At its conical peak, a skeleton of exposed beams awaited their turn to be tiled. There were no builders at work though. Adam hadn't been able to stomach the thought of all the hammering, drilling and sawing. Not today.

His gaze strayed towards the cluster of outbuildings that contained Grace's scruffy red car and the burglars' sleek black one. His forehead scrunched as he thought about what he'd said to Penny Holman – *Grace Gooden's car is probably in a ditch somewhere with her inside it.* She obviously hadn't believed a word of it.

"Do you think we should hide the cars somewhere else?" Henry asked, seemingly reading his dad's mind.

Adam showed no surprise whatsoever at his perceptiveness. "Penny Holman can't step foot through the gates without a search warrant, but she could be keeping an eye on us."

"So we wait until we're sure she's not watching the house?"

Adam nodded. "We just have to hold our nerve."

He parked in front of the porch and swiftly exited the car, shutting the door and muffling Jacob's cries. A grimace twitched on his face as Henry got out with the inconsolable baby cuddled into one shoulder and the bag of baby stuff slung over the other.

Adam watched Henry shushing and rocking Jacob. Not for the first time, he was struck by the unfamiliar sensation of looking at Henry with absolute trust. Over the weeks since Jacob's birth, Henry had proved himself to be devoted to his brother. He'd become a dab hand at bottle feeding and nappy changing. Adam hadn't detected the slightest hint of jealousy. If anything, it was he himself who felt jealous at the way Jacob's eyes lit up at the sight of Henry.

Adam heaved a sigh. Why? Why had it taken so much pain and suffering for Henry to finally come out of his shell?

Now we see things imperfectly, like puzzling reflections in a mirror.

Henry's cryptic words from the funeral returned to Adam.

Maybe it was better to see things imperfectly. He gave a little nod to himself. Yes, best to just go with the madness and accept whatever scraps of happiness were thrown his way.

"Come on, Dad," said Henry, hastening into the porch. "Don't just stand there."

"My master now knows me completely," Adam remarked under his breath, his lips curling with contempt. There could be no doubt about who the master of Fenton House was. He retrieved the mirror from the boot and carried it into the house.

The entrance hall looked the same, except that is for the mirrors.

Mirrors of every shape and size were crowded into the spaces between the paintings and tapestries. Simple wooden framed mirrors hung alongside ornate gold, silver and bronze gilded mirrors. Mirrors lined the hallway and stairs, amplifying the light and space until it was difficult to tell reflection from reality.

A sandy-coated pug with a flat black face came running from the living room, barking a welcome.

"Edgar!" Henry said delightedly as the pug jumped up at his ankles.

Adam balanced his newest addition to the collection of mirrors against a wall. The next second, Henry was passing him the baby. The lump reformed in Adam's throat as he inhaled the strawberry sweet, almost spicy scent of Jacob's hair. God, how he'd used to love that smell. Now it just made him vaguely nauseous.

"Careful," Adam remonstrated, supporting Jacob's bobbling head. "And slow down," he added as Henry broke into a run.

Taking no notice, Henry raced into the dining room with

Edgar at his heels.

"You'd better not be going where I think you're going," Adam called after him.

Once again, the words received no response. Adam gritted his teeth as Jacob unleashed a scream point-blank into his ear. "Shh, shh," he soothed to no effect. Resisting an urge to break into a run himself, he climbed the stairs.

Numerous mirrors basked in the rainbow of sunlight slanting through the stained-glass windows. Several of them faced each other across the landing, generating a kaleidoscope of images that stretched away into dizzying infinity.

Adam went into a bedroom with a balcony that overlooked the rugged coastline. An assortment of stout dark furniture – four-poster bed, chaise longue, dressing-table, bedside tables, wardrobe – almost made the large room feel small. The amateurish paintings of robins, rabbits, foxes, badgers and other woodland creatures that adorned the walls added to the sense of clutter. Patches of fresh unpainted plaster dotted the ceiling and walls. The damaged two-way mirror had been boarded up. In its absence, there was only one mirror in the room.

Adam approached a wicker Moses basket on a rocking stand at the side of the bed. Walter Lewarne's arched mirror overlooked the basket. Adam laid Jacob in the padded interior, facing him towards the mirror. He swaddled the baby in a soft blanket. Jacob flailed his arms and legs, belting out wail after wail.

Adam peered into the mirror. "Ella, where are you? Are you here?"

He searched the room's reflection, delving into the shadowy spaces under and between the furniture. Somehow, Jacob's crying grew even louder. His pointed little tongue vibrated between his gaping lips. His already flushed face turned a deeper shade of red.

"Ella." There was an edge of something akin to panic in Adam's voice. He was close enough to the mirror for his breath to mist the glass. "Please, sweetheart. Jacob needs you."

His appeal went unanswered. There remained nothing to be seen in the glass except his weary face, the bawling baby and the room. He closed his eyes, his lips moving as if in silent prayer. The screams were so loud that they seemed to shake his bones.

Ella, he called into the ether. *Ella. Ella...*

"Dad."

His eyes snapped open at Henry's voice.

"It's happened again," Henry breathlessly informed him from the doorway. Edgar stood panting at his side, nodding his wrinkled head as if to confirm the statement.

"Damn it, Henry, I told you not to go down to the vault."

"Sorry." An impertinent twist of Henry's lips made the apology ring hollow. "I just wanted to look at it." A dreaminess slunk into his eyes. "The way it glows. It's..." He faltered, unable to find adequate words to express himself.

Adam let out another exhausted sigh. "Stay with Jacob."

"Is Mum–"

"No," Adam broke in flatly, stepping over Edgar on his way out of the room.

Jacob's wails pursued him downstairs. Even in the dining room, they were teeth-grindingly loud. He hurried past the open living room door. The living room was almost unrecognisable. A new three-piece-suite had replaced the shabby sofa. A plush red wine rug covered much of the floor. The French doors had been repaired and treated to a fresh coat of gloss. A veritable constellation of mirrors dotted the walls.

Adam continued to the drawing room that looked out on the sun-splashed south lawn. He puckered his lips in annoyance. The secret panel that led into the labyrinthine passageways had been left ajar. Grabbing a torch from the coffee-table, he ducked past the panel. He blinked as cobwebs tickled his face. That was another job to add to the list – clearing the sodding cobwebs that got in his eyes every time he ventured into the passageways.

He closed the panel behind himself. After all, there were plenty of people who, like Penny Holman, would love to have a snoop around the house and grounds, but unlike her weren't bound by the letter of the law.

He turned to the narrow staircase. The broken treads had been replaced with new ones that still smelled of the varnish he'd painstakingly matched to the colour of the originals.

"Damn it, Henry," he muttered again upon seeing the gap at the side of the staircase. How many times did he have to tell Henry before it sank in? If the secret of the vault got out, they would never be able to live in peace. Every crook from Land's End to John O'Groats would be on the lookout for ways to rob them. Not to mention the inevitable torrent of begging letters that would come flowing their way.

He descended through the trapdoor and removed the stick propping it open. The stone slab began to steadily close. Goose-pimples rose on his flesh as he made his way along the dank tunnel to the vault's door. Most of the rusty bars had been sawn off. Replacing the door was yet another job that needed doing, but not one that he was about to write down on any list. A bucket containing a mixing stick, hammer, trowel and chisels sat atop a half-empty sack of 'Quick Set' mortar.

He stepped between the remaining bars and directed his torch at the vault's rear wall. Yet another sigh escaped him. A disc of rock as big as a manhole cover was lying on the floor beneath the identically sized hole. A bundle wrapped in black plastic and duct tape was protruding rigidly out of the hole.

Adam crouched to examine the brick-thick disc of granite. The mortar caked over its sides crumbled at a touch. He rubbed the porridge-like gunk between his thumb and forefinger. He'd tried half-a-dozen different types of mortar, but the end result was always the same – the hole's viscous discharge prevented the mortar from setting and, after a few days, the disc fell out.

His nose wrinkled as he watched slime dripping like drool from the plastic bundle. Its contents had ballooned, stretching the shiny black material drum-tight. Like a vet reaching inside a pregnant cow, he inserted his arm into the hole. His fingers groped along a pair of legs. A bloated belly blocked their progress.

He pressed down on the squishy flesh, triggering a sound like air sputtering from a whoopee cushion. His throat spasmed as he got a faceful of a rancid, cheesy aroma. Fighting back a gag, he forced more putrid gas from the corpse until there were several centimetres between his knuckles and the rock. He withdrew his arm and pushed at the duct taped feet.

He'd managed to shove about half of the bundle's protruding portion into the hole, when it bumped up against another blockage. He didn't need to investigate to know what the problem was. He'd inserted the bodies into the hole in ascending order of size – Grace first, followed by the witch, ghost-face and the man with no face. If he wanted to clear the blockage, he would have to remove all four bodies and expel the gas that had accumulated in their putrefying cavities. The mere thought of it made bile flood his mouth.

He retrieved the hammer from the bucket. He stood staring at the bundle for a moment, his face a mass of tics and twitches, before jerking the hammer up and down. There was a crunch of bone. Up and down, up and down arced the hammer, pummelling the corpse's legs until they hung like broken flowers. Glimpses of leaden blue flesh showed through tears in the plastic. The stench of death was thick enough to chew.

Adam took hold of the bundle again. After squashing the shattered legs back into their stone tomb, he mixed up some mortar and trowelled it around the rim of the hole. Veins swelled on his neck as he lifted the granite disc and slotted it into position. He hammered a couple of chisels under its edge. He pounded the disc with the side of his fist. Satisfied that it was firmly wedged in place, he turned towards the door.

His gaze lingered on the gold. Henry's words seemed to echo in his mind – *The way it glows. It's...* The sentence finished itself – *It's like it's speaking to you in a voice so soft that you never want to stop listening to it.*

A minute or maybe more passed. With a wrenching movement, Adam tore his eyes away from the gold. He trudged back to the trapdoor. Hesitating on the steps, he glanced wistfully over his shoulder as if seeking an excuse to return to the vault. He shrank in shame at the knowledge that he would rather be down there with only the gold for company than suffer through another second of Jacob's screaming and bawling.

He pulled the iron ring hanging on the wall. The opening mechanism clunked into motion and the trapdoor began to rise. After sidling past the staircase, he watched it slide shut. There was the click of a lock. The release button was concealed behind a false brick on the first floor. Henry had found it after a few hours of searching. Adam hadn't bothered to ask what had drawn him to that one particular brick out of the thousands that made up the maze of passageways.

Adam went into the drawing room, secured the secret panel and headed for the entrance hall. He came to a sudden stop between two mirrors that faced each other, glancing from side to side with the eerie, despairing eyes of someone trapped in an endless tunnel.

He tilted an ear towards the ceiling as he noticed something – or rather, the absence of something.

He broke away from the mirrors, his strides quickening as he climbed the stairs. Upon reaching the landing, he forced himself to slow to a tiptoe. Edgar was curled up with his head on his paws in the bedroom doorway. Cringing at every creak of the old floorboards, Adam stepped over the pug again.

Henry was holding the now empty baby bottle by its teat. Back and forth swung the bottle. Back and forth, back and forth, like a hypnotist's watch. His dark eyes appeared to be lost in the mirror.

Jacob's grey gaze was also submerged in the glass's silvery depths. His distraught wails had diminished to contented gurgles. He was reaching his pudgy little hands out as if trying to touch his reflection.

"Is she here?" Adam's voice was eager, yet there was a tentative, perhaps even fearful undercurrent to it.

"Yes," said Henry, turning to him with a smile as radiant as the gold. "She's here."

ABOUT THE AUTHOR

Ben Cheetham

Ben is an award winning writer and Pushcart Prize nominee with a passion for gritty crime fiction. His short stories have been widely published in the UK, US and Australia. In 2011 he self-published Blood Guilt. The novel went on to reach no.2 in the national e-book download chart, selling well over 150000 copies. In 2012 it was picked up for publication by Head of Zeus. Since then, Head of Zeus has published three more of Ben's novels – Angel of Death, Justice for the Damned and Spider's Web. In 2016 his novel The Lost Ones was published by Thomas & Mercer.

Ben lives in Sheffield, England, where – when he's not chasing around after his son, Alex – he spends most of his time shut away in his study racking his brain for the next paragraph, the next sentence, the next word...

If you'd like to learn more about Ben or get in touch, you can do so at bencheetham.com

BOOKS BY THIS AUTHOR

Don't Look Back (Fenton House Book 1)

After the tragic death of their eleven-year-old son, Adam and Ella are fighting to keep their family from falling apart. Then comes an opportunity that seems too good to be true. They win a competition to live for free in a breathtakingly beautiful mansion on the Cornish Lizard Peninsula. There's just one catch – the house is supposedly haunted.

Mystery has always swirled around Fenton House. In 1920 the house's original owner, reclusive industrialist Walter Lewarne, hanged himself from its highest turret. In 1996, the then inhabitants, George Trehearne, his wife Sofia and their young daughter Heloise disappeared without a trace. Neither mystery was ever solved.

Adam is not the type to believe in ghosts. As far as he's concerned, ghosts are simply memories. Everywhere he looks in their cramped London home he sees his dead son. Despite misgivings, the chance to start afresh is too tempting to pass up. Adam, Ella and their surviving son Henry move into Fenton House. At first, the change of scenery gives them all a new lease of life. But as the house starts to reveal its secrets, they come to suspect that they may not be alone after all...

Mr Moonlight

There's a darkness lurking under the surface of Julian Harris.

Every night in his dreams he becomes a different person, a monster capable of evil beyond comprehension. Sometimes he feels like something is trying to get inside him. Or maybe it's already in him, just waiting for the chance to escape into the waking world.

There's a darkness lurking under the surface of Julian's picture-postcard hometown too. Fifteen years ago, five girls disappeared from the streets of Godthorne. Now it's happening again. A schoolgirl has gone missing, stirring up memories of that terrible time. But the man who abducted those other girls is long dead. Is there a copycat at work? Or is something much, much stranger going on?

Drawn by the same sinister force that haunts his dreams, Julian returns to Godthorne for the first time in years. Finding himself mixed up in the mystery of the missing girl, he realises that to unearth the truth about the present he must confront the ghosts of his past.

Somewhere amidst the sprawling tangle of trees that surrounds Godthorne are the answers he so desperately seeks. But the forest does not relinquish its secrets easily.

Now She's Dead (Jack Anderson Book 1)

Jack has it all – a beautiful wife and daughter, a home, a career. Then his wife, Rebecca, plunges to her death from the Sussex coast cliffs. Was it an accident or did she jump? He moves to Manchester with his daughter, Naomi, to start afresh, but things don't go as planned. He didn't think life could get any worse...

Jack sees a woman in a window who is the image of Rebecca. Attraction turns into obsession as he returns to the window night after night. But he isn't the only one watching her...

Jack is about to be drawn into a deadly game. The woman lies dead. The latest victim in a series of savage murders. Someone is going to go down for the crimes. If Jack doesn't find out who the killer is, that 'someone' may well be him.

Who Is She? (Jack Anderson Book 2)

After the death of his wife, Jack is starting to get his life back on track. But things are about to get complicated.

A woman lies in a hospital bed, clinging to life after being shot in the head. She remembers nothing, not even her own name. Who is she? That is the question Jack must answer. All he has to go on is a mysterious facial tattoo.

Damaged kindred spirits, Jack and the nameless woman quickly form a bond. But he can't afford to fall for someone who might put his family at risk. People are dying. Their deaths appear to be connected to the woman. What if she isn't really the victim? What if she's just as bad as the 'Unspeakable Monsters' who put her in hospital?

She Is Gone (Jack Anderson Book 3)

On a summer's day in 1998, a savage crime at an isolated Lakeland beauty spot leaves three dead. The case has gone unsolved ever since. The only witness is an amnesiac with a bullet lodged in her brain.

The bullet is a ticking time bomb that could kill Butterfly at any moment. Jack is afraid for her. But should he be afraid of her? She's been suffering from violent mood swings. Sometimes she acts like a completely different person.

Butterfly is obsessed with the case. But how can she hope to succeed where the police have failed? The answer might be locked within the darkest recesses of her damaged mind. Or maybe the driver of the car that's been following her holds the key to the mystery.

Either way, the truth may well cost Butterfly her family, her sanity and her life.

The Lost Ones

July 1972

The Ingham household. Upstairs, sisters Rachel and Mary are sleeping peacefully. Downstairs, blood is pooling around the shattered skull of their mother, Joanna, and a figure is creeping up behind their father, Elijah. A hammer comes crashing down again and again...

July 2016

The Jackson household. This is going to be the day when Tom Jackson's hard work finally pays off. He kisses his wife Amanda and their children, Jake and Erin, goodbye and heads out dreaming of a better life for them all. But just hours later he finds himself plunged into a nightmare...

Erin is missing. She was hiking with her mum in Harwood Forest. Amanda turned her back for a moment. That was all it took for Erin to vanish. Has she simply wandered off? Or does the blood-stained rock found where she was last seen point to something sinister? The police and volunteers who set out to search the sprawling forest are determined to find out. Meanwhile, Jake launches an investigation of his own – one that will expose past secrets and present betrayals.

Is Erin's disappearance somehow connected to the unsolved

murders of Elijah and Joanna Ingham? Does it have something to do with the ragtag army of eco-warriors besieging Tom's controversial quarry development? Or is it related to the fraught phone call that distracted Amanda at the time of Erin's disappearance?

So many questions. No one seems to have the answers and time is running out. Tom, Amanda and Jake must get to the truth to save Erin, though in doing so they may well end up destroying themselves.

Blood Guilt (Steel City Thrillers Book 1)

After the death of his son in a freak accident, DI Harlan Miller's life is spiralling out of control. He's drinking too much. His marriage and career are on the rocks. But things are about to get even worse. A booze-soaked night out and a single wild punch leave a man dead and Harlan facing a manslaughter charge.

Fast-forward four years. Harlan's prison term is up, but life on the outside holds little promise. Divorced, alone, consumed by guilt, he thinks of nothing beyond atoning for the death he caused. But how do you make up for depriving a wife of her husband and two young boys of their father? Then something happens, something terrible, yet something that holds out a twisted kind of hope for Harlan – the dead man's youngest son is abducted.

From that moment Harlan's life has only one purpose – finding the boy. So begins a frantic race against time that leads him to a place darker than anything he experienced as a policeman and a stark moral choice that compels him to question the law he once enforced.

Angel Of Death (Steel City Thrillers Book 2)

Fifteen-year-old Grace Kirby kisses her mum and heads off to school. It's a day like any other day, except that Grace will never return home.

Fifteen years have passed since Grace went missing. In that time, Stephen Baxley has made millions. And now he's lost millions. Suicide seems like the only option. But Stephen has no intention of leaving behind his wife, son and daughter. He wants them all to be together forever, in this world or the next.

Angel is on the brink of suicide too. Then she hears a name on the news that transports her back to a windowless basement. Something terrible happened in that basement. Something Angel has been running from most of her life. But the time for running is over. Now is the time to start fighting back.

At the scene of a fatal shooting, DI Jim Monahan finds evidence of a sickening crime linked to a missing girl. Then more people start turning up dead. Who is the killer? Are the victims also linked to the girl? Who will be next to die? The answers will test to breaking-point Jim's faith in the law he's spent his life upholding.

Justice For The Damned (Steel City Thrillers Book 3)

Melinda has been missing for weeks. The police would normally be all over it, but Melinda is a prostitute. Women in that line of work change addresses like they change lipstick. She probably just moved on.

Staci is determined not to let Melinda become just another

statistic added to the long list of girls who've gone missing over the years. Staci is also a prostitute – although not for much longer if DI Reece Geary has anything to do with it. Reece will do anything to win Staci's love. If that means putting his job on the line by launching an unofficial investigation, then so be it.

DI Jim Monahan is driven by his own dangerous obsession. He's on the trail of a psychopath hiding behind a facade of respectability. Jim's investigation has already taken him down a rabbit hole of corruption and depravity. He's about to discover that the hole goes deeper still. Much, much deeper...

Spider's Web (Steel City Thrillers Book 4)

A trip to the cinema turns into a nightmare for Anna and her little sister Jessica, when two men throw thirteen-year-old Jessica into the back of a van and speed away.

The years tick by... Tick, tick... The police fail to find Jessica and her name fades from the public consciousness... Tick, tick... But every time Anna closes her eyes she's back in that terrible moment, lurching towards Jessica, grabbing for her. So close. So agonisingly close... Tick, tick... Now in her thirties, Anna has no career, no relationship, no children. She's consumed by one purpose – finding Jessica, dead or alive.

DI Jim Monahan has a little black book with forty-two names in it. Jim's determined to put every one of those names behind bars, but his investigation is going nowhere fast. Then a twenty-year-old clue brings Jim and Anna together in search of a shadowy figure known as Spider. Who is Spider? Where is Spider? Does Spider have the answers they want? The only thing Jim and Anna know is that the victims Spider entices into his web have a habit of ending up missing or dead.

Made in the USA
Las Vegas, NV
08 February 2024

85493994R00177